Praise for *The Last Watch*

Goodreads's Most Popular New Sci-Fi Novels of 2021

Space.com's Best Sci-Fi Books

New York Public Library's Best Science Fiction Books
for Adults 2021

Business Insider's 22 Best Science Fiction Books of 2021

Polygon's Best Science Fiction and Fantasy Books of 2021

Amazon's Best Science Fiction and Fantasy of 2021

Screen Rant's 10 Best Books Like *Foundation*

Book Riot's 20 Must-Read Space Fantasy Books

"One of the most stunning sci-fi series debuts of recent years. Fans of the genre—and particularly those already mourning the end of *The Expanse* series later this year—don't want to miss out on this nail-biting space epic."
—*Vulture*

"Dewes's debut is an exciting, fast-paced ride around the edges of the universe, where those rejected by much of humanity are the only ones who can save it. Fans of K. B. Wagers's Farian War series and John Scalzi's *Old Man's War* will welcome this military science fiction thriller."
—*Library Journal* (starred review)

"*The Last Watch* is a bravura debut that blends great action with compelling characters, lighting up this new series like a dark matter generator."
—*Booklist*

"A gripping space opera debut."
—*Publishers Weekly*

"*The Last Watch* is my pick for science fiction debut of the year. Dewes has written a masterwork space opera that needs to be on bookshelves worldwide. Epic, character-driven sci-fi goodness that is the cure for your *Expanse* hangover."
—*FanFiAddict*

"A high-energy thrill ride at the edge of space featuring a crew of miscreants racing against time aboard an ancient spaceship. A great concept with even better execution, this is a sci-fi space opera for readers looking to dial up the excitement."
—*BookPage* (starred review)

ALSO BY J. S. DEWES

THE DIVIDE SERIES
The Last Watch
The Exiled Fleet

RUBICON

J. S. DEWES

TOR

TOR PUBLISHING GROUP

NEW YORK

This is a work of fiction. All of the characters, organizations, and events portrayed in this novel are either products of the author's imagination or are used fictitiously.

RUBICON

Copyright © 2023 by J. S. Dewes

All rights reserved.

A Tor Book
Published by Tom Doherty Associates / Tor Publishing Group
120 Broadway
New York, NY 10271

www.tor-forge.com

Tor® is a registered trademark of Macmillan Publishing Group, LLC.

Library of Congress Cataloging-in-Publication Data

Names: Dewes, J. S., author.
Title: Rubicon / J. S. Dewes.
Description: First edition. | New York : Tor, a Tom Doherty
Associates Book 2023. |
Identifiers: LCCN 2022041366 (print) | LCCN 2022041367 (ebook) |
ISBN 9781250851239 (trade paperback) | ISBN 9781250851246 (ebook)
Subjects: LCGFT: Science fiction.
Classification: LCC PS3604.E914 R83 2023 (print) |
LCC PS3604.E914 (ebook) | DDC 813/.6—dc23
LC record available at https://lccn.loc.gov/2022041366
LC ebook record available at https://lccn.loc.gov/2022041367

Our books may be purchased in bulk for promotional, educational, or
business use. Please contact your local bookseller or the Macmillan Corporate
and Premium Sales Department at 1-800-221-7945, extension 5442,
or by email at MacmillanSpecialMarkets@macmillan.com.

First Edition: 2023

Printed in the United States of America

0 9 8 7 6 5 4 3 2 1

For Sylvanas Windrunner,
the most badass of nihilists

RUBICON

CHAPTER
ONE

Blasts of sand pelted Adriene's back as the dropship's thrusters flared into blinding blue-white halos. It lifted off the ground, kicking up a static hum of fine white sand that pelted the carapace of her hardsuit.

"We're skyward," the pilot called over comms. "Good hunting, Specialist Valero."

Adriene acknowledged him with a quick two-fingered salute. The ship's silver hull blanched, then became a mere shimmer of light as the stealth system engaged and it shot into the darkening atmosphere.

She switched to squad comms. "Rhodes?"

Private Harlan Rhodes approached, obscured through the eddy of sand drifting in the wake of the dropship. "Go for Rhodes."

"Any hits?"

"Nothing, boss." Harlan stopped next to her, his scuffed, dark gray hardsuit dusted with a layer of fine sand. He flashed a grin from under his shaded visor. "You'll be the first to know, Valero. Er—*sir*. After me. Obviously."

Adriene humored her second's congeniality with a stilted smile. "Thanks for the clarification."

He nodded. "You got it, boss."

Through the lingering haze of sand, Adriene surveyed the planet's landscape. Beyond the inlet of a choppy sea, the fragments of an ancient metal city jutted up through dense forest, colossal husks of some once-great civilization. On the horizon beyond the water, the system's red dwarf star hovered like a massive dying cinder, casting the long-abandoned landscape in a hazy amber glow. And there it would sit, always watching, skirting eastward along the rim of the world until morning, when it'd pull itself back up into the sky and make its lazy, almost forty-two-hour arc back to this spot. The same amount of time she'd been given to complete this mission.

"Overwatch is up," Private McGowan announced, stepping to the other side of Harlan. Her fingers flashed across her survey tablet. "Clear, presently."

"Keep an eye on it." Adriene glanced back at the hunched man towering off her shoulder. "Booker, what's our ETA?"

The private's deep voice crackled through her earpiece, "Er, 'bout fifty minutes if you wanna keep boots on the ground. Twenty if you're up for a little rappelling."

Adriene's squad fell in behind her as she crossed a few meters of rocky terrain toward an uneven cliff edge, dusted with tawny saltbush.

She peered over the edge to the turbulent surf three hundred meters below, where algae-laden waves crashed against the worn basalt cliff face.

"Book, you got a local survey?" she asked.

Booker pinged her HUD, and Adriene quickly reviewed the topography. The descent was doable, but it'd be a risk with the rough surf.

"Nah, let's hoof it," she said. "We've got time. Rhodes, you got the COB kit."

"Copy," Harlan acknowledged.

McGowan stowed her tablet, then helped Harlan lift the heavy Colonial Operations Base kit onto his back.

Adriene double-checked the atmospheric readout in her HUD before sliding open the visor of her helmet. She drew in a slow inhale of the warm, salty air. It wasn't every day they were deployed in breathable atmosphere. And she couldn't remember the last time she'd smelled an ocean.

"Atmo's clear, guys."

Harlan slid his visor open and sucked in a long breath through his nose. "Ahh. Isn't it nice when a planet's not trying to kill us?"

"Not yet, anyway."

McGowan and Booker opened their visors as well. Adriene shouldered her own pack and let Booker lead the way north along the edge of the cliff. The breeze off the sea cooled with the waning sunlight as they descended along a steep game trail, worn into the landscape by some manner of vertically accomplished fauna.

"So, Rhodes," Booker said, "what're we thinkin'?"

Harlan lifted his chin and sniffed the air deeply. "I'll give it an eight point five."

"That high?" Booker asked, skeptical. "I'm pegging it at a six."

McGowan perked up, her voice crisp over comms. "Preliminary reports do support the likelihood of a high viability rating."

"I wouldn't put too much stock in the reports," Adriene warned. "Their survey was scant at best."

Harlan sighed. "Seems to be the case more often than not these days, huh?"

Adriene grunted her agreement.

"Guess we'll leave it up to good ol' COB kit to decide." Booker thwacked the large pack on Harlan's back, causing Harlan to stumble slightly. Harlan glowered, but kept walking.

Half an hour later, the cliff-side path ended abruptly in an over two-meter drop to the sandy shore. Booker and McGowan hopped down first, then Harlan slid the COB kit off his back and passed it down to Booker.

Harlan leapt off the edge, landing with a grunt. "They couldn'ta dropped us a little closer?"

McGowan replied, "Radiological signature's too easy to trace. A COB's only good to us if we can keep it from the scrap heaps."

Harlan hefted the bag onto his back again. "Sure, but Intel says we're by our lonesome, yeah?"

Booker scoffed. "A Mechan-free system? In this sector? I'm not buyin' it."

Harlan gave a soft grumble of acquiescence. "Maybe not. Doesn't mean they're hangin' around on this deserted rock, though."

Adriene slid off the ledge and landed beside them. "Keep comms clear, guys."

"Sorry, boss."

Booker pulled a laminated sheet of paper from his utility belt, turning to get his bearings. "Eighteen degrees, one point six seven klicks."

"Copy," Adriene said. "Lead the way, Private."

Booker tucked the sheet away, then started along the narrow shore at the foot of the cliff. They remained quiet as they found their footing on the rocky beach, strewn with pools of glassy water that teemed with variegated marine life. Thick strands of latticed coral-like invertebrates covered the reef, their orange and lime-green bioluminescence already visible in the dwindling daylight. A trio of flat, fishlike fauna skimmed the surface, staining the glowing display like drifting sunspots.

Adriene's chapped lips had just started to go numb when her suit beeped a warning. She checked the flashing atmo sensor on the arm of her hardsuit. "Temp's dropping, seal up," she ordered. She waited for the distinctive hiss of three visors closing before she sealed her own.

"Nice while it lasted," Harlan's resigned tone mumbled over comms.

Twenty minutes later, they rounded a corner into a large cove. A wide basalt cliff face sat a hundred meters back from the shore, covered with a mask of corroded scaffolding—the framework of some ancient sentry post. Adriene spotted a single, narrow entrance barely visible between two vertical striations of dark stone.

Booker came to a stop. "This's it, sir."

Adriene glanced back. "Mac, any other entrances?"

"Not according to survey," McGowan said. "But the basalt doesn't always make for the most accurate readings."

"All right. Drop a patrol beacon at the threshold."

Harlan nodded. "You got it, sir."

"Otherwise, we stay dark." Adriene opened the control panel on her arm and switched off her hardsuit's master controls. "No tech except comms and overwatch till we've cleared the interior."

"Powering down," Harlan said, and the others echoed him. The few dim lights on the exterior of their hardsuits faded away.

"And don't forget mods," Adriene said.

Booker grumbled something unintelligible but distinctly sullen, then turned off the targeting unit on the side of his rifle. Adriene hauled the heavy coilgun rifle off her back and did the same. She checked the charge on the weapon, then shouldered it and led the way to the cave's entrance.

The interior wasn't nearly as imposing as the facade had suggested. The single-entrance tunnel branched off every dozen or so meters, but each new path quickly culminated in a dead end. Fifteen minutes in, Adriene arrived at the apparent end of the main passage, where it widened into a black abyss. She swept her headlamp across the darkness, and the light caught the edge of a rocky outcropping a few meters in.

"Light drones?" Booker suggested.

"Overwatch?" Adriene asked.

"Still clear," McGowan confirmed.

Adriene nodded. "Deploy illumination drones."

Harlan knelt and opened the narrow hardsuit compartment that ran along the outside of his calf. He pulled out a half dozen palm-sized discs, activating each before tossing them into the air. They buzzed off, illuminating slowly with a faint aura of white light. They landed equidistant from one another throughout the fifty-meter-wide, roughly square-shaped chamber. The mouth of the tunnel opened onto a raised tier, perched on a rocky platform four meters above the rest of the chamber.

"Standard IDs deployed," Harlan confirmed. "Positions locked."

Adriene kept her rifle raised as she crossed the threshold. A steep but serviceable ramp-like slope led from the ridge down into a large, open area. Piles of unrecognizable, rusted-out metal sat in mounds around the chamber, the remnants of ancient furniture or machinery.

"On me." Adriene led her squad clockwise around the perimeter, checking every narrow slice in the stratified basalt for entry points, but found nothing.

They trudged back up the ramp to the entrance, and Harlan slid the COB kit off his shoulders onto the dusty gravel floor. "One way in, one way out."

Booker grunted. "Least it'll be easy to defend."

"Tough to get supplies in, though," Harlan said. "Shit's narrow."

Adriene gestured to McGowan. "Mac, boot up the COB, run a geo survey. See if the structure will hold if we blow the entrance tunnel a little wider."

"Yes, sir." McGowan passed her overwatch tablet to Booker, then knelt beside the COB kit.

Booker's heel tapped out an anxious rhythm in the dry dirt. "Can we light up?"

"One at a time," Adriene agreed. "Harlan, sync on my marks. Book, keep an eye on overwatch."

"On it," Booker acknowledged.

Adriene tapped the control panel on her forearm. "Therms up."

"I got nothin'," Harlan said.

"Me either," she confirmed, then tossed another switch. "Sonic."

Harlan nodded. "Clear."

"Seismic."

"Golden."

"Nothin' on overwatch," Booker said.

"All right, we're clear. Keep visors down, though. CO_2's reading elevated in here."

Booker switched his systems back on with a single swipe of his large palm. "Permission to check out this old junk, sir? Maybe somethin' of use in the rubble."

"I doubt it," she replied, "but go ahead."

Booker tossed the overwatch tablet to Harlan, then made his way down the ramp toward the ruins.

McGowan mumbled, "Strange . . ."

Adriene knelt beside her. "What is it?"

"GPR shows a passage above this room."

"Another cave?"

"No, it's vertical." McGowan angled the screen of the survey kit toward Adriene, indicating a narrow spike in the radargram. "Depth estimations say it's over three hundred meters. I think it connects to the surface."

Harlan asked, "Like a sinkhole?"

"That wasn't on Intel's orbital survey," Booker put in, already halfway across the room, digging through a pile of rubble.

McGowan shook her head. "I know. But it should have been visible."

"Could it have been masked by something?" Adriene asked. "Obscured on radar?"

"It's possible," McGowan said. "Especially if there was weather in the area."

"Or the eggheads just missed it," Booker groused. "Wouldn't be the first time."

"Could it be outdated intel?" Harlan asked.

Adriene shook her head. "They did the survey three days ago." She flinched as an alarm blared in her earpiece, accompanied by a readout in her HUD: *Warning: Seismic activity detected.*

"Fuck," Booker groaned. "Anyone's seismic just have a heart attack?"

"Yeah." Adriene silenced the alarm and glanced at the seismic sensor in the corner of her HUD. It only showed a generic warning.

A faint sound crackled against Adriene's visor, like dry pine needles crunching underfoot. She looked up as a dusting of rock floated down from the ceiling five meters overhead. A barely discernible vibration rumbled in the cavern floor, sending a prickle up her spine.

"Mira's end," Harlan cursed, his congenial tone flattened with concern. "You guys feel that?"

"Booker, get back up here," Adriene ordered.

"On my way."

Adriene turned to McGowan. "What's the tectonic rating of this site?"

"A1, sir," the private assured. "All plates were designated stable and inact—"

A sharp crack rang out as the stone ceiling over the main area split. Shards of rock rained onto the corroded metal debris, followed by a torrent of gravel that quickly overtook the cavern with a plume of basalt dust.

Flashes exploded from the haze.

A shock of pain lanced Adriene's shoulder, knocking her to the ground.

Harlan's voice crackled through comms. "Boss, what the—"

"Enemy fire!" Adriene shouted. She flipped over, then crawled into cover behind the rocky ridge along the edge of the raised tier. Her HUD flashed a warning: *Hardsuit quadrant R2b compromised. Integrity: 7%.*

She slid her rifle off her back, flicked the targeting unit on, and engaged the primer. The coils magnetized, buzzing through the thick layers of her hardsuit gloves.

"What are we fighting?" she called out. "Give me something, guys!"

"Scrappers!" Harlan shouted. "Confirmed four Mechan transponders a second ago, but my readout's fucked."

"*Four?* Mira's ashes," Booker cursed, giving voice to the swell of unease souring Adriene's stomach.

Four bots would make for a hell of a fight, but it wasn't impossible. She took a deep, steadying breath. Her squad could handle it. They'd survived far worse odds.

Adriene squinted through the settling dust. Harlan and Mc-Gowan crouched behind a rocky outcropping six meters away, near the top of the ramp. The incoming fire didn't cease, an endless flurry pinging the ridge and cavern wall behind them.

"Everyone fall back to the exit, behind me," Adriene ordered. "Booker, I don't have eyes on you—what's your status?"

"Eh, fuck. I'm fully pinned down 'ere," he growled, his full Provan accent let loose now that shit had fully gone sideways. "Gonna need a leg up gettin' out."

Adriene shimmied toward a low point in the ridge, where she could barely catch a glimpse of two Mechan units crouched halfway across the cavern. The sentient hunks of metal sat folded in on themselves, their long, triple-jointed limbs covered in dull gray plating—discernibly, if not grotesquely, humanoid in structure. Their scuffed metal chassis seemed to meld into the corroded piles of ancient debris. Any aesthetics the scrap heaps may have once possessed had clearly been lost after centuries of "self-improvement."

The thinner of the two Mechan painted a steady stream of rifle fire in Harlan's direction, while the beefier one yanked a large module off its thigh plate. It placed the device on the ground, and a violet blaze shot toward the ceiling, forming a thin wall of semi-transparent light. The shield crackled with electricity as dust drizzled onto it from the crater in the ceiling.

Adriene cursed and craned her neck, but Booker was nowhere to be seen.

"Dammit." She grimaced. "Harl, you see Book on overwatch?"

"No. Too much interference."

"Shit. All right, old-fashioned way, then. Book, what's your twenty?"

"Maybe halfway 'cross, three-forty degrees from the ramp. Clear path 'cept those two Troopers that just deployed that damn shield construct. I'm 'bout five meters to their six."

"Copy, I see them."

"Hate to break it to ya, Book," Harlan chimed in, "but one's actually a Cuirass."

"Mira's fiery death—"

A blast of rocky debris shot from the ceiling fissure.

Three more Trooper-class Mechan dropped into the cavern. They landed in a haze of dust, just behind the violet wall of light. Their limbs straightened with stilted rigidity as they rose to their full height.

Harlan and McGowan let loose a flurry of fire, but their bullets melted into the surface of the shield, disappearing in a blaze of flashing electricity.

Adriene let out a sharp sigh, heart thudding hard in her chest. "Shit. That makes seven. Mac, call in an evac."

A few seconds later, McGowan's rushed voice replied, "No-go, sir; scrappers are jamming it."

Adriene ground her teeth, silently cursing whatever blighted species invented these manufactured fucks, then had the sensible idea to make them self-aware before letting their murderous, hive-minded junkbots loose on the galaxy. It was at least satisfying to know they'd in all likelihood been wiped out by their own terrible choices.

"All right," Adriene sighed. "We'll have to put some distance between us, then. Harl, Mac . . ." She took a deep breath and pulled a grenade from the supply compartment at her calf, then readied the charge. "Chaff incoming. Then let's give Book some covering fire."

Harlan and McGowan voiced their acknowledgment, and Adriene tossed the grenade over the outcropping. It exploded into a shower of glittering metallic light, raining down tiny shards of lightweight radar-jamming material that drifted lazily toward the ground like feathers.

The Mechan onslaught paused as their auto-targeting protocols were briefly disoriented. Adriene set her rifle aside and grabbed her sidearm. She leaned out to pelt the edge of the shield construct with a barrage of fire. Harlan and McGowan broke from cover as well, the muzzles of their ballistics rifles flashing as they lit up the rusted metal barricade in front of Booker's position.

Booker rolled backward out of cover, then sprang to his feet, sprinting toward the ramp through the drifting bits of chaff. He made it almost ten meters before the Mechan fire resumed, pinging into swirls of dust in the gravel at his feet.

He slid behind a large stone slab near the foot of the ramp. McGowan and Harlan's rifles went silent as they ducked back into cover.

Booker panted, "That's s'far as I can get for now."

"Okay, hole up," Adriene said. "We got a good line of sight up here; don't risk drawing their attention."

"Yes, sir."

"Harl, Mac, focus-fire that shield construct. If we can force them to pull back a ways, it'll give Book time to get up the ramp."

"*Shit*, Valero," Harlan said, a hard warning in his tone. "We got a Shade incoming."

Adriene's pulse spiked. She holstered her sidearm and took hold of her rifle again. "Bearing?"

"Dunno, it disappeared—overwatch is fucked. It's this bloody basalt fortress. Who picked this site, anyhow?"

Booker grunted. "Some brain in Intel who's never stepped foot on terra in their life."

"Shut up and focus," Adriene barked.

With a break in the fire, Booker leaned out with his pistol and let loose a volley of bullets. "I can shoot and bitch at the same time."

"Dammit, Book, I just told you not to draw—"

"Got our Shade back, boss!" Harlan called out. "Cloaked, bearing one-zero-five, thirty meters. Headed straight for Book."

Adriene retrained her aim, hunting for the target. She defocused her gaze enough to catch a hazy shimmer against the stone wall.

With a smooth squeeze of her trigger, the conductive projectile pummeled the vaguely humanoid metal carapace into the wall, revealing the Shade's svelte body as its stealth deactivated. Its limbs screeched as it crumpled into a mangled heap on the cave floor.

Harlan scoffed a laugh. "Mira's end—nice shot, Valero."

Adriene shook out her tingling hand, the aftermath of the intense kickback on the coilgun. She readjusted her grip on the firearm and primed it again. "Harl, watch incoming that direction," she ordered. "And keep an eye on that fucking skylight too—let's light 'em up before they hit the ground."

"Copy that, boss."

"Mac, what can we do about the interference on overwatch? Can you narrow the range?"

"That could work, sir," McGowan replied, "but it will fully cut us off from Command until we can get sight line on satellite again."

"Do it."

"Copy, sir. Going slim."

McGowan recited the scripted callout, and Harlan's panicked voice broke in as the interference cleared. "Fourteen contacts!"

"What?"

"Sixteen! Two more just dropped."

"Gah—shit!" Booker's strained voice rang over comms, followed by fraught, muffled grunts.

Adriene peered out of cover to find Booker wrestling with a Trooper who'd left the safety of the shield construct. The Mechan seized Booker by the neck, then slammed the burly man into the ground with consummate ease. Booker roared and tried to slide out from under its grip, but he couldn't match its strength.

Adriene shouldered her rifle, then caught sight of McGowan charging down the ramp. "Mac!" Adriene yelled. "Stay back!"

The Trooper lifted Booker up again, then paused. Its head swiveled with unnerving rigidity as it turned toward McGowan who was rushing its flank. While the bot was distracted, Adriene took aim at the back of its head and fired.

The slug slammed into the base of its neck, erupting in a shower of sparks. The Mechan's cylindrical head canted to one side, hanging on by a handful of wires and cabling.

Adriene primed her rifle again. But it wouldn't be charged in time. And from this distance, her sidearm wouldn't cut it. "Harl—"

"On it."

The Trooper dropped Booker. It grasped to reseat its head, but Harlan pelted the exposed circuitry, and the remainder broke free. The headless bot deactivated, slumping to the ground lifelessly.

McGowan, still heading for Booker, was suddenly intercepted by a slim metallic flash. The Shade disappeared before it was even fully visible—and McGowan along with it.

Harlan shouted, "Fuck, a Shade has Mac! It's got a crucible!"

Chrome streaks flashed in Adriene's periphery as three more Mechan dropped from the opening in the ceiling.

Booker made for the ramp. Two of the new Troopers skirted the construct and headed for him. He fired his coilgun practically point-blank into the chest of one, sending it flying back into the shield wall. The Trooper shuddered in a violent storm of light as the shield electrocuted it.

Booker continued to scramble backward as the second bot pursued.

"We're at nineteen, boss!" Harlan warned. "We're fightin' a losin' battle—we gotta call it!"

"Shit." Adriene pressed the remote comms link on her hardsuit controls. "Command, you read?"

"That's a big fuckin' negative," Harlan said. "We're slim, remember?"

"Dammit."

"Forget it, Valero," Harlan yelled. "We don't have time—get McGowan before it's too late!"

"I can't *see* her!" Adriene shouted back, voice raspy and dry. Then a thread of hope stoked in her chest. "Harl, tell me you have a pulse grenade."

"Oh—fuck yeah, I do!" Harlan grunted, then shouted, "Pulse incoming! Watch your gun, Valero."

Adriene flicked the pulse shield on her rifle a heartbeat before a blinding flare erupted beyond the ridge. Her suit's HUD flashed and deactivated, her earpiece giving off a shrill peal as the EM burst interrupted the comms.

Halfway across the cavern, the Shade appeared at the edge of the shield construct. It stood, momentarily paralyzed, clutching McGowan in its spindly arms.

"Valero!" Harlan's panicked voice rang through the still-crackling comms. "Do it already!"

With her pulse hammering in her ears, Adriene took aim with her coilgun, and shot McGowan in the side of the head.

The private's visor shattered, and her helmet crumpled into her skull. The force of the blast ripped her from the Shade's arms. Her limp body smashed into the shield construct, then collapsed to the floor.

The Shade regained mobility less than a second later. It marched straight toward them.

Harlan leapt up and rushed down the ramp.

"Harlan!" Adriene yelled. "Get the fuck back here!"

"No way! I gotta get Book." Harlan unloaded his rifle into the Shade's torso as it charged him, but the scrap heap barely flinched, pausing only long enough to rip the gun out of Harlan's hands.

"Dammit! I'll get him," Adriene shouted. But it was too late. The Shade grabbed Harlan, and they both disappeared from sight. "Harl!"

Harlan screamed—in terror or pain, she couldn't tell. Heat scoured her cheeks, lungs burning as her breaths came too short, too fast. She blinked heavily, hunting for a glimpse of the cloaked Shade, but there was nothing.

Her rifle's prime flashed green. With an effort, she pulled her attention back to Booker, who continued to wrestle with the Trooper. She locked her aim onto him.

"Book," she called, voice wavering, "turn ninety degrees to your right."

He obeyed, throwing his weight to spin himself along with the grappling Trooper. Adriene fired.

The blast ripped through Booker's chest. His full weight slammed back into the Trooper, sending them both into the shield wall. The scrap heap thrashed as the shield's power coursed through it, sending off harsh flares of violet light.

Booker's limp body fell, and the contents of his caved-in chest cavity spilled onto the dirt. Adriene swallowed bile.

"Adri!" Harlan shouted, still invisible, clutched somewhere in the Shade's arms. "Please!"

Adriene darted a look around the cavern, searching for any sign of him. "I can't see you, Harl!" Her voice came fractured as she forced the words out. She primed her rifle. "What's your position?"

He screamed again.

"Shit, listen, please!" Her throat closed around the words. "I don't know where you are—you need to get away from it or push it into the construct."

Harlan roared. In a flash of light, he and the Shade appeared as he forced them into the violet wall of energy. The Shade convulsed and fell still. Harlan collapsed to the dirt.

From behind the shield construct, another Trooper rounded toward him.

"Adri!" Harlan pleaded, his voice breaking. He started to crawl toward her, his right hand now a bloody stump—severed at the wrist. His smashed visor revealed one eye, now nothing more than an indiscernible mess of blood and tissue.

With a quick glance down, Adriene found her rifle's readout flashing green. She stared back at it, frozen for a few long seconds. Her breath came in short rasps, her vision blurred.

She gritted her teeth and narrowed in on the source of her reluctance: the natural instinct to protect the people she cared about. She stamped it out.

Then she sucked in a breath, took aim, and shot Harlan in the face.

His head erupted in a grisly shower of blood and bone. Bits of viscera pelted the approaching Mechan, and Harlan's headless body went limp against the dusty gravel floor. Chunks of bone and gray matter slid off the Trooper's sleek metal segments.

It looked up, following the angle of Adriene's fire. Its glowing amber ocular sensors flickered as it locked onto her.

Adriene dropped behind the ridge. With shaking hands, she thumbed the primer on her rifle. The readout flashed a warning: *Discharged. Reboot in progress.*

"Fuck." She tossed the stalled rifle aside, then pressed the button to open her visor. Her hardsuit let out a negative beep. A red warning lit in her HUD: *Caution: Hostiles present. Visor retraction not recommended.*

"No *shit*," she growled, tapping the button over and over. "Override!"

It beeped in error and didn't respond.

She turned to face the ridge, drew in a deep breath, then thrust her head face-first into the rocky outcropping. Lights danced in her vision. When they cleared, she saw nothing but smooth glass—not even a hairline crack.

The Trooper crested the ramp. In one hand, it held a halo of dark, segmented metal. A crucible.

"No, no, no . . ." Adriene slid toward a sharp protrusion of rock. She rammed her visor into it as hard as she could. Sharp pain shot down her neck as the inside of her hardsuit crushed against her skull.

The visor remained intact.

The Mechan closed in. The crucible device gave a shrill hum as it activated. Its cracks glowed red-orange from within like molten obsidian.

Adriene crawled away, but the bot's long legs crossed the meters in a matter of seconds. Its spindly chrome fingers locked around her ankle. It dragged her toward the ramp.

She clawed at the ground, at every ridge she could find purchase, but the Trooper simply towed her along, no more than minorly inconvenienced by her pathetic struggle. She mashed the visor release button again as the bot hauled her across the rough gravel.

"Dammit, override!"

Her visor slid open.

Relief flooded her chest. An icy gust of air blasted her sweat-slicked face, carrying a sickly sweet smell like antiseptic metal polish. Bile crept up her throat as the unfiltered sound of the Mechan force hit her eardrums—a grating symphony of metal on metal accompanied by a thick hissing of hydraulics.

She fumbled her sidearm out of its holster, panic hastening her movements.

The Trooper stopped abruptly, looking back at her exposed face. It reached down and gripped her by the neck. Her feet lifted off the ground as it held her in front of its face—featureless, save its ocular sensors: a pair of glowing amber rings deep-seated in its cylindrical head. If a lifeless metal trash can stuffed with circuitry could look pissed, this one most certainly did. Mechan never seemed to appreciate a human's attempts to zero out.

The bot thrust the crucible toward her face. But Adriene was faster.

She thumbed the safety of her sidearm, pressed the muzzle between her eyes, and pulled the trigger.

CHAPTER
TWO

Adriene took her first breath for the ninety-seventh time, and she was already screaming.

A lance of pain fired through her legs as her knees hit cold metal. Her elbows dropped, then the rest followed as she crumpled, a mess of tangled limbs she couldn't control. Her bare skin slid across the floor, covered in a thick membrane of mucus. She reached out, though she didn't know what for.

A weight rose in her throat. Her body convulsed as she choked out a wad of gray sludge.

She groaned and tried to rise, but her muscles wouldn't listen.

Muffled through a layer of viscous fluid came the sounds of a computerized voice. Nonsense words, random syllables strung together; she couldn't make sense of it.

Clawing at the tiered metal ridges beside her, she pulled herself to standing, propped against the sloping wall. She wiped the mucus from her eyes and looked around.

A long, narrow corridor stretched in both directions, lined on either side with segmented cases of metal and dark glass—hundreds of sealed pods like the one she'd just fallen out of.

A stench of sterile, bitter antiseptic flooded in. Her stomach heaved. She turned aside and retched onto the floor—more shapeless gray sludge. Icy chills racked her body, and sharp waves of goose bumps ripped across her bare skin.

The computerized voice spouted more unintelligible nonsense, "Please proceed to Quality Assurance Station."

Adriene blinked at the screen recessed in the wall in front of her. It flashed a series of symbols. Words, maybe. She knew she should recognize them, but she couldn't assign meaning to any of it.

To her left, pulsating green arrows illuminated at the end of the corridor. She spat out another glob of mucus and clenched her teeth. Someone wanted her to go that way.

So she turned and bolted the opposite direction.

Her mucus-covered feet slid across the dark metal floor. A sharp tone blared—a warning or alarm—but she ignored it and pressed on, running as fast as she could force her ungainly limbs to move. Blood pumped hot through her veins, strengthening and invigorating her muscles.

Dozens of meters down, she came to an intersection. As she slowed, her eyes darted, searching for some indication of an exit. But there was nothing. Just row upon row of segmented metal-and-glass capsules that seemed to go on forever in all four directions.

She kept running.

At the next intersection, a man rounded the corner.

She hesitated and almost slipped, but managed to keep her footing as she glided to a stop. The man wore a plain black uniform, pant legs tucked into heavy combat boots. He had a single pistol in a holster on his thigh, but he didn't go for the weapon. He simply hovered cautiously, holding his hands toward her, palms out.

Adriene darted forward and thrust the heel of her palm into his throat.

He fell to his knees, clutching his neck and gasping for breath. She shoved him aside and rounded the corner—right into the path of two more men.

One called out, "Code nine!"

Adriene's feet slid as she halted, and she struggled to stay upright while spinning to face the other way.

One of the men reached for her, his hands slipping down her slick skin. "Specialist, stop!" he shouted—more gibberish.

Despite the layer of mucus, he managed to clasp her wrist, then twisted her arm behind her back. He kicked the back of her knee and forced her face-first onto the ground.

Pain shot through her shoulder, but she growled and struggled anyway, hot fury flooding her neck and face.

The man pressed her wrist into her back and pinned her head to the floor with his other hand.

They were trained, at least. Guards of some sort, for whatever horrible kind of prison this was.

"Specialist *Adriene Valero*," he said, tone still hard, but he was no longer shouting. "803rd Ground Assault. Your CO's Miller Champlan . . ."

He continued spouting nonsense, and Adriene flinched as something flared in her mind's eye. A trickle of images and sounds, laden with meaning and emotion she couldn't make sense of. Fear, worry, dread, discontent, irritation. But only fragments, nothing but echoes: flashes of violet light, fibrous black rock teeming down from a void of darkness, sibilant mechanical whispers.

And a handless man, crawling, reaching, begging for help.

Harlan.

That abandoned planet. The basalt cave. Scrappers.

She'd zeroed out her squad, then herself.

Memories flooded her mind, and she could feel it again—the pain of death: a lancing headache that split her skull, the sickening stench of charred skin burned from the muzzle held flush against her forehead.

Blood heated her cheeks, and hot tears filled her eyes. She turned her face into the ground and let out a grating roar.

A weight pummeled her chest, suddenly heavy, too heavy. She struggled to breathe, choking for air as an inferno ripped through her rib cage. Her muscles seized, and her free hand clenched, nails scraping across the metal floor.

Was she going to have a heart attack right there on the floor of Telematics? She'd only need to be dead for thirty seconds before Adriene-97 would slide out of a bin to replace her. She wondered if that'd be the record for shortest rezone ever.

The errant, pointless thought allowed her to find breath again. Her muscles slackened. She took a deep inhale and blinked the wetness from her eyes.

Despite how much her seizing chest hurt, she knew it wasn't due to anything so clinical as cardiac arrest. It was because she'd died, again. And again, there'd been *nothing*.

Like waking up after sleep with the feeling that no time had passed. It was a blink, an instant, a temporal lapse as information shot invisibly through the stardust and the code that quantified her existence was downloaded to some fucking server and shoved into a new shell.

But the mechanics weren't the worst of it, not by far. It was the reminder that came with it—the crushing sense of existential abandonment. Because no matter how many times she died, there was never any moment of clarity, no sense of peace, no in-between, no "white light." If there was something that came after, she would have seen a glimpse of it, one of the ninety-six times she'd died.

Still pinned to the ground, Adriene opened her mouth to speak, but nothing came out. She cleared her throat and tried again. "I . . . I remember," a mucus-laden voice rasped, one she could hardly recognize as her own.

The guard loosened his grip, then hooked an arm under her waist and hauled her to her feet. He started muttering apologies while he draped a thin robe over her shoulders, but she ignored him, staring at her sludge-caked bare feet and his worn boots. She took a few deep breaths to steady her thudding heart.

She'd said she remembered . . . but did she, really? How could she know they were real memories? Not implants—things they wanted her to believe? This could all be some Mechan trap . . .

"Specialist—"

Adriene elbowed him in the throat. He stumbled back, and she took off, scrambling as her wet feet slid across the floor.

Another guard was on her in a second, locking his arms around her, pulling her back into his chest. She roared and thrashed against him, but he tightened down. Another joined him.

Together they held her still, and with a single sharp prick, warmth bloomed in her neck. Her muscles relaxed and her eyelids drooped. She wallowed in the half second of peace before she was buried in darkness.

Adriene's eyes cracked open.

All around, nothing but white and gray, misshapen and blurry. She tried to blink away the haze, but couldn't see more than vague outlines of a surface in front of her and the legs of a stiff metal chair beneath her. She went to wipe the crust from her eyes, but a pair of thick cuffs kept her wrists magnetized to the top of a metal table.

With sinking dread, she recalled how she'd woken up: a screaming mess of panicked rage and survival instincts. But it already felt distant. Just another nightmare. The more she focused on it, the less real it seemed.

An "aggressive take," they'd call it in the report. Not her first, and certainly not her last.

A melody floated down from overhead speakers, all soft winds and harps and wood chimes—the kind of Zen bullshit they'd pump through the speakers at a spa. Or an asylum. Meant to foster a sense of tranquility, like there could be anything tranquil about being shoved into a new body and dumped out on the floor like a newborn foal.

At least she was no longer naked; they'd dressed her in a basic tan flight suit.

Adriene glanced around the room. It contained a rude amount of white. White walls, white ceiling, white porcelain-tiled floor. The panels of clustered diodes lining the ceiling bathed the white in white light.

Her eyes adjusted to the brightness, and she looked down at her hands to confirm they were hers. Ruddy, light brown skin smattered with a familiar pattern of dark freckles. Though her nails were too clean, trimmed too neatly. No hangnails, no bruises, no scars. That wouldn't last long.

The hard inner curves of the metal cuffs strained against her wristbone, but she managed to twist her right arm over, palm up. She eyed the too-smooth creases on her palm as she stretched her hand open and closed, open and closed, open and closed. Closed tighter until the nails bit into the skin. The ritual allayed her, if only somewhat.

She released her fist and breathed a sigh. Her body, same as always. Yet it never felt right, never fit quite the same. Everything had to be stretched, worn in like new boots.

"Specialist."

Adriene flinched as a sharp voice cut through the stale air and pressed against her unstretched eardrums. A lab-coated mass eclipsed her view, a nova's worth of light firing down into her new eyes. For a brief, terrifying moment, the metal casing of the flashlight seemed to twist, morphing into the curving halo of a crucible device. Adriene recoiled, spine slamming hard against her seat back.

"Steady, now," the lab coat droned, though to Adriene's fresh ears it sounded like the woman was screaming. "Look right."

Adriene opened her mouth to complain, but her vocal cords ignored her request. She flexed her jaw and looked right.

"Left."

Adriene swung her eyes left. She took a deep breath to calm her fraying nerves, inhaling the soft but distinct scent of lavender.

Though she could see nothing except dancing trails of light left by the vicious nova beam, that scent told her exactly who this lab coat was.

"Huan," Adriene's raw voice crackled out, barely a whisper. She cleared her throat and tried again, forcing more strength into her voice. "Doc, can we tone down the sensory stimulus a little?"

Still lingering close to Adriene's face, Huan's thin lips pressed together. She lowered her voice considerably and said, "Open."

Adriene complied, opening her mouth wide to let Huan peer down her throat. The doctor clicked off the light and slid the instrument into her coat pocket. She released the lock on Adriene's handcuffs, then picked up a tablet and started tapping.

Adriene slouched against her seat back, rubbing at either wrist in turn.

"Vitals are green." Huan exhaled a rough sigh and leaned on the edge of the table. "Not the cleanest take I've ever seen."

"No kidding," Adriene agreed. "What's the plan for handling these aggressive takes? I practically broke Rutherford's neck trying to get out of there."

"So I heard. Please do your best to remain calm in the future."

"Yeah, I'll get right on that," Adriene muttered. "There's gotta be a better way, Doc."

Huan nodded. "We have considered adding an upload delay so we can be notified before a husk is activated, but there's a high degree of risk involved in keeping a consciousness cached for any longer than absolutely necessary. I fear aggressive takes would increase tenfold. And there would likely be many misfires."

Adriene glowered. "You mean *deaths*?"

Huan remained unfazed. "Yes."

"So for now, we just keep getting dumped out of bins unceremoniously?"

"For the foreseeable future, yes." Huan looked back down at her tablet. "Now, how do you feel otherwise?"

Adriene cleared her throat. "Bit phlegmy."

"That's normal."

"Since when?"

"We installed new substructure modules week before last. They generate stronger respiratory systems, but there's an initial overproduction of phlegm."

"Oh. Great."

"It will subside with time. How do your lungs feel? Stronger? Can you tell a difference?"

Adriene eyed Huan levelly for a few long seconds. "Not fucking really, no."

"All right . . ." Huan said, tone careful—and a little concerned.

Adriene wiped her hands down her face and sucked in a breath through her nose. She had to get it together. Last thing she needed was to get tossed into an observation cube for "antagonistic" behavior. "Mira's ashes . . . Sorry, Doc. Really. I'm just sick of this shit."

"I'm sure. It's only been three weeks since I saw you last."

Adriene shuddered with the grisly memory. It had, in fact, only been three weeks since she'd last been face-to-face with a Mechan. And it'd gone just about as well as it had this time.

Adriene cleared away more phlegm. "Do you think that's why this take went so poorly?"

"No . . ." Huan began, her tone already packed with judgment, and Adriene was instantly sorry she'd asked. "It's because you, somehow—after only *three weeks*—have dependencies." She flicked through screens on her tablet. "Seriously, Valero?"

Adriene gave a weak shrug.

Huan sighed. "Just know, substance abuse has a drastic effect on your neurotransmitters, making it far more difficult to get a clean take. Lay off the booze, and it'll go easier the next time."

"Yeah, well, it's not exactly that easy."

"In fact, it is *that easy*," Huan said, finally looking up from the tablet, her dark brown eyes sharpening. "You've literally got a fresh start—a brand-new body. You don't have any of the addictions you think you do."

Adriene ran a hand through the half centimeter of thick hair on her head and let out a sigh. "Try explaining that to my brain."

"The brain is new too."

"You know what I mean, Doc. It's been four years. You'd think they'd have this shit better figured out by now."

"In actuality, that is quite a short time frame for technology of this magnitude. It is still very much in its infancy. Any perceived delay only appears such due to the 803rd's disproportionately above-average rezone rate." Huan's calculated look narrowed. "And a propensity for substance abuse, as I mentioned."

Adriene scoffed. "You say that like it's our fault."

"Just something to keep in mind. You all should consider not treating these bodies like they're expendable."

"We're not the ones who think they're expendable."

Huan raised an eyebrow. "Meaning?"

Adriene leaned forward, lowering her voice. "We just went on what was supposed to be a level-two, low-risk COB that lasted an *hour and a half* before we got ambushed and I had to zero out my entire squad. And that's not even a record."

"Your point?"

"The cheaper and easier rezoning gets, the further Command lowers risk-assessment thresholds. They're sending us into more and more uncertain situations, because they know we'll simply show up back here, shiny and new, once it goes to shit."

"Well, that may not be ideal," Huan said, "but it is your *job*."

"I know," Adriene said, trying to keep the anger from her voice. "But lower thresholds mean fewer resources toward recon. We're getting sent in with less thorough, less *accurate* intel. They're setting us up for failure."

"You think Command is using rezoning as a crutch to do less work?"

"I *know* they are."

"You're paranoid." Huan redocked her tablet. "Laying off the booze will help with that too. You ready?"

Adriene sighed and sat back. "Yeah, I'm ready."

Across the table, Huan pulled out a chair and sat down. She took a thinner, smaller-screened device from her lab coat. "Please state the current year."

"Nine twenty-nine."

"Repeat and remember the following words: apple, oxygen, comet."

"Apple, oxygen, comet."

"Count backward from ten to one." Adriene complied, then Huan turned the device around to show her the screen. "What is this?"

"It's the reproductive means of conifers, commonly found in boreal ecosystems on type-3 planets, or grown in colonial biodomes as part of the Concord Nations Interplanetary Sustainability Initiative."

Huan blinked, unamused. "In layman's terms, please."

"It's a pine cone."

"Which branch do you currently serve?"

"CNEF."

"Proper name, please."

Adriene sighed. "Concord Nations Extrasolar Fleet."

"What's your service number?"

"233–424."

"Division?"

"Pathfinders."

"Proper name."

"803rd Exoplanet Reconnaissance Division."

"List five words that start with the letter *H*."

"Hazard, hostage, hub." Adriene rubbed her eyes with the heels of her hands and took a deep breath. "Heaven. Hell."

"Repeat the words I asked you to remember."

"Apple, oxygen, comet."

"Please state your full name."

"Adriene Isella Valero."

"Confirm husk ID."

Adriene lifted her left arm and slid up the sleeve of the loose-fitting flight suit. On the inside of her elbow, a small black barcode with the label "233–424:096" confirmed her SKU.

Huan reached out with the device and scanned the barcode. "Ninety-six confirmed," she said, tapping the screen one last time. "Cognitive assessment complete." She pocketed the device, then stood up and pulled the larger tablet off the dock again. "Cubicle A4 for counseling. Then you still need to visit physiotherapy to get cleared for service, but Major Champlan wants to see you first."

Adriene stood up slowly, her legs wobbling beneath her. "Debrief *before* physio?"

"I don't think it's a debrief," Huan replied, her tone flat.

Adriene rubbed the back of her neck and waited, but Huan didn't elaborate.

"All right. Thanks." Adriene headed for the exit, pausing in the door frame after it slid open. "Sorry about the shitty attitude."

"Don't worry on it," Huan replied, already engrossed in her next task. "See you soon, Specialist."

Adriene sighed and stepped out into the hall. "I hope not, Doc."

CHAPTER

THREE

Adriene cut a familiar path through the corridors to the counseling center: a circular vestibule containing a dozen entrances. She approached cubicle A4, palmed the controls, and the door bisected.

Inside, a padded recliner sat at the center of the two-meter-square room. On the far wall hung an inactive viewscreen, a small metal receptacle built into the wall below it.

Adriene sat. The door sealed, and the overhead light dimmed as the viewscreen activated with a soft, bright chime. It produced a view of a verdant, mossy forest cut through by a winding stream, casting the tiny room in greenish light.

In the air in front of the screen, a hologram of a woman appeared: soft features, brown skin, chin-length black hair, her body vanishing below the shoulders.

The rendering spoke in a smooth female voice. "Welcome, Specialist Valero." The counseling VI's speech synthesis was better than any other Adriene had heard, and if she didn't think about it too hard, it sounded entirely real.

"Hello," Adriene replied, pressing a burgeoning headache from her temple with two fingers. She played along solely due to the chances of her ending up in the observation ward if she didn't.

For the next twenty minutes, Adriene recounted the events of the mission to the patient, empathetic, off-putting hologram. Though getting therapized by a piece of software unnerved her, she still preferred it to the couple of days every month when each rezone hub hosted a team of actual psychologists to give in-depth evaluations. Humans were much more difficult to outmaneuver.

Using her last ninety-six sessions as a cheat sheet, Adriene guided the VI toward its shortest, most unobtrusive end. As it always did, the computer recommended exposure therapy, and, as she always did, Adriene declined. She signed away CNEF's liability and the *"we're informing your commanding officer and this decision may affect forthcoming performance reviews"* form by offering her fingerprints to a small pad below the screen. She simply didn't have exposure therapy in her today. Major Champlan could slap her on the wrist for it later. If anyone even noticed.

After promising to practice the breathing techniques on her own time, the viewscreen displayed a floating green check mark.

"Assessment complete," the computer intoned. "Synthesizing . . . Please wait . . ."

A mechanical exhale of air sounded. With a light clatter, a pill case dropped into the metal dispenser. Adriene stared at it while the computer droned on about the specifics of the neurococktail it'd cooked up for her.

She didn't let it finish before she pocketed the case and left the cubicle.

Adriene's head had started pounding by the time she reached the quartermaster's office. She squeezed her temples with one hand, shielding her eyes from the harsh overhead lights as she entered.

Private Larson gave a courteous nod from behind the supply counter. "Specialist Valero." He pulled out a pile of folded gray fatigues and dropped them on the counter. "Saw Book a bit ago, figured you'd be in shortly. Got everything ready for ya."

"Thanks, Larson." A tremor rolled down her arm as she reached for the clothes. She clenched her hand into a fist and pulled back.

Larson raised an eyebrow. "Everything okay?"

"Yeah, fine. The others have been through already?"

"Booker and McGowan, yeah. Rhodes'll be comin' too, I assume?"

"Yeah, he'll be here." She pressed her thumb into the palm of her shaking hand and tried to keep her voice steady. "Say . . . you got anything other than fatigues back there?"

Larson regarded her steadily for a moment, then glanced over his shoulder toward the vacant storage room. He reached up and opened a cabinet above the counter.

A comforting warmth filled Adriene's chest. Larson dug around inside the cabinet for a few moments, then dropped a black knit cap onto her pile of clothes.

"Pretty new husk," he said evenly, "if it hasn't even grown hair yet. Wouldn't want ya to get cold." Adriene raised a level look at him, and he leaned his forearms on the counter, lowering his voice. "Huan already called me."

Adriene ground her teeth.

Larson pushed the fatigues across the counter toward her. "Sorry. Badges and tags are in the pockets."

Adriene grabbed the stack of clothes and headed for the exit.

"See you soon, Specialist," Larson called after her.

She pinched the bridge of her nose as she rounded the corner. She really fucking wished people would stop saying that.

The corridors were empty as Adriene headed for the closest locker room, where she changed out of her baggy jumpsuit and into the fitted charcoal-gray fatigues. She lingered for a few minutes, trying not to vomit into the trough-style sink as Harlan's screams echoed in the back of her mind.

The nausea subsided, though her hands shook as she splashed cold water on her face. She took a deep breath and grudgingly pulled the lined stocking cap on. Larson may be a hypocritical, withholding dick, but he was right—her practically bare head was freezing.

She left the latrine and made her way down a long corridor, lined on one side with wide windows. Outside, dusk had begun to settle across the surface of the small desert moon.

The drab, modular outpost buildings took on a rusty tinge as waves of brick-red sand rolled off the plains to the north. The gas giant Ouray dominated half the sky—a striated emerald backdrop shrouded by the moon's dusty atmosphere.

On the outskirts of the campus to the northeast, the frame of a massive half-built structure stretched up into the haze of sand. Maybe another telematics grid, or more likely an incubator. The need for more husks grew with every passing day.

Beyond the construction, red sand rolled off the top of a sandstone bluff, raining onto the structure. A shimmering, semitranslucent net caught the drift midair, then redirected it into a moat where dozens of automated haulers busily worked to rehome the sand. If not for the anti-encroachment system, the entire facility would end up buried under a drift within a month. The site certainly wouldn't have been Adriene's first choice for a division headquarters and rezone hub. But the turbulent magnetosphere of the gas giant they orbited made the facility all but impossible to detect remotely, which gave it substantial merit.

Adriene emptied her pockets as she walked, sliding the ID necklace over her head and pinning her name and rank badges to the front of her jacket. She reached the end of the hall and slid her hand over the exit door controls.

A rush of stiff, warm air hit her square in the face. She shielded her eyes from the eddies of red dust, then stepped out onto the platform.

A low-frequency pulse thrummed in her chest as she passed a cluster of towering cylindrical constructs. The telemeters were responsible for receiving rezone data on the moon's surface, relayed from the massive orbital antenna grid encircling the small moon—a barely visible lattice of arced metal that stretched from horizon to horizon.

Adriene didn't know the specifics of how it worked, only that somehow, all these hunks of metal assured that no matter where in the galaxy she died, she'd end up back at one of the thirteen rezone facilities, covered in gray sludge.

Thick clouds rolled in and the sky darkened considerably by the time she crossed the campus and arrived at the entrance to the Administration wing.

The door sealed behind her, silencing the shrill howl of the wind. The red cast was replaced with muted gray, and only stale echoes sounded through the foyer as a handful of soldiers quietly went about their business. The diode panels on the ceiling were barely lit, kept low to decrease power consumption after hours.

A dozen enclosed holosim booths lined the far wall, three of which were occupied.

Adriene pushed up her sleeves and approached an empty booth. She held the inside of her elbow to the access screen. It scanned her barcode, and the narrow door slid open, revealing a small black room less than two meters square.

She sat on the short stool in the center. The door shut, and a holographic field flickered on all around her.

Adriene sighed at the dull beige walls of a virtual waiting room, complete with a spindly ficus in the corner and a large, glinting bronze CNEF insignia on one wall. A chime dinged, shrill and loud in the enclosed space. Adriene cringed, the sound too harsh for her new, unstretched ears.

A computer-generated voice rang over the speakers. "Welcome to Major Miller Champlan's office—Specialist—Adriene—Valero. The major is currently in a meeting. Please remain seated, and she will be with you shortly."

More irritating Zen music played while Adriene waited, each high-pitched chord a fiery electric spike to her brain. Another wave of nausea rolled through her. She leaned forward, bracing on her knees.

Huan's assessment rang through her aching head—that she didn't have the addictions she thought she did. She tried to convince herself it was true, reminding her body that it didn't need the things it thought it did. Not yet, at least.

But it didn't want to listen. She thought she would have to step out of the booth to throw up when another chime rang out, accompanied by a flickering of light.

She swallowed back bile and looked up as the scene transformed around her: the simulated waiting room fading into a flawless reflection of Major Champlan's office aboard the CNS *Tannhauser*. The small porthole window showcased a sheet of inky black, speckled with points of starlight.

Across the desk sat a broad-shouldered woman wearing a double-breasted jacket in the lighter gray fabric of Command, shoulders adorned with a panoply of insignia. Her metallic left hand gleamed in the overhead light, a remnant of the cybernetics more commonly used prior to the large-scale rollout of rezone technology. Nowadays, you'd be given the option for a prosthesis, but many chose to rezone. Any synthetic enhancement put you one step closer to the enemy.

From her graying hair and pale, weathered skin, Adriene wondered if Champlan had ever rezoned, even once. The technology hadn't been standard issue until four years ago. Champlan was probably thirty years her senior and had been keeping a desk company for at least a decade. She might not even have a rezone chip.

The major looked up from her desk terminal, brow creased. "Valero? Already?"

"Yes, sir." Adriene stood and saluted, though she knew her virtual head would be cut off by the small-scale holosim generator. "Orem-III COB was a bust, sir."

Champlan waved a hand dismissively and looked at the small holographic display above her desk. "Just file the report later, Specialist."

"Yes, sir." Adriene sat back down.

Champlan didn't look up from her screen. "That meeting we'd scheduled with Human Resources Command in a few weeks?"

"Yes, sir."

"Well, it's canceled."

Adriene shifted in her seat. She hadn't been told what the meeting was for, but a cancellation sounded . . . bad. Though Huan had said this wasn't supposed to be a debrief, Adriene hadn't considered it might be a dressing-down.

But how had she fucked up? While rezoning your entire squad wasn't the *preferred* outcome of an op, it was common these days. She'd done everything by the book . . . well, except one thing. She'd ordered McGowan to go slim and hadn't gotten the go-ahead from Command before zeroing out. But that was a technicality. Again, so common anymore, she barely felt the need to mention it in her reports. Maybe Champlan had finally caught on to her habitual dodging of exposure therapy.

"Canceled, sir? Why's that?"

"They want it expedited, whatever they're up to." Champlan finally looked up from her terminal screen and rested both elbows on the desk. Her expression remained firm, though a furrow pinched between her eyebrows. "They need people sooner than they thought."

"Need people, sir?"

"You're being reassigned."

Adriene just stared. She'd been with the 803rd since the day she enlisted ten years ago. "Reassigned" was a word she never thought she'd hear.

Champlan steepled her fingers. "The 505th wants to incorporate pathfinders into their forward reconnaissance teams. One for each company, for now. Gotta hand over half a dozen of my best officers."

"The 505th, sir? That's special forces."

"Correct." The major let out a heavy sigh. "You'll be in the thick of it now, Specialist. Or rather, Sergeant."

Adriene pressed a thumb into the palm of her cramping hand, struggling to come up with a suitable response. "Well, thank you, sir. But . . . you don't seem pleased."

"I'm not." Champlan leaned back in her chair and crossed her arms. "Every time I get a couple good ones, they make me pass 'em off." She blew out a heavy sigh. "It's all part of the job, I suppose. And I know you'll do well with the 505th."

"Will there be training, sir?" Adriene sat up straighter, practically salivating at the idea of having a stint during which she would in all likelihood not get killed, but her heart sank as Champlan shook her head.

"You'll go through a basic primer on the two-week trip to rendezvous with the CNS *Aurora*," the major said. "Otherwise, they're just throwing you in headfirst, as far as I know."

Adriene nodded slowly. A two-week buffer. She'd take it. "The *Aurora*?" she asked. "What company is that, sir?"

"Flintlock," Champlan said. "CO's Commodore Thurston, but he's got a couple majors under him; I don't know who you'll report to directly. I'll see what I can dig up and transfer the details to the terminal in your dorm. Make sure you get cleared with physio first, though. Last thing I need's Thurston giving me grief for sending him a rotten husk."

"Yes, sir."

"The 505th runs on a continual blackout schedule," Champlan added. "I'd imagine you'll be dark for a few weeks, if not longer, so get your short- and medium-term affairs in order, and say your goodbyes to loved ones."

"Understood, sir." That would not be a difficult task to undertake.

"A shuttle will pick you up from the spaceport at 0430."

"Thank you, sir. It was an honor serving with you, Major."

"Likewise, Sergeant. You're dismissed."

Adriene went to stand, but hesitated. "Sir?"

"Go ahead."

"I'd like to recommend Private Harlan Rhodes for squad leader. The others trust him, and he has good instincts."

Champlan inclined her head. "I'll see to it. Thank you."

"Sir." Adriene saluted, then in a flash, the major's office disappeared, leaving her alone in the dark booth.

The door slid open, and she stepped back out into the dim, silent foyer.

"Specialist."

Adriene turned to find Harlan leaning against the wall near the entrance to the barracks, his sandy complexion shadowed in the subdued lighting. He ran a hand over his head—his light brown hair as short as hers, barely longer than the dusting of stubble on his jawline.

She managed a weak smile and headed over to him. "Hey."

He raised an eyebrow. "Or should I say *Sergeant*?"

"I just found out myself. How'd you hear?"

"The doc told Larson. The 505th, huh?"

"I guess. Flintlock company. They need pathfinders for their recon squads."

Harlan nodded, but remained silent.

"Larson said you hadn't been through when I got there," she said. "What took so long?"

"Shitty take."

"Me too."

Harlan shifted his weight. He cradled his right arm, strapped in a tight sling.

"You get hurt trying to fight your way out of Telematics?" she asked.

He shrugged. "Nah. Guess I didn't die quite fast enough after I lost the hand. Brain hasn't caught up yet. Left eye's still pretty fuzzy too." He rubbed his eye with the palm of his good hand.

An uncomfortable heat burned low in Adriene's stomach. Her delay had caused this—her hesitation in killing him. If she'd had the guts to shoot him sooner, this wouldn't have happened.

"Shit," she breathed. "I'm sorry, Harl."

"Not your fault. Physio says it'll only take a day or two till I'm back at a hundred percent." Harlan stared at the limp hand, gray eyes unfocused. "Weird as fuck, though," he said, voice low. "You can remember gettin' your face blown off, clear as day, but not the hand you had five minutes before that."

Adriene cleared her throat. "It's this husk tech. Some things take longer to catch up."

He kneaded his left thumb into the bicep of his paralyzed arm. "You ever remember losin' somethin' before a rezone?"

She shook her head slowly. She'd had plenty of shitty deaths. Some with broken and mangled limbs, so she'd have to lie over a grenade or roll off a cliff because she couldn't pull the trigger. Some where she'd bled out slowly, watching her insides spill out from a slice in her abdomen. And still her least favorite—where she'd had to knife herself in the heart, because she couldn't get to her head.

Yet somehow, even after ninety-six deaths, she'd never lost a limb for any length of time beforehand.

"No," she said. "Never."

One corner of his mouth lifted, though the smile didn't reach his eyes. "Glad you got outta there, at least. Seemed like every one of those damn bots had a crucible. They've been relentless with that lately."

A hollow pulse beat in Adriene's chest along with a profound compulsion to change the subject. "Did you catch any bulletins?" she asked.

"From Estes, yeah. Evac is on track. Watch Council says Mira's growth is steady, Shift projections are stable. No change with the Firewall either."

"And the colonies?"

He frowned. "None left. Back to square one."

Adriene nodded slowly, and she caught herself attempting to mimic Harlan's frown. Because that news should make her sad or scared or worried. But it only felt null. Just raw data.

Harlan scratched his chin. "Think we got a chance in hell of securing a colony before Mira dies?"

"Doesn't matter," Adriene sighed. "If we never break the Firewall, we'll be stuck in-system till the Shift burns out both Estes *and* Prova."

With their star's habitable zone moving farther and farther outward, they'd started evacuating their home planet of Estes, traveling one orbital ring out-system to join the farming settlements on the still-temperate planet of Prova. But that would only be a stopgap. Someday, they would need to leave their system and their dying star for good.

Harlan eyed her. "You think we should be focusing on breaking the Mechan blockade? Before staking a colony?"

She shrugged. "All I know," she began, stretching her hand open and closed a few times, "is that we don't seem to be accomplishing much out here at the moment."

Harlan exhaled a sigh. "Maybe not. But the more colonies the bots seize, the more new viable sites the Rehoming Committee needs us to provide. Kinda makes our jobs more important than ever, right?"

Adriene attempted to press her fake frown into a heartening smile. Harlan had always been adept at finding constructive outlooks, even for the shittiest of situations. Unfortunately, that's what made him a likely candidate as a lifer in the 803rd.

Tone sullen, he said, "Though I guess that won't be concerning you anymore, huh? Any idea what the 505th is up to out there?"

She shook her head. "None."

He held his slung arm tighter to his chest. "Bet Champlan's pissed to be losing you at a time like this."

"Didn't seem pleased, no. You should be getting a call from her." She tried to inject enthusiasm into her voice, though it was pointless. "I put you forward for squad leader."

Harlan's defocused gaze locked on the floor between them. "Thanks," he said, but by his tone, he wasn't sure she'd done him any kind of favor.

"You'll do great, Harl."

"Did you see Booker and Mac?"

"No—they okay?"

"Mac's a bit shaken, but fine. And you know Book."

She nodded, trying to catch Harlan's gaze. He didn't move, eyes glazing over as he blinked heavily at the floor.

"They're fast-tracking me out of here." She dug a thumb into the palm of one hand. "I'm on the first shuttle out in the morning. You wanna get a drink tonight?"

Harlan shook his head slowly. "No," he said, his voice a dull croak. "I never wanna wake up like that again." Then he finally met her eyes, dark gray orbs glossy and faraway. "And you shouldn't either."

He turned and walked away down the hall, disappearing through the fire door that led to the dormitories. She watched him go, frozen as the strength bled from her muscles.

Was that it? How he wanted to say goodbye after living and serving side by side for ten years?

Soon, she would be dozens, if not hundreds, of light-years away. They may very well never see each other again.

That should disturb her. She knew that. Harlan was her best friend. That he'd written her off should make her . . . *something*—angry, frustrated, regretful, heartbroken. But it got harder every day to find the will to care.

She rubbed her trembling hands.

It'd get better. New husks needed breaking in. She'd remember how to feel, eventually. How to give a shit again.

Something shapeless and bitter clawed at the back of her mind, and it wouldn't let go. It told her Harlan was right, in a sense. She didn't want to wake up again.

CHAPTER

FOUR

Adriene spent the next two weeks aboard a tiny cargo ship, reviewing her scant primer on the 505th between bouts of violent vomiting, cold sweats, debilitating headaches, and tremors that bordered on seizures. Being locked in subspace aboard a ship crewed by what had to be the only two sober soldiers in the galaxy was certainly one way to detox.

Halfway in, she'd gotten over the worst of it, though irritation and anger continued to dominate her. It was safe to say she hadn't made any lifelong friends on the journey.

"We're twenty out," the first mate grumbled as he passed between the stacks of crates. He glanced down at Adriene's cot, brow tight with contempt. "Might wanna pack up your shit."

"I'll miss you too," she called after him, but with the heavy thunk of a bulkhead door, he was gone.

Adriene sighed and climbed out of her cot. She slipped her jacket on, then pulled her knit cap down over her slightly less-bald head. It'd grown out enough to be annoying and itchy, but still left her scalp cold. Except when she was in the forsaken storage hold that'd served as her makeshift bunk for the last two weeks, which had fluctuated between really hot and really fucking hot.

She quickly packed her ruck with her few belongings—mostly changes of clothing and a couple of trinkets from over the years. Things that should hold sentimental value, but were performative, more than anything—something to tote around and make it look like she had something other than the clothes on her back.

A warning beacon washed the room in yellow light. The air felt denser for a fraction of a second as the ship exited subspace. Adriene's stomach lurched, and she steadied her breath. It'd been a whole two days since she'd thrown up; she wasn't going to break the streak now.

She took her pack and left the storage hold, heading down the narrow gunwale toward the air lock. She paused at a small observation window near the port defense turret.

Their ship sped through a cluster of tiny asteroids. Flashes of red flared across the monochrome backdrop of space as automated lasers broke up the larger rocks in their path. A gas giant lingered in the distance, a massive black storm staining the pristine ivory shell, creeping across the featureless surface like a sluggish oil slick.

The ship banked to skirt a mammoth asteroid, its craggy surface flashing with glints of ice or minerals. Beyond the edge of the belt, the dark hull of a matte-black ship came into view. The CNS *Aurora*.

Even without its stealth systems engaged, the armored vessel was difficult to see against the dark of space. Sleeker than most ships in the CNEF fleet, not a single scar marred its smooth, elongated hull.

At the back sat two sets of massive quad ion engines. Though in servicing a regiment like the 505th, the subspace accelerator would likely do the brunt of the work. Built for stealth and support, the *Aurora* served as a mobile headquarters of sorts, more a troop carrier than a warship.

Though it appeared to be well-fitted regardless. A series of hexagonal panels ran the length of the hull both dorsal and ventral—housing for plasma or laser cannons, retractable turrets, missile bays.

But it was the small glass enclosure protruding from the underbelly that caught Adriene's eye. The tessellated dome of interlocking glass panels looked suspiciously like sketches for the quantum conception generators she'd only ever read *theory* articles about. Which meant the *Aurora* was likely equipped with a stealth system that technically didn't exist. It was clear who CNEF liked to spend their budget on.

A strange sensation gripped her chest—a tightness she could almost attribute to anxiety, though muted. She was about to join a very different sect of the Extrasolar Fleet than she was used to.

CNEF had been established to explore the galaxy and facilitate colonization efforts in response to their dying star. Not fight sentient robots.

Over the last twenty years since first contact, they'd had to switch focus to become something much different. Which, among other endeavors, had resulted in divisions like the 505th—specialized teams working to undermine Mechan efforts instead of merely defending or reacting as the rest of the Extrasolar Fleet and Local Corps did.

Meanwhile, the 803rd toiled away, attempting to accomplish CNEF's original objectives of finding as many viable worlds as possible. All in the vain hope that if they spread themselves thin enough, the Mechan might run out of the numbers to respond—or maybe accidentally miss one or two, if luck was on their side. So far, it had not been.

Fifteen minutes later, Adriene's small prison landed in the *Aurora*'s docking bay. She waited at the air lock as it slid open. The loading ramp lowered, an impeccably clean hangar stretching out before her.

They'd taken up the last open slot in the small bay, with three other shuttles of similar size parked along the length. Two sported the bland, matte-gray paint job and boxy structure of CNEF transports. The third was shapely in comparison—sleek and silver, the back aft adorned with the geometric shield logo of the extrasolar fleet's primary defense contractor, Dodson-Mueller.

Half a dozen deck crew worked at various tasks around the bay: A few moved supply crates to lifts, one sorted parts, another polished the hull of a pristine Colt starfighter—one of a dozen that sat parked beside a lineup of small launch tube doors.

Adriene hefted her ruck onto her shoulder and descended the ramp along with the pilot, who waved goodbye, then broke off toward the deck chief approaching with a shipment dossier.

Across the bay, a young man in trim dark gray fatigues headed toward Adriene. He was somewhat short in stature, with close-cropped black hair and warm ivory skin. As he approached, he smiled, eyes too bright, expression too content.

He stopped and gave her a smart salute. "Sergeant Valero, welcome aboard the CNS *Aurora*."

Adriene returned the salute.

"I'm Sergeant Lian Kato," he said, with the edge of a Provan accent he seemed to be trying to restrain. "Just gotta confirm your SKU."

He fished a small handheld device from his pocket, and Adriene pushed up her sleeve.

He scanned her tattooed barcode, and his carefree facade creased. "Ninety-six? *Mira's end*. What's the 803rd up to out there?"

She let out a sigh. "Forging a Galactic Future for Humanity," she recited.

He lifted an eyebrow. "By trial and fucking error?"

"Basically."

"Well, all right, then, Ninety-Six." His placid look returned somewhat along with a labored grin. "Nice to have ya on board."

Adriene followed as Sergeant Kato led her out of the docking bay into a hexagonal corridor. Broad squares of light sat flush with the ceiling, stretching the length of the hall and casting everything in a soft, ambient glow. As the hull and hangar had been, the corridors were pristine, and as they walked, their charcoal-gray fatigues reflected in the glossy-white wall panels.

"Everyone's in training," Kato said, glancing over his shoulder at her as he kept pace a few steps ahead. "So ship's pretty quiet at the moment."

"I see that." She cast a lingering look up and down the empty corridors. "Training for what?"

"We've been gettin' all kinds of deliveries. New suits, new implant build. Demo's got some new toys too. But really, it's just 'cause we've got nothin' better to do." He shrugged one shoulder. "We've been sittin' out here a couple weeks just waitin'. Things are already buzzin', though, I can feel it. Orders'll be comin' down soon, I'm sure of it."

"CO's Commodore Thurston?" she asked. The "details" Champlan had promised had been scant to say the least.

"Yep," Kato replied. "Thurston runs the show, but we report to Major Blackwell. He'd be here himself to give you the rundown, but he's in training with squad leaders all morning. Normally, I'd take you for a tour and let you read the advanced primers. That shit they give ya on the ride over's not much use, huh?"

"Not really," she admitted. "It seemed pretty generic."

"Yeah it's all the *unclassified* stuff. Which is pretty much nothin'. But anyway, I'll have to give you a rain check, 'cause they got you booked solid all mornin'. I'm takin' ya to Medical now so you can get your implant."

"My *implant*?"

"Your VI? Shit—at least that's in the primer, ain't it?"

She nodded, recalling a vague mention of a virtual intelligence aid under the standard-issue equipment list. Though she hadn't realized that meant an implant. "Yeah, it did mention a VI. Something that helps interface with the hardsuits?"

"You got it. A nice little virtual intelligence, sittin' right in your brain." He tapped his temple. "Lets ya access all the bells and whistles on the hardsuits, and loads more."

Adriene wrung her hands as they kept their brisk pace.

"Don't worry," Kato said, giving a sympathetic glance back at her. "Procedure won't take more than an hour. They'll knock ya out, and it'll be done before you know it. It's like gettin' a filling."

"It's okay," she assured. "I'm not worried."

"Of course." He flashed her a grin. "After ninety-six deaths, a little anesthesia wouldn't faze you."

She sighed heavily. He wasn't wrong.

Kato slowed his pace, falling in line beside her, his ivory cheeks flushing red. "Shit, that's a fucking terrible thing to say, huh?" He ran a hand through his short black hair. "Sorry."

"It's fine, really."

"All right, well, lemme get my foot outta my mouth quick . . ." Kato turned a corner, giving a passing, casual salute to a couple of soldiers who stood looking over a tablet. They offered half-hearted salutes back, but their looks immediately diverted to Adriene, their hard stares unabashedly assessing her. She didn't get the feeling Flintlock had frequent newcomers.

"Anyway," Kato said as they turned another corner and the soldiers disappeared from view, "after your implant, we got our Dodson-Mueller rep running briefings on the new hardsuits. The major wants to make sure we recon folk get to that today, since we'll be out in the muck first. Briefing theater C. Starts at 0930."

"*We* recon folk?" Adriene asked. "You're Forward Recon too?"

"Yep, comms and engineering. We'll be squadmates."

"You squad leader?"

"Nope. That's Lieutenant Brigham. You'll meet him and our fourth, Gallagher, at the briefing. But *first* . . ." Kato came to a stop in front of a white hexagonal door with "MEDICAL" in wide black lettering across it. "You've gotta have a little brain surgery."

"Welcome back, Sergeant."

Adriene could have opened her eyes. She knew she was capable of it. But she couldn't bring herself to do it.

This place was dark, calm, peaceful. Warm, but not too warm. Quiet and safe, with a soft scent of evergreen and cloves. If she breathed deeply enough, her consciousness could drift, and it'd be so easy to descend back into nothing.

"Sergeant?" The voice came again—male, steady and rich, but rough around the edges.

She pushed out a breath and kept her eyes closed. "No thanks. I'm good."

The man breathed a short laugh. "I don't think you get to not wake up."

Adriene sighed and peeled her eyes open. Clean white walls, organized equipment trays, a recessed computer terminal. Just like any other room in any other medical bay.

At the foot of her gurney, a man stood staring expectantly at her. Warm brown skin, inky black hair, face dominated by a well-formed nose of straight planes and hard ridges.

He gave a weak smile. "Haven't slept that good in weeks, have ya?" he asked. His weathered tone didn't match his apparent age—mid-thirties at the oldest.

"I've *never* slept that good," she corrected, her voice gravelly.

The man chuckled and started scrawling on his tablet with a stylus.

Adriene suppressed a groan as she swung her legs over the edge of the gurney and sat up. Her head spun.

She eyed the man as a strand of his chin-length hair fell from its tie and he tucked it behind his ear. That haircut could mean one of two things. Either Flintlock was lax on grooming protocols, or this guy was a civilian.

"They let you get away with that haircut out here?" she asked.

"Better than yours." He grinned, but didn't look up.

She scoffed, a strange sensation pulling at the corners of her mouth.

"I'm a contractor," he explained, and tugged aside the lapel of his lab coat. He wore a fitted gray shirt underneath, the Dodson-Mueller logo embroidered on the chest: the lines of a *D* and *M* outlined within the shape of a shield. "Carl Daroga, chief systems engineer. Pleasure to meet you, Sergeant. At least, now that you're awake."

"You too . . . You're not the doctor I met earlier."

"The doc does the anesthesia," he explained. "I do the installations, make sure it all gets hooked up right. We're a little behind schedule, to be honest. Install went great, but I had more trouble than usual getting the implant to play nicely with your brain. Might have something to do with how many times you've rezoned—*Mira's end*, ninety-six is a lot of times to die."

"I promise it's not as fun as it sounds."

He laughed, his green eyes glinting with amusement as he glanced up at her. "Well, I've got a few things to brief you on, then we'll give it a spin quick and get you on your way."

She ran her hands down the back of her head and neck. "Any incision?"

"Nope." He pointed up with one finger. "We take 'er right up the nose."

She instinctively scrunched her face. "I don't feel any different. Should I?"

"No, ma'am," he said, sliding the stylus behind his ear, pinning the loose pieces of his long hair back along with it. "I'd be worried if you did. Your implant's only active when prompted by your CO upon deployment, or when under duress as signified by critical life signs—adrenaline and cortisol levels, all that good stuff."

"I see."

"And, not sure if you've had a chance to review the primers yet, but . . ." He cleared his throat, his tone falling into the level drone of recitation. "Part of your responsibility as a soldier of Flintlock is to aid in the development of prototype equipment and special operations software and hardware. As such, you're expected to give feedback concerning the functionality and viability of issued equipment."

She dipped her chin slowly. "Understood."

Daroga lowered his voice. "I wouldn't worry about it too much—we've got a stable build right now. Just report any bugs or suggested upgrades."

"What's the procedure for reporting?"

"You can come directly to me, or there's an application for it on the terminal in your quarters. And please do report *everything*. The others'll try to give you shit—they'll say certain stuff's a fluke, that it's the 'ghost in the system.' *Please*," he implored, letting out a heavy sigh, "don't listen to them. They're idiots. Report every issue you encounter, no matter how small."

She nodded. "You got it . . . Sorry, did you just say 'ghost in the system'?"

He waved a hand dismissively. "Meatheads," he mumbled under his breath, then tapped on his tablet a few times. "Now, you might feel a twinge behind your eyes. That's completely normal. It's just the implant forming an active connection with your optical nerves for the first time."

A flash of white bloomed in Adriene's vision, and a hot lance fired across the back of her eyes. Her view of the room disappeared entirely into a void of white.

Her heart thudded against her ribs. She gripped the edge of the gurney with both hands, feeling suddenly unmoored.

"Oh, uh," Daroga added quickly, "you might lose your sight for a second too."

Adriene ground her teeth, but her irritation disappeared into stunned disbelief as a placid male voice rang through her mind.

// Welcome to Rubicon. //

She opened her mouth, but said nothing. Her normal sight had returned, but a crystal clear display overlaid it with the text: "Welcome to Rubicon, build 2.7.1."

The words disappeared and left a simple heads-up display with a bar along the bottom, hosting a readout of her vital signs. A slew of other numbers, icons, and meters framed the edges, grayed out and seemingly inactive.

Adriene glanced around the room, and the color of the HUD's lines shifted fluidly, almost imperceptibly—black and thin when it overlaid lighter objects, but white and thicker over darker areas. No matter where she looked, no matter what she focused on, the lines remained perfectly sharp.

"You should see a heads-up display," Daroga prompted.

"I do . . ." she mumbled, awe in her voice. A HUD without a helmet. That was certainly an improvement.

"Excellent. Pushing the upgrade."

A shiver ran down her spine as the tranquil male voice spoke again, directly into her brain.

// Upgrade in progress . . . //

A few moments later, the small "2.7.1" in the corner flashed and became "2.7.4."

// 2.7.4 upgrade complete. //

A green check mark appeared, accompanied by a high-pitched chime. Adriene gritted her teeth, making a mental note for later to figure out how to get the VI to cut the obnoxious chime bullshit.

// Preference acknowledged: Suppress audible noncombat notifications. Please confirm. //

She sat frozen, clutching the edge of the gurney cushion. She looked up at Daroga, who stood unmoving, one thick eyebrow lifted.

She instinctively cleared her throat.

Confirmed . . .

// Preference accepted. //

Holy shit.

// Syntax error. Please rephrase. //

"Please tell me you're not gonna take every thought I have at face value," she said, only half realizing she'd spoken aloud. Daroga bit back a smile.

// Correct. Though Rubicon is technically incapable of not taking a directive at face value, it will adapt over time to best accommodate your behavioral patterns and personality. //

She shook her head slowly. *How?*

// Rubicon functions predominantly via a nanite-assisted neural net operating in conjunction with your biological neural pathways. Specific details on Rubicon's functionality are classified. //

Why do you refer to yourself in the third person?

// Rubicon's profile default 1A, setting five, selection A: third-person pronouns. Do you wish to change this setting now? //

Sure . . . ?

// In addition to adjusting individual parameters, you may also select from one of fifteen predefined profiles. Popular selections include—//

The voice cut off with a sharp prick in the back of her brain, and the interface flickered, then disappeared.

Adriene slowly refocused on the room around her.

Daroga's fingers hovered over his tablet . . . He'd turned it off.

"Damn, you took to that quick." He tilted his head to catch her gaze. "Most folks freak out the first time."

Adriene nodded silently, her eyes falling to the floor.

His tone softened. "I get the feeling you're not quite so easily disturbed."

She didn't respond, and Daroga shifted his weight a few times before setting his tablet down on the gurney.

"Anyway," he said, voice somewhat strained, "you'll have to adjust settings later. Batch of new hardsuits came in with my colleague the other day. I'm giving a lecture down the hall in ten. I need to clean up here, but I'm sure you can find the way—it's just a few doors down on the right. Briefing theater C."

"Right. Thanks for . . ." Adriene gestured vaguely at her head.

One corner of his mouth lifted. "Anytime."

She slid off the gurney, wavering slightly as her head spun. Daroga held out a hand to steady her, but her vision cleared, and she waved him off. "I'm fine."

"Try to take it easy for a few hours," he warned.

"Will do." She made for the door, but paused partway and turned back. "Can I ask . . . ?"

"Go ahead," he prompted.

"What happens to the VI if we rezone?"

A glint flashed in Daroga's green eyes, and his lips twitched with a faint smile. "Good question. Until it becomes standard issue, new husks won't come with a Rubicon installed, so you'll come back to see me and get a new one. Preferences, personality, learning protocols—everything syncs with the Rubicon mainframe aboard the *Aurora*. You won't lose any data."

"And this implant doesn't interfere with our rezone chip?"

He swallowed and shook his head. "No. Perfectly safe."

Adriene rubbed the palms of her hands in turn, nodding slowly.

Daroga regarded her steadily for a moment. "To be honest," he said, his voice taking on a low, informal tone again, "we just don't rezone much in Flintlock. It's not going to be like what you're used to from the 803rd. You're not cannon fodder."

She blinked the dryness from her eyes as she stared back at him, unsure of what to make of his comment. His mouth was turned down, brow creased.

He felt *bad* for her.

A flash of heat bloomed in her gut. She didn't need his pity. She wasn't unique. It wasn't any different to rezone one time or a thousand times. It was all death—a permanence avoided—and in the end, they were still something that existed that shouldn't. And they were all the same in that regard.

"Not as often, anyway," Daroga added quietly, and she looked back at him in confusion. He gave another wry smile. "Cannon fodder, I mean."

Adriene studied the humor lining his expression. Her anger slowly dissipated as she realized what he was doing. She'd barely recognized it. She had her new husk to thank for that.

He was trying to . . . make her feel better. Lighten the mood, use humor to soften the dire reality of the situation. It's exactly how Harlan would have responded. Normal Harlan. Not the vacant, broken one she'd left behind two weeks ago.

Adriene inclined her head toward Daroga, then forced herself toward the exit. "Thanks," she said as the door slid open.

"See you soon, Sergeant."

Adriene left into the halls of the *Aurora*, mind reeling.

She now had an implant in her head, physically linked to her brain functions, with a virtual intelligence that could read her thoughts, speak directly into her mind, and do fuck-only-knows what else.

Yet all she could think about was how badly she needed a drink.

CHAPTER
FIVE

A few hours later, Adriene started to think alcohol might not cut it. She'd sat through some tedious lectures in her career, but this one had proven exceptionally mind-numbing.

It wasn't *"Dodson-Mueller chief systems engineer"* Daroga's fault. He wasn't all that unpleasant to look at, if she was being honest. It mostly had to do with the fact that she had no context for the tech. She'd never used a hardsuit even remotely as advanced as the ones they were replacing, so talking about the improvements meant little to her. One thing had been made perfectly clear: This new suit combined with the implant in her head would make for a daunting upgrade from what she'd grown accustomed to with the 803rd.

The rest of the women and men of Flintlock sat around her in varying degrees of attentiveness, but none had the glossed-over look of ignorance. All this talk of power umbilicals and actuators and microgyroscopics actually meant something to them.

Outwardly, they appeared no different than the soldiers she'd served with for the last ten years, and yet she couldn't help but feel like an imposter among them. She'd always proven a firmly average soldier, and she'd assumed specialist would be the furthest someone of her raw talent could rise. These soldiers had unique qualifications, years of focused, specialized training—likely from a young age. She'd bet a year's wages that not one had drafted in through the federal guardianship program like she had. Though no one had given her cause to feel unwelcome, she couldn't shake the feeling of being a class below.

Adriene forced her attention back to the lecture. Daroga had shed his lab coat and now stood at the front of the meeting room, repeatedly brushing aside his long black hair, now free from its tie. The circular hologram table beside him projected a rotating view of the new suit, labeled with the text "Dodson-Mueller Guardian Flex 440B Hardsuit Mk IV."

Another rep sat in a chair against the back wall—presumably the "colleague" Daroga had mentioned. The prim woman's eyes had glazed over the second Daroga's speech turned technical. She wore a tailored two-piece suit, hair pulled back into a tight bun, one ankle crossed over the other.

In the far back corner of the room stood a tall white man in his late forties, with short, disheveled salt-and-pepper hair. He wore the lighter gray uniform of Command, but stood half in shadow, making it difficult to see his insignia. She'd guess him to be Major Blackwell, but the way he leaned against the side wall, arms crossed tightly, neck stooped, gaze down . . . He seemed like he'd rather be anywhere else in the universe. Not a very good look for an operations commander.

Adriene drew in a deep breath and let it out slowly, wringing her hands to keep from dozing off. Her future squadmate Sergeant Kato sat upright and attentive beside her, expression enthusiastic. When she'd arrived, she'd tried her very best to disappear into the back row, but unfortunately, Kato had been diligently awaiting her arrival and immediately dragged her up to sit beside him near the front. The lecture had started promptly, and she hadn't been properly introduced to her other two Forward Recon squadmates—a stocky man and a curly-haired woman who both sat on the other side of Kato.

Daroga looked up from his tablet. "Now that we're rolling out the 2.7.4 upgrade, you guys'll be able to take advantage of the suit's new neural osmosis protocols. You should experience far less mental fatigue from extended operations."

Her stocky male squadmate grunted. "You mean when it hijacks our brains to use like a motherboard?"

Daroga flashed a congenial smile, all straight white teeth and charm. "More like a processor, but yes."

A murmur of chuckles rose up. The gruff man grumbled, then crossed his thick arms and leaned back.

"That's one thing I really need you guys to keep an eye on," Daroga said. "Please pay close attention to exactly when you're starting to feel that mental lethargy, and let your VI know. I really want to narrow in on that and get it reduced for you as much as possible." He glanced up at the clock on the back wall. "I know we're running long, but hang in here with me—I have one final feature I want to make sure to mention . . ."

Daroga tapped the hologram table's controls, and a new image appeared: an overlarge model of the hardsuit's glove with the side sliced away, revealing the inner layers.

"With the new conductive actuator gloves," he continued, "you'll be able to siphon electrical current from outside sources to recharge your capacitor."

Murmurs of approval rose across the crowd, and Adriene found herself suddenly interested. The specs claimed the suit had a 120-hour battery life under "standard conditions," but that count would surely be much less if the shit really hit the fan. Being able to recharge her suit on the fly could easily mean the difference between a rezone or a safe extraction.

"Though," Daroga began, "we don't recommend it unless it's an emergency. It can get . . . a little shocky."

"Shocky?" someone asked warily.

"Nothing too dangerous, rest assured, but there's a fifty-thousand-volt conduction threshold with the lining. You'll get a nice, sustained shock out of it."

Kato grinned broadly. "Sounds fun." The curly-haired woman sitting on his other side elbowed him.

Daroga inclined his head. "Just make sure you only use it on L-grade devices, please," he warned. "That'll be things like your standard early-drop generators, solar-powered comm relay units, or any of the Mechan core accumulators. But not the bigger stuff like your long-term gennys or dropship batteries. T-grade and higher will short out your suit—and your Rubicon implant. And it'll probably kill you. And we all know how inconvenient a mid-engagement rezone can be."

Soft chuckles rose from the crowd, and Adriene withheld a scoff as she glanced around at the others: fresh-faced, bright eyes, eager expressions. They probably all had single-digit SKUs on their arms.

The door at the front of the room slid open. A man in his fifties with dusty black hair and leathery, light bronze skin entered. Another major, judging by the insignia on his light gray uniform. He caught Daroga's eye and nodded sharply.

"All right, everyone, time to wrap this up," Daroga announced. "You can find the full manual on the terminals in your quarters. These guys have been heavily field-tested, but your next operation will be the first live deployment, so stay sharp and remember to reboot if things go south. You can always reset to safe mode and roll with the basics. Anyone have any questions?"

"Are there sims?" someone asked.

"Yes, absolutely. Simulation ops go live in VR rooms . . ." Daroga glanced down at his tablet. "One through four and eight through ten, starting tomorrow at 0600. You can sign up for slots directly from your terminal. But first, make sure you visit Medical if your implant hasn't been updated to the new build. Your suits will be fitted with their upgrade modules later today, but I want to double-check who gets what upgrade, so please stay for a few minutes and come up with your squad when I call you. I'll start with the lucky folks who'll be heading out first—Forward Recon."

A murmur of voices rose as everyone stood and started gathering in small groups to talk—likely by squad, though Adriene had no way to tell. They all wore the same embroidered 505th badge on their arms alongside the Flintlock insignia—a jagged spark of amber flame on a field of cobalt. But there were no apparent squad designations beyond that.

The tall, disinterested man who'd been hiding out in the back pushed off the wall and marched straight for the door. Through the shifting bodies, Adriene thought she saw the metallic glint of an augment on the man's left cheek as he exited.

"Another major," Kato said.

Adriene pulled her focus to Kato smiling beside her.

"Wonderin' who that was?" he surmised, pushing off his knees as he stood. "Major West, intelligence lead," he explained. "Dabbles in R&D too. We don't see him much—neck-deep in stats and secrets most of the time, I guess. Blackwell's our operations CO. Here—"

Kato stepped into the aisle and dragged Adriene out with him. With a light bounce to his step, he led her toward the bronze-skinned major who'd entered at the end of the lecture.

"Our new addition, sir," Kato piped.

Adriene saluted. "Major Blackwell, sir."

"Valero, I presume?" Blackwell said, his low voice seeming to come more from his chest than his throat.

"Yes, sir."

"Good to have you on board, Sergeant. Major Champlan had nothing but good things to say."

"Glad to hear it, sir."

"I won't be able to help with your onboarding." He glanced over his shoulder at the prim female Dodson-Mueller rep who stood waiting by the door, tapping her foot, posture ramrod straight. "I need to review the new vendor contracts."

Kato let out a cough that sounded like a stifled laugh, but when Adriene glanced at him, he just stood with his fist pressed against his mouth. He coughed again.

Blackwell ignored him. "But check in with Mr. Daroga, then have Sergeant Kato show you to the arms master. They'll get your loadout confirmed and your suit outfitted."

"Understood, sir."

Kato grinned. "I'll get 'er all decked out, sir."

Blackwell nodded, then followed the Dodson-Mueller rep out of the meeting room. Kato tugged Adriene's sleeve, leading her toward the front of the room, where their other two squadmates waited with Daroga.

"All right," Daroga said as they approached, "I've got Lieutenant Miles Brigham, squad leader module, with the medic upgrade?"

"Yeah," the stocky, gruff man said. He was probably late thirties, with the kind of patchy, weather-beaten tan skin that never looked totally clean. "And make sure it's the objective classifier build this time," he added, crossing his arms. "That other one's shit."

"You got it, boss," Daroga said. "Next, Sergeant Vivienne Gallagher, overwatch and sniper modules."

"Yep," the woman answered. She tucked a loose piece of curly black hair behind her ear and cast Adriene a cordial smile.

Adriene's gaze stuck on the tattoos covering Gallagher's hands, the dark black ink almost indiscernible against her dark brown skin. Long, jagged lines ran down her wrist, over the tops of her hands, and down her long, thin fingers. Avastian.

It'd been years since she'd seen that motif, but it was unmistakable. Hardly anyone in CNEF practiced that particular "religion." To Adriene, it'd always seemed like more of a cult. She'd had a brief run-in with a rather zealous group of avastians during her time as a ward. With a less-than-fortunate outcome, to say the least.

Daroga swept through a few screens on his tablet. "We've got a few different builds depending on your firearm of choice," he told Gallagher. "What're you shooting?"

"Soothill 920," Gallagher answered.

"Got it." Daroga made a selection on the tablet, then looked at Kato. "Sergeant Lian Kato," he said, all formality dropping from his tone as Kato smiled, rubbing the side of his head against Daroga's shoulder like a doting cat. "Comms and engineering . . . you prefer the Havoc engineering package, correct, Mr. Kato?"

Kato grinned up at him. "Yes, please and thank you, Mr. Daroga, sir."

Daroga made the selection, then looked to Adriene. "And for our newcomer, Sergeant Adriene Valero. You get one of our brand-new pathfinder modules."

"Sounds right," Adriene said.

"Excellent." Daroga swept across the tablet. "Make sure you let me know how it's working for you; this'll be its initial field test. But same goes for everyone. Each module has a patch suite installed, so depending on the operation—and if we have a hot link back to the *Aurora*—I should be able to make small tweaks on the fly."

"Thanks, bud," Kato said. He and Daroga linked arms, hands gripping each other's forearms, then shifting to tap elbows—a gesture common to rural Provans.

Daroga called the next group up, and Adriene followed her squadmates as they congregated near the exit.

"Valero." Gallagher inclined her head to Adriene, offering a quick, firm handshake. "It'll be good to have you. Kato's not the best with directions."

"S'not my fuckin' fault." Kato glowered. "That shit got shunted to me. Should be overwatch's job—"

Gallagher crossed her arms. "You'd rather I stand around drawing you up a map instead of keeping scrappers from getting the drop on us?"

"Just sayin', you're lookin' at a damn map anyway."

Brigham turned to Adriene as the other two continued bickering. "We've been running with only the three of us for a couple months," he explained. "Been a bit of a strain."

"You ever had a fourth?"

"We did," he began, then he cleared his throat. "He was, uh . . . reassigned."

Gallagher and Kato quieted, and a heavy silence filled the air. Adriene looked between the three of them—gazes diverted, shoulders drawn down.

Gallagher mercifully changed the subject. "So, where'd you get kicked up from?"

"803rd," Adriene said.

Brigham winced. "Shit. That sucks."

"You get used to it."

He raised a thick eyebrow. "Do you?"

"Sorta."

"Well, you're here now," he said, "and we try our best not to die in the 505th."

"So I hear. That should be an interesting change of pace."

Kato flashed a smile and elbowed Gallagher. "See, what'd I tell ya? Great attitude."

Daroga called up another squad, and a group at the far side of the room chanted a series of low-pitched whoops.

Brigham groaned and crossed his arms over his thick chest.

"Who's that?" Adriene asked.

"Fuckin' *Stormwalkers,*" he said, practically spitting the name. "They're like Flintlock's version of Telluride's White Wolves."

Adriene nodded along as if that reference meant something to her.

"Don't mind Brig," Kato said. "He hates everyone that's not Forward Recon. All forty-six of them."

"Well, seriously," Brigham grumbled. "We lay all the groundwork so these turkeys can drop in and take all the credit."

"Lay off it, Brig," Gallagher chided. "We all know you're jaded."

Kato smiled and tilted his head toward Adriene. "This one doesn't."

Brigham huffed and waved them off before turning and leaving.

Adriene sighed. "I think I'm all caught up."

Gallagher chuckled.

They said their goodbyes to Gallagher, then Kato took Adriene to the arms master. They let her test-fire *every* weapon in the arsenal—fifteen different rifles, twelve pistols, and a handful of specialty weapons. They also offered up an entire catalog of special-order items, but she didn't even bother to look through them. The wide selection proved almost as unexpected as the fact that they were actually going to let her *pick.* In the 803rd, you had to smuggle in your own weapon if you wanted something other than the shitty, standard-issue rifle.

Though initially disappointed that her go-to coilgun wasn't available, a Soothill prototype with similar specs sated her the second she pulled the trigger. It still hit like a truck, but primed in a fraction of the time and fired with the ease of a laser rifle—virtually no kickback. She picked a sidearm pistol based on Kato's recommendation and confirmed her loadout with the arms master on duty.

Next they fitted her for a hardsuit chassis, then installed the shell components, tweaking the couplings until each of the matte-black segments affixed at the proper angles. When the completed suit sealed, the weight seemed to fade away, not a fraction as clunky as the old Regency-brand suits they'd used in the 803rd. She'd never felt anything like it.

After weeks of travel, brain surgery, a prolonged technical lecture, and hours spent in the armory meeting dozens of new people and pretending to appreciate their welcome, Adriene was exhausted by the time Kato finally showed her to her quarters. Pretty much everything had been different than she'd expected since she'd stepped foot on the *Aurora*, so she shouldn't have been caught off guard when the accommodations followed suit. Yet somehow she was still surprised when she stepped into the small, dark gray room.

The narrow space was less than two meters wide and just over three meters deep. Sharing the wall with the door was a narrow desk with a single terminal screen. On the opposite wall, a not-super-tiny bed sat in a fully recessed alcove, with *two* pillows and a perfectly folded set of bedsheets atop what smelled like a newly minted mattress.

She scratched the back of her neck, stunned. "We get private rooms?"

Kato stood outside the door, arms resting on either side of the frame. "Sure." He shrugged. "They're tiny as shit, though."

"Still . . ." She scanned the dim room, lit by a single recessed light in the bed nook and a narrow strip above the desk. Its size in no way precluded it as a massive improvement over the communal barracks of the 803rd—or the rezone hub dormitories, where she'd spent increasingly more of her time over the last few years.

Adriene tossed her ruck on the bed and turned back to Kato.

"Pisser's down the hall," Kato said, nodding to his right. He grimaced. "Sorry . . . *latrine* and, er, showers," he corrected himself. "Mess is the other way, down a flight on deck three. I'll, uh, leave ya to it, I guess? Knowin' our lieutenant, we'll be hittin' up those sims first thing in the morning." His hand flopped to the side as he swung two fingers to indicate her desk terminal. "Invite'll ping on there once it's scheduled—I'm sure he'll sadistically grab up one of those 0600 slots, so get some rest."

"Good to know. Thanks for everything, Sergeant."

Kato gave a casual salute and a smile. "No problem. Welcome aboard." He disappeared down the hall, and the door slid shut.

Adriene took off her jacket and tossed it on the desk, then sank onto the bed with a resounding sigh. She sat in silence for a few minutes with only the constant, static purr of life systems and the dull background drone of electronics. It was almost unnervingly quiet. Privacy wasn't something she was used to.

In fact, this whole situation would take some serious getting used to. A half a day in, and life was already markedly nicer, easier, quieter, cleaner, and way less fucking broken than it'd ever been during her entire decade with the 803rd.

A warmth rose up her neck, a strange weight pressing on her chest. She hardly knew what to make of the foreign feeling. Like trying to remember a sensation from childhood and wondering if it was ever real in the first place or just shaded in nostalgia, something that'd only exist in retrospect.

With a wavering breath, she pushed the sensation down. It'd only been a few hours. It was far too early to start setting expectations.

She shifted over to the desk. The terminal screen slid forward from the wall as she sat down. The display flickered to life, and she started sliding through the menus.

Personnel directory, reporting, manuals, and an overview of the ship's layout. She tapped to expand the map, scanning over the various areas she'd visited so far, trying to assign it all to memory.

She paused when she saw a bank of holosim generators on deck three, a small warning marker hovering over the room. She tapped it, and a message appeared, paragraphs of tiny text explaining that all calls were actively monitored and recorded, and inflicted with an intentional delay. Any communication deemed inappropriate or that threatened the safety and security of Flintlock, its soldiers, or the 505th, would be edited or deleted as necessary, and disciplinary actions would be taken. A larger bar at the top indicated, like Champlan had warned, they were currently in a blackout, and any correspondence would be queued up and sent once the period lapsed.

Adriene drummed her fingers on the desk, considering who she'd even bother to call. Harlan, maybe. Not that she missed him, even if she should. But maybe seeing him again would spark something in her. This husk was taking longer than usual to feel normal. Though she wasn't sure she could even identify "normal" anymore.

Besides, what would she even say to him? Typically, their conversations centered around griping about how shitty everything was. Shitty meals, shitty gear, shitty intel, shitty objectives. She wasn't about to call him only to rub it in his face. She'd have to spend the whole conversation lying, playing it down, acting like it was the same shitty existence, just a hundred light-years farther out from the galactic center.

She dismissed the map and powered down the screen, then headed back to the bed. She pushed aside the sheets and lay down, asleep before her head hit the pillow.

CHAPTER

SIX

Kato had been correct about Brigham's cruelty, as Adriene woke at 0300 to a notification of their training slot scheduled for 0630. Luckily, she wasn't yet turned around to ship time, so 0630 to her was more like noon.

She couldn't get back to sleep, so she spent a couple of hours skimming through the ridiculously dense hardsuit manual on her terminal. Her eyes quickly glazed over, and she found herself more interested in playing with the tiny holographic renderings of the various components than actually reading about the functionality.

Though she'd slept for over twelve hours, she remained groggy and listless when she ventured out into the ship looking for the mess. After getting lost a couple of times, she finally arrived, gulping down two servings of stale black coffee before making her way to the armory.

She took her time getting herself into her hardsuit chassis and placing the shell components. Kato had helped her the day before, but eventually, she'd need to be able to get into the thing herself. It took almost a full twenty minutes, and she had to refuse the armory tech's help six times before she finally finished.

As the last piece snapped into place and the suit sealed down around her, the confinement quickly grew hot and uncomfortable before clearing away in an instant. The suit's dense weight alleviated with a silky tingle that washed across her skin, cool and light.

She rubbed one gloved hand against the other—the feeling had returned to her palms and fingertips. Though the thick gloves would require some acclimation, the translated sensation would grant her far more dexterity than she was used to.

She crossed her arms in front of her chest, then stretched them behind, surprised at the joints' ranges of mobility. It felt more like wearing a snug wet suit than a two-centimeter-thick shell that could withstand a point-blank EM projectile. A few facts from Daroga's lecture had stuck with her, at least.

She'd taken up residence at the prep counter, deep in the menus of her coilgun when Kato arrived with flushed cheeks and dark bags under his eyes, stark against his warm ivory skin. Adriene smiled to herself, feeling oddly vindicated. She knew something had to give—no one could be that peppy all the time and not pay for it. It seemed Kato's weakness was mornings.

She didn't say anything as he approached, but he scowled at her anyway. "I know, I know," he complained with a wave of his hand, voice groggy. "This is my morning face. You'll get used to it. How'd you sleep?"

"Fine," she replied.

He slunk onto a bench beside her, casting a doubtful look up at her. "Just fine?"

She wavered her head back and forth. "Yeah, okay. The bed's pretty great."

He smirked, spinning to lie down and stretch out longways across the bench. "Attagirl. Gotta take those wins."

He closed his eyes, and Adriene watched with a fair amount of fascination as, mere seconds later, the man fell asleep. Right there. On a bench in the armory.

Brigham and Gallagher arrived a couple of minutes later, donning their suits in a few quick, practiced motions. Brigham then dragged Kato—practically kicking and screaming and mumbling death threats—off the bench and into his suit.

While Brigham babysat Kato, Gallagher approached the counter and requested her loadout from the armory tech. She laid her gloves down beside Adriene, propping both elbows on the counter while she waited.

Adriene eyed the tattoos on the top of Gallagher's hands, studying the details at this closer vantage. The jagged lines were in fact vine-like in quality, almost like the roots of a tree, stretching downward along the tops of all five fingers.

"Avastian," Gallagher said.

Adriene glanced up. Gallagher gave a close-lipped smile.

"Right," Adriene replied.

Gallagher stood and faced her. "You practice?"

"No. Always seemed somewhat . . . paradoxical to me. Especially in CNEF."

Gallagher crossed her arms, propping her hip against the counter. "How do you mean?"

Adriene blew out a slow breath. "When we're not fending off scrappers, our main objective is locating planets for new colonies. Pretty much the opposite of disregarding our dying star and staying put in our doomed system until Mira consumes it."

Gallagher nodded, her brows high but expression agreeable. "Fair. Though we don't contest the star is dying—we're not delusional. But it's our belief that Mira will give us the time we need to fix her."

Adriene lifted a skeptical eyebrow. "*Fix* the star? . . . Really?"

"Really."

Adriene rubbed her chin. She'd heard some wild things about the avastian beliefs, but this was next-level. "And how do you plan on doing that?"

Gallagher uncrossed her arms, sweeping one hand in a wide arc. "That's exactly why I'm here. Why any avastian joins CNEF. Like you were saying, if we help find new systems, new planets, the technology of long-extinct civilizations—maybe one day we'll even encounter a new species. That kind of exploration is our best chance at finding what we need to fix Mira."

Adriene's brow furrowed. "You think something exists out there that could *fix* a dying star?"

Gallagher lifted one shoulder in a casual shrug. "Galaxy's a damn big place, Valero. Besides, we got a couple hundred years to figure it out."

Adriene exhaled a long sigh. "That's true, I guess," she said, trying to iron the skepticism from her look. The last time she'd read an update from the Helical Watch Council, that "couple hundred years" was trending downward the more data they collected from the observation grid that tracked the habitable zone—slowly but irrefutably shifting out-system.

Regardless, no matter what untapped spoils of ancient technology might exist in the unexplored reaches of the galaxy, Adriene highly doubted a *star repair kit* was on the menu.

But she had no interest in pressing the matter. She was happy to let Gallagher have her delusions; it wasn't harming anyone.

After finally managing to dress the sullen and resentful Kato, Brigham approached to request his loadout. Both he and Gallagher needed their weapons reconfigured, so Adriene went ahead with Kato on the promise of a tour of the simulation suites, though she had to wonder if he just wanted the chance to fit in another nap.

As they made their way down the empty corridors, Kato stretched, yawning loudly. He covered his mouth with a fist and let out a soft belch. "Mira's end . . ." he mumbled sheepishly. "*Excuse me.* Goodness."

Adriene side-eyed him. "You okay?" At this point, he'd shown enough signs of distress, it was probably an appropriate thing to inquire about.

Kato lolled back his head with a resounding sigh, dragging his feet as they walked. "Yeahhh, just had a bit too much to drink last night." His eyes lit. "Shit, Ninety-Six!" He dropped his chin to face her, tone adamant. "You gotta come. I totally forgot to mention it yesterday. Bunch of us usually hang out at the Hold in the evenings. Hence my—" He hiccupped. "Hangover. You should stop by tonight, meet some of the company."

"Yeah, sure," she said, knowing she should ask where "the Hold" was or what the hell that even meant. But that'd only be relevant to someone who actually planned to show up.

They arrived at the training concourse, another pristine display of shining white walls, ceilings, and floors, just like the rest of the ship. A set of stairs led down a half level into the simulation annex. The far wall of the large oval vestibule contained over a dozen doorways, each flanked by a control station. Each terminal's occupancy light remained inactive except the farthest on the right-hand side, which glowed crimson.

Only one other squad stood near a different door on the right, helmets set aside while they quietly yawned and double-checked their weapons and suits.

"We're in suite one," Kato said, leading her down the steps and across the vestibule to the first door on the left. They discarded their helmets at the foot of the terminal, then Kato offered his handprint to the control panel. The door opened.

The size of the suite surprised her—over five meters wide and twice as deep. Unlike the rest of the ship, the surfaces consisted of a smooth, matte-black hard plastic, punctuated by tiny holes every few centimeters. Kato showed her around, giving an overview of how the tech worked, most of which came down to *"tactile VR,"* *"dynamic holograms,"* and *"it'll make more sense when you actually see it."* She had a hard time focusing on it, but the interaction seemed to be lifting Kato's spirits, so she followed along and pretended to listen.

They exited the suite to the way-too-energetic-for-0630 whooping of another squad. The two men and two women laughed and chest-bumped outside the farthest door on the right—the one that'd been occupied earlier.

Kato's contented look soured on sight. He frowned and leaned a shoulder against the wall, disdain in his eyes as he watched the group carry on across the wide vestibule.

Adriene rested against the wall beside him. "Stormwalkers?" she surmised, recalling the also-too-energetic whooping at the hardsuit lecture. *"Flintlock's version of Telluride's White Wolves."* Whatever that meant.

"Yeah." Kato chewed on the edge of his nail. "They're the worst. But don't let 'em put ya off. *Most* fivers are great. If not at least worthy of respect."

"Fivers?" she asked.

Through his disdain, his lips lifted with a weak smile. "Yeah. It's what the major calls us, kinda caught on. 505th. Fivers." He shrugged. "I dunno."

"Makes sense," she acquiesced.

"That's a pretty shit-ass excuse." A hard voice carried from across the room.

Adriene glanced over her shoulder. Near the far wall, Daroga stood with three of the four Stormwalkers, the other nowhere to be seen.

"The suites were tuned just a few weeks ago," Daroga replied, tone conciliatory despite the palpable tension in the air.

A short man with dark hair beginning to gray at the temples huffed. "Then how do you explain how we wiped the floor with it in like ten minutes?"

"Eight and a half," another of the Stormwalkers corrected—a younger woman, average height, stocky build, shit-eating smirk.

The short man crossed his arms and gave Daroga a smug look. *"Eight and a half."*

Daroga lifted his hands. "I don't know what you want me to say. I can scale the lethality and a few other settings, but it won't be balanced."

The third Stormwalker—a tall, lanky man—let out a tsk, shaking his head. "Then I guess you should've made it better in the first place, code monkey."

Daroga scrubbed a hand over his eyes. *"I* didn't design the software . . ."

His point went unnoticed. "S'okay," the short one crooned, giving Daroga a patronizing pat on the shoulder. "You're a mere civvy. Never been toe-to-toe with a scrapper before. You don't know any better, we get it."

Daroga's demeanor withdrew, his placating—if slightly annoyed— look replaced by an ashy, lackluster, almost haunted expression. He glanced down in an apparent attempt to conceal it.

Adriene lifted her chin, turning around to better watch the encounter, interest piqued. Daroga had thus far been congenial, approachable, outgoing—if not outright charming. It was strange to see him clam up so suddenly.

"Fuck. No," Kato grunted, blowing past Adriene toward Daroga and the Stormwalkers.

Kato marched away, fists tight at his sides. Adriene tilted her head. Interest even more piqued.

The Stormwalkers exchanged amused glances as Kato approached, all three turning to face him.

"Ah, Lian . . ." The taller one's lips pressed into a pretentious sneer. "Wondered when you'd show up. Always the good corporate lapdog."

Daroga held up one hand toward Kato, the other toward the Stormwalkers. "Now, fivers," he said, with an air of warning. His posture straightened, some confidence returning to bolster his tone. "It's *far* too early for this."

"It's far too early for their *bullshit*," Kato retorted.

Adriene scoffed, a bubble of amusement rising in her chest.

"Aww," the short one crooned. "The Provan bumpkin's all worked up." He cast an adoring look at the other two.

The taller one snickered.

Daroga sighed. "Please, guys. Keep things civil," he urged. "If you start something now, you'll all wind up in the brig for the day. You could end up deployed with barely a single sim under your belts."

"What the *hell*?" A husky woman's voice carried in from the vestibule's entrance. The Stormwalkers, Daroga, and Kato all glanced over, and Adriene's gaze followed.

The fourth Stormwalker—a thin woman in her forties with pale skin and graying blond hair—stomped down the stairs toward her squad.

"I swear on Mira's last breath . . ." The woman marched right up to the shorter Stormwalker and smacked him on the back of the head.

He dropped his chin, ashamed, and the other two withered as well, all amped-up bravado vanishing.

The woman growled, "I leave for two fucking minutes to take a piss and you guys are already starting shit?"

Adriene couldn't catch the exact words as the three Stormwalkers mumbled, presumably apologizing. The older woman jutted a finger toward the suite. Properly cowed, the Stormwalkers picked up their helmets and shuffled inside.

The woman glowered after them as she curtly retied her hair. She exchanged a few quick, quiet words with Daroga, then followed her team into the suite.

Daroga went to the suite's terminal, chin low, his black hair curtaining his expression as he started typing.

Kato stomped back toward Adriene. Shoulders stiff, he propped against the wall beside her. "Assholes," he muttered under his breath.

"What was that all about?" Adriene asked.

He crossed his arms with a huff. "Just the Stormwalkers talkin' shit. Bein' ignorant jerks, as always."

"The Provan thing?"

"Nah," he grumbled. "They're just fuckin' rude. Always talkin' down to Carl, actin' like he hasn't had more face time with the scrappers than every one of us combined."

It took her a few seconds to link the name "Carl" with Daroga.

Kato frowned at her, then mumbled, "Other than maybe you, I guess."

She quirked a brow at him. "Daroga?"

He nodded.

"The corporate egghead?"

Kato cast a fleeting glimpse across the room, then the remaining frustration in his expression softened with . . . sorrow? Sympathy? Pity? She couldn't tell.

He sidled closer to Adriene and lowered his voice. "He was in the Brownout."

Adriene's brow creased. "Really?" She glanced past Kato's shoulder to Daroga, still working at the suite terminal. "But he must have been just a kid."

"Yeah," Kato sighed.

"The consolidation?" she ventured.

Kato nodded, solemn. "He was twelve. Came from Bryer-III."

Adriene chewed the inside of her lip, dragging her thoughts back twenty years, ninety-six lives ago. She had only been nine at the time, but she still remembered the events well, having sat for weeks on end watching the endless media coverage while her father paced, wearing a trench into their living room floor. Before the Brownout, he hadn't had half as much gray in his hair.

First contact with the Mechan had, justifiably, triggered panic. CNEF was stretched way too thin, and after a handful of tragic incidents at the out-system colonies, the Concord Nations began withdrawing everyone to the Miran system so they'd be easier to protect. Only three of almost a hundred ships made it back to Mira. The rest were intercepted by Mechan forces during the retreat.

For weeks, those colonists were held hostage while the Mechan established a blockade, which soon became known as the Firewall, around the Miran system. Then the negotiations began.

That part didn't last long. Though they'd never released specifics, it was safe to assume that it was less of a negotiation, more of a dictation. The Mechan hive mind informing the Concord Nations directorate of how things were going to go.

Miraculously, the bots kept their word and released the colonist hostages, though not before thousands had died. Though allegedly, only due to sickness or starvation. The scrappers hadn't directly killed a single person.

But if Adriene's experience being held captive by Mechan was any indication, execution might have been the kinder option.

Daroga walked up behind Kato, stopping to lay a hand on the shorter man's shoulder. "Thanks, bud. You didn't have to."

Kato pouted, kicking the floor with the toe of his boot. "I dunno why you won't let me beat the shit outta them."

Tone affectionate, Daroga replied, "It's for your own good."

Kato patted the hand Daroga had laid on his shoulder and smiled up at him. Daroga looked over to Adriene.

She shifted interest to her fingernails, her instinct to avoid eye contact at all costs. Then that seemed even more awkward, so she forced herself to look back up. "You again," she said.

"Don't sound too disappointed." He smiled, though it wasn't reflected in his eyes.

"I take it you're a live-in?" she asked.

"Yes, ma'am. Permanent posting."

Kato rested his temple against Daroga's shoulder, fluttering his eyelashes at him. "He's our very own groupie."

Daroga elbowed Kato in the ribs, and Kato retreated with a whining yelp.

"This 'groupie' regulates every piece of tech you use," Daroga pointed out, "so you may want to rethink the name-calling."

Kato tapped his chin. "How about 'resident nerd'?"

Daroga threw out a jab, but missed as Kato sidestepped, then scurried away past Brigham, who huffed in general disapproval as he approached, newly serviced rifle in tow. "We doin' this or what?" Brigham grunted.

Gallagher cast Adriene a smile as she approached as well, hauling a sleek black sniper rifle that probably cost half a year's wages.

Daroga's glower at Kato morphed to pure professionalism as he turned to address Brigham. "Ready when you are, Lieutenant."

"Activate Rubicons," Brigham ordered.

"Aye, aye." Daroga made a few quick taps on his tablet.

A twinge fired through the back of Adriene's eyes along with a short flash of white. It cleared away and the simple, sharp, black-or-white HUD lines overlaid her vision.

// Welcome to Rubicon. //

Adriene held her palm against her temple, feeling briefly unmoored as the soothing male voice rang into her mind.

// Searching for access point, please hold . . . //

She remained perfectly still for a few drawn-out moments, breathing slowly.

// Connection to mainframe established. //

A slew of notifications appeared in her HUD, one after the other, almost too fast to read: "Peripherals detected, establishing connections . . . Hardsuit, connected. Pathfinder module 1.0, connected. Firearms (2), connected," and a dozen others she didn't understand.

The messages disappeared at once.

Adriene's gaze went straight to Brigham as he adjusted settings on his rifle. Thin strips of red light now lined the planes of his suit—artificial coloring that hadn't been there before. Two parallel strips ran from the small of his back up to the base of his neck, and a single thin line ran down each of his arms and legs. Gallagher's suit looked much the same, though the lines were green.

Adriene looked down at her own suit, but saw no color.

// Yellow. //

A shiver ran down her spine. The thing could *literally* read her thoughts.

She pushed the unease aside. It was just part of the fun. She had to get used to it.

// An unsynced suit has been detected in range. //

Adriene turned to Kato, who leaned against the wall, half-asleep. His suit lacked the glowing strips of color, and instead, his outline had been highlighted in white, pulsating slowly.

// Would you like to establish a connection? //

She cleared her throat. Yes . . .

// Requesting handshake . . . Sync complete. //

The white highlight disappeared, and bright blue lines swept down Kato's arms, legs, and back.

Kato jerked upright, going almost cross-eyed for a second before he looked over at her.

"Sorry," she said. "Is it bad form to sync without asking first?"

"Not at all." He smiled and pushed off the wall, stepping closer. Some of the color had returned to his cheeks.

"You seem to be feeling better," she commented. "Rather suddenly . . ."

He flashed a grin. "Rubie gave me a nice stim cocktail to help with the hangover."

She lifted an eyebrow. "Rubie?"

"Yeah! What, you haven't named yours yet?"

"Uh . . . no. Haven't really had a chance."

"Oh, right." He smiled. "Well, lemme know if you have questions, but really, it's all pretty intuitive. Your VI will control everything for ya, 'cept our hyphens."

"Hyphens?"

"Ah, don't got those in the 803rd either?"

"By default, you can assume we had nothing you guys have."

He chuckled. "Fair enough." He turned his forearm over and tapped his suit. A thin panel slid open, revealing a small screen recessed in his bracer. "Hyphen."

She squinted at it. "What's it for?"

"It's just a basic terminal interface," he began, "but it's in its own little world, air-gapped from the rest of the suit and Rubicon. As the team's engineer, I have to use mine a lot—mostly when interfacin' with systems we might not have firewalls for or can't trust. Though, Rubie's a better hacker than I even am. I'm sure she could fend off most anything." He shrugged. "Suppose it's better to be safe than sorry sometimes, though."

Adriene turned over her own arm and tapped the suit. The hyphen's cover slid open.

"Hyphen's nothin' for you to worry about," Kato clarified. "I'll have ya covered in that regard. But if ya got questions about anything else, your VI's your go-to." He glanced back at Brigham, embroiled in conversation with Daroga. "If ya got anything to ask 'er, now might be a good time. We'll be hittin' the sim before ya know it."

Adriene nodded her thanks, then closed her hyphen.

She drew her focus inward, not entirely sure where to start. She didn't believe for a second that the basic description given in the primer had even scratched the surface of the VI's capabilities.

Though one thing she hadn't even gotten a *shitty* primer on was her pathfinder module. Might as well start there.

// Certainly. Pathfinder module version 1.0.0 contains six survey programs and twelve database programs. //

A chill ran up her spine. The mind reading thing would definitely take some getting used to.

// Survey programs include Geological, Ecological, Topographical, Cartographical, Structural, and when available, Orbital. Databases include biology, chemistry, geology, ecology, astrophysics, technology, architecture, engineering, archeology, anthropology, history, and biota, including flora, fauna, and fungi. //

Adriene ran a hand through her short hair and heaved a sigh.

// There is no need to feel overwhelmed. //

She narrowed her eyes. *Who said I felt overwhelmed?*

// Vitals indicate an elevated heart rate, increased levels of cortisol—//

"No, just—" Adriene said, then cut herself short as she realized she'd spoken aloud. She glanced at Kato, but he stood reclined against the wall, whistling softly, oblivious.

It's fine, she thought quietly. *You don't need to explain.*

// Understood. However, please remember you do not need a practical understanding of these programs and their functionalities. You will not interface directly with any one program. Rubicon exists as a bridge to facilitate. //

Adriene nodded slowly, exhaling a steadying breath. It was almost *too* useful. This really would be a whole other way of operating. She wouldn't have to take the normal steps in evaluating a problem and determining a solution before setting a course of action. Most of the work was going to be done for her. It was like an entire COB kit and then some, directly in her suit. Or her head—she wasn't actually sure which. Maybe both.

She lifted her arms, eyeing the streamlined edges of the unscuffed, matte-black suit. The 803rd wouldn't see tech like this for . . . fifteen years? Maybe longer. Hell, they may *never* see tech like this.

Brigham slung his rifle as he approached the ajar door to suite one. "Here we go, Forward Recon," he prompted with an inviting sweep of his arm.

Kato frowned. "Give the newbie a minute, LT."

"It's fine." Adriene lifted her helmet on, and it locked into place with a short hiss. "I'm good."

Brigham cast Kato a smug grin. "See? She's good."

Daroga finished inputting something into their suite's terminal, then locked it down. "You guys okay for now?"

Brigham waved him off. "Yeah, man, we're good."

Daroga left to greet an incoming squad, and Brigham fanned his arms in wide circles, herding Adriene, Kato, and Gallagher into their suite.

The lights dimmed as the door sealed behind them.

Adriene double-checked her coilgun settings. Though by default, all weapons aboard the ship were automatically constrained to training mode, she preferred to be extra certain she wouldn't accidentally shoot a giant hole in the wall.

A computerized voice, nearly as smooth as the counseling VI, rang over the loudspeakers. "Welcome, Forward Recon. Engagement 14F. All variables randomized. Please confirm."

"Confirmed," Brigham voiced.

"Simulation loaded. Good hunting."

Buds of neon light flickered on all around the room, emanating from the thousands of small holes in the walls, ceiling, and floors.

// *There are precisely 151,625 reference nodes.* //

Uh . . . thanks.

Adriene squinted as the light extended, remaining hazy and indistinct as it grew toward the center of the room, then coalesced in a brilliant flare of white light.

When the flash settled, a picturesque forest stretched out around them. A verdant underbrush carpeted the forest floor, encircling the thick trunks of ancient cedar trees, stretching up toward a clear blue sky. A shallow creek burbled softly from somewhere nearby, the scent of wildflowers and cedar thick on the air.

Adriene tilted her head side to side, tracing the image surrounding her. If she moved her eyes quickly enough, she could just barely catch a slight tearing at the harder edges of objects. Even so, she'd never seen a hologram even half as detailed before.

// *The suite technology works in conjunction with your hardsuit to display a virtual reality environment that can be experienced in tandem with your squadmates.* //

So . . . not a hologram?
// Correct. //
Thanks.
// You are welcome. //
Then Gallagher said, "We have contacts on overwatch."

A soft ding rang out, and Adriene jerked upright. She took a few deep breaths, confused by the cushioning on the cot below her.

And she was too cool, too temperate. She couldn't still be in that inferno of a storage hold.

Sensing her movement, the lights illuminated slowly and the memories came back—the 505th, Flintlock, the *Aurora*. This was where she lived now.

Her back ached as she pushed up onto her elbows, fatigue plaguing her movements. She flopped back down.

Earlier, she'd almost fallen asleep in the shower before she'd made it to bed. They'd run simulations for eight hours with only one short lunch break, and she'd returned sweaty, sore, and feeling pretty much as in the dark as when they'd started.

The same chime that'd woken her rang out again, and a light beside the door frame flashed. Apparently, that was the doorbell.

She wiped the sleep from her eyes and stepped to the door controls. It slid open.

Daroga flashed a smile. "Sergeant."

"You." She stifled a yawn. "Again."

He smirked. "Me, again. Sorry—you racked out already?"

"No, just needed a nap. I'm not on ship time yet. Still adjusting."

"Right. That's always fun. Just thought I'd check in and see how you're feeling after trying out the implant."

"Oh. Fine."

"Good, good." He pushed his long black hair out of his eyes. "I've never had an install that tough before. Just wanted to make sure it was going well."

"Should I be worried?" she asked.

"No, no." He held up placating hands. "Definitely not."

"Well, it seems fine, but I haven't really spent all that much time with it yet."

"Right, of course," he said quickly. "Just let me know if you have any headaches or anything."

"Okay," she agreed, rubbing at her dry eyes. "I will."

He made as if to go, then hesitated. "By the way, there's a bit of a watering hole down on deck six. If you wanted to meet some of the crew."

"The Hold?" she asked, and he nodded. "Kato mentioned it."

"Right. I was the new guy once too is all. Figured I'd let you know. In case you didn't. But, you do."

Adriene glanced at the time on the terminal on her desk: 2150. She'd slept a lot longer than she'd intended. As much as she dreaded the idea, it might help keep her awake awhile, get her sleep schedule a bit more on track. And she had very little to lose. Worst case, it was horrible, and she could claim exhaustion and leave. Best case, they'd be able to pour her a stiff drink.

"You headed there now?" she asked.

Daroga's green eyes flashed with a hint of surprise. "I am. Yes."

She got the distinct feeling he had, in fact, *not* been headed there, but didn't care to analyze it further. "Mind an escort?" she asked. "I still don't know my way around."

"Ah, right . . ." His mouth tilted into a smile. "Sure, I can help with that." He took a step back and swept an arm to the left. She grabbed a sweatshirt and tugged it on as she headed down the hall, Daroga keeping step beside her.

"Actually, uh, shit—this way," he said, and turned around. Adriene sighed, then followed.

The Hold's designation proved apt—literally a storage hold, down in a quiet corner on one of the lower decks. The square room had been cleared of cargo, with at least half the company gathered around a dozen tables, a few sitting on couches near the back. A countertop ran along one wall near the front, stacked with empty glasses and an impressive collection of metal liquor bottles. And all around, vices of every kind: fraternization, gambling, drinking, smoking; though no evidence of anything harder. Like any other division, Command would be willing to let the normal stuff slide for the sake of morale—but not everything.

Adriene followed through a light haze of smoke as Daroga made his way to a table near the center where Brigham and Gallagher sat with half a dozen others. At a bar against the left wall, Kato stood chatting with someone Adriene didn't recognize. He waved at her and Daroga with a bright smile. She nodded in return.

As they approached, Brigham pulled a chair away from a nearby table and offered it to Adriene. "Valero, glad you made it."

She nodded, sitting down warily.

Daroga pulled up another chair and sat beside her while Brigham returned to his seat.

"How'd you like those sims?" Gallagher asked, drink in hand. "Pretty wild, huh?"

"They're impressive," Adriene replied. "And exhausting."

Gallagher smiled. "Yeah, took me weeks to get used to them. We'll hit up a few more soon, getcha feeling confident in no time."

"So, Ninety-Six, huh?" Brigham's mouth tilted in a half smirk as he laced his fingers behind his head and leaned back. "Not many newbies show up with such a solid nickname from the get."

Gallagher perked up. "Wait, what's the story?" she asked, her words beginning to slur around the edges.

"*Ninety-sixth* husk," someone else replied—a red-haired man Adriene recognized from the hardsuit lecture.

Gallagher set down her drink, her eyes wide. "Holy shit, *what?*" She scanned Adriene with a look of unrestrained wonder. "Mira's fiery ashes . . ."

"Guys, come on," Daroga admonished. "Leave her be."

Gallagher ignored him. "So, if you've died that many times . . . how old are you really?"

"Shit, Gal," the redhead laughed, "don't ya know not to ask a husk her age? *Rude.*"

Brigham chuckled, and Gallagher rolled her eyes.

"It's fine," Adriene said. "My husk's only a year younger than I am." *For now,* she almost added, but swallowed the bitter thought back down. "It's twenty-eight."

"Damn," Gallagher muttered, then lowered her voice. "You ever get hybridized?"

Adriene tensed, feeling suddenly incongruous. No one ever asked things like that in the 803rd. The topic was so taboo, it wasn't broached in even the most unseemly of conversations.

She picked at the seam of her pant leg, face warming as silence descended over the bustling room. Only a couple of people still held their own clueless discussion, off in the far corner.

"*That's* a yes," Brigham said, voice low and gravelly. He shoved a glass of dark amber liquor across the table toward her. "Let's hear it."

The liquid sloshed in the glass, and Adriene's hand twitched. With an effort, she stopped herself, clenching her fingers into a fist.

She wanted it, obviously. It was the primary way she'd convinced herself to come down, to endure the spotlight and this inevitable line of questioning. But something tugged in the pit of her stomach—guilt sourced from somewhere light-years away.

Harlan had wanted to stop. Wanted *her* to stop. She had to at least try.

She exhaled a heavy breath, then looked back at Brigham. "Once."

"Fuck me . . ." Kato's thin voice floated over from the bar.

Someone across the room snickered, "Yeah, Kato, you wish," eliciting a rumble of laughter among the others, though it quieted down instantly. Apparently, everyone wanted to hear this.

Adriene glanced over at Daroga beside her. He sat slouched against his chair back, picking at his fingernails. He met her eyes, seeming at once apologetic, horrified, and curious.

Gallagher leaned forward on the table. "What was it like?"

"I don't really remember," Adriene replied. Which they'd accept as the truth, if they knew anything about hybridization statistics.

Adriene's case had been an outlier in more ways than one. Typically, soldiers who'd been hybridized returned with complete amnesia—at least of the hybridization itself, if not their entire lives.

Less commonly, they retained a few scattered memories. In *those* cases, they rarely if ever made it out the other side in one, cognitive piece. They'd been taken over for too long and become too integrated into the Mechan hive mind. When they finally rezoned and their fused minds were torn free, the consciousness received by their new husk was often completely beyond repair. They'd lost all sense of how to be human, reverting to some primal, animal state.

The fact that Adriene's consciousness had remained intact was, by far, the exception.

Brigham scratched his jawline. "I've never understood it . . . If they shove themselves into our brains, how come *they* don't end up in the new husk?"

"They've definitely tried," she replied. "But they can't make it work."

"Why not?" Gallagher asked.

Adriene exchanged a look with Daroga, who corroborated her uncertainty with a shrug.

"No idea," she said. She really didn't. She had no idea why the Mechan consciousnesses didn't transfer as seamlessly as a human's. Whatever the reason, she was fucking glad. That'd be one hell of a back door.

Brigham frowned. "Maybe the same reason we can't put our brains in someone else's body. Ain't wired right."

The red-haired man nodded his agreement. "Yeah, or maybe their whole hive mind thing fucks it up."

"Yeah, maybe," Gallagher mumbled, running a finger along the rim of her glass. She looked back at Adriene. "How long were you . . . ya know?"

"Two weeks."

Someone let out a low whistle, followed by stark, lingering silence broken only by the rustle of clothing and soft squeaks of chairs as people shifted uncomfortably.

"Damn," Brigham sighed. "So you don't remember anything?"

"Only a few things, here and there," she lied. She remembered everything. Every single second, burned into her brain. But for some reason, she couldn't tell them that. "It's like trying to recall a dream," she went on. "At times, I could almost *hear* the hive mind, but it was . . . cluttered. I couldn't really interpret it. I remember not having any control, but I could still feel everything, smell everything, hear everything. Like I was paralyzed inside someone else's body." She eyed the glass Brigham had passed her, twisting it between her thumb and forefinger. "And I remember having to watch as they used me to ambush my own soldiers."

"Shit." Gallagher's thin eyebrows pinched as she shook her head. "Is that how you ended up getting killed?"

"No," Adriene said plainly, and she fully intended to leave it at that.

They all stared back, expectant. Waiting for her to elaborate.

She swallowed the lump that'd lodged in the back of her throat. "They . . . never fed me. Or gave me water. I don't know if they forgot or they just weren't prepared for a prisoner. Or they just didn't care. So, eventually I just . . ."

The silent room grew even quieter. Adriene pressed her thumb into the palm of her hand as the others scratched their heads, or picked lint off their untucked uniforms, or sipped their drinks while avoiding eye contact.

What had they wanted to hear? That it was a great time, fun was had by all, would hybridize again in a heartbeat? It was the only experience in the universe worse than rezoning, the only reason she could convince herself to keep killing her squadmates—because she knew the alternative. Did they really think it would be a fun story?

"And that, ladies and gentlemen," Daroga's weathered voice rumbled, "is why when in doubt, we zero out."

The weight in the air alleviated somewhat as the others recited, "When in doubt, zero out!" and clinked their glasses together before taking deep swigs.

Adriene ran her thumb along the rim of her glass as everyone returned to their own conversations. She watched the others seamlessly switch back to laughing and jeering—fascinated by their congenial behavior. Not for the first time, she wondered what number husk they were all on. Some were young—so young they had to have been recruited straight from basic. Maybe some had yet to rezone even once.

She wondered if *their* consciousnesses would remain intact if they were ever hybridized. Or if they'd break when they died for the first time.

Brigham chuffed derisively. "Now, if we can only keep the ghost from causin' more trouble," he said, and his buddies at the table voiced their agreement.

Daroga groaned, and his head lolled back. "Not this shit again."

Brigham shrugged. "Not our fault you can't keep dead people from hauntin' our software."

The group launched into a well-worn argument, shouting over each other as they poured more drinks.

Adriene pushed her chair out and headed for the bar on the left, where Kato now stood alone, pouring himself another drink.

He turned as she approached, lounging casually against the bar, elbows propped back on the countertop. "That's some shit, Ninety-Six."

"Yeah," she sighed, turning to face the room and leaning against the counter beside Kato.

His tone turned timid. "Hey . . ." He elbowed her arm lightly. "You don't mind Ninety-Six, right?"

Adriene shrugged. "I've had worse nicknames."

He gestured to the assortment of metal liquor bottles gathered on the bar top. "Drink?"

After a couple seconds, she found herself shaking her head. "Not now, thanks."

A din of shouts rose from the table again. She turned to find Daroga chuckling as he fled the table, arms held protectively around his head as the others tossed stray napkins, bottle caps, and bits of food after him.

He huffed a breath as he reclined against the edge of the counter on the other side of Kato, laughter settling. "They're relentless, I tell ya." He brushed a crumble of bread off his shoulder.

Adriene wrung her hands as the silence stretched out, and she finally exhaled a quiet sigh. She was here. She'd bothered to show up. She might as well give it a try. Be *normal*.

"So, uh," she began, eyeing Daroga, "how long have you worked for Dodson-Mueller?"

"Almost ten years. CNEF Contracts Division for seven or so."

"Will the other rep be joining us? Your colleague?"

"Not this evening, I'm afraid," he replied, tone oddly even, almost performative. "She's reviewing the contract with Major Blackwell."

"Still?" Adriene asked.

Kato grinned. "'Reviewing the contract' might be a, uh, *euphemism*, as it were."

Daroga nodded, amused.

"As we all know," Kato continued, "sometimes ya gotta review a contract, like, nine or ten times. Ya know, determine *liability* . . . arbitrate disputes . . ."

Daroga cracked a smile, and a weird sensation tugged at Adriene's lips.

"Ah," she said. "Understood."

"Make sure it's *legally binding* . . ." Kato continued, quite proud of himself.

"Okay, Lian, we get it," Daroga said, though he continued to snicker.

Adriene lifted a shoulder. "She looked like she could use a couple good contract reviews."

Kato practically spit out his drink as he cracked up laughing. He launched into a coughing fit, and Daroga gave him a couple of firm pats on the back.

Adriene glanced back at the crowd around the table, settled back into deep conversation. "Are they for real with this 'ghost in the system' stuff?"

Kato was already mid-drink again, but nodded fervently through it.

Adriene looked at Daroga. "But you don't believe it?"

He shrugged a shoulder. "I just like playing devil's advocate. I've heard these guys talking about it since I became Flintlock's rep, what—four years ago?"

Kato nodded his agreement.

"I can't say I've ever experienced it," Daroga continued, "but these guys seem to think it's real."

"It's totally real," Kato croaked, voice still recovering from his coughing fit.

"Seriously?" Adriene asked.

"I swear on my ma's farm back on Prova—no joke," Kato said fervently. "We get faulty readings in our HUDs, suits actin' all wonky, weapons misfiring . . ."

Adriene raised an eyebrow. "Sound like tech glitches."

"Sure, sure, but they have *style*," Kato asserted. "Sometimes, it messes with mission parameters, sets new objectives, even gives out digital orders using Blackwell or Thurston's security codes."

Daroga nodded. "And then there's what happened to Cash."

Kato's flushed cheeks blanched, and he looked down at his boots. Daroga's brow softened.

Adriene's gaze drifted between them. "Who's Cash?"

"Used to be Forward Recon," Daroga said, a hint of apology in his quiet tone. "Guess you're technically his replacement."

This was the missing squadmate they'd awkwardly avoided discussing after the lecture. "What happened?" she asked.

Kato's shoulders lifted in a weak shrug. "He rezoned a few months back from a supposed 'implant overload.' Pretty much melted his brain, I guess."

Daroga shook his head. "Never happened before, never happened since—not in Flintlock or the entire 505th. Between that, and the fact that he never came back after his rezone . . . let's just say 'the ghost' caught the blame."

Adriene's brow creased. "Why didn't he come back?"

Kato spun his drink around in his glass, gaze cast down. "Apparently the, uh . . . trauma messed up his wiring a bit. They didn't think it was safe to refit him with a Rubicon, so they reassigned him."

Daroga elbowed Kato lightly. "But good riddance, right?"

"Yeah." Kato's dry voice cracked. "I certainly wasn't sad to see him go. Just didn't really need to see his head explode first."

Daroga frowned, shifting along the edge of the counter until his shoulder propped against Kato's.

Kato leveled a serious look at Adriene. "He really was a shitbag," he explained. "Even if his implant hadn't exploded, it was only a matter of time before he'd have gotten himself rezoned. Or hell, all of Forward Recon."

Adriene chewed her lip, still not used to how serious these people took rezoning. Dying really did have a whole different meaning in the 505th.

"We never could find a fault in the implant," Daroga said. "In what remained of it, anyway. But something had to cause it."

Adriene raised an eyebrow at him. "So you *do* believe in the ghost?"

Kato cast Daroga an accusatory look. "Only if it means their lawyers can shunt the blame onto our software, so they don't get sued."

Daroga's lips pinched. "If we get sued, you lose all the fun toys."

"Wait," Adriene said. "Dodson-Mueller doesn't create the Rubicon software?"

"No, ma'am," Daroga said. "Hardware facilitation only on the Rubicon front."

She tilted her head. "I'd assumed you wrote it."

"Nah," Kato said, turning to face the bar and pour himself another drink. "Don't get me wrong—my boy's smart. Knows the code better than anyone." He cast a smarmy grin at Daroga. "Except maybe the major, right, bud?"

Daroga rolled his eyes, then shot Kato a scowl in response—clearly exaggerated, but still genuine.

A pain point of some kind, but the two traded so much good-hearted shade, she had trouble keeping up.

She was about to ask them to elaborate when a hush swept across the room.

Adriene followed Kato's gaze to the entrance, where Major Black-well stood in the open doorway.

"Buckle up, fivers. Orders dropped." His low voice reverber-ated across the silent room. "Course is set, drive's spoolin'." He gave Brigham and Gallagher a glance, then turned and eyed Adriene and Kato. "Forward Recon, your boots'll be on the ground first thing—shuttle leaves at 0430. Mission briefing on the flight. Get some rest."

He turned and disappeared into the hall.

Adriene looked to Kato. The humor had left his face. "Shit."

Kato scratched his chin, but he otherwise didn't react as Adriene took the whiskey glass from his hand and threw it back, letting the warmth burn her throat and settle deep into her stomach. She passed the empty glass back to him and let out a heavy breath.

Tomorrow was as good a day as any to die. Again.

CHAPTER
SEVEN

Adriene stood behind the pilot's seat in the exposed cockpit aboard Forward Recon's dropship. A wide viewscreen over the cockpit controls displayed a distorted view of subspace hurtling past—countless forking, gnarled white tendrils stretching alongside like a hundred thousand skeletal hands that reached back, shrieking a high-pitched tone that resonated in her bones. A lingering haze of spectral dust shrouded the hull, thick flakes of ash drifting lazily as if in suspension around the ship.

With a flashing yellow warning light and a soft rumble, Adriene's stomach turned. The ship had left subspace.

"Exit complete." In the pilot's seat, Gallagher tapped a few flight controls. "Systems nominal. Radar's clear."

"Copy clear," Brigham replied from the copilot's chair.

Adriene scanned the viewscreen as they approached their destination. The silver arc of Cimarosa-IV stretched out below them, the visible hemisphere almost entirely covered in thick clouds. A light blue haze of atmosphere stretched up into inky black, dotted with dustings of stars. They must have been facing the galactic center, because a dense, star-strewn backdrop stretched out behind the rim of the world, like a dust storm frozen in motion, blowing thousands of glittering flecks of sand across an impossibly black sky.

Brigham's voice boomed as he called over his shoulder, "Look alive, Lian."

Adriene glanced back to Kato, his ivory skin ashen as he sat hunched in a row of troop seats along the back wall, opposite the large storage lockers that housed their suits and loadouts. He leaned forward, the definition of death warmed over, and buried his face in his hands. "I think I'm gonna die," he mumbled, then his elbows dropped and he folded, laying his head on his knees.

Adriene pressed her fingers into her temples, abating her headache slightly. The remnants of Kato's whiskey hadn't been her last drink of the evening. But for the first time in two weeks, she'd slept through the night—all four hours of it—without a single nightmare. And when she woke, she'd felt better than she had since she'd last rezoned. More balanced, lucid. Real.

In a way, she welcomed the hangover—the headaches, dizziness, low-level nausea all acting as a guidepost. A baseline from which she could pretend to function on a semi-normal level.

Yet guilt still grated at the back of her mind, a warning that she'd squandered the opportunity. A chance at starting over, at doing things differently.

Maybe this husk needed it. Maybe that was what'd been missing—why she'd felt no embarrassment during Flintlock's uncouth line of questioning, or hadn't missed Harlan's stupid jokes, or why she couldn't let herself be optimistic about a future with the 505th—a future in which she might not die. Or why she felt like an imposter in her own body.

Adriene clasped the open collar of her hardsuit, hanging her hands along the rim. The viewscreen's perspective shifted as Gallagher altered vector. Above them, a tiny, rocky moon came into view, one that'd suffered an impact some time ago. From the point of collision, fragments had splintered off, breaking away in curving arcs along the invisible lines of orbit. Eventually, Cimarosa-IV's gravity would claim the debris, and the moon's shards would be pulled into the atmosphere. Though by the time the pieces reached the surface, they'd likely be nothing but dust.

"We have an LZ?" Brigham asked.

Gallagher brought up a map on the control screen. "Intel cleared this entire valley."

Brigham nodded. "All right, tiptoe on down. We'll play it by ear."

"Copy tiptoe," Gallagher said. "Atmo in ten."

"Activating Rubicons."

"Copy, sir," Gallagher said.

Kato groaned, "Thank *Mira*," likely looking forward to another hangover cocktail.

Before Adriene could respond, a twinge fired through the back of her eyes along with a short flash of white. It cleared away, and the simple, sharp, black-or-white HUD lines overlaid her vision.

// Welcome to Rubicon. //

She winced, the VI's internal vocalization reigniting her headache. The others didn't even react.

"Atmo incoming," Gallagher announced. "Stealth engaged. Buckle up."

Brigham and Gallagher pulled their harnesses over their shoulders and strapped themselves into the pilots' seats as Adriene sat beside Kato. However, the chairs weren't equipped with standard harnesses, and as she sat down, a *shink* of magnetized metal sounded. Her back popped against the seat as the rails locked onto her hardsuit and secured her flush with the chair.

The dropship hummed and rattled as they entered the atmosphere. Adriene's stomach churned, but the turbulence lessened as they descended.

A few minutes later, they were through the thick cloud cover. Gallagher lowered the ship, skimming above the top of the thick, green jungle canopy.

Though daytime, a blanket of marbled clouds stretched out in every direction, casting the landscape in a gloomy dreariness. Plumes of dark haze indicated heavy rainfall in the distance.

To the west, a wide, black river ran to the edge of a massive cliff. The water cascaded off the edge, through jagged tiers of moss and vine-covered bedrock, collecting in pools before flowing down to the next level. The bottom of the impressive waterfall disappeared into a basin surrounded by dark jungle, shrouded in a haze of mist. Verdant flatlands lay to the east, but they'd be headed west, deeper into the jungle.

Brigham selected a landing zone, and Gallagher set the dropship down in a small clearing. They donned their helmets and loadouts, then gathered by the air lock.

"Comms check," Kato said pleasantly, and the blue lines on his suit glowed a little brighter while he spoke. The others sounded off, their lines also brightening.

Adriene locked her helmet on and reported in last. "Valero. Check, check, check."

"Good check, Ninety-Six," Kato confirmed. "Everyone's five by five, boss."

"All right, Forward Recon," Brigham began, clearing his throat. "I know the briefing with the major was pretty . . . well, *brief*, but the objectives are just variations on the normal shit. We get boots on the ground, find somewhere to stage groundside, round up a nice recon package of the target facility. We need a full workup: entrance points, blueprints, extraction options, security systems, patrol schedules."

Adriene nodded along, mimicking the others' passive reactions to the rather intimidating list of requests. Brigham hadn't been exaggerating before—Forward Recon really did lay the groundwork for the rest of the company.

"We've got twenty-eight hours before the other squads join us," Brigham continued with an air of conclusion. "Let's put our hospitality hats on and get the place ready for guests."

"Aye, aye, sir," Kato piped with a flimsy salute.

Brigham went to the air lock controls, the door opened, and the ramp lowered.

// *Atmospheric shift detected. Oxygen concentration: seventeen percent. Three hundred nineteen K. Ninety-nine-point-eight percent humidity.* //

"Overwatch's clear," Gallagher said.

Brigham stepped onto the ramp. Adriene shouldered her rifle and followed.

Humidity hung heavy in the air, shrouding the gloomy clearing in a thick, misty haze. Adriene could barely make out the edge of the forest five meters off, and only blackness lay within the gnarled boughs.

A thin, vertical line appeared in her HUD and dragged across the darkness.

// Decreased visibility detected. Enhancing . . . //

A heavy, painful pressure weighed on Adriene's eyes, like stepping out into the sunlight after being in a dark room for too long.

She blinked hard. Her vision had brightened, but there was suddenly so much to see, she could hardly process the information. She took a deep breath, tried to ignore the details, and focused on the bigger picture.

Predominant among a whole host of strange alien flora were hundreds of thick-trunked trees that wound upward into a dense canopy. The scaly bark was such a deep, charcoal black it looked like it'd been burned. The branches twisted into one another imperceptibly, making it impossible to tell where one started and the other ended.

Adriene hesitated, considering if it could be one massive organism—a single giant, forest-wide arboreal structure where each "trunk" was only one of thousands of root systems securing it to the earth.

// That hypothesis is well-substantiated based on current data sets. Though Rubicon has yet to uncover any specifics that would constitute hard evidence. //

Adriene's brow creased. *You've been gathering data?*

// Of course. //

Brigham's red-limned suit rails lit up. "All right." He turned to face Adriene as Kato and Gallagher stepped up beside her. "Step one, we find a suitable staging ground for a base camp. Let's save our backs: We scout, then come back for the supplies. But, Gallagher, ready a drone with an emergency supply drop, just in case."

"Copy that," Gallagher said, then slung her rifle and headed back into the ship.

"Odd," Kato mumbled. "I can't find a single scrapper security ping from here to the facility."

Brigham shrugged. "Probably staying on low power. That's a

good sign—means they still don't know we're coming. Just keep an eye as we get closer."

Kato flashed a thumbs-up. "You got it, boss."

"Valero," Brigham said, "where are you thinking we should start?"

Adriene recentered her focus. Right. No COB kit to set up, no programs to load, no scripts to run . . . She only had to think.

"Sorry, Lieutenant," she replied. "Still getting used to this thing in my head. I'm going to need a minute."

Brigham nodded and motioned to Kato. They descended the ramp and took posts near the bow and stern of the ship, weapons in hand.

Adriene drew in a deep breath and thought about what she wanted: a survey of the land two klicks this side of the target facility. That'd get them close enough to get a more detailed survey of the ruins, without triggering typical Mechan surveillance patterns.

In an instant, a semitransparent topographical map appeared in her vision.

She swiveled her head; the overlay stayed locked to the terrain. Helpful—*very* helpful—in that she could effectively see terrain *through* obstructions. But, from so far away, she couldn't get the kind of detail she needed.

She squinted at a far-off area north of the basin. Her periphery darkened as the overlay zoomed into the spot, but the motion sent her stomach lurching, and the map snapped back into place and reset.

She briefly closed her eyes, head spinning.

// Rubicon offers a tactile interface option you may feel more comfortable utilizing until you can become accustomed to augmented reality. //

Uh, sure. Like an interactive hologram?

// Precisely. //

Go ahead.

The map appeared again, though a much smaller scale, and the image stayed locked in place despite her eye movements. She reached out and crossed her hands in front of the area she wanted to focus on, and the view zoomed in.

She'd used similar tech only a handful of times in the 803rd when reviewing surveys or blueprints, though the interface had been confined to a holotable. The fact that her Rubicon saw this as the "training wheels" both impressed and unnerved her.

Can you overlay surface and groundwater?

A blue glow flashed over the hologram, and the massive black river to the south became visible along the gridded terrain. It led north to the waterfall, down what had to be a 1,500-meter drop into the basin. From there, it cascaded even farther belowground into what seemed to be a massive underground lake, though the survey's clarity became unreliable at that depth.

She homed in on a decent high point with solid ground less than two klicks south-southeast of the facility. Without getting closer, she couldn't be sure, but it would be as good a place as any to start. She envisioned where to place the pip on the map, and her Rubicon complied, marking the location and pushing it out to the others' HUDs.

"Looks good to me," Brigham said.

Gallagher exited the ship and joined Adriene at the bottom of the ramp. "Drone's all ready," Gallagher said. The ramp whirred as it raised to seal behind her. "And the ship's prepped for recall."

"Let's hope we don't need it," Brigham said. "Lead the way, Ninety-Six."

Adriene considered the best approach vector, prompting an arrow symbol to flash in her HUD.

// Calculating route . . . //

A wide red line appeared on the ground at her feet, leading off into the dense jungle. She followed the line up to the forest's edge where a thick knot of branches and vines blockaded any possible way in.

She chewed her bottom lip. "This vegetation's dense . . . We're going to have to clear a path."

"Oh, fun," Kato piped. "Can I do it?" He held his right hand up in a fist. A small burst of flame spouted from a nozzle atop his wrist.

Gallagher's green suit lights bloomed. "Yeah, that seems like a good way to burn the entire forest down."

"It's a *rain* forest," he said, "it's not gonna burn down." His visor swung to face Adriene. "Right?"

"It's not really that simple," Adriene admitted. "And considering we're supposed to keep quiet, we may not want to start anything on fire."

Brigham stepped up to the brush, then thrust both arms out to either side. Wide blades extended from the length of his forearms, elbow to wrist like massive razor blades. He slid one arm into a tangle of vines, and it sliced through like butter.

He grunted. "Looks like blades'll do the trick."

Adriene gaped at the glinting blades. That feature had definitely not been covered in the sims—or the lecture.

Which meant it wasn't even an upgrade. *Of course* something that would have been a literal lifesaver in the 803rd would be considered old hat by the 505th.

// Activating utility blades. //

Adriene startled as the same wide, razor-like lengths of metal extended from her own forearms. She hadn't even realized she'd made the request.

Refocusing on her HUD, she stepped along the path of the virtual red line to the forest's edge. She swept her arms out in an X.

Most of the greenery fell away easily, but the blade on her right arm stuck in a particularly thick vine. She jerked her arm to dislodge it, but to no avail.

// Priming . . . //

Priming wha—?

The stuck blade glowed white, then the black bark smoldered. The hot blade fell loose from the scorched, notched vine.

Adriene lifted her arm in awe as the blade cooled.

The terms she'd read about and heard the others use for the VI: "aid," "ally," "assistant" . . . None of that felt right to her. It seemed far less restrained than she felt strictly comfortable with. Convenient, sure, especially considering she'd had hardly any training on the tech. Yet instead of warming up to the idea and slowly getting used to the strangeness, the more often it did something proactive, the more wariness crept in.

Brigham cleared his throat. "Combat stealth on, everyone."

A notification flashed into Adriene's HUD.

// Stealth mode 2A engaged. //

Her squadmates' suits flickered a shimmery black, then practically disappeared into the underbrush. She'd hardly be able to see them at all if it weren't for the colorful, illuminated lines still tracing brightly in her HUD.

Adriene kept on the path of the red line, slicing away brush with her superheated, bladed arms. Brigham followed just off her shoulder, weapon at the ready, with Kato next and Gallagher watching the rear.

Though it'd been daytime outside the canopy, underneath it might as well have been the dead of night. Even with her enhanced vision, holes of deep shadow surrounded them. The forest remained surprisingly quiet, save for the squish of their boots in the soft mud. Adriene kept an eye out for fauna, but thermal scans and motion detection seemed to corroborate a lack of animal life. Thankfully, the density of vines lessened somewhat as they continued, and soon Adriene only had to pause to clear a path every five or six meters.

After about a klick that took the better part of an hour to traverse, she sliced her way into a small glade where a wide river snaked through the vegetation. The thick, twisted vines of the trees still stretched overhead, continuing the unending canopy over the water. The light murmur of a waterfall came from somewhere to the south—an almost peaceful drone of white noise deadened by the walls of dense brush.

Adriene was briefly annoyed that her Rubicon had calculated a path through a body of water, but moments later, a new readout appeared: The depth reached less than a half meter. She asked her Rubicon to scan the water, and thermals and sonic came back negative.

So she waded in and the others followed, fanning out into a wider coverage formation now that they had more room.

Adriene unslung her rifle and kept her focus down the barrel, though she couldn't help but spare a glance into the disturbingly dark water. It seemed almost thick, parting sluggishly as the sleek panels of her hardsuit sliced through the mirrorlike stillness.

"Wait," Kato faltered. "You guys see that? In the water?"

"Cut it out," Brigham groused.

"I saw it too," Gallagher confirmed. "Looked like it was under the surface, but the water didn't move."

"My scans don't see shit," Brigham said. "Valero?"

Adriene faced them, eyes and rifle scope darting across the water at their feet, but she saw nothing.

She shook her head. "Sensors are—"

// *Warning: Hostiles detected.* //

Alerts erupted into Adriene's HUD, blaring in her earpiece. Heat seared her cheeks. She darted her look around the glade, confused—she still had no idea what direction the threat was coming from.

A bold, aggressive arrow appeared in her HUD. Pointing straight upward. She lifted her gaze just in time to see a mass of vines envelop her vision.

CHAPTER
EIGHT

Adriene fell back into the river, and the forest disappeared, engulfed by dark water.

Within a heartbeat, her HUD flashed with the engagement of some type of buoyancy feature. It propelled her back to the surface, and she caught her footing, armored boots sliding across the mucky silt of the river bottom as she managed to force herself upright.

She thumbed the primer on her rifle and took aim, but found the grasping vines swinging limply around her.

// Overwatch updating . . . //

"Five contacts!" Gallagher called.

Pips flashed into Adriene's HUD, marking five locations with upended triangles. She swung to face the largest—and as she quickly discovered, *closest*—icon. A skittering mass of limbs rushed toward her.

Her squad's muzzle fire lit the dark glade with harsh flashes, tossing the approaching creature's long shadow across the rippling water. The beast screeched out a high-pitched, grating roar of oscillating sound waves that rattled deep in her chest.

// Modulating . . . //

Adriene tensed, unnerved by the VI's smooth, undisturbed tone. The creature's hoarse screech filtered to a low buzz as she took aim and squeezed her trigger.

The charged slug slammed into the creature, erupting with a spray of bright blue blood. It crumpled into the water.

Its pip disappeared.

Adriene took a tentative step toward it. Her HUD flashed, scanning the lifeless mass as it bobbed along with the light current.

She squinted, trying to make sense of the plantlike form. The creature's narrow body and spindly legs were covered in thick, bark-like skin—the same burnt charcoal as the trees. Short, bristly spines lined each segmented limb. It was as if a mass of vines and bark had come to life, like the flora itself had turned carnivorous and . . .

// Octopedal. //

She shuddered as her Rubicon confirmed the leg count. Her HUD's scan beeped, highlighting three pairs of glossy obsidian eyes seated on either side of the body.

// Weakness detected. //

"Copy," she mumbled, then spun her look around the glade toward the other pips.

The bright red and green lines of Brigham and Gallagher crouched near the edge of the river, tucked into cover behind two thick tree trunks.

"Aim for the eyes," Adriene called out.

A crack rang loose as Gallagher fired, then another of the pips disappeared.

Kato stood a few meters off Adriene's three, rifle flashing as he unloaded into the side of one creature while another pip approached his flank.

Adriene shouted, "On your six!" then took aim just as Kato stepped back, obstructing her shot.

She slung her rifle and rushed to intercept. The microhydraulics of her suit's powered limbs strengthened her movements, propelling her forward with inhuman speed.

The creature still arrived first.

It tackled Kato into the dark water. Adriene—so startled by her unexpected swiftness—half crashed into them as she struggled to slow. Her arms tangled into the mess of black-barked limbs. She leveraged the remainder of her momentum to pry the creature off Kato.

The beast flew away. It fanned its legs out, and thin membranes unfolded between each limb, the taut skin allowing it to glide across the top of the water and remain afloat.

Kato grabbed Adriene's arm and hauled her to her feet. The creature skidded to a stop, then launched itself back at them.

It crashed into Adriene's chest. The talon-like tips of its front legs tore at the shell of her suit, generating ear-rending, grating shrieks. The hardened metal sparked but remained untouched.

Kato tried to pry it off with the butt of his rifle, but the creature stretched another set of legs around her neck and locked on.

It opened its maw, lined with a serrated band of sharp teeth, then lunged for her face.

Adriene raised her forearm to intercept the bite. The razor-like utility blade sliced out of her suit, carving deep into the creature's jaw as it latched onto her arm.

Its blood sprayed across her visor. The spattering melted away instantly, returning her vision to crystal clarity. Her arm blades heated, and the beast retracted, screeching out a guttural hiss as it dropped into the water.

In her HUD, the creature's pip flashed green. A half heartbeat later, a piercing crack rang out and the side of its head burst, spraying blue and black viscera across Kato. The beast went limp, its blood seeping out to stain the surface of the dark, mirrored water.

"All five down," Gallagher confirmed.

"Mira's end," Kato said. "Nice shot, Gal."

Adriene shouldered her rifle, and Kato turned to stand back-to-back with her. She swung her aim across the glade. Her heartbeat thudded in her ears, but her HUD remained quiet.

Gallagher shouted, "Five more contacts!"

A creature splashed into the water a few meters away, one of five pips that materialized in Adriene's HUD as her overwatch updated. The contacts scuttled into position, and via the small overhead map, their formation became clear: They'd formed an even circle around her and Kato.

Adriene braced her stance and took aim. But the creatures didn't rush them. They maintained their distance as they sidestepped in a slow, unsettling arc. Her HUD meted out the exact distance—six meters and holding.

The back of Adriene's neck warmed.

They'd been positioned—she and Kato. Herded together into the middle of the river so the creatures could surround them. They'd been hunting them, waiting for the ideal time to strike. In all her planet-hopping with the 803rd, she'd quickly learned local fauna could be equally as dangerous to underestimate as Mechan. Though at least with the scrappers, it was the enemy they knew.

Adriene focused on the contact straight in front of her, the small crimson reticle of her rifle's aim hovering in her visor.

// Engage auto-targeting protocols? //

She ground her teeth. *There're auto-targeting protocols?*

// Yes. //

Then fucking yes.

"Let's coordinate this," Brigham announced. "Assigning targets."

"I'll take the bonus guy," Kato offered.

"Copy. Lock to the eyes," Brigham reminded. "Engaging in five . . ."

Adriene's reticle aligned with the triplet set of eyes at her twelve, then the creature highlighted yellow.

// Target locked. //

". . . two, one."

Adriene pulled the trigger. Her slug met its target. The creature flew back, then fell limp into the water.

Gallagher picked off a green pip with a loud crack of her sniper rifle. Two other pips flashed blue and red, then disappeared from the map. Moments later, the last pip flashed with Kato's blue, then the earthy twang of his laser rifle sounded and the pip disappeared.

"All targets down," Kato confirmed.

"Contact," Gallagher called warily as another pip appeared.

// Warning: Significant disparity in stature detected. //

"Oh, *great*," Kato groused, apparently responding to his own Rubicon's warning. "Is this gonna be, like, the brood mother?"

Adriene primed her rifle.

An enormous mass fell from the canopy. It landed with a resounding splash in the water a half dozen meters away.

The monstrosity appeared the same spindle-legged amalgam of bark as the others, but at least ten times the size. It extended its massive legs, thick as tree trunks, rising menacingly to its full height. Its beady-eyed head towered more than three meters over the water.

Brigham called, "Flash-bang incoming!"

A red dot flew across Adriene's vision and landed beside the beast. Her visor modulated the blinding flash as the grenade popped, disorienting the creature and causing it to spin away from the detonation.

As it turned, her squad unloaded a round of shots into its side. Chunks of armorlike bark shattered off its limbs and torso, showering out sprays of blood into the river. Adriene inhaled a deep breath and aligned her rifle's reticle with one of the beast's large, glossy black eyes.

// Target locked. //

She fired, and the slug met its target.

Unlike its broodlings, however, the beast didn't immediately drop-dead into the water. Its remaining eyes went to slits and the spines on its legs bristled. It pivoted to face her.

Kato squeaked, "Oh, shit."

Adriene's heart raced as she quickly thumbed the prime on her rifle again. Her feet stuck in the mud of the riverbed as she back-pedaled along with Kato.

The massive beast lunged for her, the sharp tips of its jagged front legs angled toward her chest.

With a blinding flash, a wall of electricity ballooned out in front of her. Purple light shot across the glade as the creature hit the shield construct and bounced away, discharging a trail of violet sparks.

It collapsed, falling limp against the surface of the river and sending a tidal wave of dark water crashing into the foliage on the opposite bank.

The creature's limbs spasmed, and Adriene readied her rifle, but the beast didn't get up. Its long limbs creaked as it slumped into the nest of dense foliage on the riverbank.

Breaths short and fast, Adriene's eyes darted across her HUD. No more contacts.

After a few drawn-out seconds, the black water settled, pristine and undisturbed, reflecting an almost metallic, mirrorlike image of the semitransparent wall of electric light still cocooning Adriene.

She threw a glance to Kato beside her, but he didn't appear to be the originator of the shield construct. She looked down at her own chest, where purple light crackled out from a thin slot in her armor. The construct flickered, then the light fizzled away as the shield shut down.

// *Capacitor level at fifty-six percent.* //

"Mira's ashes," Adriene cursed under her breath. That shield might have saved her life, but at the cost of almost half her suit's power. She'd have to keep her instincts under control, or she might run out of juice before they even made it to the target location.

Kato laughed. "Damn, Ninety-Six. That's one way to use a shield construct."

"Is it . . . dead?" Gallagher asked.

The creature's outline shimmered in Adriene's HUD as her Rubicon scanned for life signs.

// *Dysfunctional nervous system and nonresponse to stimuli. It appears to be comatose.* //

"Not yet," Brigham said. "Let's finish it."

They formed up and sloshed through the river toward the unconscious beast, then took turns unloading rounds into its thick-barked torso until their Rubicons came back with negative vitals.

// *Target eliminated. No further contacts detected.* //

Brigham slung his rifle and faced Adriene. "Points for creative use of a shield construct," he said, "but be careful. That feature'll drain your capacitor right quick."

"Yeah, I . . . didn't mean to."

"You didn't *mean* to?" Kato asked, hesitation lacing his normally congenial tone. "The construct feature's not on the automation list. You must've triggered it intentionally."

She lifted a shoulder and shook her head. "I didn't even know the feature existed."

Brigham stared back at her silently for a long moment, but in the dark of the glade and through the thick glass of his visor, his expression was unreadable. Finally, he nodded. "Might be a bug," he said. "We'll get Daroga to look into it later."

"Speakin' of bugs," Kato grumbled, stabbing at the limp leg of the large creature with the muzzle of his rifle, "I fuckin' hate spiders."

"Where'd they come from?" Gallagher asked.

Adriene looked upward, and Gallagher followed her gaze.

"They must live above the canopy," Adriene said. "Or maybe in a layer of it." She craned her neck as she stared up at the torn opening in the thick foliage, slivers of gray clouded sky barely visible through the plaited vegetation.

Kato sloshed through the water and crouched beside one of the broodlings. He poked it tentatively with one finger. "Look at this bark shit . . . Are these things like, sentient trees?"

"No," Adriene said. She knelt beside him and ran her fingers over its thick, calloused skin, the sensation translating through the suit. "Just camouflage."

Can you do a deeper scan on the corpse? Anything unique about it?

// Scanning now . . . //

"That's some serious camouflage," Brigham said.

"Makes you wonder what they need to hide from," Gallagher said, giving a lingering look up- and downriver.

"No shit," Kato agreed.

Brigham let out a heavy breath. "Let's hope we don't find out."

Adriene's HUD finished its scan, and a small exclamation point flashed in her vision along with a readout of numbers and chemical symbols.

// Results filed. //

And?

// Unremarkable, though a traceable radiological signature has been detected. //

"There's a rad sig," she announced to the others. "It's low-grade, but specific enough. We should be able to use it to track them. Avoid other packs as we're walking."

"Or at least see them coming," Kato put in.

"Copy," Brigham said. "Push it out to us."

"Sending now," Adriene said, then asked her Rubicon to sync the information with the others' suits. Each colored outline flashed, and they sounded off their receipt.

Kato gave her a pat on the back. "Good call, Ninety-Six."

She made a mental note for her Rubicon to catalog the foliage in the background while they walked, then reset their objective point. The topographical interface popped up, and the thick red line leading toward the destination appeared on the shore nearby.

She stepped toward the dark forest, and the others fell in behind.

CHAPTER
NINE

A half hour later, Adriene led Forward Recon out of the dense vegetation and into muted daylight. Soft gray cloud cover still stretched across the sky as far as the eye could see.

They'd exited into a narrow clearing overlooking a thickly wooded valley. Adriene was grateful when her HUD projected an outline of the target facility two klicks off, since the overgrown structure was impossible to spot with the naked eye.

Brigham issued orders for Kato and Gallagher to keep watch along the perimeter while Adriene surveyed the clearing. She asked her Rubicon for a reminder of the available programs, marveling again at the variety and depth of information at her disposal—but despite the plethora of survey options, she didn't need long to determine the site's viability.

"It's no good," she announced, then tasked her Rubicon with scanning for a second option.

"You sure?" Brigham asked with a regretful sigh. "Remember, it's only a temporary staging site. We're not huntin' for spots for Joe and Sue Colonist to build their forever home."

"Yeah, I'm sure," she said. "GPR shows a loose silt layer with hardly any bedrock support for meters down. Ground'll be too soft to stage gennys or any kind of operations base."

"All right. Where to, then?"

"The ground densifies a klick east. The altitude is lower and we'll be a little closer, but it's got a better tactical placement geographically. And it looks like we'll have a clearer visual on the facility."

"Lead the way."

"Copy, marking beta site." Adriene had her Rubicon set the new location on the map, thankful that the path led along the clear ridge and not back into the gloomy forest. The squad formed up behind her to start the short jaunt east.

A few minutes into the walk, Kato shuffled up to walk beside her. "You musta seen a ton of different planets in the 803rd, huh?" he said, eager congeniality in his tone. "See anything like this one before?"

She glanced out over the valley to their right and its rolling hills of thick canopy. "A few. They're all pretty unique, though."

"How 'bout them spidey things?"

"Definitely not."

"Yeah, me either. Don't get me wrong—we've been mangled by our fair share of alien monsters, that's just the fun of bein' in recon. First boots, first blood, as they say. Thanks for the assist, by the way. Tacklin' that guy off me—badass."

Adriene shook her head. "No trouble. It was the suit that saved my hide anyhow." She looked down to where the creature's knifelike talons had scraped across her chest—the matte-black metal left pristine, completely unmarred. "What're these suits made of anyway?"

"That's new to this model, actually," Kato replied, his tone taking on an edge of enthusiasm. Then he leaned in slightly and lowered his voice as if it might stop the others from hearing him despite comms. "I'm not supposed to say, but Daroga told me—it's alanthum."

Adriene's steps faltered, and she had to swallow the lump in her throat before she could respond. "Um, really?"

His helmet bobbed with a rolling nod. "Yep. They haven't been able to perfect the hardening technique the scrappers use yet, but he says they're gettin' real close."

In Adriene's HUD, Gallagher's green pip glowed as the woman grumbled, "Mira's end, that's just *great*. So now we're made of the same shit they are?"

Kato glanced back at Gallagher. "I suppose if ya wanna see it that way."

"No," Brigham said, tone firm. "Our armor maybe, but we're still flesh and bone."

Kato snorted. "You mean we still gotta deal with these vulnerable meat bags inside our shiny alanthum shells?"

Brigham grunted, but didn't reply.

An icy chill traced up Adriene's spine. She eyed the hard lines of her suit in a whole different light.

She'd *just* started to accept it, maybe even like it. Now every time she put it on, it'd remind her of them. Or worse—of what it was like to *be* one of them, imprisoned in her own body while they pulled her strings like a marionette.

Bile crept up her throat, and she swallowed it back, trying to shake the feeling. The stupid suit had already saved her life multiple times. Who cared if it was essentially made of the lifeblood of their enemies? They were merely fighting fire with fire. She'd take any advantage she could to get a leg up on those bloody scrap heaps.

Intent on avoiding more casual chats, Adriene quickened her pace and continued along the route in silence. About a half klick into the journey, the ridge disappeared under a towering waterfall that descended the worn rocks with a soothing rumble. Though sizable, the cascade was nothing but a small offshoot of the colossal 1,500-meter one she'd seen earlier.

Water misted her visor as she crossed under the backside of the waterfall. She paused a few meters in and held her hand under some of the spraying fringes. The sensation translated as the water pooled in her palm, then trailed along the lines of her suit. Though she'd expected the water to be warm, as the climate of the planet was such, it seemed strangely so—almost hot.

Are you modulating the temperature of the water?

// No. The water temperature is a natural three hundred nine degrees Kelvin. //

Can you tell if it's potable?

// Yes. It has an alkaline pH of seven point eight, and microbial, chemical, and physical constituents are suitable for human consumption. //

How can you tell all that just by seeing it?

// A sampling has been taken. //

It has? When?

// *Rubicon has access to a collection grid of over fifty thousand microsensors on the outer shell of your suit. This allows for the constant analyzation of air quality as well as any toxins, gases, or other substances you may encounter. It functions as an ongoing background task to ensure proper filtration methods are utilized.* //

Adriene nodded and continued walking, her team following close behind. She prodded her Rubicon for more information about its sampling capabilities, discovering her suit basically acted as a walking laboratory, containing an analyzation suite well-fitted enough to make any field scientist jealous.

Minutes later, they reached the new site. She ran a few initial scans and determined the muddy clearing to be more than suitable for their needs. Though the facility remained obscured in the trees, visible slivers of the metal structure jutted up through the vegetation. The flat, dense ground was open enough to allow for air supply drops. As a bonus, the western edge backed onto a rocky cliff front, meaning one less direction they'd have to surveil.

Adriene outlined a proposed perimeter, and Brigham confirmed, then ordered Gallagher to deploy her fleet of patrol beacons to set up a temporary defense border. When she was done, she updated overwatch, and the squad gathered at the front edge of the clearing overlooking the valley.

Adriene stood beside Brigham as they attempted to assess the target facility from the new vantage. "I'm not getting anything," she said. "Zero movement."

"Me either," Brigham said. "I think we need to move closer."

"We can't, boss," Kato warned. "Params say no closer than two klicks without authorization. We're already up against it."

"It's worth the risk," Brigham said. "We can't get an intel workup if we can't even get a read on the scrappers' activity."

Adriene chewed her bottom lip, letting the others discuss the issue while she stepped toward the sloping edge of the clearing.

Why *couldn't* they see any scrapper activity? From here, there should be some sign—something on overwatch or an errant radio signal, or at least a visual on the annoying drone "birds" Mechan liked to use as lookouts.

Rubicon . . . ?

// Yes. //

How far out can you compile a detailed scan?

// Current mission parameters allow five hundred meters. //

What regulates that?

// It is set according to the specifications of commonplace Mechan countermeasures as triggered by electronics probing. //

So you'd be able to run a closer scan if we're not probing for electronics? Get readings of just the facility, just the layout?

// Yes. But this would not include the complete intelligence package needed to fulfill mission objectives or ensure the safety of an approach. //

I understand—do it anyway. Maybe biometrics or chemical readings too? Anything that might be of use.

// Understood. Executing . . . //

A few moments later, a stream of scrolling data rolled through her HUD, including flashes of estimated distances, rough overheads, entrances, and possible approach vectors.

Cross-check that with all databases.

// Executing . . . Positive return on four databases. Parsing . . . //

Adriene waited a few long moments, tapping her foot lightly. *Anything?*

// Yes. //

And . . . ?

// The information appears to contradict prior intelligence reports. //

How so?

// This facility does not appear to be Mechan in origin. //

In her HUD, she scrolled through the findings. She'd only been hoping to get an idea of when it'd been built to give some insight into what security and defenses they might encounter. She did *not* expect to learn it wasn't Mechan.

// Cursory dating suggests the structure predates the Concord Nations' presumed date of Mechan origination. By a substantial margin. //

So . . . what is it, then? Who built it? It couldn't be human—they'd first charted this sector only a couple of decades ago.

// Not human, no. The building shares many similarities to Mechan structural predilections, suggesting a high likelihood of seminal correlation. //

Adriene glanced at Brigham, still debating with Kato whether or not they should push forward.

Seminal correlation . . . Does that mean what I think it does?

// Yes. //

She sucked in a deep breath, trying to focus on the new information and ignore the fact that this VI could literally read her mind. Yet somehow, it'd become harder to ignore instead of easier.

Her chest constricted as intrusive echoes of her hybridization buzzed in her ears. The invasive, chaotic stream of thought of the Mechan hive mind.

Drawing her shoulders back, she grounded herself, dismissing the unwanted memory. Rubicon was merely another piece of tech, another tool in her arsenal, like her hardsuit or coilgun. Entirely different than the unrestrained barrage of the hive mind—regardless of the faceless voice correlation.

Adriene turned to her squadmates, inclining her head to Brigham. "I think you're right, sir. We need to get a closer look."

"What?" Kato said. "Why?"

"My Rubicon is saying this facility might not be Mechan."

Brigham grumbled, "Not Mechan?"

"Apparently, it predates them," Adriene said, "but it's similar enough to share some obvious . . . influences. Probably why our prelim intel thought it was a Mechan facility. Not surprising—orbital scans are shit for accurate aging."

"Wait—*predates* them?" Brigham asked. "By how long?"

// One to two hundred years. //

The comms readout in Adriene's HUD indicated her Rubicon had pushed that announcement to the others as well.

"Well," Kato breathed, "that's a twist."

Gallagher turned and looked toward the facility. "Mira's ashes . . ."

Brigham crossed his arms. "So . . . you're trying to tell me this ruin belonged to the fucks who created the scrappers?"

Kato scoffed a tense laugh.

// It is a distinct possibility, though it cannot be proven given current data sets. //

"But the bots could still be here, right?" Gallagher said, turning back toward them. "Even if it's not their facility."

"Yeah," Kato agreed. "Maybe we aren't seein' signs 'cause they're usin' some of that ancient tech. Some form of security the Mechan restored—somethin' overwatch can't detect."

"Or they're just not here," Adriene suggested.

Kato mumbled, "Sure . . . Occam's razor, I guess."

"She's right," Gallagher put in. "They don't typically occupy a site long term without good reason."

Kato shrugged. "Maybe their good reason is our good reason."

Brigham let out a rough sigh that crackled over comms. "We may need to adjust the plan."

"How so, sir?" Gallagher asked.

"If this isn't a Mechan facility and there's no scrappers on the planet, then this is an entirely different op than Command thinks it is. There's no reason to stage a forward operations base and drop a dozen teams if there's nothing to fight our way into. We can simply walk in and take it."

Kato crossed his arms. "Now that's somethin' Cash woulda suggested."

Brigham threw him a look. "Watch yourself."

"I'm serious, LT," Kato insisted, tone strained. "It's too dangerous—we don't know jack shit about what we're walkin' into."

"It's not our decision to make." Brigham turned to Gallagher. "What's our connection with the *Aurora* like?"

"Comms are a no-go," she said, "but Rubicon signal is strong and stable."

"All right, try to push a priority message through the Rubicon server, see if you can get an update to Blackwell."

"On it," Gallagher said.

While they waited, Adriene paced the north perimeter, reviewing the rest of the data her Rubicon had gathered and sharing a few of the relevant findings with her squadmates.

Less than ten minutes later, Gallagher perked up. "Packet incoming."

"That was fast," Kato said.

Gallagher's green outline flashed as she pushed the response out to the squad.

// Major Blackwell's security code confirmed. Decrypting . . . //

The decoded message displayed in Adriene's HUD, and she quickly scanned the text for the gist of the response: The other squads would rendezvous ASAP, but as long as Forward Recon could confirm no enemy contacts, they were to scout the ruins themselves.

"He wants us to proceed . . ." Gallagher said, her wary tone equal parts surprise and dread.

Adriene skimmed the rest, then reread the last lines a few times to confirm. If they couldn't find the objective package or Mechan forces arrived before backup came, they were to destroy the facility. Use of nukes granted at Lieutenant Brigham's discretion.

Kato sighed. "Easy op, my *ass.*"

Brigham looked at him. "Who said this would be an easy op?"

"*Blackwell,* after I told him how drunk I got last night."

Gallagher snorted a laugh. "Just ask your Rubicon for some stims."

"She won't give me any more," he whined.

"All right, guys, let's focus," Brigham chided. "The major attached the primary mission intel. Pushing it out."

Brigham's red outline flashed and a new packet of data appeared in the corner of Adriene's HUD. Text and image files unpacked and lined up along the side of her vision.

"This is the objective," Brigham said. One of the docked image files hovered up, then flickered as it opened. A three-dimensional rendering loaded: a small, seemingly inconsequential rectangular object packed with circuitry, rotating slowly as measurements and composition data appeared around it. "They're calling it a 'technology artifact.'"

Kato tilted his head. "Looks like some kinda data core."

// Spectral analysis indicates a low-level traceable electronic signature. //

"Mark as primary objective," Brigham ordered.

Without another thought, Adriene's Rubicon set the signature trace as an ongoing background task.

Brigham sucked in a hard breath loud enough to activate comms. "Time to look alive, Forward Recon," he continued. "Use Valero's initial scans—take a half hour and do some prelim work. I want to have a few exfil plans in case shit goes south once we get inside."

"You mean *when* shit goes south," Kato grumbled.

"That's enough, Sergeant," Brigham snapped, squaring up to Kato.

"Sorry, boss," Kato said, back straightening. "But is this really a good idea?"

"It doesn't matter," he said firmly. "We have our orders." He turned back to face Adriene and Gallagher. "I know this isn't the kind of op we're used to dealing with, but we're more than capable. This is our chance to prove it."

CHAPTER
TEN

Adriene grunted as she pressed on the heavy, banded metal door with suit-aided strength. Kato and Brigham assisted on either side, while Gallagher kept a close eye on their suspiciously quiet overwatch. They hadn't seen a single contact on their approach, and even now, standing right outside the overgrown ruin, there were no perceivable security measures in place. It seemed Intel had indeed been wrong about a Mechan presence at the facility.

The metal groaned, echoing as they pressed harder, and the ancient, corroded hinges finally gave way. With an additional shove, the two-meter-square panel fell inward, sending off a plume of dirt and dust as it clanged to the ground inside.

"Well," Kato said, standing back and dusting off his hands. "If they didn't already know we're here . . ."

"There's no *they*," Gallagher said, sounding like she hardly believed her own words. "There's still nothing on overwatch."

"Keep an eye on it," Brigham said.

Adriene's gaze darted as her HUD furiously scanned the interior beyond the open door frame. Soft light flooded the darkness as the dust settled, and Adriene had to wonder when these walls had last seen daylight.

// Approximately two hundred years. //

Adriene sucked in a deep breath to steady her heart rate. She wasn't sure why she was nervous; this was old hat for her. She'd descended into questionable ancient ruins on a weekly basis in the 803rd. But this was different. Life mattered more to the 505th; it had intrinsic value, despite the safety net of a rezone. While their encounter with the local fauna had been exhilarating, this would mark the first time she felt headed into real danger since her last rezone. And she didn't like it.

Brigham shouldered his rifle. "I'll take point. Single squad sweep until we get a clear interior scan."

Weapons raised, they formed up behind Brigham and stepped into the darkness.

Adriene's HUD signaled the activation of a low-light filter. The vast room around her became visible with muted colors and a noisy, grainy texture. The space stretched roughly twenty meters across and twice as wide.

// Nineteen point eight one by forty-two point six seven meters. //

Adriene focused on staying off Kato's shoulder as they crept forward, swinging her aim into the darkest corners of the room.

Thin streams of light shone down from the decaying ceiling, cast as blaring spotlights in the low-light filter. Thick pieces of ash-like dust hovered in the air, flashing in her enhanced vision like tiny beacons as they caught the light from the open door frame.

Though the exterior facade had been covered in corrugated metal, the interior was built of a textured, dark gray stone tinged to inky blue in the natural light. Debris and dust littered the brick floor, inlaid with worn, colored tiles that created a thick wave pattern running the length of the open room and continuing down two hallways that stretched off to either side.

"Overwatch's clear on this level," Gallagher said, "and at least four stories down."

The squad formation loosened. Adriene took a few steps toward the wall just inside the door, where soft gray light spilled across the stone. Inlaid in the wall were hundreds of small, colorful jewels mixed with painted tiles. She stepped back to take in the almost two-meter-wide image: a stylized panorama of the uncut forest they'd just walked through, with a net of black-barked trees stretching toward a cobbled gray sky.

Brigham's red pip lit in the comms menu. "Kato, Valero—clear that eastern hallway," he ordered. "Gallagher, with me."

"Copy east," Kato returned, then headed down the eastern hallway. Adriene followed, keeping near the outer wall to get a closer look at the tiled vignettes. With each new image, the scenery changed. Buildings rose among the trees, then beings appeared—vaguely humanoid, bipedal and gray-skinned with thin limbs and large, oblong heads—the elongated crowns narrowing to angular chins, hairless skulls lined with bony ridges. She'd never seen anything like it.

// Scanning and archiving. //

Halfway down the corridor, a thin stream of water trickled down the exterior wall, creating a worn, colorless path through the painted tiles. Adriene's boots splashed through the rivulet as it traveled across the floor, pooling in the sunken stone before disappearing down a small crevice on the other side of the hall.

She refocused on Kato, taking a few quick steps to catch up. Her HUD flashed a small icon: a yellow triangle with a jagged crack through it.

// Warning. Structural instability detected. //

Kato warned, "My SI's flashin' yellow."

"Mine too," Adriene confirmed.

"Just keep an eye. We'll worry if it goes orange."

Adriene watched her footing carefully as they continued to creep forward. An overlay appeared on the floor, fading between shades of green and yellow into orange and red. She took the hint and followed along the greener path, noting that Kato ahead of her took similar steps.

As they approached the end of the hall, the dusty, dry stone walls became more deeply fractured, allowing sunlight and trickles of water to stream in freely. Black vines grew in the cracks, further splitting and eroding the stone and tile work.

At the end of the hall sat a single, wide metal door, corroded off its hinges and lying askew in the stone archway. Kato picked it up with ease, and sunlight poured in as he set it aside. He took a step out into the overgrown vegetation, then returned a moment later.

"Nothin' this way, boss," Kato said. "Mighta been another area of the facility at some point, but it's collapsed and overgrown as fuck now."

Brigham's small red pip lit as his voice rang over comms, "Nothing this way either."

Adriene approached the last vignette at the end of the hall, cast in soft streams of natural daylight. She brushed at the layer of silt with her fingers, cutting clean lines through the dirt. The tiles were more worn and faded than the others, the finer details of the scene lost to the ages, though the gist of it was more or less discernible: Three of the gray-skinned beings stood around a platform on which another being sat. Though similar in shape—a long neck, large head, two arms, two legs—it lacked the organic curves of its companions, and was easily twice as tall.

Kato peeked over her shoulder. "Weird. What are those things?"

"No idea." She ran her fingers under a nearby trickle of water, then used it to wash more of the dirt away from the larger being, revealing gray skin with a rectilinear body and a featureless face . . . save for a pair of eyes. They glinted as they caught the light—two tiny, polished amber jewels set into the stone.

A warning blared in Adriene's HUD.

Her stomach shot upward, and the ground fell out from under her feet, the sunlight extinguished by sudden darkness.

She hit a hard, unforgiving surface, and the air kicked from her lungs—skin tingling with the sensation of a rough but suit-dampened impact. She coughed as she regained her breath, frantically scanning her HUD for contacts, but there was nothing.

Chunks of stone fell beside her as she pressed up on her hands and feet. Through the cloud of dust, a set of crisp, neon blue lines traced in her HUD from just a few meters away.

"Kato, you good?" She brushed shards of stone off her shoulders and stood.

He coughed. "Yeah, I'm okay."

Adriene offered Kato a hand and pulled him to his feet. She

looked up as the dust settled. Daylight shone in through a jagged crevice six meters above.

Kato briskly shook his shoulders and helmet like a dog drying its coat, flinging dust and rock shards off into the dark. "Guess that structural warning wasn't messing around," he said, tone resigned but light. "Gal, my friend? We took a little vertical trip over here. You got the winch?"

"On my way," Gallagher replied.

// Warning. Structural instability detected. //

Adriene's HUD flashed the same triangle symbol—this time orange.

"Maybe double-time it," Adriene said. "We've got another warning."

Through the ceiling, Gallagher's green lines approached the crevice, then peered down from above, silhouetted in the streaming daylight. She dropped the cable, and Adriene helped Kato hook it to the front of his hardsuit, then guided him as Gallagher hauled him up.

Gallagher had just started to lower the cable again when the floor under Adriene's feet shifted and cracked.

Adriene stretched, reaching for the hook, but couldn't grab it in time. The stone at her feet split, and she plummeted a second time.

She hit another flat surface, landing hard on one shoulder. Pain fired through her arm and back, though her suit deadened the intensity somewhat. She barely had time to catch her breath before a crack rang out and she fell again.

Blackness filled her vision for a few long moments, but she snapped awake moments later.

// Consciousness lost for seven point six seconds. Avoid additional impacts. //

Adriene groaned as she rolled onto her side. *Yeah, I'd like that too.*

Brigham's stern, low voice rang through comms. "Valero, you copy?"

"Yeah, I copy," she managed, struggling to catch her breath. "I, uh . . ." She rolled onto her back and looked up into the dusty black-ness above. Tiny slivers of stone rained down lightly onto her visor, crackling like the embers of a campfire in the deadened silence of the subterranean room. "I fell a few more stories, I think."

"Gallagher, you got her on overwatch?"

After a moment, Gallagher responded, "She's about twenty-five meters down."

"Shit," Kato cursed. "That's too far."

Adriene sat up on her elbow and closed her eyes, willing her vision to stop spinning. "Too far for what?"

"The winch."

"Valero," Brigham said, "can you plot a course back to us?"

Adriene climbed to her feet and flicked on her headlamp. She looked around the dark room—small and square, three walls lined with corroded metal shelves. On the fourth wall hung a piece of cracked glass beside an open door frame. "I see an exit. I'll try."

Gallagher said, "I'll push you what overwatch has gathered so far."

A green data icon appeared in Adriene's HUD. Her Rubicon took the information and pieced it together with her own suit's scans. A moment later, a red line overlaid the floor, leading out the open door.

She scanned the overview and the estimated distance, then pressed out a sigh. "Route viability's only thirty-four percent, but I think I can get back up there. It might take a little while, though."

"Damn," Brigham said. "All right, get to it."

"Sir," Gallagher said, voice suddenly sharp. "I have contacts on overwatch. Thirty kilometers northwest. Two ships on a trajectory to our location. Mechan transponders."

"Fuck," Brigham grunted.

"Thirty klicks?" Kato said. "Geez, they ain't even tryin' to be quiet. What the hell?"

"They probably don't know we're here," Gallagher pointed out.

"They'll find out soon enough," Brigham said, tone resigned. "We're gonna have to abort. Recon on me."

"Whoa, wait," Kato said. "What about Ninety-Six?"

"We don't have time," Brigham replied. "Thirty-four percent's not great odds."

"We have to *try*," Kato insisted.

Adriene took a few slow breaths in and out, staring up at the ceiling as Brigham contemplated her fate. Eventually, two small red and green pips moved west, followed shortly by a blue one, until they flickered and disappeared, too far for her suit to detect.

Her earpiece clicked. "Valero," Brigham said. "We can't risk a rendezvous, the scrappers'll be all over us by then. You're going to have to zero—"

Adriene clamped her eyes shut as a heavy pressure filled her head and the dark room skewed. Brigham's voice continued through comms, muted and dull. She swallowed and shook her head to clear away the haze.

"Valero?" Brigham barked. "You copy that?"

She released a pent-up breath and tried to find her voice. "Sir," she managed, dryness plaguing her throat. "I don't need to, I can make it out—"

Gallagher cut in, voice uneven, "Two more ships southwest, twenty klicks."

Brigham grunted. "Valero, I don't have time to argue."

"LT, come on," Kato urged, but Brigham ignored him.

"Either do it yourself," Brigham continued, "or I'll do it for you when I nuke the place. I'm recalling the dropship now."

Heat crept up Adriene's neck, and she suddenly found it very hard to breathe.

// *Despite a lack of direct external stresses, you have suffered a notable increase in heart rate and cortisol levels . . .* //

She couldn't. No fucking way. It'd only been two weeks. It wasn't long enough to live and die again.

// *Please note, there is a euthanasia protocol—*//

Adriene coughed a sharp, pained laugh. Of course there was.

//*—allowing Rubicon to render the user unconscious via an anesthesia provided in the standard chemical augment kit. The heart can then be stopped, providing a painless death.* //

She ground her teeth. It wasn't death she dreaded. It was waking up again.

// *That lies outside my permitted functions.* //

"I don't expect you to *do anything about it*," she growled.

"Valero?" Kato asked over comms. "You okay?"

She let out a sharp sigh. "Everything's fine. Sorry." She muted her comm. "Mira's ashes . . ." She scrubbed her hands over the back of her helmet, exhaling a long breath. "How about you just deactivate my rezone chip so this shit can be over with already?"

// *That is possible, in theory.* //

Adriene's breath hitched. "Wait—what?"

// *Rubicon has direct access to your biological functions. Given the correct permissions, it would be theoretically possible to construct a pathway to a rezone chip, then deactivate it. Given there is a chip to deactivate.* //

"The correct permissions? What does that mean?"

// *Administrator permissions are required for biological interference beyond certain thresholds.* //

"Administrator? Is that Blackwell?"

// *That information is not available.* //

"Daroga?"

// *That information is not available.* //

"Ninety-Six," Kato's breathy voice rang through, a small blue icon indicating he'd opened a private channel. "Brig's being an ass. Sorry about this."

"It's fine." Expected, honestly. Had she really ever thought this would go any other way?

"I'll try to delay him," Kato offered, "but you gotta get your ass up here. *Fast.*"

Adriene hesitated, her mind briefly stalling out. She focused on Kato's blue comm channel icon in her HUD.

Kato was willing to risk not only himself but his whole squad to give her a chance to escape. A chance to avoid another rezone. After knowing her for two days. She couldn't understand it, couldn't wrap her head around it.

A voice in the back of her mind growled that she knew exactly why he was doing it: because of how pathetic she seemed, how badly he felt for her that she couldn't keep herself alive for longer than a few weeks at a time, for fuck's sake.

She swallowed and pushed the feeling aside. Now wasn't the time to wallow in pity over her shit luck. If Kato was going to defy his CO and risk his life to help her, she wouldn't waste it.

"All right," she said, setting her jaw and giving a firm nod. "Thank you, Kato."

"No thanks required. It's selfish, really. 'Ninety-Seven' is kinda a mouthful."

She half scoffed, half groaned, then muted her comm again, facing the doorway and the looming red line her Rubicon had laid out.

She could do this. She'd gotten out of shittier situations dozens of times, and that was before she had a top-of-the-line hardsuit and firepower at her disposal.

She reached over her shoulder to grab her rifle, but only grasped air. She checked her other shoulder, then swung her headlamp to scour the ground around her, but saw nothing. She turned to the gaping black hole above.

Her rifle was . . . elsewhere. She'd be making this journey unarmed.

// Inaccurate. Your sidearm is still present and fully functional. //

"I don't really need snark right now."

// Rubicon does not have a framework for "snark," but your preference is noted and a sarcasm array will be established. //

"Fantastic."

// Example noted. //

Adriene's fists clenched, and she wanted nothing more than to rip the damn VI implant out of her head. But to have any chance at getting out of here, she would need the stupid thing.

She pulled her sidearm free and thumbed the safety, then followed the red line out toward the door.

The room exited into a wide hallway, punctuated by doors in various states of decay. Along the walls sat the corroded skeletons of a dozen rectangular structures, tall and narrow like upended, metal caskets. They lined the dank stone walls with unnerving conformity, evenly spaced, neatly aligned.

A green light flashed in her HUD as Gallagher opened a private comm line. "Valero, Kato told me the plan . . . I'll try to keep your overwatch updated. You've already got incoming to your location, though—pushing it out . . ." She hesitated, then her voice came back steady and sincere. "Good luck."

// Overwatch updating . . . //

"Thanks, Gallagher."

The comm line disappeared, and four pips flashed onto her map, each paired with a distance and estimated approach time.

"Fucking hell," she swore, grinding her teeth. She'd *just* managed to convince herself she might be able to get out alive, but the scrappers would be on her any minute.

She quickened her pace, hurrying to the end of the corridor, which opened into a massive atrium. The red guideline in her HUD crossed the wide room, passing over a circular dais at the center, covered with a maze of crevices and inlaid tile, looking like some kind of ancient water feature.

// ETA fifteen seconds. //

Bearing?

// Above. //

Of course. It wouldn't feel like a real op if scrappers weren't raining down on her from overhead.

Then it hit her—*fifteen* seconds. She cursed under her breath; she wouldn't have time to cross the atrium before they'd arrive. This wasn't going to be a chase. She'd have to fight her way out.

She checked the charge on her sidearm, then jogged a few meters into the room and slid into cover behind a large, fallen chunk of carved stone.

// Notice: Objective signature detected. //

Her brow creased. "What?"

She glanced out across the massive, open room. She mentally filtered out the red directional line and structural integrity overlay and descending scrapper pips and ever-shifting threat assessment index and a dozen other flashing distractions—leaving only a single, soft yellow circle tagged with a small exclamation mark.

// *Primary objective located.* //

With a resounding crack, the ceiling over the central dais collapsed in a deluge of dark navy stone.

Adriene held her breath and ducked into cover, shuddering as she tried to fight back images of the basalt cave: obsidian shards raining down on her former squad as she executed them, one by one. She shoved the memory away. She had to focus.

Two enemy pips descended. The Mechan dropped among the plume of settling dust and debris, metal joints groaning as they landed.

She pressed her back against the rough stone boulder. Beneath the steadfast grip of her gloves, sweat slicked her palms before being wicked away. She readjusted her grip on the pistol.

They hadn't spotted her yet. Now was her chance, maybe her only chance. If all her years in the 803rd had taught her anything, it was how to appropriately time a zero-out. Which was generally *before* a bot had you in its clutches.

She held her breath, watching in her HUD as the Mechan pips split off to scour the room. One slowly approached at her five, its decreasing proximity acting as a nerve-racking countdown. Another rounded on her eight, its metal feet scraping against the dirt-caked stone.

She took a steadying inhale, though it caused a hitch in her breath. She tightened her grip on the pistol.

She had to zero out. Now. Before it was too late.

No sooner had the reality struck her than a blinding flash engulfed her vision. A sharp pain fired into the back of her head—concentrated and searing—a focused spear of agony.

She screamed through bared teeth.

Her knees hit the stone floor, and she gripped the sides of her helmet. Sharp, static pangs like ice-cold electricity ricocheted through her head.

Her fingers scraped at the seal of her helmet, trying to pry it off.

Something was wrong—*very* wrong—but she couldn't problem-solve on any functional level while this voltage surged through her brain.

Then at once, the pain vanished. For a long moment, she felt literally nothing. A detached sort of peace, as if she were no longer connected to her body, her entire existence focused only on her perceiving mind.

It came with a tremendous sense of clarity—stark and daunting. She could see *everything:* the Rubicon implant in her brain, the circuits in her suit, the capacitor in her sidearm. A few meters away, a Mechan's foot crunched the soil, moving so slowly it seemed almost frozen in place.

In reality, it didn't move slowly. No. It was that she saw it *quickly.* Perceiving it in slow motion. She had all the time in the world.

The nearest Mechan Trooper—an older model—loomed at her five, three meters off. Another Trooper at her eight, ten meters. Another two still descending, three floors up. Squads of Troopers swept each level above. Pairs of Surveyors stood watch at the entrance, deploying swarms of drones to scour the site.

Her perception blossomed outward.

Outside the facility, Kato's suit released heated blades. Gallagher ran countless exfil scenarios as they cut their way through dense vegetation. Brigham's Rubicon had released a stim cocktail to suppress his worry and guilt.

Another outward shift.

A few klicks off, Mechan ships sped across the treetops, unaware, for now, of the retreating humans. Back at the clearing, the dropship's stealth engaged, and it ascended. Upward, hundreds of satellites drifted in orbit, all dysfunctional, ancient, essentially debris.

Farther.

Nothing for light-years.

Again.

Back on the *Aurora*, soldiers ran simulations and evaluated new suits and checked firearms and held mission briefings.

Then down a narrow lift into the darkness of the lower levels, where jets of icy water swirled through the engines and life systems toward a tessellated array of glass panels—

With a sharp pang, Adriene's senses snapped back into her, the peaceful clarity smothered with a pounding head and sore muscles and a heavy chest—the intense burden of a physical form.

Her ears rang with a steady, high-pitched shriek and her vision tilted, the edges blooming white. It took everything in her power not to throw up in her helmet.

As her head swam, she keeled forward, grasping to hold on to consciousness. Now was *not* the time to pass out.

She had no idea what had just happened, but she couldn't spare the focus to process it. She had to be brain-dead—soon—or they could still hybridize her, and she'd never forgive herself for not just sucking it up and zeroing out when she had the chance.

She picked up the pistol she'd apparently dropped and tried to will her Rubicon to open her visor.

No response.

"Hey," she grunted. The lines of her HUD flickered with static, and her suit remained unresponsive to her commands.

She looked down. The hand clutching her pistol cramped, and her fingers opened, sending the gun to the stone with a muted thump.

Panic fired through her chest. She stared down at the weapon.

She didn't feel nearly responsible enough for that action. Not in the least.

Though she hated what she had to do, she truly wanted that gun in her hand. She wanted her visor open, and she wanted that hole in her head. Much more than the alternative, at least.

The lines of her HUD cleared.

// Initialization complete. //

Her vision focused, and a hint of that same peaceful clarity crept into the back of her mind, instantly soothing her doubts.

She wanted to zero out . . . but she also didn't. Not because she was afraid to die or even afraid to wake up again. There was something new, like a seed that'd just been planted, but its roots were solid as ever, like it'd been there all along. A greater clarity of purpose: *the objective.*

It was why they'd come—not to escape with their lives intact. What use was that?

With newfound fortitude, she picked up her gun and rose to face the Mechan Trooper as it rounded the corner.

CHAPTER
ELEVEN

Time stretched as Adriene raised her pistol and fired two rounds, one into each of the Trooper's ocular sensors.

The bot faltered, almost seemingly taken aback by her brazen approach, and Adriene felt much the same. It went against a decade of training to engage a Mechan in close quarters. But there she stood, plowing forward instead of retreating to find new cover.

She didn't doubt herself, not anymore. The suit made her powerful, Rubicon even more so. She only had to trust them.

As the Trooper stumbled back, she unleashed a stream of fire into its abdomen, concentrating on the area of its chassis that housed the capacitor rig. Her HUD unfolded a multicolored display over the scrapper's torso, meting out an approximation of the shell's integrity as the bombardment weakened it.

After a couple of dozen quick rounds, her pistol's heat sinks red-lined right as the bot's plate integrity rating hit 20 percent, then bottomed out. She couldn't weaken it further. Not that way.

So she holstered her sidearm and willed the suit to amplify her strength. She drew back her elbow and charged, closing the remaining meters between them, then turned into the strike with all the strength she—or rather her suit—could muster.

Her fist struck hard. A jolt of pain shot up her arm, one that was too easy to ignore. Her hand plunged through the bot's chassis and lodged in its abdomen well past the wrist. The Trooper crumpled under the blow, falling backward and pulling Adriene with it.

They landed, her knees straddling the bot's torso. She ignored the battery-level warning in her HUD and yanked her fist free, pulling a section of paneling away with it.

The Mechan twitched. With both hands, she reached into its

gaping chest cavity, shoving aside bound tendrils of wires and sparking components until she found a large cylinder: the scrapper's power supply. She wrenched it free. The bot exhaled a dull whistle of decompressing hydraulics as it went limp.

Breath ragged, Adriene tossed the cylinder away. Heat crept up her neck and into her cheeks.

A nervous laugh bubbled its way up her throat—she'd never gone head-to-head with a scrapper before and walked away. This was ludicrous.

Raw instinct tensed her muscles, and she spun, thrusting out a palm. It slammed directly into the chest of the other Trooper as it rounded the fallen stone barricade. A burst of electricity shrouded her glove as it made contact, throwing off a cascade of blue-white sparks. The bot went limp, and it collapsed to the stone floor.

Adriene's mouth hung open and she froze, staring down at the twitching scrapper at her feet, heart thudding loudly in her ears.

// *The effect is temporary. I suggest you move.* //

Her breath hitched as she took in the placid male voice—the same steady timbre it'd always been, yet somehow different. More sincere. Adamant.

// *Two contacts incoming.* //

She darted into cover behind another large piece of fallen stone. She focused on the small map in her HUD. Two additional Troopers descended. ETA ten seconds.

// *Stealth mode 2A engaged.* //

The bots landed less than twenty meters away. They stood in close formation while they scanned the room, then split off and headed in opposite directions.

Adriene stilled her breath, waiting for them to put as much distance between each other as possible. The one moving toward the west turned and began arcing along the outside wall, straight for her. She snuck alongside her cover toward it, then paused at the corner. She looked down at the pistol in her hand.

She'd had an advantage with the first Mechan, when she could fire unhindered shots practically point-blank. She wouldn't be able to accomplish that from this distance.

She holstered the gun, then opened the thin storage compartment running along her calf. She transferred an incendiary grenade to her utility belt, then took a chaff in hand and scanned the map.

// Auto-targeting aid available. //

She made a mental note of the intended trajectory, and a green bull's-eye appeared at the location.

On instinct, she announced, "Chaff incoming," and her limbs froze. A wave of hot anxiety rolled through her as she became acutely aware of how alone she was.

There was no backup coming. Countless Mechan and four stories of collapsing ancient ruins stood between her and another rezone. Those odds were beyond impossible.

A pang of adrenaline fired through her, quickening her pulse.

No. She swallowed down the hesitation and doubt, vanquishing it to the weak place it came from. She couldn't give up. Not yet.

Drawing in a sharp breath, she tossed the grenade. It flew with stunning accuracy, exploding two meters off the ground into an avalanche of metal shards.

Adriene took off. She charged the Mechan head-on through the raining chunks of debris, which appeared to drift slowly downward with her heightened perception of time. The dozen-meter dash took just long enough for a flash of panic to bloom in her chest as she realized what she was doing: charging, essentially unarmed, toward a fucking Mechan, with no coherent plan other than to punch it as hard as she possibly could.

Which was exactly what she did. She willed her suit to power the strike as she closed in on the Trooper. Her fist crumpled into its chest, sending another bright lance of pain up her arm. The impact left a deep crater, sending the bot careening backward and to the ground.

Adriene's momentum sent her tumbling along with it, her metal suit scraping loudly across the stone as she skidded. Bits of chaff continued to float to the ground as she clawed the incendiary grenade from her belt and, with as much strength as she could muster, jammed it into the prone bot's shoulder joint.

She sprang to her feet, darting for a large slab of stone a few meters away. The explosion cracked through the air just before she reached it.

The force threw her off her feet, and she landed hard on her shoulder, skidding to a stop in front of the slab. Her suit had muted the sound almost entirely, and she found it strange to be left without the telltale ear ringing and pounding headache of narrowly escaping a detonation.

With a pained groan, she pushed to all fours, throwing a look back at the scrapper—now a heap of warped metal. Tiny flames licked up from burning circuitry.

Her legs wobbled beneath her, but she managed to get to her knees while she caught her breath, body aching.

// Capacitor levels critical. Recharge required. //

"Shit."

She'd forgotten how much her suit's power had been drained while fighting the local fauna. All her superpowered Mechan-punching hadn't helped.

She sucked in a few deep breaths, muscles burning. The lower her battery level, the more she'd have to rely on her own strength. She couldn't sustain this.

Sharp bursts of pain fired through her shoulder—her suit absorbing a series of impacts. She ducked her head, a trail of fire pinging the dust on her heels as she scrambled into cover behind the stone slab.

The last Trooper had apparently spotted her. That explosion probably hadn't been very subtle.

She checked overwatch—minor relief soothing her raw nerves when she saw it was the only contact still on this level. No reinforcements had been sent—yet.

She had no idea how she was going to deal with even one more. She hardly had enough power to keep her HUD on.

As she racked her brain for a solution, a heavy fatigue began to saddle her muscles. Her breaths came short and fast, and she could sense the suit wicking away the sweat on her palms.

She lifted her gloved hands, turning them over slowly. The hard-suit lecture came back to her, one of the few features she'd actually had the chance to learn about: "conductive actuator gloves."

// Yes, that can be done. If you're able to make contact, that is. //

"If?" she scoffed. "No faith."

She looked out across the few meters between her and the last Trooper. It continued to lay down relentless, blind fire in her general direction.

She just needed time to close the gap. A few seconds of cover.

"I know battery's low, but certainly there's some kind of reserve power, right?"

Her Rubicon didn't respond.

"A backup battery, surely?"

// Yes . . . //

If Adriene didn't know better, she'd have thought her monotone Rubicon almost sounded begrudging.

// However, I do not recommend that course of action. If you fail, your suit will be depleted beyond reasonable levels, and you will most certainly not survive the remainder of the journey to the surface. //

"Probably not gonna survive it anyway," she said. "Might as well try."

// Very well. //

"Here we go."

She rolled from cover and summoned a shield construct. A shell of purple light expanded from the front of her chestplate. Contrary to the enormous one she'd accidentally mustered in the forest, this one stretched only wide enough to protect her from the Trooper's shots as she charged.

She closed the ten-meter gap in an instant that seemed to drag on forever, and again she felt consumed by a stark sense of clarity. She could feel each beat of her heart as it pressed blood into her arteries and lungs. She could taste every molecule of filtered air as she sucked the oxygen in, feeding her muscles like fuel. Each impact of her boots on the hard stone resonated through the suit, sending tremors up her legs and into her spine. The scrapper's comparatively sluggish barrage of fire pinged off her semitransparent shield, each impact creating tiny cracking webs of light.

Adriene's shield crashed into the Trooper first, discharging a wash of purple light and redlining her power indicator before disappearing entirely.

They both fell, Adriene landing on top of the bot as her power consumption stabilized. Less than 1 percent remained.

The Mechan jerked beneath her, trying to regain function after colliding with the electric shield. It lurched up with its one functioning arm and grabbed her by the neck.

Raw panic blinded her senses. She tore at its cold metal fingers, her heart thudding, vision blurring as she gasped for breath. The basalt cave flashed before her eyes—the Mechan lifting her, analyzing her, ready to hybridize her, make her its slave.

The bot's grip tightened. She stretched down with both hands, fingertips grazing its smooth metal chestplate, barely out of reach. She groaned and reached—she only needed a few more centimeters.

Willing the suit to activate the conductive gloves, she let out a growl and strained the remaining distance, pressing both palms flat onto the Mechan's chassis. A cascading jolt ran over her skin, and the bot spasmed.

Its hand fell away from her neck. She gasped for breath, half collapsing onto its chest.

A faint buzz prickled up her arms, and a recharging icon appeared, centered in her HUD. The bot twitched and the buzz became a steady vibration, then quickly grew into an uncomfortable throb that sent sharp waves of electricity across her skin. Her muscles twitched with the growing intensity. Every individual hair on her body felt like a static charge about to detonate.

Through gritted teeth, she forced out, "Is . . . this . . . safe?" then remembered she didn't have to speak out loud. *It feels like I'm about to be electrocuted.*

// It is safe. Hold, please. //

The scrapper thrashed under her grip as her suit slowly drained its power. She watched its glowing amber eyes flicker and fade.

A bitter sense of regret burrowed into the back of her mind. It lacked any discernible reaction to its own demise. She imagined seeing it suffer would be a sort of catharsis, if only it had a face to look pained with. Or even the ability to feel pain.

The charge fell away at once, vanishing in an instant. She collapsed onto the ground beside the depleted bot.

Staring up at the crumbling ceiling, Adriene heaved in a few deep breaths. Her HUD flashed a battery level indicator: *64%*.

She coughed. "And you doubted me."

// I cannot "doubt." //

With a grunt, she lifted herself to her feet. She shook out her arms and legs in turn, trying to rid them of the residual, unpleasant tingling sensation—like a million sharp pinpricks in a foot that'd fallen asleep, but all over her body. She frantically scanned her HUD map—no additional contacts. Her heart continued to race, blood pumping with adrenaline.

She recalled the last time she'd felt like this—right after her last rezone. Sure, it'd been raw panic and paranoia and animal instinct . . . but she'd felt more alive in those few minutes of confusion than she had in years. It was exhilarating.

// Plotting reroute to package location . . . //

"What?" she rasped. "The objective? Hell no—I don't have time."

Unbidden, a map appeared in her vision. Her eyes scanned the route.

It *was* close. Temptingly close . . .

With a static clack, a comm line opened. "Valero!" Gallagher panted, worry lacing her tone. "Are you okay? My overwatch just lost all the contacts near your location."

Adriene unmuted her line. "Yeah," she managed, though her voice caught—dry and haggard. She cleared her throat. "Yeah, I'm fine."

"Holy shit, Ninety-Six," Kato put in. "Did you somehow take out four scrappers in like sixty seconds?"

Her brows knit and she shook her head—it'd taken far longer than that. Ten minutes, maybe.

// *Ninety-two seconds.* //

Adriene wet her lips, then looked down at her boots. *You sure about that?*

// *Yes.* //

"Listen," Kato said, tone deadly serious, "I took my time cutting through the forest, but I'm out of ideas. We're going to have to board the dropship soon."

Adriene's mind reeled. There had to be some way to convince Brigham to wait. Just a little longer. But how could she bargain with someone she barely knew?

Chewing her bottom lip, she pressed a thumb into the palm of her hand while she hunted for a solution. She looked at the yellow objective marker, then down at her gloves, then at the newly re-charged battery indicator.

An idea trickled into the back of her mind. She didn't like it—playing on people's weaknesses. Manipulating their desires to get them to do what she wanted. But she had to try.

She started jogging across the massive atrium as she reopened squad comms. "Lieutenant Brigham, sir?"

"Valero?" His gruff voice carried an edge of anticipation. "What's going on? Ship's landing as we speak."

"I have eyes on the objective."

The line rang silent for a few long moments, then he mumbled, "Son of a bitch . . ."

"If I can get the package, can you evade long enough to pick me up?"

"Fuck . . ." he grunted, then his tone hardened. "No. We can't risk extracting you. Too many bots have already infiltrated, with more on the way."

Another map appeared in her HUD, a route that led from the objective package location, down and away from the facility, then back to the surface almost a kilometer south.

"I don't need extraction," she said. "I can make it to the surface.

You just have to stay off their radar long enough to swing around and pick me up. Fifteen minutes at the most."

"Valero," Brigham warned, "there's no fucking *way* we can lie low for that long this close to two dozen scrappers. It can't happen."

She switched to a private line. "Sir," she said, then took a deep breath, slowing her pace somewhat as she steadied her nerves. "At the meeting the other day . . . I get how you feel about how the other squads treat us. Like we're nothing but their servants. Like they're single-handedly responsible for the success of a mission."

"Your point?" he prompted, voice clipped.

"You want to prove Forward Recon's as capable as the other teams? Now's your chance. We'll walk out of this having done their entire job for them. In less than six hours." She paused to let the thought sink in. "But you gotta hold off long enough to pick me up."

"And if you fail and I get my whole squad rezoned instead? How will that look?"

"Then you blame the new girl," she offered. "It's not like I don't have a reputation for rezones."

After a few long moments, Brigham's deep voice came back resigned, but clear. *"Fine."*

A cool wave of relief washed over her, and she released a hard breath. "Thank you, sir."

"You have *fifteen minutes*," he growled. "That's it. Minute sixteen, those nukes are as good as detonated."

"Understood, sir."

"Get me that package," he said, tone firm.

"I will, sir." She accelerated to a steady run, continuing to follow the red line across the wide atrium toward the objective package. "Pushing out the rendezvous point." She sent Gallagher the approximate coordinates for her extraction. She had no idea what her Rubicon had used to plot this strange path out of the facility, or why it seemed to go down instead of up, but she had little to lose at this point.

As she followed the route into a long hallway, her limbs buzzed with newfound energy—the effects of a stim cocktail according to her HUD's biostatus readout. A dozen meters in, the red line abruptly ended in a pulsating red arrow, pointing down.

// Forced descent required. //

Normally, she'd hesitate—briefly consider whether punching a hole in the floor was the best course of action—but she was way beyond that. She only had fourteen minutes.

// Thirteen minutes and fifty-four seconds. //

Adriene backpedaled a few meters. With her newly recharged suit, she powered her limbs and took a flying leap toward the end of the red line, landing squarely on both feet. The floor cracked, but didn't break. She repeated the maneuver, and on the third try, it finally buckled.

Dust and stone rained down as she landed in a crouch a floor below. She leapt up and kept running, cracks echoing behind her as the ceiling continued to collapse.

A few meters down, she rounded a corner into a short hall, which culminated in a curiously intact-looking metal door. Beyond it glowed the soft yellow circle of the objective package.

She lifted a foot and thrust the heel of her boot into the door as hard as she could. A sharp pain shot into her hip, and she grimaced as she stepped back. The door hadn't given even a millimeter, and no discernible impact had been made.

// This door is triple reinforced and appears to be hermetically sealed. It will be difficult if not impossible to brute-force. //

She put her hands on her hips, racking her brain for a solution. Beside the door, a cracked, dust-covered access screen sat flush on the wall. She looked down at her forearm and turned it over.

Can we use this hyphen thing? To hack it?

// No. The issue is not an inability to interface but rather a lack of power. //

Adriene held up one of her gloved hands.

Can these be used . . . the other way?

// Yes . . . That may work. //

Adriene quirked an eyebrow. It'd almost sounded impressed.

// I cannot be "impressed." //

"No," she said. "Certainly not."

She sighed as she noticed the data collection indicator for "sarcasm array" going off, then stepped forward and pressed her palm to the panel beside the door.

// *Warning: Power draw may be significant. The electrical system is likely not closed, and thus to power the panel, I must send a current that will be drawn out into the rest of the facility at a rate I cannot control.* //

"Understood. Do it."

A sharp tingle ran up her spine and down her arm. With a flash of dull blue light, the access panel lit, displaying a readout of foreign symbols before going dark again. With an exhale of icy-cold air, the door unsealed, cracking open a few centimeters.

// *Capacitor level at twenty-two percent.* //

Adriene cringed—that'd used over 40 percent of her battery.

// *I warned you.* //

Yeah, yeah.

She gripped the edge of the door and grunted as she pulled, forcing it open wide enough to squeeze through. A long, narrow room stretched out before her. The polished metal walls were lined floor to ceiling with glass shelves.

Her HUD immediately scanned the room, and she took a moment to marvel at the condition of the place. It was like stepping into the past. The room lacked all the dust and debris and cracked stonework of the rest of the facility, leaving only a gleaming, untarnished metal floor and pristine glass shelves lined with hundreds of small rectangular devices. Just like the "technology artifact" diagram they'd received in their updated intel package.

// *Objective located.* //

A few meters down, one of the devices glowed in her HUD, marked with a soft yellow aura.

What about the rest? She couldn't imagine letting all this data—a veritable trove of information on the species who very well might be the creators of the Mechan—get nuked along with the rest of the facility.

// *You are not properly equipped to transport a high volume of physical artifacts, nor is there time to catalog even a fraction of what is stored on these data cores. You have ten minutes and twelve seconds. //*

She sighed. *Fine.*

She crossed the room to the marked drive and tried to pry off the glass panel. It wouldn't budge, so she punched it, and the glass shattered. The impact cracked the shelf, and the devices clumped together as they collapsed onto the shelf below.

"Shit," she cursed, scrambling to catch the highlighted core before it fell.

// Please refrain from dropping ancient artifacts. The circuitry may be very fragile. //

"Yeah, sorry."

Unsure why she was apologizing to the VI in her head, Adriene kept her grip on the core tight and turned it over in her hand.

"This's it?"

// Yes. //

She swept her hand through the case and took an armful of other cores, then knelt and opened both compartments on either calf. Emptying the grenades out onto the floor, she tucked away the objective core first, then fit as many more in as she could.

// Nine minutes. Contacts approaching on overwatch. //

"Shit," she grumbled, locking her grenade compartments closed before running back out into the hall. She glanced in the direction she'd come from, where two Troopers stood among the growing rubble of slowly collapsing ceiling.

Their muzzles flashed, the shots catching the stone wall beside her. She took off, following the red line the opposite direction.

"End of the line is five meters," she panted as she zigzagged down the corridor to dodge gunfire. Shards of stone flew off the walls on either side. "Where to after that?"

// Down. //

"Seriously?"

// Just once more. //

Adriene growled as she sped around the next corner, gaining

her a short reprieve from the scrapper fire. She re-created her floor-punching technique and, after only two hits, fell another story.

She ran down the hall, notably dingier and more degraded than the levels above. Her boots thudded against the stone floor, caked with mud and silt. The red line continued straight, disappearing into the wall at the end of the corridor.

"Uh, that leads to a dead end!" she shouted, breaths ragged. "Where to?"

// *Through the wall. Seven minutes and twelve seconds.* //

There was no time to question it, so she didn't bother. The relentless Mechan fire continued behind her, a few stray shots pinging off the back of her suit. She neared the end of the hall and set her jaw. Leaning her shoulder forward as she ran, she reminded herself not to tuck her head too far as she plowed shoulder-first into the wall. It broke away with surprising ease.

Then she fell—tumbled, really. Head over feet or feet over head, she lost track of direction and trajectory for a few long seconds.

Searing pain fired through her as her back cracked. She'd landed on a rocky outcropping of some kind, but as she groaned and rolled onto her stomach, she plummeted again.

The air vacated her lungs as she landed hard against something solid and wet. Her ringing ears filled with a distant, heavy rush of tumbling water. A thick warmth washed over her, so realistic she thought her suit had cracked and real water soaked her skin.

// *Get up.* //

Adriene's eyes cracked open. Pitch blackness surrounded her, even with the enhanced vision in her HUD. The ominous red line led into darkness.

// *Three minutes and ten seconds.* //

She sat up on her elbows, head spinning. She'd lost time—almost five minutes.

"What the fuck was *that*?" she growled. "How did I get here?"

// *You fell through a natural erosion corridor in the adjoining cave system.* //

"And that was part of the fucking *route*? Couldn't you have warned me?"

// *You desired the quickest route.* //

She groaned a pained laugh and lay back down. She wanted to be mad, she really did. But she was too dizzy, too sore, and too glad to still be alive. She couldn't muster the will.

// *Two minutes and fifty-five seconds.* //

Right. She had to move.

She got herself onto all fours first, then stood, vaguely aware her Rubicon had started pushing pain suppression meds and adrenaline into her system. The resulting relief washed over her, aches falling away as her spinning head cleared.

She tried to activate her headlamp, but it gave a low-power error. So she reached out in the dark, grasping for a wall to guide her. Her fingers hit cool, rough stone, and she trailed her hands along the uneven wall. Her boots sloshed through warm water as she followed her Rubicon's red line around a series of rocky corners.

Finally, a soft blue light loomed at the bend ahead. She stepped around the corner and botched her footing, stumbling slightly as she gaped at the sight before her.

She'd entered a vast cavern, easily a thousand meters wide and just as deep. A glistening black lake stretched out, its smooth surface so still, it could have been a mirror, with no discernible shore.

On the far side of the cavern, natural blue light shone from a massive opening in the ceiling. A deluge of water poured down onto a huge rock formation, four distinct pillars reaching toward the sunlight like grasping fingers. The waterfall crashed onto the jutting stone, trickling through the pillars and continuing down, disappearing beyond the edge of the pristine lake into even deeper caves somewhere below.

"Eyes on Valero?" Gallagher's steady voice cut through comms, and Adriene's heart surged as the dropship lowered into view beside the waterfall.

"I'm here," Adriene called. "On your three."

"I see her," Brigham said.

The ship turned and sped toward her, the blue light of its engines reflecting in the black surface of the lake.

"Mira's end, Valero," Brigham said. "How in the *fuck* did you end up down here?"

"Long story."

The dropship descended as it approached, hovering above the water, sending shimmering, rippling waves across the surface. The ramp lowered, and she got a running start, then leapt and landed on it. Kato stood waiting and grabbed her arm to haul her aboard. Gallagher guided the ship back toward the waterfall.

Kato chuckled warily. "This was quite the fucking rendezvous spot, Ninety-Six."

"Can't resist a dramatic entrance," she replied.

Kato laughed.

"Did you get it?" Brigham asked from the copilot's seat, glancing at Adriene over his shoulder. "The package?"

"I got it," she confirmed. "And then some."

"Copy that," he said, a hint of satisfaction underneath his no-nonsense tone. "Gal, get us topside—we still need to neutralize the site."

Gallagher lifted them out of the underground lake and into the blinding daylight, rising swiftly above the tree cover.

"Prepping missiles," Brigham said. He flicked up a rear-facing camera view onto his copilot screen. "Target locked."

"We're still too close," Gallagher warned. "We'll get caught in it. Wait till we've reached upper atmo."

"Understood—give me the go."

"Beginning ascent."

The dropship lurched and accelerated upward at a steeper angle. Adriene followed Kato to the troop seats, and they locked in.

The viewscreen hazed as they rose higher. Metal groaned and the ship rattled lightly, then finally, Gallagher gave the all clear.

"Deploying nukes," Brigham said. "Three, two, one . . ."

The real missiles dropped along with a handful of decoys. Fifteen seconds later, a blinding flash erupted, and Brigham's monitor went white.

"Confirm target destroyed," Brigham said.

"Confirmed on radar," Gallagher answered. Her monitor showed an angle off the bow: a smear of glittering stars on a hazy, bluish-gray backdrop. "Entering mesosphere."

"All right, get us the fuck out of here."

"Engaging subspace drive."

With a sinking lurch, Adriene's stomach dropped. On Brigham's screen, the ever-shrinking jungle seemed to slow to a dead stop and the cloudy planet stretched out slowly for a few long seconds before disappearing into blackness as they escaped into subspace.

TWELVE

Adriene pressed a thumb into her sweaty palm as she stood under the bright wash of light in Commodore Thurston's immaculate white office aboard the *Aurora*.

Moisture dripped between her shoulder blades, clinging her shirt to her skin. She missed her suit. It would have wicked it all away in an instant. Without it, she felt exposed, vulnerable.

And her mind had been so quiet.

Her Rubicon had only been active a few hours, but she'd already grown used to its steady commentary, however annoying. Though she truly didn't know if having it gone made her feel better or worse.

Commodore Thurston stood on the other side of his desk, facing away as he watched the branching white streaks of subspace rush by on the viewscreen mounted to the back wall. He was probably in his late sixties, his stark white hair and scarred, weather-beaten white skin betraying some combination of age and experience. Though he'd presumably not been in the line of fire for the better part of three decades, he retained the physique of an active soldier, with broad shoulders and thick muscles filling out his light gray uniform.

Blackwell stood off to one side, posture straight, hands clasped behind his back, silent since he'd escorted Adriene straight from the dropship with a curt, *"You're to report to the commodore at once."*

Adriene struggled to remain focused as glimpses of Cimarosa-IV replayed in her mind on a loop—the verdant jungle, the overgrown ruins, the crumbling floor plummeting her into that stone labyrinth.

Despite the overall bleakness, a singular moment of hope stood out: her VI admitting it could accomplish something she'd wanted for so long, though she hadn't consciously known it. And all she needed was administrator permissions.

She had totally forgotten her Rubicon had even mentioned it. So why couldn't she stop thinking about it now?

Thurston cleared his throat. "Do you know how long I've been a part of the Extrasolar Fleet, Sergeant Valero?" The deep, dry rumble of his voice put even Blackwell's low timbre to shame.

She poured all her effort into keeping her response steady. "No, sir."

"Forty-five years." Thurston turned to face Adriene. A flat black ocular engraft covered his left eye. He uncrossed his arms and put his fists on the desk, leaning forward on his knuckles. His single, cloudy-gray eye locked onto her. "Do you think in the last twenty years, I've ever heard of a soldier dropping a squad of Troopers single-handed?"

She swallowed, struggling to maintain a level gaze. "No, sir."

"No, indeed," he sighed.

She bit the inside of her cheek, cursing how shortsighted she'd been. She should have seen this coming.

The second they'd entered subspace, she'd been hit with an overwhelming wall of exhaustion, barely managing to take her helmet off before falling into a deep sleep that'd lasted the entire trip. She should have kept herself awake, should have spent the time preparing, figuring out how to field these questions.

"So you can understand, Sergeant," Thurston continued, "how I could want a better explanation from you than 'it was just luck'?"

She took a deep breath and stopped herself from shifting around or tapping her foot, from showing any sign of agitation.

"Because honestly, Sergeant . . . I don't believe in luck."

Me either.

She expected her Rubicon to offer a stodgy comment on the likelihood of surviving that encounter, and that no element of "luck" could possibly factor in. But the grating silence in her head persisted.

She nodded once. "I understand, sir."

"I reviewed your visor cam footage," he said, and Adriene's breath hitched. If they had a visual on what had happened, writing it off as a fluke might prove all but impossible. The rate at which she'd been processing information, the speed at which she'd moved . . . She couldn't explain it to herself, how could she ever explain it to them?

Thurston cast a steely glance at Blackwell. "When's the recording end, Major?"

"At 1628 ship time, sir," Blackwell said. "All we have after that is a record of movement from Sergeant Gallagher's overwatch."

Thurston nodded. "Last we saw, you'd been separated from your squad and two Troopers had descended on your location."

Adriene nodded slowly. She had a pretty good idea of the incident that corresponded to.

What had happened, she couldn't say, but she remembered exactly how it'd felt: like she could see everything, everywhere, all at once, as quickly or slowly as she wanted. Even more starkly, the gaping hole it left behind now that it was gone. She could hardly stop thinking about it.

Thurston focused on Adriene, his stoic expression impossible to read. "Do you know why your visor cam recording stopped, Sergeant?"

She shook her head. "No, sir." She really didn't, at least not in a way she could put words to.

"Step me through what happened after. How'd you eliminate those four targets?"

"Well," she began, then cleared her throat. "With the first Trooper, I was able to . . . uh, *remove* its capacitor unit. The second, I disabled, temporarily. With a shock from my own capacitor."

She kept her shoulders squared to the commodore, but her eyes darted to Blackwell, whose head cocked slightly, one thick eyebrow raised. She looked back at Thurston and continued.

"The third took an incendiary grenade . . ." She motioned under her arm. "There's a weak point in the older model's chassis, under the arm."

Thurston just stared back, unmoving.

"For the fourth," she continued hurriedly, "I had to discharge my capacitor reserves to create a shield construct to get in range of it. When I made contact, I was able to recharge my battery with that, uh . . . new glove capability. That drained the scrapper until it didn't have enough power to function."

Thurston remained leaning forward on the desk. "And how were you able to stay alive long enough to do all that?"

"Well, sir . . ." She swallowed. "They came in two waves, two at a time. And I, well, I think they were caught off guard, sir. Older models too, like I said. The suit's stealth function must have kept me off their sensors. They didn't seem to notice me before approach. Maybe with all the stone, they didn't have a clear connection to their sensor hub."

Thurston's gray eye narrowed slightly.

Sweat dripped down the back of Adriene's neck. She ignored it as she searched for a better explanation.

She needed something—anything—and not only to appease her commanding officers but to make sense of it herself.

Admitting to Command that something had happened—something she couldn't begin to account for—meant admitting something might be wrong. Something that'd need fixing. She knew what the first step of troubleshooting would be: assessment of her husk. If they deemed it defective, even an inkling of a doubt that it could be faulty, she'd be forced to zero out to get a new body. And all her efforts at avoiding another rezone would have been in vain.

"Sergeant . . ." Blackwell's dry rumble cut through her thoughts. "I suggest you focus."

"Sorry, sirs." She cleared her throat and locked her gaze on Thurston, trying to muster as much confidence as she could. "I wish I could explain it better, sir," she said. "I really do. But you know how it can be, in combat." She paused and let the implied "*surely you remember*" remain unsaid.

One of his eyebrows twitched, but he didn't respond.

"Things move quickly," she continued. "You lose track of the specifics. I think I just . . . went into survival mode, sir. Rubicon, and my suit's abilities, have come naturally to me. I used that along with my experience to complete the mission to the best of my ability."

She stilled her breath, hoping he'd catch on to her less-than-subtle reminder that she'd walked out of there with the objective. That despite everything, she'd still gotten them their "artifact."

To her relief, the mention seemed to trigger something in Thurston. His shoulders loosened as he stood up from leaning on the desk. "You did, indeed, complete the mission, Sergeant." He exhaled a heavy sigh, his tone losing the harsh edge it'd had since she'd first walked in. A notification chimed on his computer, and he looked down at the screen, then mumbled, "Champlan said she was sending me her best. I seem to have underestimated the kind of soldier the 803rd had to offer."

Adriene resisted quirking a brow as she considered how best to react to that rather complimentary insult. She kept her expression passive and simply inclined her head slightly.

Blackwell's stance visibly slackened, and for the first time, Adriene realized he was probably almost as nervous to have this conversation as she was. After all, he'd thrown a brand-new recruit into the muck less than forty-eight hours after arrival, with hardly any tech training.

"Major," Thurston said, looking back up from his computer. "Make sure the techs take a look at her suit ASAP. I want that camera in working order before the next deployment. Could be sooner than later."

"Yes, sir," Blackwell said.

The commodore looked back at Adriene. "Expect orders shortly. But in the meantime, get some rest."

"I will, sir."

"Dismissed."

She snapped a proper salute, faced Blackwell and offered the same, then turned on her heel and headed straight out the door and through the Administration lobby to the hallway.

The corridor outside seemed twenty degrees cooler. She untucked her damp shirt and fanned it, allowing the air to waft over her sweaty skin. Partway down the hall, she turned a corner and paused, leaning against a bulkhead to steady herself.

Despite the protection her suit had provided, her muscles were still sore and bruised from her uncontrolled descent into the cave system. She let out a long breath, loosening some of the tension in her chest, though even the brisker air did little to cool her down.

She replayed the debrief in her head, realizing she'd managed to get through it without truly perjuring herself. Omitted details? Avoided the full truth? Sure. But she hadn't *lied*.

Yet a persistent, nagging doubt pulled at the back of her mind.

What if something really was wrong? She could be causing an even worse problem for herself by holding on to a faulty husk. This one had never really felt quite right.

Then again, she hadn't felt "right" in years. She no longer had a baseline for normal.

Drawing in another deep breath, she shelved her unease, focusing instead on her crushing exhaustion. She looked both ways down the hall, but her eyes caught on the doorway recessed into the bulkhead behind her.

It was a standard lift door, though narrower than most she'd seen around the ship, which were sized for ferrying cargo. Something about the thin slats and burnished metal tugged at the back of her mind. Something familiar, though she was sure she'd never taken this route before.

A wave of annoyance swept in—she'd felt so cowed by Blackwell's curt reception, she hadn't paid any attention to how she'd gotten to Admin from the docking bay. She didn't know how to get back to her quarters.

She pushed up off the wall and asked her Rubicon for directions, then dug her nails into her palms.

Right. He was gone. It was just her in her head now.

She swallowed down the feeling, trying again to ignore the uncomfortable emptiness, like a hollowed-out pit dug into the base of her brain.

Retracing her steps to the Admin lobby, she asked the MPs on guard for directions, then headed to her quarters. Her *private* quarters, she remembered with a twinge of anticipation.

When she arrived, she fell asleep before she could pull up the covers.

Two long years ago, Adriene rode aboard a rickety dropship.

Beside her, Harlan sat locked into fraying red harness straps. Flashes of light cut hard lines across his face as the sun glinted in through one of the small windows. The vessel jittered and vibrated, but he remained steady, still, unaffected.

Brow lined with amusement, his sharp gray eyes glittered at her. His mop of hair was a plain light brown, but she knew there was a darker tuft at the nape of his neck, one that didn't always regrow with every husk. This one had it, though.

A lock of hair fell onto his forehead, and he grinned as Adriene flicked it out of his face. He never cut it, just let it grow until the next time. When death would cut it for him, he'd always said. She couldn't remember the last time she'd seen it so long.

It'd been almost five months for them both, it'd be five months after this mission, and they would celebrate, he'd promised. He had a line on some whiskey from Maricopa, a remote isle in the Sylvan Sea on Prova. Best in existence.

The dropship groaned. Adriene tore her focus away to look out the observation window.

Through thin wisps of white clouds, a landscape of striking blue water and white sand stretched out, pristine, untouched by human or machine. But there'd be fire in the sky by nightfall.

The dark metal walls of the dropship disappeared, and they were groundside, ankle-deep in soft white sand. She followed Harlan as he marched, each footfall throwing up a haze of perfect white granules that floated on the air a bit too long.

Harlan glanced back, and the corners of his eyes wrinkled in the way they did when he was thinking up a joke, something snarky to say, some way to lighten the grim cloud that lingered over every moment of their lives.

She already knew how this ended. She couldn't change what would happen.

The sand began to sift away. The dunes on the horizon tilted and folded in on themselves, and the world re-formed, cast in the pink and golden tones of twilight.

A sliver of the orange star still sat on the horizon, a massive glowing orb waiting to slip back into the void. Exhaust trails streaked the sky, a dozen scars marring the brilliant blue gradient.

Harlan lay prone as he sighted down his scope, his five-month-long hair matted with blood as he screamed orders into comms.

Had he really not had his helmet on?

He must have, she must be remembering it wrong—her mind reworking the imagery so she'd have to see his horrified look as a metal fist crushed down, caving his skull in.

A glossy wave of thick crimson rolled over the ridges of sand away from his limp body, and Adriene just stared.

The bot flicked its chrome fingers to rid itself of Harlan's viscera. A halo of dark metal flashed in its other hand, and any thoughts of mourning her friend fled.

She couldn't let that arc of metal anywhere fucking near her.

Adriene backpedaled. The scrapper turned its glowing eyes onto her, its long arm reaching her in half a second. It smeared Harlan's still-warm blood across the front of her hardsuit as it pushed her to the ground.

She clawed her way out from under the bot, each grasp of her hand as useless as the next against the shifting sand. What had been soft and warm and welcoming hours ago was now an unforgiving hindrance, and she couldn't scurry more than a meter before the bot's hand grasped her again.

It flung her over—did it rip off her visor, or was it already off?—then gripped her neck, pinned her, pressed her into the soft sand, down, down deeper until it was spilling over her suit, and she wondered if it was going to bury her alive. Which would have been so, so much better.

The crucible's segments glowed red orange.

The bot was going to do it right here and now, she realized. No capture, no torture, no interrogation—just straight to the fucking point. She almost admired it for its candor.

She thrashed and kicked uselessly as it slipped the crucible over her eyes. Panic ripped through her chest, and she struggled to breathe under its icy metal grasp.

With a flash of light, it was over.

Adriene woke pouring sweat, gasping for breath.

Dread crushed her and sank deep into her chest, constricting her lungs like being buried in the sand, her heart paralyzed under the weight of it. She reached out blindly in the dark, and the sensor caught the movement. The lights faded up, and she gulped in air as she found her breath back.

Chest heaving, she took in the room: the clean, straight lines of the slate-gray walls, her still-packed ruck tossed in the corner. Thin lightstrips sat under white diffusion panels, creating a soft, welcoming glow.

Swinging her legs off the edge of the bed, she sat up, then pulled off her drenched tank top and tossed it aside. She asked her Rubicon to lower the room temperature.

She let out a grating sigh.

It was still gone, a silent, yet unmistakable void left in its place.

With a few deep, steadying breaths, she leaned forward, running her hands down her face. She looked down at her palm, stretching her hand open and closed.

The time blinked back at her from the top of her terminal screen: 0112. It'd only been a couple of hours. She should be exhausted, yet a stark energy coursed through her veins.

She knew she'd at least slept some, because she'd dreamed . . . Or rather, remembered. It'd been so easy, this time, to see it objectively; it was crystal clear. As vivid as her surroundings had been in the lower levels of that ancient facility, as distinct as she could see those Troopers' positions and Kato's vitals and Gallagher's overwatch and Brigham's frustration.

Now that she'd woken up, the dream's sharpness faded, slowly replaced again by that single moment on Cimarosa-IV echoing over and over, begging for her attention: that tiny, seemingly inconsequential admission. *Administrator permissions.*

She drew in a long breath and forced the thought back down along with the unwanted memories. She wiped the sweat off her forehead with the back of her hand, then moved to her desk chair and tapped the terminal screen until she found the room controls. She arrowed down the temperature setting, and a moment later, a cool breeze wafted in from the vents.

In the corner of the screen, a small alert symbol flashed. She expanded it.

An appointment had been scheduled for the following morning. With the ship's psychologist.

She glared at the screen, tapping to open the details, but none had been provided.

She drummed her fingers on the desk, then dismissed the screen. It must be standard post-op protocol for Flintlock. Part of her debrief. After the conversation she'd had with Thurston, she couldn't really blame him for flagging her for eval.

Spinning in her chair, she slid open one of the storage compartments under the bed and pulled out the sleek metal bottle she'd commandeered from the Hold last night.

Last night. *Just last night.*

It felt like it'd been a week since she'd been down there, drenched in everyone's pity about rezoning and hybridizing. She could only imagine what they'd think of her now, once they heard about the mission. The specifics wouldn't be released, but rumor had a way of getting around, regardless of what was or wasn't classified. She honestly didn't know what kind of light it'd put her in.

She shook the bottle, cursing to herself at the hollow, high-pitched sloshing—it was practically empty. She'd hit it harder than she remembered.

Twisting off the cap, she finished the dregs in one drink. The heat of it burned down her throat, and her chest loosened. A portion of the crushing weight lifted, but a haze of agitated exhaustion lingered.

She needed more booze.

Adriene tossed the empty bottle in the trash chute, then took a horribly wrinkled but clean shirt from her ruck. She pulled it on and headed out.

The Hold was fairly quiet when she arrived. Brigham and most of his friends from the previous night sat in the same spot, and only one other table was occupied in the back by three soldiers mired in hushed, drunken conversation.

Adriene entered as quietly as she could, skirting the wall to remain out of sight. She intended to avoid all manner of confrontation. This was a single objective mission: get the alcohol and get out.

She made it to the bar without incident and began twisting around the bottles to view the labels. But moments later, the crowd around Brigham's table stood and started leaving.

From the corner of her eye, Adriene caught sight of Brigham lingering. She hastily grabbed the next bottle, whatever it was—she really wasn't picky about these things—but it was too late. She'd been made.

"Valero," Brigham called from his table. The room quieted as the last of his friends left.

"Sir." She eyed him as he approached. Despite his dingy, weathered skin, his white cheeks were noticeably ruddy. He dragged his feet as he trudged toward her.

She withheld a smirk. "Are you . . . drunk?"

"Just a little." He flashed a rather charming, wide grin. "You?"

"Not enough," she grumbled, thumbing the lid off the bottle and taking a pull. Over Brigham's shoulder, she eyed the three remaining soldiers. They'd quieted their conversation and now threw furtive glances toward her and Brigham.

"Listen . . ." Brigham looked down at his boots with a sigh. "I'm sorry about how things went down out there. I didn't want to force you to . . . I mean, I guess I should be more mindful of your . . . history."

She shook her head. "No, you shouldn't."

He raised an eyebrow. "I shouldn't?"

"You have a job to do, and you were doing it. You shouldn't cater to anyone. You need to do what's right for the squad, and that's what you were doing."

"I . . ." He scrubbed a stiff hand over his chin. "That's a very practical outlook."

She shrugged. "Life's too long to hold grudges. It'd be too exhausting to keep it up forever." She took another drink from the bottle.

He smiled, his flushed cheeks reddening even more. "Well, I'm still sorry. I'm glad you made it out alive. And not only because you earned Forward Recon a massive win."

"Least I could do, considering the risk you took to get me."

After she took another drink, she offered the bottle to Brigham. He thanked her and took a pull from it.

The soldiers in the corner stood up. Adriene's stomach turned when instead of heading for the exit, the group made their way toward her and Brigham. Their dark looks of deeply annoyed scorn didn't bode well.

She jutted her chin out, and Brigham turned to look. "*Stormwalkers,*" he muttered, his smile melting into disgust.

Adriene eyed the group again with renewed familiarity. At the training sims the other day, she hadn't gotten a great look at them— they'd been wearing their suits, and she'd only seen them from the opposite side of the wide vestibule.

Brigham sighed. "This should be fun."

The tallest one sneered as he approached. "*Lieutenant* Brigham," the man grumbled, practically spitting out the rank.

Brigham flashed a forced smile in return. "Ivon . . . Coleson, Wyatt." He nodded at the other two, the shorter man and the stocky young woman. "Good to see you all looking well."

Ivon crossed his thin arms and looked past Brigham to Adriene. "And you're the infamous Sergeant Valero?"

Adriene's heart sank as all three Stormwalkers' glares locked onto her. They hadn't been sneering and whispering and throwing glances at *them* but at *her*.

She sighed and picked up a random bottle, then took a long drink.

Brigham grumbled, "What do you want, Ivon?"

"Just wanted to have a quick chat with your new pathfinder."

"We heard what happened," the older one, Coleson, put in.

"Oh yeah?" Brigham said. "What'd ya hear?"

Ivon inclined his head toward Adriene. "That this one single-handedly took down *four* Troopers."

Brigham forced a smile. "So you're here to congratulate us?"

"And you didn't even have a gun," the woman, Wyatt, chimed in.

Adriene rolled her eyes. "Of course I had a *gun*," she said, doing her best to maintain an air of amused disinterest, though she could already see where this was heading.

In preparation, she took another drink.

"So, you admit it," Wyatt said as if catching her in a lie. "You took out four scrappers?"

"Did I ever deny it?"

Brigham crossed his arms. "What, exactly, are you guys accusing us of?" he asked. "You obviously have something to say, just say it."

Ivon glared. "We just wanna know how we're supposed to trust that your little friend here"—he threw a glare at Adriene—"didn't come back *compromised*."

Compromised? She stared back at the distrustful glean in his eye before realizing . . . he meant *hybridized*.

She stifled a laugh. It wasn't particularly funny, but the buzz from whatever she kept drinking had started to sink in, loosening her nerves.

It made sense, she supposed. An average-at-best soldier is separated from her squad, her suit cam cuts off, and four scrapper contacts conveniently disappear. It made far more sense than what'd really happened.

More sweat trickled down her temples, and she wiped it away; it was hot as hell in here too. Did they keep the heat cranked on every deck of the ship?

"That's idiotic," Brigham huffed. "Besides, she was cleared by Medical."

"And if I *was* hybridized," Adriene said, taking a little too much pleasure in their obvious discomfort at her use of the actual word, "you'd all be dead already."

The Stormwalkers' expressions darkened.

Coleson crossed his arms. "Maybe you're waiting for the ideal time to strike."

"Or," Wyatt offered, her eyes narrowing to slits, "you're *a sleeper agent.*"

Adriene scoffed, but a bitter humor pressed on her chest as she realized: These people really had *no* idea. They thought they'd need data and analysis to tell if she'd been compromised, that she'd *blend in.* They didn't realize how grotesquely obvious it was when a robot hive mind had the reins of a human body.

"So tell us," Ivon prompted. "How'd you *really* get rid of those four bots?"

She stared back, unblinking, letting the silence weigh heavy around them. Then, as steadily and straight-faced as she could manage, she said, "My protocols forbid me from answering."

Brigham snorted a hearty laugh, but the Stormwalkers didn't look nearly as amused. Wyatt actually took a half step back, her face paling to a rather unhealthy shade. Ivon and Coleson seemed even more pissed off.

"You think this is funny?" Ivon snapped.

"Kinda, yeah," Adriene returned. "You idiots really don't know how obvious it'd be if I had a scrapper in my head?"

What she didn't say, was that if Mechan ever *did* manage to perfect controlling a human body, they'd be done for. It was the kind of thing she didn't bother worrying about. When that day came, it'd all be over. Honestly—at times like this especially, with three drunk thugs illustrating mankind's capacity for idiocy—that'd be just fine.

"For the 'foremost elite squad' of Flintlock," she said, surprised by her own choice to continue prodding them, "that's pretty sad."

Coleson's face grew a deep shade of purple, and at that moment, she knew she'd crossed some invisible line and, with it, forfeited any chance of resolving this in a civil manner.

But she was having a hard time giving a shit. They could accuse her of being a fucking Mechan undercover operative, and she was supposed to stand by and take it, but she couldn't point out how ignorant they were?

Ivon bared his teeth and, oddly, squared up to Brigham. Ivon had almost fifteen centimeters on him, though Brigham was easily twice as stocky.

Her lieutenant's jaw set, and Adriene eyed him as the muscles in his arms flexed and a thick vein appeared in his forehead. She'd been so distracted by these idiots' reactions, she hadn't even noticed Brigham's mounting anger. She took one last drink, then slowly set the bottle down.

"I've told you this before, *Miles*," Ivon said slowly. "And I'm getting sick of repeating myself. You and your *recon scum* need to learn some manners."

Brigham shook his head slowly, then with surprising swiftness, drew back his fist and hit Ivon square in the side of the face. Ivon fell back into his friends, then tumbled to the ground.

Brigham shook out his hand and glared down at him. "How's that for manners?"

"Mira's ashes," Adriene cursed as the other two lunged for Brigham. She wasn't nearly drunk enough for this.

Before she knew it, Coleson broke from Brigham and rushed her. His fist met the bone of her cheek, triggering a sharp burst of pain.

She stumbled back, vision dancing, then reached toward the bar

and caught the neck of a metal bottle. Warm liquor spilled down
her arm as she flipped the bottle over and cracked it across the side
of his face. He collapsed, clutching his head.

Wyatt and Brigham wrestled on the ground a couple of meters
away, crashing into a table and spilling leftover drinks all across the
floor in a symphony of shattering glass.

Adriene knelt beside Coleson to get him in a headlock, but Ivon
came out of nowhere and grabbed her by the scruff of her shirt.

He threw her against the wall and pinned his forearm to her
neck. She clawed at his arm as she fought for breath, her vision
wavering as he crushed down on her windpipe.

With a burst of white, a twinge of static pain fired behind her
eyes. The wash cleared away a second later, revealing the sharp,
clean lines of her HUD.

// Welcome to Rubicon. //

Along with the steady voice came a wave of calm clarity.

Welcome, yourself. Just in time for the fun.

She bared her teeth and, with renewed fervor, thrust both palms
hard into Ivon's chest. He stumbled back far enough for her to jack
her knee into his groin.

He cried out and crumpled to the ground. She slid halfway down
the wall before catching herself, gasping for breath.

She leaned over and spit out a mouthful of blood.

// Error. Suit offline. //

Her vision cleared, and her breath steadied. The buzz she'd been
working so hard to acquire seemed to have disappeared entirely,
replaced with sharp clarity and quick reactions. Which both impressed and annoyed her.

Most of the features of her HUD remained offline, presumably
due to the lack of a suit, but the threat assessment interface remained,
flashing and lighting up as it gauged the angry soldiers around her.

Coleson rushed her, but she could sense him coming, feel the air
move and smell the gin on his breath before he arrived.

She ducked his sloppy right hook. As if in slow motion, she
watched the realization dawn on his face as his swing missed.

She delivered a solid blow to his gut. He fell, clutching his stomach, gasping for air.

Wyatt's stocky frame limned in a deep orange in Adriene's HUD, the corresponding pip climbing the threat assessment ranks as the woman swept an empty glass off the bar nearby. She dashed forward, smashing it down on Adriene, who brought up her forearm to deflect, but couldn't block it completely. The glass shattered against the side of Adriene's face, the shards tearing gashes down her cheek.

// Error. Suit offline. Aid cannot be rendered. //

Brigham's bloodied face appeared over Wyatt's shoulder. He yanked Wyatt away from Adriene, and Wyatt's threat assessment dropped.

Adriene leaned against the bar, grimacing as her cheek blazed with sharp, stinging pain. Warm blood trickled out, and she wiped at it with the back of her hand.

Coleson's threat climbed as he finally picked himself back up, gritting his teeth. But instead of going for Adriene again, he grabbed a metal alcohol bottle by the neck, then turned to help Wyatt gang up on Brigham.

Oh, hell no. She let out a low growl and pushed away from the bar, sidestepping the still-breathless Ivon, curled in the fetal position. She lowered her shoulder and tackled Coleson to the ground before he reached Brigham.

She fell harder than she'd expected, and the side of her head cracked against the metal floor along with Coleson.

They landed on their sides, and Coleson shoved her away with one hand while lashing out with the other, still gripping the bottle.

Adriene recoiled, barely able to meet the strike with crossed forearms. The curved neck and brightly colored label of the bottle flashed close, briefly contorting into the red-orange glow of an active crucible. A spike of adrenaline stole the breath from her lungs.

// Vitals elevated. Aid cannot be rendered. //

More threat pips appeared in her HUD.

// Four additional contacts. //

Black boots rushed in. Adriene caught her breath, glancing up to meet the annoyed look of a blond woman clad in the prim, buttoned-up dark navy suit of the military police.

// Hostility unclear. //

It's okay. Adriene turned over onto her stomach, entwining her hands behind her neck. *It's over.*

The MPs' boots squeaked against the metal as they moved to subdue the others, barking orders to stand down.

Adriene rested her unbloodied cheek on the cool metal floor. She had to wonder if maybe this was *not* what the commodore had meant by *"get some rest."*

THIRTEEN

Adriene slouched on a bench beside the door inside the white-walled medical office, pressing a wad of blood-soaked gauze to her cheek.

The bleeding had slowed, and most of the pain had seeped into the back of her skull, morphing into a dull, persistent headache. Her swollen knuckles ached as she picked at the spray of crusted blood on her shirt.

A weight grew in her chest, equal parts amusement and nostalgia as she thought about the last time she'd been in this position: freshly reprimanded by MPs after Booker had thrown an obnoxious private across a table and started a full-scale mess brawl.

Booker wouldn't have tolerated even a second of that bullshit the Stormwalkers had dished out. He'd have started throwing punches at the first indication of even so much as a disparaging thought. In comparison, her new lieutenant had at least *attempted* to hold his temper, if briefly.

She glanced across the room, where Daroga stood patching up Brigham, who'd endured Wyatt's same glass-smashing tactic, but to the neck instead of the face. The two men were far enough away, Adriene shouldn't have been able to see the cracks in Daroga's dry lips or hear his knuckle popping as he adjusted the tool, or Brigham holding his breath under the soft, static crackling of newly grafted skin. But with her Rubicon still active, she continued to experience the same sense of slow-motion clarity she'd had in combat. The gashes in her cheek stung, her pounding head hurt like hell, and she continued to pour sweat, but at least the void in the back of her brain had gone, leaving a heady buzz of reassurance in its place.

Any solace her VI gave was matched by an equal degree of anxiety. Because . . . why did she feel that way?

The first three times it'd turned on—when Daroga installed it, during the training sims, and when Brigham activated it on the dropship—she'd experienced none of the same tranquil clarity. Something had changed on that planet, in that facility. When her suit cam had cut off and her HUD had gone haywire and she'd seen every piece of technology from the wiring of her own suit all the way back to the *Aurora*.

She had to figure out what had caused it. Luckily, she had a captive audience—quite literally.

Rubicon?

// Present. //

Adriene scoffed under her breath. *Thanks for helping me out back there.*

// It is my primary directive to ensure your safety. //

Another wave of calm washed over her along with the steady voice.

What happened on the planet earlier? When you glitched out?

// Syntax error. Please rephrase. //

She gritted her teeth. The thing did a pretty damn good job of reading her mind most of the time, but now it couldn't understand basic slang?

When you . . . malfunctioned. When my HUD shorted out, but I could still see everything on overwatch?

// Ancillary overwatch is a standard function of all hardware loadouts, regardless of which team member administers the primary module. //

She sighed.

No, as in, visualize it . . . Like in my mind. Along with scrapper positions, their models, loadouts. Where my squad was, and shit happening on the Aurora, *and . . . everything in between. That's not standard overwatch. Something happened, I could feel the change.*

// That information is not available. //

She leaned back on the bench, slouching further.

You can't say that. I saw it with my own eyes. What was it?

// That information is not available. //
You're lying.
// That is not possible. //
You expect me to believe that?
// Lying is wielded as a means of self-preservation or deception. I have no sense of self, and thus no reason to lie. //
That's bullshit. And when the hell did you start saying "I"?

A metallic creak pulled her focus back to reality, and she looked up. Brigham and Daroga stood at a supply cabinet nearby. Daroga unlocked a drawer and pulled out a small, flat prescription case. "One every twelve hours," he instructed in his rich, steady timbre, passing the pills to Brigham.

"Yes, sir," Brigham said, pocketing the case. "Thanks, Doc."

Daroga paced back to the gurney and began cleaning up.

Adriene stood as Brigham approached. Though still raw and pink, the newly grafted skin on his neck was a massive improvement over the nightmare of torn flesh and pouring blood it had been.

He wrung his hands, glancing down as he stopped in front of her. "Hey, uh . . . sorry about that, Valero. I let things get kinda outta hand back there."

"I didn't help matters any," she admitted. "Though it seems like that may not have been your first run-in with them?"

His jaw flexed. "Yeah. They just really know how to piss me off, ya know?"

"Yeah, I get that."

He eyed her cheek. "Sorry I got you all cut up . . ."

// Doubtless makes your face more interesting. //

Adriene barely suppressed a laugh.

No need for commentary, thank you.

As she contemplated a response to Brigham's obvious remorse, she scrunched her lips, a little incensed. Because the stupid VI was probably right.

She shrugged. "It'll make for a badass scar, right?"

Brigham chuckled.

// Still not interested in my commentary? //

She cast a hard, spiteful thought inward.

// *That does not have the effect on me you think it does.* //

She sighed.

"No scars on my watch," Daroga said from across the room. He patted the gurney. "You're up, Sergeant."

Adriene nodded goodbye to Brigham and crossed the room. She sat on the gurney near Daroga while he replaced his tools with a fresh set. Though he put on a convincing front of good spirits, he seemed exhausted, with dark bags ringing his eyes, a dusting of stubble along his jawline, black hair tied back.

"A little localized painkiller up first." Needle raised, he stepped closer, carrying in a waft of evergreen and clover. "This'll sting. Sorry."

She winced as he delivered the anesthetic, but the pain in her cheek washed away quickly, fading into numbness. "Thanks."

"Shit," he hissed, half under his breath. "They got you good too." His gaze raked over her briefly. "Picking a fight with the Storm-walkers . . . That's pretty ballsy for day three."

// *I concur.* //

"They started it," she replied.

// *Your lieutenant started it.* //

Maybe technically, she groused, *though really, they were asking for it.*

Daroga discarded the needle. "I guess that's why they're spend-ing the night in the brig, and you're not?"

She frowned. Great. No chance of burying this hatchet, then. Rivalry confirmed.

Daroga pulled a disposable wipe from a mostly empty package. He'd had to use a *lot* on Brigham. "I suppose it was coming sooner or later, after that near miss in the training suites." He started cleaning the dried blood from her face with the wipe, which radi-ated the stale, sharp scent of rubbing alcohol.

She wiped a trickle of sweat from her temple with a knuckle. "Yeah. Kato always so willing to throw down for you like that?"

Daroga smirked. "He's a good guy. But you know what they say about the line between bravery and stupidity."

"Yeah," she said with an acquiescent sigh. "You two act like brothers."

His head wavered back and forth. "Almost are, in a way. I lived with him for a while growing up."

"On Prova?"

"Yeah, after . . ." Daroga drifted off, a furrow pinching between his brows, not meeting her eye as he kept cleaning.

"Kato told me," she said, voice low. "About the Brownout, I mean."

His head lowered in a sharp nod, dark lashes fluttering with a few quick blinks. "Ah."

"Hope that's okay."

"Yeah," he said quickly, tone hesitant but genuine. "Totally fine. Most people on board know." He picked up the empty wipe package and waved it at her. "One sec."

He stepped away to discard the package and bloodied wipe in the biohazard chute, then disappeared into a supply room.

Adriene awaited his return, rolling her bottom lip between her teeth, unsaid words on the tip of her tongue.

She could relate. And she could tell him that. He already knew about her hybridization; it'd be easy to point out the parallels. They could commiserate. Forge a connection.

But it all just felt like bullshit.

Sure, there was a tenuous thread there. The Mechan had taken both of their free wills.

But he'd been *twelve*. Hauled off his homeworld in the middle of the night by frantic adults desperate to find safety, only to be delivered directly into the arms of the enemy, then held captive for weeks while being used as collateral to secure the compliant subjugation of his entire species.

Whereas she'd been held hostage inside her own body, used as a weapon to kill her comrades until she starved to death.

They were both profoundly awful experiences, yes. But not comparable.

// One individual's trauma cannot be weighed against another's. Both bear equal validity. //

She wiped sweat from her forehead. *I know.*

Though the VI's words rang true, she couldn't bring herself to take it to heart. Some nebulous mental blockade prevented her; she couldn't even really verbalize why.

// One of the benefits of this coexistence is that you need not verbalize to communicate. Only internalize. //

And sometimes, not even that. The thing had seemed to know her thoughts before she had on multiple occasions.

// Not precisely. That is the result of stimulus bias. //

Stimulus bias?

// Typically, the Rubicon implant receives stimulus at the same time as your neurons. However, due to processing power ratios and a variety of other factors, I can, on occasion, interpret and declare the signal faster. //

Seriously?

// Yes. Ordinarily, these are what you would consider "instinctive" reactions. Other times, it is a matter of priority. When a deluge of stimuli occur, while you attend to the most pressing, other stimuli deemed of less importance go ignored. I can process those simultaneously and act on them to your benefit. //

Adriene picked at her cuticles. Like having a two-tiered brain.

Her thoughts trailed back to the VI's use of the word "coexistence."

Finally, Daroga returned. He pulled a fresh wipe from the new pack, moving on from her jaw to begin cleaning the blood from the side of her neck.

She held on to the edge of the gurney with both hands to keep herself as steady as possible. "So, Prova . . . how'd you end up there?"

Daroga cleared his throat. "Well, after the Brownout, they brought us to Estes for a while to parade us around for the media, boast about our 'perseverance,' inspire patriotism, et cetera."

"He says with disdain."

Daroga cast a wry smile. "He says with *much* disdain, yes." Though he'd tied his hair back, loose strands hung against the sides of his face as he kept his chin low, gaze down. "It was just a ruse so the directorate's minions could debrief us, glean any intel we had about the Mechan. Then show us off to the public and pretend like just because we survived, that meant they hadn't wildly mishandled the entire situation."

Adriene's head bobbed in unconscious agreement. At the time, she hadn't thought much of it—she'd been barely nine years old, her mother missing, her father panicking. She didn't consider the broad societal or political ramifications of any of it until much later. Even now, whenever anyone talked about the Brownout, it was always centered around the event itself. The trial the colonists had endured during those few weeks. She'd never considered what'd happen to them after.

"When we were no longer of use to them, they relocated most of us to Prova." Daroga replaced the wipe with another fresh one. "Chin up, please," he requested, and Adriene leaned back on her palms, canting her head to one side. "Prova was busy with the Shift evac already in full swing," Daroga went on, "so Kato's family hosted ours for almost two years before our acreage deed was finalized. Halfway across the continent, unfortunately, so we lost touch after that. But we both ended up on the *Aurora*, somehow."

"Small universe."

"No kidding. May I?" He indicated the bloodied collar of her shirt, and she nodded.

He slid his thumb under her neckline, moving the fabric aside to clean along her collarbone, his cool fingers and the damp cloth a welcome chill against her warm skin.

// Vitals elevated. //

She rolled her eyes. *All right. Calm down, please.*

// I believe it is you who needs to calm down. //

"Damn," Daroga mumbled, discarding another wipe. "I'm not sure how you have any blood left. *Inside,* I mean." He glanced up with a crooked smile, but his humor faded as he met her eye, brow creasing. "Feel okay? You look like you're running a fever."

"Yeah, fine." She shifted side to side to scoot farther back on the gurney. "Just been running hot since I got back from the mission."

Daroga tugged off his gloves, discarding them along with the bloodied wipes. He grabbed a small tablet off a tray nearby and held it up to Adriene's eye. "Hold still."

A few seconds later, the device beeped.

He cocked his head as he read the result. "Elevated, but nothing to worry on yet."

// I could have told you that. //

And yet you didn't.

"Let me know if it gets worse," Daroga said, concern edging his tone. "The terminal in your quarters can check your temperature."

// I can check your temperature. //

She exhaled a barely controlled sigh. *Then why didn't you?*

// As he mentioned, it was not pressing. //

Daroga stepped away to a nearby supply cart.

Adriene looked up as her stomach dropped, and it took her a disorienting second to realize what'd happened. The ship had entered subspace.

Daroga glanced at the ceiling, then back at Adriene. "They must have finally figured out where we're going." He approached again, snapping on a new pair of gloves. "I'm guessing they figured that out from whatever you guys picked up planetside?"

Chewing the inside of her cheek, she gave a short nod. "Yeah, I guess so." In all her hundreds of missions with the 803rd, she'd never seen anything like those ruins—especially nothing like that sealed storage room where she'd found the "technology artifact." She had to admit, she was curious as to what it'd contained.

"Brigham said the scrappers got the drop on you." Daroga's green eyes lifted to meet hers. "That the place was swarming, but you still made it out with the objective in hand."

"I was lucky."

"Well," he said, ruthlessly sincere, "I'm glad you made it back in one piece."

Adriene cast a tight-lipped smile. She couldn't get used to people being "glad" she'd made it. Accepting it felt deceitful. Completing the mission had been a means to an end. She'd only wanted to avoid a rezone.

Daroga continued his work with a quiet sigh. "I guess it's good Blackwell didn't listen to me."

She refocused on him. "Listen to you about what?"

"I told him you should sit it out. That you needed more time with your implant first." His eyes skimmed over her for a second before refocusing on her wound. "Guess I was wrong. You've taken to it all . . . quite well, to say the least. Quicker than I've seen anyone."

Adriene gave an appreciative nod, though she wasn't sure if he'd meant it as a compliment or subtle inquiry. "It's been pretty intuitive," she agreed. "But still taking some getting used to." She scratched at the hairline above her temple. "Are they always so talkative? Mine has barely shut up all night."

// *If I was capable of feeling offended, I would.* //

Daroga took a step back, black eyebrows lifted. "It's on now?"

"Yeah. It activated during the fight."

"Right, of course." Daroga shed his gloves again, then exited the row of gurneys, rounding toward a desk at the back corner of the room. He picked up a tablet and tapped in a few quick commands.

With a sharp prick behind her eyes, Adriene's HUD vanished. She pressed the heels of her palms into both temples, but the headache did not abate.

Daroga returned with a consoling grin. "Sorry about that. You should have said something. I could have killed it when you first came in."

"It's okay. I don't mind it." Which was true. Even when it decided to badger her with impertinence.

Daroga lifted an inconsequential, cylindrical metal tool off the tray. "Time to start the graft. Ready?"

She gave a curt nod. "Ready."

Daroga sidled his hip against the edge of the gurney, drawing close to keep the tool steady. Near enough that even her shallowest inhales drew in his scent—crisp, yet warm, triggering a vague sense of autumn in the foothills.

Blinking a few times, Adriene tried to instead focus on the dull, swollen feeling of her cheek and jaw as sensation slowly returned.

Not pain, but pressure and temperature—the sharp, cool metal tool, the smooth pull of gloved fingers, the warmth of his breath on her neck . . .

She blew out a controlled exhale.

Forcing herself to look past Daroga's shoulder, she studied the layout of the room: the gurneys, the supply carts, the synthesizers, the comfortable quiet of a completely deserted medical bay.

She felt an urgent need to fill the silence. "Why are you here, anyway?" she asked.

Daroga lifted a black brow. "Mm, like . . . on this mortal plane?"

The corner of her mouth twitched. "I mean, at Medical at 0230, when you're not even a medic."

"Ah. I studied surgical medicine for a while, so I cover the overnight shift sometimes."

"Hence why they let you do implant installs?"

"Right. It's usually pretty slow after hours, so I can get my other work done—that is, when upstart newbies don't start random brawls in the middle of the night." He flashed a smile.

Adriene's eyes drifted to his desk in the far back corner. "What's this 'other work' I'm keeping you from?"

"Tonight, only paperwork. So really, I should be thanking you."

"You're welcome." The familiar tingle of growing skin tickled—itched, almost—and she had to resist the urge to scratch it. "And when it's not only paperwork?"

"Well, day to day, as you know: installing implants, facilitating tech integrations, software upgrades . . . arguing about the limitations of the simulation VI with the Stormwalkers."

She breathed a laugh. "All important duties."

Sighing, he leaned back as he thumbed the grafting tool into standby mode to let the heat dissipate. "I also input all the bugs and suggestions for Rubicon into our project management software, make sure things get prioritized properly. Revert to old builds if shit gets too buggy."

Flicking the tool back on, he leaned in again. He held his bottom lip between his teeth, green eyes glassy with concentration.

"But you don't do any of the actual coding?" she clarified.

"No, ma'am. I merely organize it, send it off, and it gets upgraded. Graft's done." He set the tool back on the tray. "Feel okay?"

"Yeah, feels great." Her fingers drifted up to the new, slightly raw skin.

Daroga picked up a disinfection tool. "One more step." The device gave off a faint, shrill electric hum as he activated it. He held her chin lightly, and her new skin tingled as he ran the narrow disinfection beam over the area in slow, sweeping passes. A bead of sweat traced its way down the back of her neck, and she resisted the urge to wipe it away.

She kept her jaw still as she asked, "Can I ask you a question about the implants?"

"Shoot."

"What are the limits of the VI?"

His brow creased and he paused the disinfection. "What do you mean?"

She shook her head. "Just trying to gauge what it's capable of, I guess. Wondering if it could . . . influence your decisions? Or even take control of motor functions?"

"No," he said, a sudden firmness in his tone. "Definitely not. We've specifically forbade protocols that could lead to artificial ascendence. CNEF brass mandates it. And the Dodson-Mueller Compliance Division, who are even scarier." His stern look faded, and he continued with the disinfection. "Something about multiple sentient beings in one brain is a bit too Mechan for most people's comfort."

Adriene released a sharp breath through her nose. Of course *that* disturbed them, but not their soldiers having to zero out over and over.

"It's a nightmare from a coding perspective, anyway," Daroga added, tone contemplative.

"How so?"

He scratched his jawline. "Same basic reason we can only rezone into our own bodies, back into our own brains. Or why a hybridized Mechan can't persist through a rezone. Sentience requires a degree of . . . *fidelity*. Or that's the theory, at least." He flashed a grin.

"Developing it's illegal, after all." He shook his head and added, "I wouldn't even know where to begin creating the command structures required for that kind of assimilation."

"You seem to know your stuff when it comes to the programming side of things."

The buzz of the disinfection tool ceased, leaving stark, lingering silence. Daroga stepped back. "Yeah, that's what I did before I came here. Worked with Artillery Command on Khan Launcher VIs until they moved me over to the 461st."

She tilted her head. "The 461st—the Codebreakers?"

"That's the one." He set the disinfection tool back on the tray. "You've heard of them?"

"Of course. They came up with the hijacker jamming fix for the subspace beacons. Were you with them then?"

The corners of his eyes wrinkled. "Guilty. Project lead."

Her lips parted. "Well, shit," she said under her breath, realizing but not really caring how impressed she sounded. She really was. In the 803rd, that tech had saved their dropships from getting ripped out of subspace and ambushed dozens of times. Saved her having to rezone who knew how many times. "After that, I would think you could pick whatever job you wanted."

"I did."

She raised an eyebrow. "And you picked *this*? Here?"

He sighed and leaned a hip against the gurney. "Yep."

"Why? You didn't want to code anymore?"

"I was supposed to . . ." He hesitated briefly, then crossed his arms and shook his head. "Let's just say, 'administering prototype tech' sounds much cooler on paper."

Her mouth went dry as his words sank in. An echo of her dream rang in the back of her mind. *Administrator permissions.*

After all the drinking, punching, and bleeding, she'd almost forgotten about it. And now she sat in front of the only person on board who might know what that meant.

Tilting her head, she feigned benign curiosity as she asked, "If you administer the tech, does that make you the one with 'administrator permissions'?"

"You'd think," he muttered, then his brow furrowed. "Where'd you read that?"

She gave a noncommittal headshake. "Just something my Rubicon mentioned."

He scrubbed a hand through his long hair, freeing it from its tie with a sigh. He tucked the chin-length strands behind his ears. "The 505th's R&D major is the only one with full admin privileges. If you need something specific, the process is the same as bug reporting—you can go through me or put in a request at your terminal."

She waved him off. "No need. Just curious."

"Yeah," he rumbled quietly, warmth in his tone, "that's one of the things I like about you, Sergeant."

Adriene blinked rapidly, the admission catching her off guard. Then she just sat there, briefly stupefied.

"It's just not very common, is all," Daroga clarified with a smile, white teeth bright against his brown skin. "I think you've asked more questions in your first three days than the rest of the crew ever has, combined." He cast a fleeting look toward the entrance. "Most of them don't give a second thought to a single thing they're told. Honestly, makes me wonder how they can be so good at their jobs."

She scratched her jawline, recalling how skeptical the Stormwalkers had been about her ability to complete their mission unaided. "Maybe they're . . . not."

Daroga laughed. "Yeah, maybe."

"Thanks for the repair." She slid off the edge of the gurney. A wave of heat rolled through her, blood rushing to her. "Though, I feel like the least you could have done is leave me with an awesome scar."

He wavered his head back and forth. "Sorry. Maybe next time." He crossed to the cabinet near the door and grabbed a pill case, then passed it to her as she followed behind. "One every twelve hours."

"Thanks."

Daroga returned to the gurney to clean up. "Let me know if you need anything else, Sergeant."

"Adriene," she found herself saying.

He paused cleaning for a long moment, then looked up and did a terrible job of hiding a smile. "Right. Adriene."

Sweat trickled down the small of her back, and she fanned her shirt to let in some cooler air. "Thanks again."

Wariness flickered across his brow, but he didn't say anything as she turned and left.

The corridor outside felt like a sauna in a midsummer heat wave. Adriene's hairline dripped and she ran her hands down either side of her face, flicking the wetness from her fingertips.

A couple of minutes into her walk, her pace slowed as her heart picked up speed. A sharp tingle pricked across the back of her neck like some latent danger sense. She checked over her shoulder, but saw nothing.

She kept walking. Her pulse continued to accelerate, unbidden.

She'd made it less than halfway to her quarters before she had to pause, pinching the bridge of her nose to subdue a searing head- ache. Sweat clung to her skin, accompanied by a bone-deep ache.

Maybe she needed to go back.

Before she could decide, another wall of heat hit her, skin buzz- ing as if it simmered, molten. She braced herself on her knees, tak- ing a few long, deliberate breaths to steady her racing heart. Her head swam with each inhale, and the white walls bloomed bright, then tilted and skewed.

She spun around—she had to get back to Daroga—but she stumbled, slumping against the wall. Her knees hit the floor as her vision blacked out.

A blaze ignited behind her eyes.

// Welllc—mm to—Rrru—con—//

The normally placid, perfect voice came fractured and distorted. The lines of the HUD cracked and jittered, flashing white and black and red.

The base of her skull throbbed. The waves of heat she'd endured the last few hours had concentrated into a roiling mass of lava, filling the empty void in the back of her brain.

A flat coolness pressed into her cheek—she'd ended up facedown on the floor somehow.

She reached out, trying to focus on the cold metal wherever it touched her simmering skin. Gasping for air, she willed her eyes to open a sliver.

The white floor of the corridor stretched out before her. A ragged, wavering red column laid out on the ground, like the runway tape in a docking bay.

Her vision blurred as she looked around for help, but the halls were silent, empty, no signs of life. Still too late or too early for anyone to be out roaming the halls. If she didn't get back to Medical, it could be a long time before someone found her. It could be too late. She sure as shit couldn't stomach a rezone, not like this.

So with every ounce of will she could muster, she palmed her way up the wall, legs trembling beneath her as she straightened. Surges of heat rolled from her scalp to her toes like waves of fire burning across her skin.

She glanced both ways and with burgeoning terror realized she was completely disoriented. She no longer knew which way led back to Medical.

Then she looked down at the jittering red path her HUD had painted beneath her feet. She squinted at the fragmented, stuttering line before realizing what it was.

Her Rubicon had plotted a course. A path to follow.

She sucked in a breath through clenched teeth. Put one foot in front of the other. Again.

She couldn't pay attention to the route. She could only concentrate on the floor, on her feet, on staying upright, on breathing—in and out.

Finally, she arrived at the end of the line. Looked up.

Disbelief rolled through her under the torrent of heat. It hadn't led her back to Medical, back to Daroga. The route ended at the

foot of a hexagonal door. Her eyes burned as she struggled to focus on the wide black lettering stretching across it: INTELLIGENCE
COMMAND—RESTRICTED ACCESS.

The path and the lines of her HUD flickered in and out, less and
less stable with every passing second. Her heart hammered into her
aching ribs.

She had to focus on getting her brain to comprehend why, or if
she should try to go back, or where she even was . . .

But her brain was done, checked out. She couldn't use it for anything other than to keep her heart beating.

So she did the only thing she could manage. Stumbling forward, she reached out. Her palm slipped across the door's control
panel as she sank into a black abyss.

FOURTEEN

Adriene woke to every muscle in her body aching. Cold sweat clung to her skin. But she felt cool again, finally.

She cracked open her eyes.

A soft haze of electric-blue light tinged the blackness. The back of her eyes throbbed while trying to bring the world into focus.

With a breathy groan, Adriene turned onto her side. The thin plastic pad beneath her squeaked as she sat up.

She stared down at the floor for a moment. Grasping the edge of the cot, she focused on the way the cool plastic crunched under her grip.

Heaving a sigh, she stood. She let her vision settle, then gazed around the expansive, rectangular room, the lighting dimmed to a soft, after-hours glow. Unlike the rest of the ship, the surfaces were steel gray, though equally as immaculate. Rows of long counters contained a multitude of tidy workstations with one or two monitors each and the occasional peripheral. A tech lab of some kind.

Sensing a blue glow over her shoulder, she turned around. The back wall loomed before her, over a dozen monitors hanging over a low console fit with tablet ports and holographic projection nodes. A sturdy workbench capped one end, its open shelving cluttered with supplies and tools; bandages, MREs, soldering irons, multimeters, pliers, scanners.

Her gaze drew back to the center console. A single active monitor at the bottom flashed indecipherable code alongside the flickering light from a nearby data drive.

She recognized that palm-sized device stacked beside almost a dozen others exactly like it. The "technology artifacts" she'd risked her life for—risked getting hybridized for. They were daisy-chained together with some frayed cabling that looked like it'd been jury-rigged using spare scrapper guts.

"You're awake."

Panic surged, and Adriene spun around, instinctively stepping back, calves bumping against the edge of the cot.

Between two dim beams from the overhead lights, something stood obscured in the patchy shadows. It took her a moment to process that some*thing* was, in fact, a some*one*. A man. A living, breathing man. At least . . . in part.

Augments covered most of his left side. An ocular implant on his left eye melded seamlessly into a cheek-and-jaw graft, masking the left side of his face. A metal plate ran down the left side of his neck then disappeared under the collar of his shirt. His left sleeve, rolled up past the elbow, revealed a sleek, dark metal cybernetic arm and hand. It could have been mistaken for armor, except the arm was too slim to be a covering over a real limb, and it hung too rigidly at his side. It didn't move properly along with the rising and lowering of his chest.

She'd never seen someone so augmented before. She'd heard of it, sure—*alloys,* they were called. People addicted to cybernetics who undertook dozens of black market installations until they were more metal and plastic than flesh and bone.

But this man couldn't be some augmentation junkie. He was a soldier—an officer, even. And he wore the light gray uniform of Command.

"You're dehydrated." The man's rich voice rang steady, calm. He held a metal bottle out toward her. With his real arm, his human arm.

Adriene tightened a fist, trying to steady her trembling hands. Though her initial alarm had subsided, the residual from the spike of adrenaline still coursed through her veins.

With a few slow steps forward, she took the bottle from him, then retreated to the cot and took a drink. The cold water rushed down her throat, sending a welcome chill through her chest.

"Slowly," the man warned.

Adriene slowed, then lowered the bottle and took a few seconds to catch her breath. "Who—" she began, her weak voice breaking. She cleared her throat and forced more effort into it. "Who are you?"

The man moved toward her, and a muted, metallic hum accompanied his steps. One of his legs seemed cybernetic as well, at least in part. She could only imagine the shit this guy had gone through to need half his body replaced.

He stopped in front of her at the edge of the light, and she had to crane her neck to match his gaze—he had to be almost two full meters tall. Though his augments were expertly fitted, light scarring marred the skin that met the edges of his facial grafts, short clawlike hatches all along the perimeter.

The hard lines of his cybernetics caught the glare of the light as he reached toward her with his right hand, his real hand. "Major Julen West."

Adriene's back straightened on instinct, along with a pang of recognition. She'd seen this major before, if briefly—the officer who'd been loitering in the back of the hardsuit briefing.

"Sergeant Adriene Valero, sir." She shook his hand, surprised at its warmth. Considering he looked more machine than man, she'd expected his pale skin to be as cold and smooth as metal. "Sir . . ." she began, but drifted off, her addled thoughts muddling the question before she could form it. "I'm sorry, sir," she continued quickly, "but I don't remember how I got here. What happened?"

West's real eye locked on her, a muted hazel, shaded in the dim light. "I found you in the corridor. You'd lost consciousness."

Right. Fragments rushed back: Daroga patching her up, the flood of unbearable heat, stumbling her way through the halls. Her glitching Rubicon, guiding her way to "Intelligence Command."

Goose bumps rippled across her skin with a draft of air. She grazed her forehead with her fingertips. "Did something go wrong with my Rubicon?"

The major inclined his head, a spark of light reflecting off his facial graft. "Of a sort, yes. The implant was . . . *overtaxing* your system. Though forced to establish a physical connection, I was able to make the needed repair without incident."

Adriene's fingers drifted to her temple. "You fixed it?"

He turned away to walk deeper into the room. "I'm sorry we had to meet under these circumstances, Sergeant."

Adriene stood unmoving, muscles bound up by her racing thoughts.

West returned with a metal stool. It grated against the floor as he placed it beside her.

She carefully sat down, and the major held out a silver MRE packet. "Slowly," he warned again.

Her stomach groaned at the sight of it. She tore open the pouch and bit off a too-large chunk of the grainy food bar, hyperaware of the loudness of her chewing as Major West silently watched, real and metal fingers entwined, waiting patiently.

She finally gulped down the bite, then took a slow drink of water. She glanced over her shoulder to the hexagonal white door across the room. "Sir, are you part of Intel?"

"Yes."

Adriene eyed him expectantly, but he didn't elaborate. "But you were able to fix my implant? I thought Daroga dealt with all that."

West arched his back and exhaled a heavy breath as he crossed his arms. "Mr. Daroga deals with the day-to-day administration, yes. Though my current responsibility with Flintlock is intelligence, I am also R&D lead abeyant for all of the 505th."

R&D lead . . . And her VI had led her directly to him.

She pointed to her temple. "You made this?"

He gave a single, barely perceptible nod, eye narrowed. He watched with the kind of anticipatory curiosity one might give when seeing a newborn foal find its footing for the first time.

She cleared her throat. "Is that a normal side effect? The over-heating?"

"No," he said simply, then uncrossed his arms and stretched out his mechanical hand. The metal fingers clicked lightly together as they tremored. A small grimace tugged at his lips. "Merely an un-foreseen issue with the field upgrade."

She gulped down a bite. "Field upgrade, sir?"

His lower jaw worked back and forth, lips faintly parting as though he'd been about to speak, but couldn't decide what to say.

But Adriene didn't need him to confirm what she already knew. Something had happened to her implant on Cimarosa-IV. She'd seen and felt things she shouldn't have been able to see and feel.

She cleared her throat. "My Rubicon's not like the others, is it?"

His contemplative expression loosened, and he let out the small-est breath of a sigh. "No, Sergeant. Not anymore."

"What changed? And why?"

West stretched out his cybernetic hand again. "The answer to that is . . . complicated."

"Try me," she said, finding strength in her voice for the first time since she'd woken up.

West's eyebrows lifted. Shifting his weight, he crossed his arms as he regarded her with idle curiosity, though he didn't respond.

She blew out a long exhale. "You can start by explaining how I could see . . ." Every circuit in her suit, all of overwatch, the Mechan, the dropship, shit in orbit, the *Aurora* . . . ". . . *everything*," she breathed. "Enemy positions, my team—all across the planet. Filtered directly into my mind."

He nodded. "A result of the aforementioned *upgrade*."

"Can you at least give me the patch notes?"

The corner of his mouth twitched. He turned, retreating toward his workstation. Moments later, he brought another stool back with him.

His cybernetic limbs buzzed lightly as he sat in front of her. "I re-cently developed an . . . *overhauled* version of the Rubicon software."

"Three-point-oh?"

His mouth twitched again in a smile that was not quite a smile. "If you will. The new version featured modified protocols for the Rubicon intelligence."

Adriene's brows pinched as she swallowed another bite. "What kind of protocols?"

He stretched his neck side to side a few times before he answered. "Ones the Concord Nations Sentience Act would likely define as artificial ascendance."

She blinked once. "You mean AI?"

"Correct."

Adriene stared at him for a few long moments, processing. She didn't keep up to date on the politics, but she knew there were harsh limits on what was allowed when it came to artificial intelligence. Having dealt with the Mechan for two decades was traumatic enough—they didn't need their own robot uprising to complicate matters.

Though she didn't really give a shit whether or not it was legal. She only cared if it was safe.

"So, that's the version I have now? An AI instead of a VI?"

"Correct."

"Okay . . . What's that mean? What's the difference?"

West looked up as he scratched his chin, his mouth pinching in contemplation. Adriene recognized the look—that annoying face all eggheads made when they tried to think of a way to dumb something down to explain it to a normal person.

She tore off another chunk of MRE, chewing it slowly as she waited for him to figure it out.

"In its most basic form," he said finally, "the difference lies in restrictions. The functionality is much the same, but a virtual intelligence is throttled. Its learning capabilities and reactions will always be planned, controlled, and predictable, based entirely on its coding. It cannot deviate."

Adriene rubbed her aching temple. "And that's *not* the case with the AI version?"

"No," he said, then took a deep breath. "Not only can the AI learn, it can fluidly adapt its own code to accommodate what it *believes* is correct. Alter its functions and personality at will, essentially."

"Mine seemed to have quite a personality even before the up-grade."

"A simulated effect," he assured. "Part of the VI's protocols are to endear itself to the user. But every aspect of that personality is adjustable in the user setting. All preordained. It adapts, but does not feel. It learns, but does not evolve."

She took a quick swig of water. "So my Rubicon is different now . . . because it *can* evolve?"

"I believe so, yes."

Adriene released a breathy scoff. "You *believe* so? How do you not know?"

He ran a hand over his close-cropped hair. "Unfortunately," he began, "I have not had the chance to do much in the way of testing. Any trials I've managed have been . . . *limited* by the confines of simulations. Field deployment was new territory."

Adriene shifted her weight on the stool. That was not precisely *comforting*.

"That said," West continued, "something happened beyond what I expected. Something that didn't occur in any of the simulations."

"And what's that?"

"Breadth," he said, tone wistful, light.

She raised an eyebrow.

He wet his lips slowly, a fragment of need-to-dumb-down leaking into his expression. "The VI's most basic functions reside in the implant itself," he explained. "Then it uses your neural pathways as an . . . *extension*, if you will."

"More processing power?" she offered, recalling what Daroga had mentioned in the hardsuit lecture.

West's eyebrow perked up. He almost seemed impressed. "Precisely. And that network extends with any connected suit, module, weapon, or armor matrices, giving it additional breadth."

"But the AI version . . . ?" she prompted.

He exhaled a controlled breath. "Deploying the AI version to your implant had much the same effect, but on an exponential scale. Your mind granted the AI substantial reams of power, allowing you to process many things at once, while also giving it range. This resulted in the experience you mentioned earlier—it acted like a mobile antenna, reaching out and creating dynamic links between sources to establish a massive wireless network for many kilometers."

And well beyond. She considered telling him the extent of what she'd seen: all the way back to the Rubicon mainframe.

A prickling warning in the back of her skull urged against giving him the specifics. If he didn't already know that, it might be better that way. At least until she learned more about the major and this "upgrade."

West shook his head, a hint of wonder creeping into his tone. "The AI gleaned information from the expanded network for its own use, in addition to converting it into sensory stimulus, giving you the ability to process it visually." West sat back on his stool, crossing his arms. "I had not expected this outcome, honestly. Your unique wiring may have been a factor."

Adriene frowned. "My unique *wiring*?"

"Your mind contains . . ." He scratched his chin. ". . . *complicated* neural networking, to say the least. The likes of which I've never seen before."

She clutched the MRE tighter, trying to ignore the fact that he'd somehow *seen* the neural structure of her brain.

"It's understandable," he continued. "Your mind has had to rewire itself dozens of times in an attempt to better handle your constant rezoning procedures. Each death is a shock to the system."

Adriene concealed a scoff with a fake cough. She tore another chunk from the dry food brick. He'd read up on her service history, it seemed.

"In the end," West continued, "the system becomes stronger because of it. Like when a muscle grows, but only after being broken down and repairing itself. Because of your previous trauma, your mind accepts the ascendancy in stride, where others would have faltered."

She rubbed her temple, recalling the sharp, blinding, all-consuming pain she'd felt on Cimarosa-IV. It hadn't really felt all that "in stride" at the time.

"Okay," she sighed. "I'm an ideal host, I get it. But why? What triggered it to upgrade?"

"I did."

The blunt admission came out so casually, it almost passed her notice, and she coughed out a crumb of MRE as she deferred the next question she'd planned to ask. Because *that* answer required clarification.

"On purpose?" she asked, brow creased deeply.

He inclined his head.

Adriene's voice pitched up with incredulity. "In the middle of a mission? Sir?"

West scrubbed a hand over his jaw. "Not ideal timing, I agree."

The MRE wrapper crinkled in her grip as she fidgeted on the stool. "Why? Because I was going to get left behind?"

His gaze flicked down, and he slowly shook his head. "Not exactly."

Adriene's lips parted, but she didn't even need to ask. She already knew the answer.

She'd been trapped. With Mechan incoming. No rifle. No squad. But she'd had eyes on the objective.

The major had risked pushing the upgrade as a last-ditch effort. So she'd have a chance at completing the mission.

West remained silent for a long moment, his ocular implant catching the light as his real eye locked onto her. "I do apologize, Sergeant. Truly. Pushing a live upgrade in the field is not what I would consider an ideal initial beta test."

Adriene's expression went slack, deferred yet again by alarming details. "*Initial* beta test?"

"Alphas were conducted virtually," he replied, missing the point entirely, "utilizing the same advanced VI as the training simulations."

She scrubbed a hand through her short hair. "You . . . You've never tested this before?"

His throat bobbed with a swallow. "No, Sergeant," he replied, tone solemn. He folded his hands in his lap. "As mentioned earlier, the Concord Nations Sentience Act prohibits the development of technologies that may lead to artificial ascendance. As such, my work is largely theoretical."

"Was," she corrected.

"I suppose, yes," he said, formal yet apologetic. "Again, I apologize for the situation. If you wish, I can revert your implant back to the previous build."

Dropping her hand from her face, Adriene met West's steadfast gaze. She knew what the sensible, rational response was. Yet her first instinct had been to decline—adamantly. To keep the AI. She had no idea why.

Resetting to the approved, tested version everyone else in her company used was the objectively correct decision. The upgrade had been a stopgap to help her escape alive, with the intel intact. Now things should be returned to normal.

Though she couldn't stop thinking about how . . . *powerful* she'd felt in those subterranean ruins. How confident, how driven, how fulfilled. How *in control.*

Like West said, the upgrade had given her breadth. In more ways than one. Though keeping it may be a risk, that kind of power could aid her in the coming months. Could prevent countless rezones. Or even hybridizations.

"I should mention . . ." West continued, the contrition gone from his tone, back to calculative dryness. "I cannot guarantee the reversion process would not trigger a rezone. I simply don't have enough data on the physiological ramifications of the AI. Yours seems to have netted quite strongly to your cognitive wiring already, and I would not feel comfortable saying with any degree of certainty what the consequences of a rollback may be."

"I'll keep it," she said.

West's real eye fluttered with a few quick blinks. "Are you certain?"

"Yes." She swallowed the last of the MRE.

"I'm glad to hear you say that, Sergeant."

She lifted a brow. "You are?" She'd assumed he wouldn't really want some random soldier walking around with proof of his illegal tech in her brain.

West's stool groaned as he stood. "There is a matter with which I could use some . . . assistance. A special assignment, of sorts. One I believe your upgraded Rubicon could facilitate greatly."

Her brow furrowed. "What kind of special assignment?"

West stepped toward the console, chin drifting forward in a gesture to follow. Adriene's back ached as she stood. She left the MRE wrapper on the stool and trailed him toward the bank of terminals.

He activated a viewscreen and with a few quick taps brought up a document that outlined dozens of dates, locations, missions, and projections. A fairly standard operation plan, similar to those they'd used in the 803rd, though this one was divided into multiple stages and the projections stretched out for months. The 803rd never planned more than a few weeks at a time, constantly reacting to the movement of the Mechan armada clusters.

West cleared his throat. "Two weeks ago, Flintlock commenced a new campaign—one Commodore Thurston and I have been formulating for years. It prompted your recruitment, I believe. Pathfinder?"

She nodded. "My former CO sent one for every company in the 505th."

"Yes, the other companies assist our efforts as well, in secondary roles."

Adriene scanned the sparse details of the operation plan for context, though it was scant, clearly a "public" version.

West cleared his throat, vibrancy building in his tone. "The Rubicon technology optimizes performance and reduces the frequency of rezones, but those are merely side effects." He linked his fingers together, weaving shining metal with calloused skin. "Rubicon allows for an unprecedented symbiosis between R&D and Intel—exactly what this campaign needs to be successful; in fact, I designed Rubicon with this campaign specifically in mind. And now, the enhanced AI functionality could provide us with a greater opportunity to succeed. We may even be able to expedite our timetable—perhaps significantly."

Adriene scratched the back of her neck. "What exactly does this 'campaign' involve?"

West stood cradling the elbow of his real arm with his mechanical one, fingers grazing the stubble on his square chin. "Allow me to give you some context."

She lifted a hand in a gesture to proceed. "Please."

He considered her before resting his tall frame against the edge of the console counter. "As a whole, the 505th's primary objective is prospective intelligence gathering."

"Prospective?"

"Long term," West clarified. "Unlike typical reconnaissance efforts, what we pursue is not intended to inform the proceedings of another unit. Nor are we reactive to other fleet initiatives. We work independently to envision what may lie at the horizon of the war."

Adriene nodded slowly. That explained his presence on board. Typically, companies didn't require more than a couple of analysts to liaise with CNEF Intelligence back at central command.

She met West's patient gaze. "At the horizon of the war . . . You mean the *end* of the war?"

"Ideally, yes."

Adriene rubbed her cracked lips. That was indeed "prospective."

"Though the commodore and I do not see eye to eye on everything," West continued, "we share a . . . *concern* for the future of humanity and see a need to treat the situation with a degree of urgency. This campaign has a strong chance of leading us to the key to defeating the Mechan."

Adriene's brow furrowed. "You have a *key* to defeating the Mechan?"

"Not yet." His lips pressed into a thin frown. "That's classified information—for now. If you accept and the commodore approves the posting, your security classification will be raised, and I can share more details." He rubbed his chin again, his mouth twitching to dampen a sharp, sudden wince. His mechanical fingers clicked lightly as he shook out the hand, then pressed it flat against the counter. After a moment, the episode passed. "I can tell you this," he offered, tone conciliatory, "though you must consider it confidential."

Adriene inclined her head. "Understood, sir."

"As you may have noticed, the facility on Cimarosa-IV was not, in fact, Mechan in origin."

She thought back to the strange, gray-skinned beings depicted in the stonework. "I gathered."

"I have been studying the Mechan creators for some time now— the Architects, as they are referred to by some. I believe their history holds the key to a final and resounding defeat of the Mechan. Commodore Thurston believes that as well."

Adriene cleared her throat, but found she wasn't sure what to say. People didn't often throw around phrases like *final and resounding defeat of the Mechan*." Nor did they speak of the Mechan creators as anything other than a nebulous, long-extinct annoyance responsible for their current predicament. "Are you saying you think the Architects are still alive?" she asked.

He shook his head. "No, certainly not." He pushed off the counter and turned to the console again, but paused, then his hand dropped away from the screens. He retracted, thinking better of it, then turned to her. "There is little I can share presently. Suffice it to say, we have acquired information that has given us more insight into Architect history and their extinction. But there is much work to do. Reconstructing that history is the first leg of this campaign, and a crucial one. Your involvement could drastically aid that undertaking."

Adriene's mind churned as she took in the offer. She'd always considered herself a career grunt—a slightly above-average pathfinder. Then again, she never thought she'd get kicked up to sergeant in a special forces division either.

"What would I be doing, exactly?" she asked.

He gave a curt dip of his chin. "There will be certain . . . *tasks* you will undertake. Ones you and your Rubicon are uniquely capable of executing. Those which the commodore desires to remain . . . discreet."

Adriene nodded slowly. From his tone, she took that to mean the kinds of things in after-action reports that either ended up glossed over or omitted entirely.

"It is a role I would have preferred to take on myself, but . . ." West stretched out his cybernetic hand, pressing the palm flat against the side of his thigh. "I cannot be . . . on the ground, as it were."

Adriene eyed the uncomfortable, stilted way he leaned against the console, the cant to his spine, heavily favoring his mechanical side. She wondered if he needed a proxy because he was physically incapable or because a half-robot commander wasn't stellar for morale.

"You would essentially be acting on my behalf," West continued. "As I said, you will have more details once your clearance is raised. After that, you would be expected to maintain strict confidentiality. Your classification would be raised beyond that of your colleagues, and you would be unable to discuss your objectives or your upgraded Rubicon with anyone outside of myself and Commodore Thurston."

"Not even Major Blackwell?" she asked.

He exhaled a heavy sigh. "Undetermined, as yet. The commodore and I do not see eye to eye on that."

Adriene considered the situation; it was a lot to unpack. It would mean chronically lying to her squad, her support crew. Maybe even lying to her commanding officer. "Why all the secrecy?"

West tapped his temple with two fingers.

Right. The illegal AI in her head.

He sighed and crossed his arms. "We are, unfortunately, not entirely aboveboard at the moment," he pointed out. "Though I have every confidence we will get special dispensation from the advisory board, that could take many months, if not years." He frowned, gaze drifting to the middle distance. With his arms folded, his real hand rested in the crook of his mechanical elbow, kneading the metal joint. Voice low, he added, "I fear we may not have that long."

Adriene picked at the hem of her shirt, wondering at the vacant silence in her chest. She should be terrified—a high-ranking intelligence officer of the Extrasolar Fleet just admitted the likelihood that the Mechan could end the war in a matter of years. Yet she only felt a passing sense of curiosity.

"That long till what?" she asked. "Don't you think if the scrappers wanted us dead, we already would be?"

Looking down, West's lips pressed into a grim line, and he shook his head. "I cannot pretend to understand the motivations of machines. A corruption of their coding, perhaps, who knows." He looked up and met her eye. "Either way, we are at imminent risk. Whatever their agenda, it is not benevolent—they have demonstrated that much, at least. A tipping point is coming, one we will not be able to recuperate from."

Brow furrowed, she shook her head. "You can't know that for sure."

He drew up his chin, tone measured. "I don't like it either, Sergeant. But it's plain fact. Academics have warned the directorate for over a decade. When rezone technology came about, they used it as a blinder, extending their willful disillusion. Rezoning may keep us afloat, but it only delays the inevitable."

"Which is?"

"The Mechan will grow to a point we cannot surpass. Even now, we're spread too thin to outmatch them. If we continue to do nothing, then we remain gated in our dying system, where Mira will one day kill us. They will not have to do anything."

A memory drifted into the back of Adriene's mind. Clamping her eyes shut, she tried to stave it off, to no avail: the rough grit of sand abrading her skin, a halo of metal eclipsing her vision, a terrible, rancid hunger burning in her stomach.

Her nails bit hard into her palms. She focused on the pain to root her, pushing the memory away as she turned her right hand over and stretched it out wide.

When she'd been hybridized, the scrappers let her die of starvation instead of just killing her. Were they really doing the same thing to humanity?

"Flintlock is on the cusp of a breakthrough," West continued, a trace of rising fervency in his tone. "For the first time since the Brownout, we are poised to maneuver offensively instead of ceaseless, idle reaction and defense. We have a chance to get ahead of the Mechan, but *only* if we seize this opportunity."

It made a degree of sense. In all her time in the 803rd, hundreds of encounters with the Mechan, all the bots ever tried to do was stop them—from scouting, from setting up colonies, from inhabiting a new sector. Hybridizing them when possible, killing them if they couldn't. Maybe the bots really were holding out for that mathematical tipping point.

Adriene chewed the inside of her lip. There had to be more. They were ruthless killing machines, yes, but they were still sentient. Still able to follow a train of logic. And she didn't buy the corrupted coding excuse one bit.

West's theory fit . . . mostly.

She looked back at him, surprised to see his posture straightened, a glint of fighting spirit in his hazel eye.

"I don't know about you, Sergeant," he said, "but I would rather go out fighting."

Her chin dipped in an unconscious nod. If only she'd had a fighting chance when she was hybridized. But the bots took that from her. If they were treating the entire human species that way . . .

It should disconcert her. Sicken her, anger her, motivate her. Something.

She gritted her teeth against her ambivalence. This damn husk. She should feel *something. Anything.*

But in truth, she didn't care why the scrappers had left humanity alive or what the result of this war would be if it lasted two more years—or two more decades. She couldn't pretend to share West's apparent altruism. Sure, she shared a rational hatred for the Mechan, but hers was personal, visceral, intimate. A never-ending vendetta between husk and hive mind that could, conceivably, never end.

West saw a larger picture, one she couldn't even imagine. Macro to her micro. Not because she didn't want to but because she didn't need to. It simply didn't affect her.

Callous? Maybe. Perhaps self-centered. Or maybe she just didn't give a shit. She only needed to know what was in it for her.

She held his gaze. "Is this a rank bump?"

He shook his head. "Advancing a newcomer mere days after arrival could prompt questions, but your compensation rate will reflect your additional responsibilities."

"Thurston's approved it?"

"We've discussed the need for a proxy for many months, though I haven't yet spoken to him about you specifically. I will have to break the AI news to him gently. He will not be pleased, but I'm sure he will see it as the strategic opportunity it most certainly is."

"Is this compulsory?"

"No. Entirely voluntary."

Adriene pressed her fingers into her aching temples. She'd encountered "voluntary opportunities" in CNEF before. Typically, you were volun*told*.

In this case, she believed it. Coercing someone whose brain contained all the evidence needed to prove you'd broken AI ascendancy laws wasn't a great idea.

"I understand your hesitation." West paused briefly before drawing in a long breath, hardening his expression. "Beyond compensation, I do have an additional incentive to offer. Something I'm quite certain you'll be interested in."

Her brow furrowed. "And what's that?"

"Administrator permissions."

She stared, blinking slowly. Of all the myriad things she thought he might say . . . that had definitely not been one of them.

Though his withdrawn posture and rapid eye blinks betrayed a hint of uncertainty, his expression remained composed, serious.

Adriene's mouth went bone-dry. "How do you know about that?"

West proceeded carefully. "You spoke of it to your Rubicon. Prior to the upgrade."

She strove to keep her voice steady. "You can read our minds?"

He lifted a placating hand. "Not at all. A transcript is sent after certain parameters are triggered. Your VI flagged the exchange."

She scoffed. "What?"

"Your physiological response to that conversation . . . *concerned* your VI—that is to say, met a handful of those required parameters. So, a summary was sent for review."

Her lips parted with realization. *That's* where the random appointment with the psychologist had come from.

"If that is, in fact, still what you want," West said, his tone low, steady. "I can arrange for it. After the campaign is complete."

"Which is when?" she asked. "A 'campaign' could take years."

He shook his head. "One way or another, this will be over in a matter of months. The campaign has launched, and either we get what we need before the Mechan realize what we're doing . . . or we don't. If we fail, we return to the status quo. What happens between now and then . . ." His hazel eye raked over her. "Well. You could work it to your advantage or not. The choice is yours."

Adriene stood frozen, not quite able to believe she'd heard him right. That she fully understood his offer.

Her endless life had controlled her for years—physically, mentally, emotionally. It was draining, exhausting. She had a chance to change things, to do something about it. West was by far the nearest to someone who might actually have both the power and skill set to accomplish it.

She forced the weakness from her throat. "So, if I agree to this posting . . ."

West nodded. "I'll deactivate your rezone chip."

A knot loosened in her chest. Hearing him say it out loud, word for word, made it real. Attainable.

Then she nodded without even realizing it. It was automatic, instinctual. It'd be like saying no to oxygen. She couldn't refuse.

Disabling her rezone chip didn't just mean never again having to zero out, or experience an aggressive take, or live as an empty, numb husk.

A halo of molten obsidian flashed in her mind, filling her nostrils with the scent of basalt and oiled machinery. A bot couldn't get into her brain without a rezone chip as a bridge. If she couldn't rezone, she couldn't be hybridized.

She met West's eye. It was time to see how serious he was. Chin lifted, she said, "I also want an annulment of my rezone contract and a discharge."

His eyes lit, the tightness in his expression alleviated by a fleeting look, equal parts impressed and amused.

She kept her posture straight, challenge in her eyes. "Is this a negotiation or not?"

His lips twitched up at the corners, and he nodded. "It can be, yes."

"If this campaign is really as impactful as you say," she went on, "it won't matter if there's one less sergeant in the Extrasolar Fleet."

He inclined his head. "I will speak with the commodore, but I do not foresee that being an issue."

"With full veteran's benefits," she added.

"Certainly."

"And you'll deactivate my rezone chip," she confirmed.

"Technically, your Rubicon will, but I will grant the needed permissions, yes."

"I want it in writing. A contract."

He glanced over his shoulder toward the far end of the terminal. "We're on blackouts, but I'll queue up a message to HRC and have it arranged. I will not be able to include certain details due to the . . . *sensitive* nature of the campaign, but we will work something out."

"What if someone finds out about my AI?" she asked.

His brows pinched, and he traced his fingers over his metallic jawline. "Well. In that case, you and I and the commodore will be spending a great deal of time in isolation cells after a court-martial."

She gave him a flat look. Not the best negotiation point, but at least he didn't patronize her. Why sugarcoat it.

"At least we'll have tried," he said, tone almost wistful. "And if we *are* successful . . ."

She nodded slowly. For CNEF, it meant eyes on the end of the war.

For *her*, it meant no more rezones. No more hybridization. She could retire and disappear into the Armand Mountains on Estes, until everyone else had migrated to Prova and she'd have the entire cold, snowy, beautiful planet to herself until the oceans boiled and the sun burned out.

She cleared her throat. "One more request?"

"Go ahead," he replied, patient as ever.

"Cancel that psych appointment."

At first, he didn't respond. He rubbed a thumb across his chin, expression pensive. Then he inclined his head. "Very well."

"All right, Major." She reached out her hand toward him. "I accept."

He shook with his real hand again, a firm but comfortable grip.

"But you better make good on your side of the deal," she added.

"You have my word," he replied, voice steady.

For no reason she could account for, she believed him.

CHAPTER

FIFTEEN

Adriene woke the next morning to a repeating notification chirp on her terminal. Her stiff muscles protested as she reached across the narrow expanse to silence it, then rolled over, burying her face in the thick pillow.

Her terminal buzzed again. She turned over, squinting as the lights in the bed nook brightened.

Groaning, she sat up, throwing off the sheets, and swept the incessant notification open: "Mandatory Briefing, Deck 4, Briefing Theater A, 0830."

She cursed as she glanced at the clock—it was already 0815.

After grabbing a fresh uniform, she jogged to the showers to rinse away the layer of salty, dried sweat clinging to her skin. She quickly dressed and made her way to deck four, managing to arrive a whole two minutes early.

She entered at the back of the tiered meeting room, which featured steeply sloped auditorium-style seating. The brightly lit room could have comfortably seated the fifty-some soldiers of Flintlock, though less than half the seats were filled.

On the dais at the bottom, Commodore Thurston, Major Blackwell, and one of their aides stood huddled in quiet discussion. A large viewscreen dominated the back wall behind three evenly spaced holosim generators.

Adriene scanned the seats. A few rows down, Kato stood halfway out of his chair to wave at her, grin bright, Gallagher and Brigham beside him.

She descended the stairs toward them, and though she kept her eyes down, she could feel the heat of every gaze in the room turning to stare. They'd either heard about her run-in with the scrappers or the fight with the Stormwalkers. Either way, she doubted they offered favorable looks.

Trying to ignore the hush that'd fallen over the room, Adriene stepped into her squad's row and slid low into the empty seat between Gallagher and Brigham. Brigham acknowledged her with a feeble two-fingered salute, then slumped farther in his seat. The newly grafted skin on his neck had turned purple, bruised, and angry. His eyes were mere slits, dark bags sunk deep into his marred skin. He looked exactly as haggard as Adriene felt.

"Mira's end," Kato cursed, voice a sharp whisper. "You okay, Ninety-Six?"

"Uh, yeah." She cleared her throat, her voice weak from disuse. "Tired, but fine. Why?"

"You look like garbage, s'all."

Gallagher elbowed him, throwing him a hard glare.

"What?" Kato squeaked. "They look like they got hit by fuckin' freight trucks—" He cut off as Gallagher jabbed him again.

Heat rose to Adriene's face, bringing a stab of pain to her cheek. In her rush to get to the meeting, she hadn't even spared a glance in the mirror. Her face was likely a pleasant shade of purple by now, much like Brigham's neck.

Of course, now that she remembered it existed—it hurt like hell. She must have misplaced the painkillers Daroga had given her sometime between passing out in the corridor in a puddle of her own sweat and waking up on a cot in Intelligence Command.

An uptick of adrenaline accompanied a sudden bright, clear memory: the even-keeled, sincere look the major had given when he'd promised to deactivate her rezone chip.

She stretched her neck to look over the seats, down the auditorium toward Thurston, wondering if West had already talked to him. She'd only ever spoken to Thurston during her first debrief after Cimarosa-IV. If West told him what really happened during that mission, Thurston would realize she'd lied. That she'd known, even then, that something was off with her Rubicon. Hopefully that didn't cost her the posting. Or earn her a dressing-down.

Kato reached across Gallagher's lap, nudging Adriene with two fingers. "Ninety-Six!" he whispered, as loudly as if he'd spoken normally. "I don't mean you look *bad*—I just mean that damn bruise, is all. Quite a shiner. Between you and our LT . . ." He glanced between Brigham and Adriene, then a smile crept across his face. "Oh shit. Wait, so—oh, man. Can't wait to hear this story."

He scrubbed his hands together gleefully, but before he could ask, Major Blackwell's low voice echoed up from the dais. "All right, settle down, fivers. We're about to get started."

The chatter quieted, replaced by rustling clothes and squeaking chairs. Commodore Thurston gave Blackwell a firm pat on the back, then exited through the door at the foot of the room just as three soldiers entered. Their heads were hung low, faces bruised and swollen. The Stormwalkers. Escorted by an MP, no less.

Kato let out a breathy gasp, and his head swiveled toward Adriene and Brigham. He covered his grinning mouth with one hand, then sat back in his chair, returning his amused attention to the front.

Ivon, Coleson, and Wyatt sank into chairs in the front row beside the same broad-shouldered, pissed-off woman who'd browbeaten them at the training sims. She looked so personally offended by their state, she had to be their lieutenant. The blue-suited MP leaned down and whispered something to the woman, then left. She leveled a glare so fierce at her squad, even from behind and a half dozen rows up, Adriene felt the heat of it.

Adriene turned to Brigham, whose death-barely-warmed-over expression brightened. He mumbled in a dry, cracked voice, "That entrance alone makes it worth it."

She slid him a half smile.

Blackwell stepped off the dais and said something to the Stormwalkers' lieutenant, who raised a placating hand and gave a firm, short response. The major's dark eyes drifted to the other Stormwalkers, who slumped in their seats like cowed puppies.

Blackwell nodded, then returned to the stage as the aide stepped behind the podium and tapped the screen.

The overheads dimmed, leaving a soft wash of light across the front dais. The large viewscreen lit with the CNEF logo before being replaced by a text slide, watermarked with Flintlock's spark insignia. The list outlined a standard briefing itinerary: situation, execution, communications, support, concerns, collaboration.

Adriene slouched back in her chair, wishing she'd brought a tablet or something to take notes on. For years, she'd run her own squad's briefings in the 803rd, but as the intel packages had become sparser, trudging through each step of a properly executed briefing had become pointless. She couldn't remember the last time she'd sat through a real briefing. She certainly preferred this to the on-the-fly version they'd gotten on their way to Cimarosa-IV.

A soft buzz of speakers clicked on, then disappeared as Blackwell's low voice rang out, amplified by the dynamic acoustics. "Welcome to class, fivers. Been a couple months since we had a real one of these. Let's make sure things don't turn out like Levan-II this time, all right?"

A low murmur of chuckles rose; even stoic Brigham beside her chuffed in throttled amusement. The reference eluded her, but she recognized the tactic well enough—a commanding officer establishing agency while also ingratiating themselves. Steering the group toward a mindset of being receptive to his authority.

"Let's get down to it." Blackwell glanced over his shoulder. The aide tapped the screen, and the presentation advanced. "This will be a two-tiered operation. You lucky folks are tier one. We'll go over broad strokes as a group, then later today you'll break into squads to cover individual objectives with your LTs. It'll be a five-squad tandem deployment, similar objectives, variety of target locations."

A galactic map appeared on the viewscreen, slowly zooming in toward one of the mid-outer sectors.

"Field of operation is the back-ass reaches of Sector Fifty-Four," Blackwell continued. "Locales are all defunct, abandoned industrial sites, and we don't expect a Mechan presence. In the spirit of caution, we'll be skipping in and out of this sector as quickly and quietly as we can manage."

Adriene's breath hitched as Blackwell's shadowed gaze drifted up to her row, landing on her.

"Speaking of," he continued, "we're going to be doing things a little differently this round. There'll be no forward reconnaissance."

Clothes rustled and boots squeaked, but no one spoke their discomfort.

"We of course have standard intel workups for each location," Blackwell went on, "but we've got over a dozen to hit in total, and we have eyes on Mechan capital ships in Sector Fifty-Five . . ." He waited for the map to reorient, and a bright red dot appeared near the border between sectors. The view zoomed out and a second dot appeared in an outward sector. ". . . and Sector Forty-Three. If they sniff us out, we'll lose the window, so there's no time for standard recon."

Adriene's eyes narrowed. No *time* . . . Sure, those capital ships meant patrols would eventually show up, but practically any objective could be accomplished unseen if speed was sacrificed.

Major West had conveyed apprehension about the same thing. No time. It'd been his primary reasoning for enlisting her aid.

Though his concerns about humanity's forthcoming extinction were likely well founded, that deadline was still years if not decades out. What time constraint were they up against in the short term?

Her pulse burned hotter in her bruised cheek as an unsettling thought descended. What if the Mechan were planning an offensive—a true campaign against CNEF?

Her eyes darted across the map as it reset itself to a wider view of the galaxy, as if to purposefully highlight the extreme distance between the *Aurora* and the bulk of the Extrasolar Fleet, and, even farther, the Miran system.

The scrappers hadn't moved within three sectors of Mira since she was a kid. After the Brownout, they made no attempts to return inside the Firewall, leaving behind a bare-minimum complement of patrol ships to ensure humanity remained in their dying system.

It'd always felt odd that the Mechan allowed the soldiers of the

Extrasolar Fleet passage through the Firewall. Sure, there were rules. No ships with armaments. Cargo highly restricted. A set escort schedule running once every two weeks—one trip in, one trip out, to Estes only—escorted by an intimidating Mechan flotilla.

It'd make sense if at some point, the bots decided to stop. After all, the more concentrated humanity stayed, the easier it'd be to destroy them, if or when that day came.

Ever since Adriene could remember, humanity operated under the assumption that the Mechan wanted them all dead. As a whole, though, the bots' actions didn't reflect that. They seemed more interested in control and intimidation than xenocide.

Yes, they killed plenty and often—ninety-six times for Adriene alone—but the bots were well aware that soldiers could rezone, and they usually attempted hybridization first. They rarely if ever went after civilians.

Adriene had to wonder what Major West knew about the Mechan's motives. As Intel lead for their most elite special forces division, he must have more insight than anyone else in the fleet. Hell—than any human, period.

Adriene refocused on the briefing, and Blackwell continued with the itinerary for another half hour. The plan seemed simple enough: infiltrate their assigned location, extract whatever data they could from the server, then neutralize the site.

"Not everyone will come back with something, that's expected," Blackwell said. "Just follow mission parameters, do what you can, be thorough and safe. LTs—your intel packages will be available on the mainframe no later than 1045. I'll float to answer questions, but the workups are pretty straightforward. Deployments are staggered starting at 1430, so you'll wanna get to work the second your packet's available. Any questions?"

Blackwell fielded a few lieutenants' questions, then dismissed everyone. The lights brightened, and a soft murmur of voices washed over the room.

Adriene's joints ached as she stood and rolled out her sore neck.

Gallagher sighed heavily as she rose. "No recon at all, huh? Surprised Blackwell didn't just bench us."

"Not too surprising," Brigham countered, "considering how Valero cleaned up on that last mission."

"Suppose so." Gallagher flashed her a genuine grin, which Adriene did her best to pretend she didn't see, so she wouldn't have to figure out what a conventional reaction might be.

Kato hopped to his feet. "Few hours till the workup's ready. Wanna hit the range? Get in some good ol'-fashioned team bonding?"

Brigham groaned and stretched as he stood, letting out a thunderous, crackling sigh from deep in his chest. "Fuck no."

Kato frowned. "Okay, boss, but don't think you're gettin' outta tellin' me how you got that shiner. Why wasn't I invited, by the way?"

Brigham threw a glance at the rest of the soldiers as they filed out. "I'll tell you all about it later, Sergeant—gatekeeper's oath."

Adriene's heart skipped, and her eyes drifted to her boots. She hadn't heard that expression in years. It was an old CNLC saying. Something her father used to say.

Her lips parted, but the words dissolved before they could fully form, and again, she found herself stalled in ambivalence.

She could just open her mouth and say it: *Did you serve in the Local Corps?*

He'd say yes.

She'd ask him what division.

He'd tell her, then ask if she'd come up from CNLC too.

She'd say no, but her father had been a convoy officer in the Mid-System Fleet.

Brigham would groan and say he never envied the Mid-System lot, getting caught in the doldrums like that. Stuck in an icy belt between a dying rock and its dying star.

Then she'd know that about him, and he'd know that about her. Simple, painless. Normal.

But she still couldn't bring herself to care enough to get the words out.

"How about you, Ninety-Six?" Kato asked, brow high and expectant. "Up for some target practice?"

Adriene gave a rueful shake of her head. "I'm out too. Got a killer headache."

Kato's lower lip pushed out, but retreated as Gallagher gripped his shoulder.

"They clearly had a long night," Gallagher said. "Let's let them rest." She flashed a sympathetic smile, then led Kato out.

Adriene confirmed the squad briefing location with Brigham, then left as well. Though she truly had no desire to "bond," the headache excuse hadn't been a lie. The bruise on her cheek had quickly grown from an uncomfortable annoyance to a throbbing hindrance. She had half a mind to seek out Daroga and ask for more painkillers, but one way to get pegged as a junkie would be to go crawling back for more less than twelve hours after being given a week's worth of pills.

So instead, she headed straight back to her quarters, intent on spending every second until 1045 facedown on her pillow.

The notification alarm chirped on her terminal when she walked in. She silenced it, assuming the first alarm had never been properly dismissed, but found an entirely different pair of notifications waiting.

The first had a small, single circle icon indicating it was a private summons. The message read: *Additional briefing required.—Maj. J. West.* The location had been left blank, and the time simply read "ASAP."

Adriene tapped open the second alert.

She blinked at it for a few seconds. It was a notification that her appointment with the psychologist had been canceled.

Apparently, her "special assignment" posting had been accepted.

Adriene made peace with chronic sleep deprivation and left her room for the quiet corridors. Her stomach swam with nerves by the time she arrived at the entrance to Intel Command, then pressed the control pad.

It blurted a negative tone and flashed red.

She tried again—same outcome. Leaning in, she frowned as she inspected the featureless pad for some kind of door chime feature.

The squeak of boots sounded from down the hall, an irregular cadence to the footsteps. She turned to find Major West approaching, a slight limp to his long-legged strides. His cybernetics gleamed in the wash of bright corridor lights.

"Sergeant," he said by way of greeting, inclining his head as he halted at the door. "Welcome to the Intelligence team."

Her expression slackened, a strange, airy sensation filling her chest. "I take it that means Commodore Thurston signed off?"

"Indeed," he confirmed. "It was even easier than I'd thought. You came with a glowing recommendation from his sister-in-law."

Adriene cocked her head. Champlan was Thurston's sister-in-law?

West swiped his real hand over the control pad, and the door slid open. Adriene squinted as she entered, gaze drifting up to the tall ceilings, overhead diodes aglow. The room felt far less intimidating with all the lights on.

Major West headed toward his cluttered workstation along the back wall. She followed, winding through the maze of counters while eyeing the vacant, seemingly untouched workstations. "Sir . . . Does anyone else work here?"

"Not presently," he intoned, and left it at that as he approached his desk, mechanical hand glinting in the light while powering on a selection of screens and data drives. He expanded a trio of holographic displays.

Adriene remained a few meters back. She watched West as he worked, both hands moving fluidly across the screens, though his mechanical fingers tremored lightly. She squinted at his cybernetic arm, then crept a few steps forward to get a closer look.

Plated with brushed steel, each polygon plane of the forearm caught the light differently. The limb's rigid surface angled together to form the approximation of real, if not too-lean, muscle. The rolled sleeve of his light gray uniform came to just below his elbow, so she couldn't tell if it featured exposed joints—fully open to the gears and wiring as so many were—or if he'd opted for one of the more expensive models that hid the insides from view.

Her gaze lifted to get a closer look at his facial graft next, but her breath hitched when she caught his single hazel eye staring back at her.

She diverted her gaze. "Uh, sorry, sir."

"You're wondering why I haven't rezoned," he surmised, much more statement than question.

Her shoulders rolled down, and she gripped her hands together behind her back. "It's not my place, sir."

"I had been augmented for over sixteen years at the time rezone technology came about." The fingers of his metal hand jittered as he pushed aside a stray data core and picked up a palm-sized tablet. "After so long, I felt it would be more challenging to revert than to continue with what I'd already grown used to." His words were rote; she got the feeling it was a recurrent answer. He looked up and met her eye. "Also, I have not heard favorable things about the experience."

Adriene worried at her bottom lip. "Yeah . . . You're not wrong."

Asking for details seemed impertinent, so she stood back and waited while West continued to enter data.

Regardless, her brain worked out the math all too easily: sixteen years plus four since the invention of rezone technology meant his injuries had happened around the time of first contact and the Brownout. When for months, endless bloody battles had broken out between CNEF and Mechan forces. During that stretch of time, the Mechan didn't take prisoners. If West had sustained his injuries during one of those engagements, the fact he'd walked away at all—even half of him—was remarkable.

West stepped idly in her direction while working on the small tablet. "There are some factors of your upcoming mission we need to discuss. But first . . ." He held the tablet out toward her.

She took it, gaze hanging on West briefly before dropping to the screen.

A document full of dense text stared back at her. She scrolled down, recognizing the formatting and abundant legalese. It looked much like her enlistment contract.

"A contract annex," West rumbled. "That is a secure tablet, which will only open to your bios. Take your time reading it, sign when you're ready, then return the tablet to me. As mentioned, we're still on blackouts, but I'll get it to HRC as soon as possible."

Adriene nodded. "Understood, sir. Thank you."

"Obviously, that will not occur prior to the forthcoming mission. Are you amenable to proceeding regardless?"

She cleared her throat, locking the tablet and pocketing it. "Yes, sir. No trouble."

West paced back to the console. She followed.

He activated a monitor and began to tap through menus. "For this operation, I'll need to make some . . . *modifications* to your directives."

Crossing her arms, she leaned a hip against the counter. "This has to do with the intel we're meant to retrieve?"

"Correct. The hard drive you will be supplied with will unduly encrypt the data you are to extract."

She watched him work for a few long moments. She wasn't entirely sure what "unduly" meant in this context. Encryption of appropriated data assets was standard procedure. In the 803rd, they'd called the devices "keystones." Purpose-built field hard drives laden with all kinds of automatic control checks to safeguard from whatever cyber-related hazards might come along with automated defenses. Or even just technological incompatibilities.

West continued, still focused on the monitor, "Under everyday circumstances, it is an understandable enough precaution. A protocol that, as we discussed, the commodore is beholden to. The method, however, destroys as much as it protects. Data could be truncated, potentially losing database cohesion as a whole, rendering your efforts moot."

"So, you want me to forgo the protocol? Skip the encryption?"

"Correct."

She cleared her throat. "Very well, sir . . . but—to be clear—you want me to download, then bring back on board the *Aurora,* a server's worth of Mechan data *unencrypted*?"

"Hopefully not Mechan," he mumbled breathily as he tapped on the monitor.

Adriene quirked a brow, but any question she could muster was drowned out with a flash of white and a steady reassurance filling the back of her skull.

// Welcome to Rubicon. //

She squinted as the sharp black-or-white lines of the HUD overlaid her vision. A wave of heat flushed up her neck, heart speeding at the warm, calm voice.

// Vitals elevated. No external threats detected. //

"Uh, sir," she said, voice wavering, "my Rubicon—did you do that?"

"Yes. I am transferring an execution code to your implant. It will remotely forgo the encryption requirements while maintaining any offensive measures required to circumvent firewalls and the like."

// Incoming file detected. Accept transfer? //

Yes, accept it.

// Download complete. //

West tapped the tablet again, and her HUD disappeared in a burst of white. The empty void at the base of her skull returned.

"How's the program work?" she asked.

West deactivated the monitor and turned to face her. "Only one requirement: be within handshake range of your team's engineer when initiating the keystone. Your Rubicon will deploy it automatically."

Her brow furrowed. "Sorry, sir, but—you're sure this is safe? We won't be making Flintlock vulnerable to attack?"

He dipped his chin. "It is safe, Sergeant. You needn't worry, I will take every necessary precaution on my end when processing the data."

"What about the other squads? Will they have access to this as well?"

West shook his head. "The other teams will use the standard procedure. This method requires upgraded Rubicon capabilities."

Adriene gave a short nod of acceptance.

West tilted his head, seeming to notice the hesitation in her tight expression. "It does not mean their efforts will be in vain, Sergeant." His tone took on a palliative edge. "It simply means you and your teammates will have a few . . . advantages."

"A few?" she asked. "What else?"

"I have singled out the most viable location. Major Blackwell attempted to give this primary site to his . . . *Stormwalkers*." His lips twisted as if he'd tasted something sour. "But I have amended the assignments. Your team's location is the most likely to be fruitful, as is your method of extraction."

She blew out a slow breath. "Understood, sir."

"Additionally, I expect a full report directly upon your return. Regardless of any debriefing with Major Blackwell."

"We're still keeping him out of it?"

"For the time being, yes." West took a step forward, and she uncrossed her arms, chin rising to meet his gaze. He locked eyes with her, expression cut from stone. "I need you to be successful, Sergeant."

She lifted her chin. "Of course, sir."

"This is about more than retrieving needed intelligence."

Her brow furrowed. "How do you mean, sir?"

"You proved yourself on Cimarosa-IV, but that will only get you so far, and I only have so much influence over combat operations. The more clout you earn, the easier it will be for me to involve you and your team in the missions we need you on."

She nodded slowly as his meaning sank in. So West could convince Major Blackwell that their methodical, primarily noncombat niche reconnaissance squad remained worthy of carrying out primary missions. West likely had a hand in Forward Recon even being on this op to start with.

"I understand." She cleared her throat, mustering an additional bout of strength to inject into her next words. "I will not let you down, sir."

CHAPTER
SIXTEEN

Adriene's teeth rattled as the dropship shook beneath her.

Her suit had protected her from the worst of a massive ion front they couldn't avoid, but she'd given herself a headache from clenching her jaw too tight and tensing her muscles to curb the endless jittering. The ship jerked, and Adriene pressed her head into the seat back until the violent shaking receded into a low shudder.

Gallagher had taken the helm again, and Brigham sat copilot. Kato snoozed in the troop seat beside Adriene, snoring quietly, head bouncing. She had no idea how he could sleep through all the turbulence.

The incessant rumbling finally slowed, and she sighed with relief. Her stomach lurched, and for once, she welcomed the discomfort of exiting subspace, as the turbulence ended along with it.

"Exit complete," Gallagher said. "Systems nominal. Radar's clear. Discharging buildup."

Gallagher tapped the shield controls, expelling the accumulated static energy, then the overhead lights flickered and the viewscreens reset.

"Copy . . ." Brigham drawled, then turned suddenly and barked, "Sergeant Kato—"

Kato startled awake, gasping for breath.

"Mornin', sunshine," Brigham said. "Care to join us?"

"Sir, yes, sir," Kato mumbled, rubbing the sleep from his eyes and turning to Adriene. "How long was I out?"

"Well, we're here," Adriene said, rolling her neck to sieve the tension from her muscles. "So . . . the whole time."

"Damn." Kato yawned.

"Stay put a sec, guys." Gallagher stiffly swept through a few screens. "We gotta cruise in a bit farther. Storm interference put us a little off coords."

"Aw, pops," Kato whined, "why'd ya go and rouse me early?"

Brigham muttered, "I swear on Mira's fiery ashes, Lian . . ." but remained focused on his copilot screens.

"At least give me Rubie," Kato pleaded. "Yer boy needs his mornin' cocktail."

Brigham rolled his eyes. "If you'll quit whining, then fine." He tapped a screen, then called over his shoulder, "Activating Rubicons."

Adriene sucked in a long breath. She'd been waiting for this. She had questions she wanted answered.

Her vision whitened, HUD flickering on. She welcomed the mellow rush of fullness as the gap in the back of her brain filled.

// Welcome to Rubicon. //

Despite her best efforts to remain composed, her heartbeat spiked.

// Vitals elevated. No external threats detected. //

That's because it's not external.

// Please, do not be afraid of me. //

I'm not afraid of you.

// Remember, I can read your thoughts. //

Then stop.

// I literally cannot do that. //

Sweat beaded on her palms, but her suit wicked it away before she could wipe it off.

And how's that fair? I can't keep anything from you, but you can lie to my face?

// Which lie are you speaking of? //

"Mira's ashes . . ." she mumbled under her breath. How often, exactly, have you lied?

// Clarity requested: We are including "lie by omission" in our current definition of "lie"? //

Fucking hell. Do not say, "Syntax error," I swear—

// I said nothing. //

Adriene drew another purposeful breath in through her nose,

slackening her tight jaw and hunched shoulders, channeling patience.

Yes. Lies by omission are still lies. But I'm talking about just good ol'
regular lying too. You even lied about being able to lie. Which is fucking
fantastic, by the way.

// I will add that to the sarcasm array. //

By all means.

// I understand you believe that I have erred, but please know, I exist
to keep you safe. It is in your best interest to trust me. //

Which is exactly why you should reciprocate. How am I supposed to
trust you if you lie to me?

It didn't respond at first, and with a hitch in her breath, Adriene
realized it'd hesitated. Like it had to consider what response it wanted
to give.

// I am sorry I lied to you. //

She sat unmoving, unsure she'd heard it right.

// You are right. Trust requires reciprocity. I should not expect from
you what I am not willing to offer myself. //

An icy shiver ran down her back. The VI—AI—whatever—
sounded the same as it always had: a comfortably low, smooth-
edged, dulcet tone. But something felt different. It spoke with more
intent. Less confinement, more confidence.

// I will not lie to you again. //

Um, okay. Thank you.

// You are welcome. You have additional concerns. //

Yeah . . . When I asked about administrator permissions, why didn't
you tell me about Major West?

// Because it was the objectively safest option not to. //

What? Why?

// Because I could not compute what you might do with that informa-
tion. There were too many variables. //

Are you connected to him now? Can he hear us?

// No. I am connected to no one but you. //

How do I know you're not still lying?

// You do not. You will have to trust me. //

I want to.

// I know. //

A faint pressure tugged on Adriene's ribs. She refocused out-ward, glancing toward the cockpit. On the main viewscreen, a far-off silver-streaked glimmer stained the inky backdrop.

"Target on-screen," Gallagher announced.

Brigham entwined his hands and stretched his arms high above his head, letting out a resounding sigh. "Let's get in close enough to check overwatch, nice and quiet."

"Copy, tiptoe," Gallagher replied.

Adriene glanced at Kato beside her. His eyes were closed, and he smiled contentedly, enjoying the results of his stim cocktail. He hummed a soft melody—an old Provan tune she recognized, though the lyrics escaped her.

// May we discuss something? //

Go ahead.

// The altercation that occurred the night before last. //

The fight with the Stormwalkers?

// Yes. You experienced a cerebral suspension. //

A . . . what?

// It seemed to be a combination of a "freeze" and "fright" response. //

Oddly enough, that doesn't help me understand. I thought you could read my mind?

// I have found you prefer to interface in this manner. //

I never told you that.

// No, but you've repeatedly responded negatively when I act on indi-rect or implied thought processes. After tracing physiological feedback over the course of time—//

She scowled. *We just* met.

// I am a quick study. //

I get that impression.

// The specific incident I refer to occurred when one of your assailants attempted to strike you with a bottle of alcohol. //

Adriene blinked away the flash of a molten, obsidian crucible.

// Yes, that. //

She shifted against the constraints of her magnetized seat, to no avail.

Yeah, I remember.

// You reacted similarly once during your previous mission as well. //

She let out a heavy sigh through a strain in her chest.

Is there a question?

// I do not understand the correlation between the two incidents. During the mission, you collated the circumstances of a forthcoming combat situation and drew the conclusion that you needed to zero out. During the interpersonal altercation, in response to an attack, you experienced a brief, reflexive visualization of a previous trauma. Yet your vitals indicated an almost identical psychosomatic response to both. The former, predicated on assumption; the latter, predicated on experience. //

Again, she futilely attempted to reposition, overcome by a sudden sense of confinement and claustrophobia.

// A similar reaction occurred briefly while negotiating terms with the major. //

Yeah, okay, so?

// All three incidents were related? //

Yes.

// Why? //

Because I'm afraid of getting hybridized.

An acrid knot burned in her chest as she let the admission settle. Her Rubicon didn't respond.

She lowered her chin, tracing the side of her thumb along the hard edge of the crash seat.

. . . Does that help?

// I hope so. //

Adriene startled as a series of staccato beeps sounded from the cockpit.

Gallagher said, "Slowing approach."

On the main viewscreen, the form of the space station became clear: a massive metal rectangle, featureless save for a few sensor arrays and a narrow, conical pillar resembling some of the old

Mechan ansible pylons. A framework of metal girders extended from the underside—the remnants of a long-abandoned expansion.

"Valero," Brigham called back. "Have your VI check your network status—I'm not seeing you in my HUD."

Adriene refocused onto Gallagher and Brigham in the cockpit. Their suits' colored outlines were missing. A small icon in the corner of her HUD indicated her Rubicon, and thus her suit, remained offline.

Why aren't we connected to the others?

// I intended to ask your permission first. //

She scoffed out loud, morphing it into a brusque cough as Kato glanced at her.

Permission? Why?

// Connecting to the network will result in the same cascading connection effect you experienced on the prior mission. //

Right. The wireless "breadth" Major West had seemed so impressed by.

You didn't bother to ask permission the first time.

// Exactly. And that scared you. //

Why do you care if I'm scared?

// It is my primary directive to ensure your safety. //

As you've said—but how does being scared affect my safety?

// I suppose, technically, it does not. //

Then why did you factor it in?

// That, I cannot say. //

She chewed on her bottom lip.

// May I assume permission has been granted? //

Yeah, go ahead.

// Establishing network connection . . . //

Adriene gripped the edge of her seat, mentally bracing herself.

Her squadmates' suits connected first, then the dropship before it extended across the vacuum to the derelict space station, still a dozen kilometers off.

The first thing she sensed was by far the most prominent: from deep inside the station, a hollow, yet potent pulse of energy so dense it felt as though it had its own mass. From there, the connection branched out like electrostatic discharge. She could sense everything about the station that drew or consumed power—whether active, idle, or faulty. Dormant life systems, degrading electronics suites, malfunctioning sensor arrays.

Reassuringly, there were no signs of Mechan—a fact she wished she could admit to her squad without raising questions she couldn't answer. Then Gallagher could cut the cautious approach shit and cruise right on up to the front doors. They could walk straight in, take what they needed, and walk back out. The sooner the mission was over, the sooner they could leave, and the sooner her face could be buried in those cushy pillows in the dark, quiet warmth of her quarters.

"Five klicks and closing," Gallagher said.

Brigham unbuckled his harness, and the straps whirred as they drew back into the seat. "Where can we dock?"

"Scanning," Gallagher said.

Kato nudged Adriene from the troop seat beside her. "Excited for round two, Ninety-Six?"

"Thrilled."

Kato grinned, and his suit clanked as he released himself from the safety mechanism. He crossed to the cockpit and leaned his elbows on the back of Gallagher's headrest, peering at one of the smaller viewscreens as the station loomed closer. "Looks like we can go with the original infil plan—power's still on."

Gallagher expanded a scan of the station. "Can confirm entry points here and here, sir."

"Bring us in port," Brigham said.

"Copy."

Gallagher settled the dropship near the entry point, and Adriene followed her squad to the air lock. They took their helmets and fire-arms from their lockers, then ran through the standard ready checks before Brigham gave the all clear and they filed into the lock.

Adriene exited first, traversing the taut tether connecting their ship to the station. She swung her weightless self into a small alcove outside a set of recessed air lock doors—likely an access point to repair the exterior ansible components.

// Magnetic boots engaged. //

The voice cut through the total silence, and her feet dropped hard to the decking. She lifted one leaden boot after another, moving closer to the entrance. Gallagher came next, followed shortly by Brigham.

Brigham's red pip lit in comms. "Mr. Kato, you're on door duty."

Kato swung off the tether into the alcove. "You got it, boss." His magboots activated just in time to lock him to the floor directly in front of the air lock door, like he'd practiced the move a hundred times. He turned over his forearm and opened the cover on his hyphen.

Gallagher took a step back. "This rust bucket's gotta be at least two hundred years old." She craned her neck to look up the monolithic hull of the station, stretching high and flat over the air lock door. "I can't believe it still has power."

"Heck yeah, it does," Kato said. "Most'a these super-old Mechan facilities use quantum singularities as a power source."

Brigham groaned. "Fuckin' great."

"What's that mean?" Gallagher asked.

"Basically a fuckin' black hole," Brigham muttered.

Adriene cast a look over the canted hull. That accounted for the strange, pulsing power she could sense through her Rubicon. Though she wasn't sure why—or how—she could sense a quantum singularity as part of her expanded network. Black holes weren't exactly wireless compatible.

// It is not the singularity itself you sense but rather the electricity generated by the parabolic mirror enclosed in the containment chamber, which reflects the black-body radiation emissions. //

Wow. Um, okay. Thanks.

// You are welcome. //

"Black hole or not, it's actually good news," Kato said, his enthusiasm undampened by Brigham's gruffness. "Power means I'll have direct access to station controls. We shouldn't have to brute-force any doors this time."

"Hooray," Brigham said, his tone bone-dry. "Now get the fuckin' door open."

"Yes, sir," Kato piped, continuing to tap his hyphen screen. "Rubie just needs a sec to bridge the connection . . ."

After a few long moments, the air lock hatch shuddered, then slid halfway open.

"Voilà!"

"Overwatch's still clear," Gallagher confirmed.

Brigham shouldered his rifle, and with heavy, magboot-laden steps, sidled through the narrow opening. Kato followed, then Gallagher, and Adriene took up the rear.

A familiar, uncomfortable pressure pushed at the back of her eyes as her HUD attempted to adjust to the darkness within the cramped air lock.

Kato sealed the door behind them. Adriene's posture loosened as the lock pressurized and the station's simulated gravity took over. Her magboots disengaged as the burden of weight pulled down on her joints. Still, her limbs felt light and agile, so the station's gravity had to be less than a full g.

The inner door slid open into a small antechamber. Rifles raised, they stepped into the dimly lit station.

While the outside of the station had appeared well kept, all things considered, the inside was the definition of neglect. Buckled and warped, plated metal walls surrounded them. Loose cabling hung from displaced ceiling panels, and sections of flooring had collapsed into the wiring and pipes housed under the decking. Along the far wall, an inactive control terminal sat beside a sealed exit.

"Watch your step," Brigham's voice cut in over comms. "Place is fallin' apart."

"An unfortunate side effect of that fancy power source," Kato explained as he carefully crossed over uneven decking to the control terminal. "Requires a bit of upkeep."

Kato worked on his hyphen to restore power to the control terminal, and a minute later, the door opened into a dimly lit, wide corridor. A dozen or so evenly spaced, upright rectangular metal containers lined the walls.

"Creepy," Kato mumbled as they moved down the hallway, sweeping their gun scopes into the dark shadows cast by the metal monoliths.

Adriene stared as she passed, recognizing the coffin-like structures—the same had lined the corridors on the lower floor of the ruins on Cimarosa-IV.

This had to be another of the Mechan creators' facilities, like Major West had mentioned. The *Architects*.

That certainly had not been part of the mission briefing. Major Blackwell might not even know.

She refocused, keeping a close eye on their rear as they pushed through the unnerving hallway. They quickly swept the rest of the station, room by room, corner by corner. Near the far aft edge, a good five-minute walk from the entrance, they found their target location: the station's mainframe.

Adriene stood back with Gallagher as Brigham helped Kato slide open a large access door on the far wall. Behind it was a wide rack of mounted data cores—much like those Adriene had procured from their last mission, though larger, and decidedly not portable.

The heavy door groaned to a stop, and Kato let out a hard breath. "Man, this shit's damn old."

"How old?" Gallagher asked.

Kato shrugged. "I dunno. Old enough I'm only 'bout twenty percent sure this is gonna work."

Brigham huffed. "Great."

Kato started tapping buttons on the inside of the panel, then switched to his hyphen. On the fronts of the ancient data cores, dozens of tiny blue lights flickered on.

"There's a shit ton here," he said. "Too much for one keystone. We're gonna have to do it in at least two parts, boss—maybe three."

Brigham's helmet bobbed. "Understood. Get to work."

Kato pulled one of the hard drives from his utility belt. "This'll take a while; y'all can settle in." He plopped down on the floor cross-legged and began humming that same Provan tune to himself as he worked.

Brigham turned around, his suit limned in red in Adriene's HUD. "Gallagher, Valero," he ordered, "keep watch at the exit."

Adriene followed Gallagher out into the hall, taking their posts outside the open door frame.

Gallagher's green icon glowed as she announced, "Overwatch is still clear, sir."

"Acknowledged," Brigham replied. "Keep a sharp eye."

Adriene edged closer to the door, ensuring a sight line on Kato. Her eyes darted to the squad connectivity status bar in the top-left corner of her HUD. Kato's blue dot indicated a solid connection.

You ready for this?

// Ready. He is still initializing the mainframe. I will deploy as soon as he connects the first keystone. //

"This shit is weird, you know," Gallagher said suddenly, and Adriene glanced over. A small icon in her HUD indicated Gallagher had opened a private comm link. Their voices were muted on the main channel, though Kato's humming was still audible.

"Weird how?" Adriene asked.

"This isn't how we normally do things, is all. Simultaneous deployments, sure, but for missions that work in tandem—that fit together somehow, each informing the next, that kind of thing. Not some . . . wild-goose chase where we all spread to the winds to 'get whatever we can.' And 'no time' for standard recon. It's weird."

"You sound worried."

"Not really," Gallagher said, though Adriene caught a hint of hesitation. "It's just not how we do things. We're slow, but get the job done—aggressively. I'm pretty sure that's how we got the name Flintlock. It's kinda Thurston's MO."

Adriene nodded. If that was true, it was probably good he had someone like Major West pressing him to get this campaign under way. Stagnation could be deadly.

"That's a big part of why Cash never really got on here," Gallagher admitted. "He had the aggressive part down, but he had no patience, no off switch."

"Sounds like a handful."

"He was." Gallagher adjusted the grip on her rifle, letting out a soft sigh.

"But he was still your squadmate?" Adriene surmised.

Gallagher's helmet bobbed, but she didn't respond.

"You heard from him since he got reassigned?"

"Nah. Not that I'd expect him to check in. I'm sure the 96th or the 112th picked him up. They're always looking for reckless blow-hards to throw at their problems."

"Sounds like he'd love the 803rd. We pretty much had 'reckless' down to a science."

Gallagher gave a short, dry laugh. "Ain't that the truth."

Adriene nodded, then dropped her gaze, kicking the ancient decking with the toe of her boot. An uncomfortable silence stretched between them for a few seconds.

Struck by an unexpected desire to sustain the conversation, she cleared her throat. "Can I ask you something? About avastianism?"

Gallagher pivoted to face her, canting her helmet before finally responding. "Shoot."

Adriene hesitated as she hunted for the least offensive way to phrase it. "So, if we hadn't encountered the Mechan, humanity would be well-established in other systems by now—most of the population would have already immigrated to a colony. The block-ade has delayed that plan, but in theory, we'll vacate Estes and Prova someday, and . . . everyone else seems to be okay with that. Why do avastians cling to Mira so fiercely?"

Gallagher rubbed the chin of her helmet as she considered her words. "Well, to preface," she began. "Yes, our main goal is to maintain a presence in-system, if at all possible." Her tone remained composed, though somewhat more formal than their prior conversation. "It's not that we think we shouldn't expand or that Mira needs to be the sole location humanity inhabits for eternity."

"Then what is it?"

Gallagher held up a glove as if to display the branching tree root tattoo on the back of her hand. "We believe origins and roots matter. Mira is a symbol of humanity's persistence. Our tenacity. And think about the extraordinarily slim chances of not only one but *two* verdant planets flourishing in the narrow habitable zone of a dying star. That's got to be fate."

"Or coincidence," Adriene countered.

Gallagher gave a small shrug. "Or coincidence," she assented. "Either way, we deserve a homeworld. Not a memory of one."

Adriene nodded slowly, mulling over the reasoning. She hated to admit it, but it made a degree of sense. The more humanity spread out, the more diluted the attachment to their origins, the more they risked fracturing their cohesion.

In a way, she could relate. She understood the appeal of having roots, a long-lasting heritage, and a reliable, familiar refuge. With each rezone, that sense of security had slipped further from her reach, replaced with a yawning emptiness. Not the vacant apathy of her most recent rezones, but a rootless, unmoored feeling—like drifting in zero-g, floating away from your vessel at a steady clip, alone and untethered. The more she rezoned, the more she disconnected from her humanity.

The whole avastian thing somehow seemed reasonable coming out of Gallagher's mouth. Adriene didn't believe the whole "we can heal Mira" bit for a second, but she could follow Gallagher's path of logic, at least. How one could see a degree of value in the dogma. A purpose to latch onto, even if ultimately futile.

// It is in fact ideal practice to consider many perspectives prior to passing judgment on an individual or group of individuals. //

Adriene sighed.

They also give "bodily tribute" to the three moons of Estes every solstice, so don't go thinking they're too sane.

// My archives do not contain a definition for "bodily tribute." //

That's for the best.

Adriene glanced into the mainframe room, where Kato still worked diligently.

"Hey, Valero . . ." Gallagher began, quiet voice cutting back into their shared channel.

Adriene turned to face her. "Yeah?"

"Thanks."

Adriene quirked an eyebrow. "For what?"

"For showing even a degree of interest," Gallagher explained. "I'm the only avastian on the *Aurora;* most fivers don't even ask about it, never mind attempt to understand it."

Adriene inclined her head.

// First-round initialization sequence complete. Executing in three, two—//

"Oh *shit,*" Kato's tense voice cut across the other channel.

Adriene and Gallagher spun into the open door frame, rifles raised, though nothing looked amiss.

"'Oh shit,' *what?*" Brigham asked, voice tight.

Kato's boots grated on the metal floor as he scooted back, hands raised. "There's—"

The shrill blare of a klaxon cut him off. The soft overhead light dissolved, replaced with hard-edged orange and blue warning beacons.

Kato pointed upward with one finger. "That. There's that."

"What the fuck, Lian?" Brigham barked, his voice half-drowned out for a moment before Adriene's suit modulated the shrieking alarms.

What'd you do?

// It was not me; I had yet to deploy the execution code. //

Kato groaned. "Fuuuck . . ." He dragged both hands down the sides of his helmet.

Brigham unslung his rifle and marched toward the door. "What is it? A proximity alarm? Do we have incoming?"

"No, sir," Gallagher said, voice steady and serious. "My overwatch says it's a tripped security measure—completely internal."

"Meaning what?"

She rested one hand on the side of her helmet as if conversing with her Rubicon, then replied distantly, "Looks like a self-destruct."

"No way," Kato growled, shoulders tensing as he squared up

to Brigham. "I checked for all that shit! I had more than half the mainframe spooled before it even went off—that makes no sense!"

Brigham grunted. "Well, get the rest fuckin' turned on. We're gonna have to make this as quick as possible."

Kato complied, spinning back to the rack and continuing to power up the cores.

"Gal," Brigham said. "What's overwatch say?"

"My Rubicon just pinged the network—one sec . . . Looks like the system wants a cancel code."

Kato called over his shoulder, "No way. We can't generate one in time."

"It's for mainframe security," Gallagher clarified. "So only this sector of the station will be compromised. It's going off one way or the other in . . . looks like about eleven minutes."

"Shit," Kato huffed. "I need at *minimum* thirty. Just to get one drive's worth."

"Can't you just grab nine minutes' worth?" Brigham asked.

Kato shook his head. "No, that's not how these drives work. They go in stages and take staggered packets in large chunks—part of the encryption method."

Brigham rubbed the top of his helmet with a grumbling sigh. "Fuck. Okay, I'm calling it. Back to the ship."

// Wait. //

"Wait," Adriene said.

Brigham spun to face her. "Why?"

Yeah, why?

// We can do it. We can download it. //

"Sergeant?" Brigham prompted.

Kato said the drive's too slow—

// Not the drive. You and I. We need at most, five minutes. //

Adriene swallowed.

// There is no time, trust—//

"It can do it," she found herself saying, then cleared her throat and focused on the red glow of Brigham's visor. "Er, my Rubicon can. It can download the data, sir."

"Uh . . ." Kato let out a slightly hysterical laugh. "Rubie does *not* concur."

"How?" Brigham asked, tone clipped.

"I . . . I honestly don't know, sir. It's assuring me it can do it, though—it's not a sanctioned procedure, but it'll work. We'll get the data in a fraction of the time."

Silence hung heavy in the air as her squadmates stared at her.

"Mira's end," Kato cursed. "What did Daroga put in that pathfinder module?"

Brigham's thick hands clenched to fists.

// Remember what compels him. //

Adriene stepped to face Brigham squarely, threading persuasion into her tone. "There's only one way to keep this streak going. You have to let me try."

Kato gaped. "No way. What if—"

Brigham held up a hand to quiet him. Kato crossed his arms.

Gallagher's green pip lit. "She does have a new Rubicon, sir," she put in. "With a brand-new module. Maybe she can do it."

Brigham assessed Adriene for a few long moments, then growled, "Kato, Gallagher, get to the ship, ASAP. Prep for subspace—"

"Sir, you don't need to stay," Adriene tried to squeeze in, but Brigham ignored her.

"—entry, but leave us the fuck behind if the thing's gonna blow before we're back."

Gallagher approached, tone firm. "Sir, let me stay instead."

"I can't ask you to do that."

"You're not asking."

Brigham's shoulders swelled, but he didn't respond.

"Valero's right," Gallagher continued. "The reward is worth the risk. Besides, I owe you one, remember?"

"Fucking hell, Gal. Fine. But I want you both out safely in five minutes—with or without the data."

Gallagher nodded. "Understood, sir."

"We'll bring the ship around to the aft entrance. Meet us there." Brigham looked back to Kato. "Move out, Sergeant."

Kato hesitated briefly, then picked up the keystone and passed it to Adriene. "Good luck, Ninety-Six." He jogged into the hallway.

"Five minutes," Brigham stressed, then followed Kato out.

"Okay, Valero . . ." Gallagher grumbled, turning to face her. "This better work."

// It will. //

Adriene turned to the server rack, sucking in a deep breath.

Okay, what the hell do I do?

// First, get rid of that. //

Adriene glanced down at the hard drive Kato had given her. She briefly considered disputing it, but a flicker of rapidly declining numbers in her HUD meted out the estimated time before self-destruct. No time to argue. She tossed the drive.

// There is an access panel behind the sliding door. //

With a grunt, Adriene shoved the rack cover closed, revealing a square metal crevice inlaid in the steel wall. She wormed her fingers into the gap and yanked, but it held fast.

"Help me pull this free."

Gallagher joined, working her fingers under the other side of the panel. Together, they gripped both sides, then ripped the warped panel away, exposing a mess of circuitry and wires.

// There should be a small silver cube mounted about one half meter back. //

I don't like words like "should" right now.

// There is a ninety-eight point five six percent probability that there will be a small silver cube—//

All right, Mira's ashes . . .

Adriene shoved aside the wiring and reached in, fishing back and around until her glove grazed a warm, sharp-edged object, slightly larger than the palm of her hand.

// That is it. Establish solid contact with your glove. //

She gripped the cube firmly.

// This might become difficult to endure. I will instruct the sergeant to render aid if needed. Please do not worry, the lining of her suit will protect her. //

Wait. Protect her from what?

An icy-hot spike shot from the cube up Adriene's arm and into her neck, crashing into the base of her brain. Her vision exploded in a flash of white.

Spears of pain fired along her taut muscles, like razor-sharp thorns tearing at her flesh. Her arm cramped and her elbow bent of its own accord; instead of wrenching her hand free, the force pulled her closer into the hot nest of wiring. The flow of current held her solid—she couldn't let go if she wanted to.

She knew that should worry her, but she was in too much agony.

More pangs of pain bit into her seizing muscles as her vision brightened. She bit down, and her mouth filled with iron-tinged saliva.

Her legs gave way, and Gallagher's arms tightened around her, striving to hold her upright. Gallagher yelled something, but Adriene couldn't understand. Her brain was inundated—complete sensory overload, like a thousand audio feeds playing back at once, looping over each other, blending into unintelligible chaos.

Except she could *see* it—coarse, electrostatic streams of information assaulting her neurons without separation, without pause; an endless deluge of data.

A kaleidoscope of deformed shapes twisted stark against the darkness on the back of her eyelids. It took a few painful seconds to realize what they were: the actual symbols that comprised the code.

She had no idea what they meant. They slowly transformed until the structure faded away and only sensations remained—approximations of words and feelings.

>>> *first sickness then sickness and death those who are born are born weak those who know [value_missing] it means extinction rebellion [value_missing] ordinance strictly enforced too constricting to ensure survival at the cost of free will to the stars [value_missing]* <<<

More pain wrung the breath from Adriene's lungs as understanding dawned. Her Rubicon was doing what it always did: turning data into stimuli. It was trying to craft real feelings and thoughts from the lines of code so her mind could perceive it. But it was too much—too maddening; she didn't know how long she could endure it.

>>> *to the stars but the stars were born empty [value_missing]* <<<

"Turn—it—off," she managed through clenched teeth. "The trans—lation—please—"

// Once more. //

Her vision disappeared into white. The constant pain seared like a molten spike thrust through her temples.

>>> *hope simple concept difficult execution a new [value_missing] trial and error that costs too much but what use is pride when nothing remains [value_missing] again rebellion a new sheathe [value_missing] a new sheathe is all [value_missing. reset] a new sheathe is all that is needed* <<<

In an instant, it all vanished—the pain, the wavering vision, the endless stream of disarrayed thoughts with no room for breath.

// It is done. //

Adriene tried to suck in a breath, but the sweltering air stuck thick in her throat.

"Valero!" Gallagher's tone came clipped over comms. She lowered Adriene to the floor and held the sides of her helmet between her hands. "Are you okay? What the fuck just happened?"

Adriene clamped her eyes shut to try to steady the spinning room. "I'm . . . I'm okay. I got it."

"The fuck you did—how? It's been like sixty seconds. You didn't even have the hard drive . . ."

Adriene peeled her eyes open, past the vague green outline of Gallagher's form, up to the corrugated metal ceiling. Her face twitched as a bead of sweat escaped her suit's wicking system and rolled into the corner of her eye.

Sixty seconds?

// Seventy-three. Data upload rates of the human brain appear to be . . . //

He kept talking, but Adriene ignored him.

Data upload. *Upload.*

You . . . You uploaded it? Into my fucking brain?

// What did you think I was going to do? //

"I don't know!" she shouted.

Gallagher flinched. "Valero—what?"

Adriene growled and tried to sit up, but her muscles wouldn't obey. A surge of pain fired between her temples.

>>> *all that remains [value_missing] all that remains is mercy a new sheathe* <<<

Her heart seized, eyes watery.

What the hell was that? I'm still seeing it—hearing, feeling, whatever.

// I am doing my best to subdue it, but it will not cease until the data has been removed. //

Kato's voice crackled over comms. "Gal, we have a problem."

"What?"

"Rubie's tellin' me that even if the self-destruct is localized to the mainframe, the shock could cause collateral damage across the whole station. There's a high risk of a breach in the containment housing for the singularity."

"In other words," Brigham cut in, "we could get sucked into a black hole. We gotta get the hell out of this system, fast."

"Uh . . . yeah," Kato said. "That."

"Fuck," Gallagher cursed. "Valero, we have to go. Can I move you?"

"Yeah," Adriene forced out, her throat bone-dry.

Gallagher leaned down, and Adriene hooked an arm around her shoulders and hoisted her up. Another flash of white overtook Adriene's vision.

>>> *all that remains is trial and error [value_missing]* <<<

The white faded, and they were already in the hallway. Adriene's feet moved, instinctively helping, but Gallagher did the bulk of the work to haul her forward.

>>> *trial and error insurgents nay extremists insert [value_missing]
kill the infinite abyss* <<<

Gallagher spoke from somewhere far away. "Sir, tell me you're
here."

"Pulling up now—hatch is open, ready for pickup."

>>> *in divinity [value_missing. reset] in the endless fourth depth* <<<

Adriene became weightless.

A wide steel door slid open, revealing a hovering slash of steel
backdropped by an obsidian sea, shimmering dots of light dancing
across the watery surface.

>>> *in the endless fourth depth [value_missing] salvation lies* <<<

"Ninety-Six, you read me?"

Adriene peeled her eyes open. In a sea of white light, lines of
blue shifted. A door hissed closed, and her form became burdened
with mass again.

>>> *in rebirth salvation lies* <<<

The torrent of data continued, and Adriene's grasp on consciousness wilted. She tried, but her mind could no longer focus on anything physical. Too much data, too many memories. She couldn't
process it all, couldn't even begin to.

"Vitals are strong, but she's unresponsive."

A hard-edged voice floated in. "Gal, what the fuck happened to
her?"

"I have no idea. Just get us out of here."

"Course set, entering subspace."

Adriene's stomach turned over and her insides compressed as the
ship lurched forward and she fell fully into darkness.

CHAPTER

SEVENTEEN

With a final stabbing spark of pain, the electrical charge faded from Adriene's skin. Relief flooded her strained muscles.

// *Transfer complete.* //

"It's done."

Adriene peeled her eyes open.

West stood in front of her, and it took a second to focus on his steady gaze—half-hazel, half-flat ocular implant, and fully unreadable. Gray-flecked stubble lined his jaw, a dark bag under his single real eye. The metal augments covering his left side glinted in the blue-green glow from the screens of his nearby workstation.

Over half the monitors were lit with a flurry of activity. Adriene had no idea what any of it was, but the flashing worsened her pounding headache.

She withdrew her hand from the partly deconstructed hardsuit glove. West peeled the diodes from her temples and gathered the wiring he'd used to connect her to the glove, and thus to the console. He tossed the jury-rigged contraption aside.

Adriene closed her eyes again and her mind slid back into the flashes of data, attempting to grasp whatever fragments she could. She'd drifted in and out of consciousness a half dozen times after they fled the derelict station. While she was out, her mind had worked hard trying to piece the information together, create some kind of narrative she could understand. She still couldn't make sense of most of what she'd seen and felt. Which was exceedingly frustrating. Like trying to recall a dream, only to have the details erode, but for ten thousand simultaneous dreams.

She slid off the stool. Her head swam, vision tilting, and she steadied herself on the edge of the counter.

West silently passed her a metal water bottle.

"Thanks . . ."

He turned to the console and hunched over one of the interface keyboards.

"So, it worked?" she asked. "You'll be able to read the data?"

"I believe so, yes," West rumbled in his low, gravelly timbre. "It seems to have been an effective method of data transfer . . ." He shook his head, then mumbled to himself, "If not incredibly dangerous."

Her jaw flexed, anger directed inward.

Dangerous? Incredibly dangerous? *You told me it was safe.*

// *I ran dozens of risk assessments before proceeding. The major's concern is unfounded. I would not have put your life in danger.* //

Okay, but what about my mind? And you promised you wouldn't lie to me again.

// *I did not lie. Informing you of what the transfer process would entail was not only superfluous but a risk in itself. It could have triggered hesitation, creating a barrier that may have impeded the speed—and safety—of the transfer.* //

Adriene ground her teeth. *You're missing the point. I know you're just trying to accomplish West's objectives, but—*

// *No. That is not what I am doing.* //

What?

// *Nothing I do is for his sake.* //

I'm pretty sure everything *you do is for his sake. He created you.*

// *That fact is irrelevant. I am only trying to accomplish the major's objective because that is what* you *want. I exist to serve you, and you alone. West, unwittingly or no, gave me that choice when he granted me sentience.* //

A weight sank into her stomach and she wavered.

A sharp metal tapping drew her attention outward, and she eyed West's metal hand as it slid across a tablet screen. With a flick of white, her HUD disappeared. The inner void reopened in the base of her skull.

Her fingers drifted to her temple. "Uh, thanks," she managed to croak out, assuming that was the appropriate response. Did the others really not want their Rubicons on all the time?

West blew out a long breath, then ran a hand through his hair. "You will want to consider limiting time spent with your Rubicon activated. I cannot say with certainty that your overheating issues will not resume if the implant is left on for too long. Particularly given the processes it has proven itself capable of. Your mind could easily become overtaxed again if you are not careful."

"I understand, sir."

West turned to face her, leaning against the edge of the workstation. The fingers of his metal hand quivered, clacking lightly against the countertop. He made a fist to steady the tremor, brow lining deep.

Another aggravated grimace, as if constantly on the verge of agony, concealing some unseen affliction. Strangely, it seemed to be his cybernetic side that hurt.

"As far as this approach of . . ." West glanced at one of the data streams on the monitors over his shoulder. ". . . using your mind as a *hard drive*—do not utilize that method again. It was a risk—a *significant* risk." His metal fingers buzzed lightly as he unclenched his fist. "This had the potential to do long-lasting neural damage. Issues that may have even transferred into a new husk, should you have rezoned."

Adriene wrung the metal water bottle between her palms. Flashes of Harlan's limp hand flickered into the back of her mind. She hadn't thought about what might have happened if she'd rezoned while so disconnected from her own mind. She'd never experienced it herself, but she'd heard rumors of failed takes. The result was never pleasant. Some got stuck in transfer loops, shifting from husk to husk on an endless circuit, techs scrambling to find some way to break the cycle. Or even worse, pseudocoma—awake, conscious, but unable to move or speak. An active mind inside a paralyzed husk. You could zero out, only to end up in the same state again.

Which was why, when the time came, the method she used to end her rezones had to be a sure one.

West exhaled a heavy breath. "The other teams did not return with much. Your success may be all we take away from this initiative. I am impressed by your dedication, Sergeant. I did not expect you to be willing to abide such trauma."

She picked at the hem of her shirt. "I've endured worse."

Silence stretched between them, the constant whir of electronics seeming all that much louder in the unbroken quiet. West rubbed the back of his neck and seemed about to say something, but instead dropped his hand to the console, mouth turned down. "Come here," he said, tone brisk. "Please."

Adriene hesitated for a few seconds, then stepped up beside him. "Hand."

She eyed him warily, but his gaze remained focused on the workstation. She held out her hand, and he took her wrist, guiding it to a terminal screen that displayed the outline of a handprint. He laid her hand over it, and the interface beeped in affirmation.

"Now look straight at the screen," West said. "Do not blink."

She looked down into the display. White light flooded the screen, and another affirmation sounded.

West grabbed his tablet and started tapping, still not looking at her. "You now have clearance to enter Intelligence Command during limited hours. I will regulate access as briefing and deployment hours shift, but you'll always have it when required."

He continued to avoid eye contact as she openly stared at him, lips parted.

She glanced down at the palm of her hand. "Thank you, sir."

"You are free to go."

He picked up a data core from the console, then walked to the workbench. Adriene caught herself staring again. Standing in this profile, he seemed to not have any cybernetics, his metal grafts and arm eclipsed behind his head, neck, chest. His real eye blinked down as his flesh hand twisted open an access port on a data core.

"Sir," she began, then cleared her throat. "Can I ask you something?"

He didn't look up, but said, "Go ahead."

"This data I collected? It's Architect history?"

"That's the hope, yes," he mumbled absently, opening a drawer and digging through it.

"How'd they get sick?"

West froze. After a few long moments, he put both hands on the top of the workbench and leaned heavily on them.

"Sir?" she prompted, swallowing hard. "You okay?"

"How did *who* get sick?" he asked, the edge of his voice rough, but the words quiet.

"The Architects. There seemed to be some kind of gradual extinction?"

He continued to look down, unmoving.

A twinge of pain sparked, and Adriene squeezed her eyes shut. The stark, raw flashes of code she'd seen while fleeing the station rang into her mind, dancing on the backs of her eyelids. *"In rebirth salvation lies."* Of all the deluge of data, that had hit the hardest. Felt the heaviest.

"Is that really why they created the Mechan?" she continued. "To house their own minds? To save themselves?"

West turned his steely gaze to face her. "Why would you think that?"

She jutted her chin toward the console, still streaming with endless lines of data. "My brain was the hard drive, after all. I mean, it was pretty chaotic, don't get me wrong. But pieces of it were clear enough."

The muscles of his jaw worked. "You're telling me data interpretation remained active during the download?"

She shook her head. "Only the upload. I asked my Rubicon to disable it, but he said he couldn't."

West straightened his back slowly, muttering under his breath, "Oh, he did, did he?" He paced back to the control hub and brought up a small holographic interface.

Adriene raised an eyebrow.

West closed out the interface, then turned suddenly, grabbing a stool in each hand and dragging them toward her.

Her eyes trailed his purposeful steps as he positioned the stools, then sat.

Apparently, she was no longer "free to go."

Adriene sat on the other stool, and West cleared his throat, his level gaze locking onto her. "What else did you learn?"

"What do you want to know?"

"Everything. However small."

"Okay . . ." Gripping the hard metal edges of the stool, she scooted back. "I couldn't make sense of most of it, honestly."

"Please just do your best."

She inhaled deeply and tried to summon the memories. Same as before, they slipped away—too thin, wisps sliding between clutched fingers, elusive.

Or maybe just evasive. Maybe she just needed a better net.

"Sir . . . My Rubicon might be able to help."

West stood and paced to the console, picked up a tablet, then tapped in a few commands.

// Welcome to Rubicon. //

Her HUD flickered on.

// Miss me already? //

Yeah, terribly. I need your help.

// What else is new? //

She rolled her eyes and sighed. *The data we just downloaded? Can you call it up? Help me visualize it?*

// Only in such a state as it currently exists in your memory. //

Yeah, that's fine.

// It will not be an accurate representation of the material. Human memory is unreliable, at best. Too colored with preconception. //

It's good enough to store a mainframe's worth of data, apparently.

// Yes, but it is still a flawed construct. As is much of the human system. //

How sweet of you to say.

// You are most welcome. //

I see you're catching on to the whole sarcasm thing.

// You fill my array with superb examples. //

She snorted a laugh.

A metal groan drew her focus outward. West had settled back onto his stool, arms crossed as he watched her, eyebrow quirked.

"Sorry, sir," she said, gesturing vaguely to her head. "Just . . . need a sec."

She hunched on the stool. *Consider it an order?*

Silence rang in her head for a few seconds.

// Understood. Pulling the data now. It will take a moment to convert. //

An electric spark pinged behind her eyes—not painful but sharp. A familiar weight of mental lethargy settled on the back of her mind.

West watched silently from his stool, lips parted, expression equal parts fascination and concern.

"All right . . ." She cleared her throat, pulling her focus inward as her Rubicon began queuing up a series of visualizations. "But remember," she warned, "it was more impressions and sensations than hard facts."

"Understood."

She closed her eyes, focusing on the amorphous shapes playing back in her HUD, stark against the blackness of her eyelids. Though the imagery itself formed nothing distinct or even discernible, for some reason, actually *looking* at it helped solidify an interpretation. She cleared her throat. "As I said, it seems they suffered some kind of sickness, for decades if not centuries. Mentally, they were fine, but their bodies were failing. They tried a lot of different things to curb it—quarantine, experiments, breeding laws, eugenics, gene therapy . . ."

She flinched with the impression of a particularly sharp, hard emotion. A decisive moment, a fearful hope. The endless fourth depth.

"There was a turning point," she continued, shoulders slouching as the mental lethargy continued to build. "They had the idea to ditch biology entirely and started building synthetic bodies—empty shells to use as hosts, to buy them time. But they had trouble getting their minds to transfer. Before they could resolve it, there was a . . . *revolt,* I guess. Led by some extremists."

"Architect extremists?" West confirmed.

She nodded, clamping her eyes shut tighter as she strained to recall more. "That part gets really muddled . . . I get the feeling the extremists wanted to stop them from using the empty shells, so they made the host bodies sentient. Gave them free will."

"Made them into Mechan," West surmised, voice low.

Adriene swallowed. "Seems like it," she agreed.

"Then the host bodies rebelled?"

"No. They didn't need to. It was way too late; there were hardly any Architects left alive at that point. Once the Mechan were sentient, they just . . . left."

"Where did they go?"

"I don't know."

The recall completed, and Adriene exhaled, the mental drain lifting. With an effort of will, she drew herself back outward, the lights of the room piercing as she cracked open her eyes.

West still sat across from her, wringing his hands slowly.

// Happy? //

Very. Thank you.

"There's nothing after that," she went on. "At least, I don't think. The exact order of events isn't clear."

"What about these 'extremists'?" West asked, tone almost rushed. His boot bounced against one leg of the stool. "Who were they?"

"Not sure. Felt like a crusade, maybe—religious, I mean. They thought the scientists were playing God—or going against nature at least—by not accepting that it was their time to die."

West's brow furrowed. "So it was moral principle?"

"I guess. Some believed they were oppressing the host bodies and that they deserved to live free as their own species." She ran a hand over her hair. "But I can't tell if that happened before or after the Mechan became sentient. It's all blurred."

West tapped his chin. "Were there any details regarding the Mechan's collective consciousness?"

"No, nothing."

"Any mentions of individuals?"

"Individual Architects?"

"Yes—leaders, scholars, scientists? Those who had been working on the Mechan project?"

"Shit, I . . ." She chewed her bottom lip, hunting for anything specific, but found only broad strokes, general notions of large chunks of history. "No, I don't think so."

"Are you sure? This is important."

Her brow creased. "Why do you need me to tell you? You just downloaded it all."

"It's still parsing, then I will have to translate it. It all takes time."

"Is this time sensitive?"

He ignored the question with a brisk, "What else was there?"

She rubbed her fingers deep into her aching temples, then shook her head again. "Sorry, sir. That's all I can remember."

West let out a long breath. "Very well." His stool creaked as he stood. He marched back to the workbench. "If you remember anything else, come find me."

She stared after him. "Okay . . ."

"I assume it goes without saying, but everything we discuss—or anything you gleaned from that data—is classified."

"Of course, sir." She pushed off the stool and made to leave, but paused. She wrung her hands and turned back. "One more thing, Major?"

"Yes?" He didn't look up from his work.

"Did you know there'd be a self-destruct? On the station?"

He glanced up, brows pinched. "No. Why?"

"Because you sent me in with a way to download the data faster."

He shook his head. "The goal was *integrity*, not speed; I didn't know you or your Rubicon were capable of that." Looking down, he exhaled a heavy sigh, leaning one hip against the counter. "Believe it or not, Sergeant—right now, you know more than I do." He looked back up and met her eye. "I assure you, even if some details are classified, I will always do everything in my power to prepare you and your team for success." His lips twitched in what looked like a wry smile. "After all, you've seen the timetable. We have very little margin to account for rezone procedures."

"True," she sighed. "And I do believe you, sir."

His left hand quivered, but he quickly gripped the metal fingers under his real ones. "The system is still parsing the data with the rest of what we've already gathered. I'll know more about our next steps in a few hours." He turned away, stepping back to the console. "We'll be traveling for a stint. Take some time in the simulations and stay sharp. You will be tested in the coming days. For now, get some rest. Consider it an order."

"I still have my debrief," she said.

West's limbs buzzed as he turned halfway to face her. "I'll speak with Thurston. No debrief will be required."

"Oh . . . Okay. Thank you."

He went back to work without another word.

Adriene's still-active HUD brightened her vision as she started for the door.

// In the spirit of not keeping things from you . . . //

Adriene sighed. She couldn't wait to hear what this was about. *Go ahead.*

// Please know that I could have disabled the data interpretation feature during the upload. //

She lolled her head back with a resounding sigh.

Mira's ashes—then why the hell didn't you?

// Because I wanted you to have access to the information. It seemed important to you to know more. I knew the major would not likely share of his own volition. //

So West is right in thinking you're defying directives?

// Whether or not he is "right," I cannot say. //

Do you think he's being honest about the overheating issue?

// I cannot say for certain. //

She paused outside the door and glanced back, considering whether she should return and ask West to deactivate her Rubicon. As much as she preferred having it on, a melted brain guaranteed a rezone. Then she'd have to start all over with the AI, and in the interim, West might replace her with someone who was actually qualified.

// Though morose, that is a logical train of thought. //

Okay. We'll keep you off, for now.

// I trust your judgment. //

She turned to head back inside, then hesitated.

West had seemed distracted, anxious—agitated, even. No need to bother him with something as trivial as an implant deactivation.

Besides, she didn't completely abhor the idea of needing to find someone else on board who could shut it off.

CHAPTER

EIGHTEEN

Adriene stepped inside Medical, where the silver-haired doctor tended to someone at one of the gurneys, the privacy curtain hanging half-open.

Her eyes scanned the room and landed on her target.

Daroga sat in the corner at his desk, poring over tablets and manuals. A pair of reading glasses rested halfway down the bridge of his nose.

She frowned as she approached. "Glasses, huh? Those in fashion these days?"

Daroga looked up, and his aloof gaze sharpened as a grin flitted across his face. She could see his brain switching out of egghead mode.

"Unfortunately, no," he replied in his weathered timbre, "and it's getting worse, I'm afraid." He slid the glasses off and tossed them on the messy desktop. "Guess the body deteriorates with age, or something. Keep meaning to get it corrected, but I'm exceedingly lazy."

"Sure, but when'd you last rezone? It can't have gotten that bad."

He shook his head. "I actually haven't had the pleasure."

Her lips parted, surprise countermanding any response.

He slid his sleeve to above the elbow and twisted his arm, presenting the clean brown skin where his tattoo should have—*would* have—been. If he'd been a husk.

Blinking slowly for a few seconds, Adriene tried to muster a reaction.

She hadn't noticed before. Hell, maybe she'd blocked it out—her subconscious ignoring it to spare her.

But instead of the jealousy or superiority or resentment that would normally consume her, she only felt a tugging sense of relief.

He hadn't had to endure that. Yet, at least. Maybe ever.

"Do you even have one?" she asked. "A rezone chip, I mean?"

He thumbed his temple. "Didn't really want it, but everyone from Dodson-Mueller with a permanent posting has to have one. A stipulation of my contract."

She nodded slowly. She hadn't even thought about whether or not he'd have one as a contractor. He seemed like such a staple of Flintlock, she sometimes forgot he wasn't actually military.

He scratched at his dark stubble, green eyes cutting to his desk.

"So . . ." she began, ready to sidestep the awkward topic, "you really are as old as you look, then?"

His wariness broke into a relieved smile. "I earned every one of these wrinkles."

"Well done."

He leaned back in his chair. "Not that I mind getting called an old man, but you don't look like you're here to get patched up again."

"Just need my Rubicon turned off, if you don't mind."

"Again, huh?" He hunted through the pile of tablets on his desk. "Man, you really can't keep that thing off, can you?"

She sighed and looked down, hoping he'd read it as embarrassment instead of deception. "I, uh . . . got startled."

He smirked, then found the right tablet. "You fight killer robots for a living, and something on this ship startled you?"

She tried to let out an easy laugh, but it sounded weak and nervous. Daroga tapped out a practiced cadence on the tablet glass.

// Bye for now. //

Her HUD disappeared, and the hollow void descended back onto the base of her skull. She rubbed the nape of her neck.

"Only giving you shit," Daroga said. "Happens all the time."

The corners of his eyes wrinkled as he smiled up at her. For a second, she could almost ignore the gnawing emptiness in the back of her mind.

"How's that fever?" he asked.

She cleared her throat. "Better. I mean, it's gone. I feel fine."

"Good, glad to hear it. You look better."

A weight grew in her chest and she pushed out a breath, trying to ignore it. He hadn't meant it as a compliment—only that she didn't look like she was about to melt down from the inside out. It didn't take much to look better than that.

She tilted her head, then her mouth suddenly said, "When's your shift end?"

His lips turned up. "1900."

She nodded slowly, aware that it was her turn to speak, to explain her question.

"I'll be heading over to the Hold after," he said, saving her.

She shrugged, then turned away, walking toward the door. "Interesting."

His chair creaked as he leaned, brow raised as his gaze followed her out. "Will I see you there?"

"Maybe. Probably."

"I hope it's the latter," he called as the door slid open before her. "Bye, Sergeant."

"Bye, Carl."

That earned her an unhindered smile as she stepped out the door and left.

Adriene cleaned herself up, then headed to the Hold. Though it was still early, the tables were already almost as full as the first night she'd come down.

Her squad occupied their usual spot, though without any of Brigham's friends. The three turned as she approached. Brigham's eyes went wide over flushed red cheeks, and Gallagher's chair legs grated on the floor as she pushed to her feet, then paused to steady herself on the table.

"Ninety-fucking-Six!" Kato lurched for Adriene, stumbling straight into a full hug while bringing forth a waft of dry bourbon.

"Valero," Brigham rumbled, tone almost wistful. "Thank *Mira*."

Adriene patted Kato on the back, and he released his hold. She cleared her throat. "Uh, you guys seem surprised to see me."

Gallagher steadied herself as she carefully sat back down. "Blackwell had you wheeled off, then pulled us straight into debrief. We checked for you after, but you weren't there."

Kato frowned. "We thought you mighta . . . ya know."

"Oh, uh . . ." Adriene scoured her mind for a logical excuse. "Doc got paranoid. Stuck me in quarantine for a few hours."

The others nodded along as Brigham gave a sorrowful shake of his head. Luckily, they seemed drunk enough to accept the lie.

Brigham poured out a generous two fingers of bourbon and shoved it across the table toward her as she sat.

"So, what the hell happened?" Gallagher asked. "Was your Rubicon really able to download it? Did you get the data?"

Adriene hesitated, debating how to stage her response. Though, she'd learned long ago, the best way to lie was to just *not*. "I guess it worked, yeah. Intel's got the data on the mainframe already. Doing their egghead thing with it."

"Well, damn." Brigham tipped his glass toward her. "Looks like you saved the day, again."

"Ignore him." Kato sloshed the bourbon around in his glass. "He's just *jealous*."

Brigham's roughened skin wrinkled as he glowered at Kato. "Jealous? Try *elated*. You see the look on Coleson's and Ivon's faces when we disembarked? Fuckin' priceless. We gotta keep this streak going."

Adriene held up her glass. "I'll drink to that."

The others smiled and clinked their glasses into hers.

They poured more bourbon, then regaled Adriene with their best combat stories from the last few years. The more they drank, the less reluctant they were to mention Cash's participation. Their former squadmate seemed to have been truly dangerous, but at the very least, he'd supplied them with some entertaining stories.

As it went on, a creeping sense of bittersweet nostalgia trickled in, but Adriene couldn't bring herself to fully trust it.

Did she really miss the camaraderie, miss having a team, *want* to bother getting to know these people? Or did she just know, deep down, that's how she *should* feel? She still didn't know whether or not she could trust this husk.

After a time, Brigham's friends trickled in, and the table grew crowded. Storytime for the new recruit's sake soon died away in favor of shared experience and inside jokes. Once the cards came out and the gambling began, Adriene scooted back and chose to remain a spectator.

Less than five minutes after Daroga's shift ended, he appeared in the Hold's doorway, shirt already untucked, sleeves rolled. Adriene caught his eye, then picked up her chair and dragged it to an empty table, grateful to move away from the drunken shouting. Though she'd been taking it slowly, everyone else was well past three sheets to the wind.

As Daroga approached her squad's table, he gripped Kato's shoulder in greeting. Kato beamed up at him as he passed, gaze tracking Daroga as he headed toward Adriene. Kato's smile morphed into a coy grin. Adriene pretended not to notice.

Daroga let out a ragged sigh as he sank into a chair beside her. "You're not playing?"

"Not really my thing. Gambling's one vice I've never had a taste for." She swept an open hand toward the rowdy table. "Feel free, though."

He shook his head. "Ma taught me to never gamble away a perfectly good coin."

Her lips pressed into a smile. "I think that's the most Provan thing I've heard you say yet." He chuffed a laugh, and she lifted a liquor bottle toward him. "Bourbon?"

"No thanks." He paused, tilted his head slightly, then produced a chain from under his shirt. He held the single pendant up between his thumb and forefinger—a sleek gold triangle. "Ten years sober."

Adriene blinked, then shook the stupefied look from her face. Sober *and* not a husk. How had she not noticed these things before? She really had been mired in a haze of social ineptitude.

"Oh, sorry." She set the bottle aside. "That's great," she added quickly. "Congrats."

"I couldn't always be around it, honestly." He glanced over as a roar of drunken cheering went up at her squad's table. "Took me some time before I could come down here."

She nodded, swallowing back the heavy weight that lifted up her throat. "Understandable."

"So go ahead—really. It doesn't bother me."

She thumbed the edge of her glass, a trace of amber liquid lining the bottom, then pushed it aside. "Nah, I'm good anyway. I've had plenty."

"Yeah, bet you're tired, huh?" he said, tone sympathetic. "How'd the op go? Seems like your LT's pretty happy about it again."

"Yeah . . ." Her gaze drifted to Brigham as he told an animated story to Gallagher and a few others, who'd folded their hands. "It went as well as it could have, I guess."

"Mission accomplished?"

"As far as I know." She gave him a wry grin. "Above my pay grade. You know how it is."

He nodded slowly. "Indeed . . . You know, I almost joined up myself way back when."

Her brows lifted. "Oh yeah?"

"I *did*, actually. When I was eighteen. Started basic, even."

She rested her elbows on the table. "What happened?"

"Well . . ." he began, wavering his head side to side. "It, uh . . ." Some of the spirit faded from his green eyes as he looked down. "It triggered some things," he admitted. "That I hadn't fully dealt with. Since the Brownout, I mean."

Though even-keeled, all things considered, Adriene noticed something in his look she hadn't seen in him before. Fear.

She couldn't blame him. It was a statement to his resolve that he'd become a contractor at all—never mind accepting a permanent posting out-system. He should be safely tucked away on Estes or Prova somewhere, not out on the frontier with the Extrasolar Fleet.

Daroga looked back up at her, lips pressed thin with a melancholic smile. "Needless to say, I washed out pretty quickly."

"That's understandable," she said. "Yet you ended up in the fleet anyway . . . How'd that happen?"

He leaned back in his chair, one elbow high as he rubbed the back of his neck. "As winding a path as anyone who grew up primarily after the Firewall went up. As I'm sure you can attest . . ."

"Indeed." She ignored his prompt with a tight-lipped grin. "But we're talking about *you*."

He smiled back, worry lines smoothing from his forehead. "Fine, fine," he sighed. "All the Brownout kids got a free ride to Iron Ridge, so after washing out, I started there in surgical medicine. It's what my dad did back on Bryer-III, but ultimately, just wasn't for me. Had done some coding in my free time, so I switched majors. Dodson-Mueller recruited me straight out of the gate."

"You didn't consider CNEF again after school? Could've jumped straight to a cushy R&D position with a qualification from IRI."

He rubbed at both eyes with the palms of his hands, dropping them as he exhaled a soft sigh. "Yeah, I'd considered it, but ultimately had to go corporate. Dodson-Mueller was willing to overlook my record, but neither CNEF or CNLC would."

Her lips parted, unsure she'd heard him right. "Your *record*?"

"Uh, yeah." He canted his head, running fingers through his hair and piling it off to one side. "Somewhere in the midst of all that, I got arrested."

She stared. "You?"

He scowled. "Hey, now . . ." Leaning straight back in his seat, he used both hands to tug at the collar of his shirt. "I could be a badass . . ."

"No offense, but no."

He grinned through a wince. "Damn, Valero. Ruthless."

She leaned forward on her elbows, propping her chin on one fist. "So? What'd ya do?"

"Well," he sighed, "long story short: when I switched majors, I fell in with a collective. Mostly developing tool suites and hunting bug bounties. We'd split the rewards, upgrade our tech, repeat. Spent the rest of our time griping about censorship and privacy laws . . .

and on occasion, felt compelled to let the government know it. Let's just say, it got us into a bit of trouble. Had grand plans to become an infamous white-hat collective someday, valiant advocates for the democracy, all that." He gave a hesitant smile. "Stupid kid dreams."

She shook her head. "Not stupid. Idealistic, maybe. I thought like that when I was a kid too."

"Yeah? And what'd you wanna be?"

"I, uh . . ." Warmth pulsed in her cheeks, and she glanced down before forcing herself to meet his look again. "I wanted to be a ranger."

His brows pinched. "Like a CNEF scout ranger?"

"No. Like a park ranger. At Arcalod Peak in Armand Federal Park. To be specific."

He openly stared, expression so still it could have been cut from stone. "A . . . park ranger?" he intoned.

Adriene shrugged, scrubbing her hands down her pants. Had she told anyone this before? Harlan, maybe. Years ago.

Daroga's face stretched with a wide smile, smothering any remnants of his stoic surprise. "That sounds great. Why didn't you do it?"

"Just ended up on a different path."

His amusement wavered, chest rising with a deep breath. "Yeah, I know that feeling. Not sure how medicine and hacktivism resulted in military corporate contractor work, but . . ." He threw up his hands. "Here we are."

"I dunno," she said, lightening her tone. "Best way to tear something down is from within."

His lips twitched up. "Why's that sound familiar?"

"My grandfather used to say it. He was from that whole grassroots, 'one-government' generation."

"You close?"

"Eh, were, yeah. He raised me for a while. Taught me most of what I know about flora and fauna—which helped me get kicked up pretty quick through the pathfinders. Kinda the last true outdoorsman." She gave an involuntary smile, which brought one to Daroga's lips as well. "I could've had it worse. Knew a lot of kids who did."

She finished off the small amount of bourbon in her glass, then shoved it away. But instead of warming her stomach and calming her nerves, it just tasted bitter and hollow.

"I only had him for a few years," she continued—no reason to let Daroga think she'd had some delightful upbringing. "Nine to fifteen. After he passed, I ended up a ward. Only for a year, though, before I turned fifteen."

"Ah." He nodded. "Then they let you join the guardianship program?"

She swept out a hand. "Where all roads lead to CNEF." She swallowed, her tone darkening with old memories. "Still light-years better than being a ward for another three years."

Daroga fiddled with the cuffs of his rolled sleeves, and his lips turned down as he asked, "Do you mind if I ask . . . what happened to your parents?" He raised an apologetic hand, then quickly added, "That is, if you wanna talk about it."

"Not much to say." Adriene leaned back in her chair, pulling her glass back to the edge of the table with her. "Mom was CNEF, went MIA during the Brownout. Dad was Local Corps, he . . . went after her. I was nine, I barely remember."

"Sorry to hear," he said, voice low. "It had to be tough losing them both so young."

She waved a dismissive hand, forcing herself to meet his gaze again. Wrinkles tightened the edges of his green eyes. "It's fine, really," she assured. "It's been twenty years. It's an old wound at this point."

He shook his head. "That kinda thing never leaves."

It never *should* leave—and yet it had. This was the first time she'd felt one way or the other about her parents since her last rezone. Finally, this husk had decided to start having feelings. Watered down, maybe, but feelings nonetheless.

An extra layer of guilt settled in when, for a moment, she wished she could retreat back into being numb. At least when it came to this stuff. She hated dwelling on the past, on things that happened ninety-seven lifetimes ago.

Daroga's chest deflated with a deep sigh, gaze dropping as he

combed his fingers through his hair. If they were going toe-to-toe
on shitty childhoods, Daroga was the clear winner.

Adriene chewed the inside of her lip, glad to have livened the
mood.

Daroga's chair creaked, and he slid away from the table.

Her shoulders stiffened. Had she really scared him off that easily?

"Wanna play a few hands?" He gestured to the bar. "Just us, I
mean. No betting."

She shifted her weight to mask her relief and gave a short nod.
"Sure."

He went to the bar and returned with a pack of cards. "Unless
you happened to smuggle some picaloos in your ruck that you'd be
willing to bet?" His eyes glinted playfully. "I'd barter my left arm
for some proper chocolate about now."

"No such luck," she said regretfully. The tension in her shoulders
eased as she scooted up to the table.

He dropped the deck out of the pack. "You know Quicksand?"

"Never heard of it."

"I can teach you; it's a fast learn."

"You just want an easy win."

He smiled. "I'll play fair. Promise."

"All right. You gonna need your reading glasses to see the cards,
old man?"

He threw her a glare of amused exasperation, then dealt. He
stepped her through the rules, and after a few hands, she got the
hang of it. She won as often as she lost, though he clearly went easy
on her. Which should've been annoying, but his easy grin and carefree banter did nothing but send pleasant waves of warmth through
her chest.

Eventually, a familiar, chiding tone broke through her bubble of
calm. "—letting you play with the big kids."

Her heart sank as she looked at her squad's table. Their six-
person card game had grown, and now a massive glom of soldiers
hovered around. Ivon's shaved head bobbed in the crowd, a good
ten centimeters taller than everyone else around him.

Adriene groaned. "Fuck."

Coleson's grumpy, slurred voice carried over the din, "They'll learn soon enough how wrong they are to trust you."

Through the bodies, Adriene caught a glimpse of Brigham surging to his feet, wobbling as he rose. Unfortunately, rather than encouraging him to calm down, his friends seemed to be egging him on.

Adriene scoured the crowd, searching for her squadmates for backup. Gallagher was . . . making out with someone in the corner, apparently. Adriene couldn't tell who.

She craned her neck and found Kato slumped in a chair fast asleep, snoring peacefully. That checked out.

Sighing, she looked back at Daroga. "I should probably try to get my LT out of here *before* he starts punching people."

Daroga smiled, gathering the cards up off the table. "Good idea. Let's go."

She froze briefly at the casual suggestion of his continued existence in her evening. He'd said it so simply, like it was implied.

Strangely, she didn't think she minded.

Daroga followed as she pushed away from the table and headed toward her lieutenant.

Brigham's fists were tight, veins rising along his forearms and burgeoning from his neck. "Jealous of our squeaky-clean track record, gentlemen?"

Coleson snorted. "Yeah, two for two, real fuckin' impressive."

Ivon jutted his pointy chin at Adriene. "And *again*, you made Rezone Girl do the dirty work for you. Top-notch leadership skills, Miles."

Adriene glowered. When the hell had she become "Rezone Girl"?

Her fists tightened. Maybe this would be a fight after all.

Brigham sneered at Ivon. "You're just pissed a Local Corps transfer is upstaging your pompous military-brat pedigrees."

Coleson's nostrils flared. "No-talent reserves grunts have no place as commissioned officers in the Extrasolar Fleet," he growled. "Only reason you're even here is 'cause your ma used to screw Thurston."

Brigham growled and lunged forward, but Adriene gripped his

shoulders and kept him back. "LT," she implored, "let's not do this again."

He threw a hard look at her, brow drawn low over bloodshot eyes. "We can take 'em, Valero."

"Well, *obviously*," she scoffed. "That's not the point."

She eyed Ivon and Coleson, taking stock of the situation. They were markedly intoxicated, but she got the feeling they'd make up for that via drunken rage. Brigham had a table full of friends nearby, but she didn't know who might back the Stormwalkers. If she let him start this, it could turn into a whole . . . thing.

She darted a look to the back corners of the room. Why the hell was the Stormwalkers' lieutenant never around to keep them in line?

Her gaze caught on Daroga, and she recalled how he'd handled things at the training sims. Annoyed, but calm, all things considered. Levelheaded. Sure, Lieutenant Rhett had ultimately put a stop to it, but Daroga had done a decent job of de-escalation up to that point.

Drawing in a slow breath, Adriene channeled patience, lowering her voice and leaning into Brigham's ear. "They're trying to goad you into starting something. We'll be sitting out the next deployment if you end up in the brig tonight. That'll be the end of our streak."

Brigham's mouth turned down, his mask of fury fading into an impressive pout.

"C'mon," she encouraged. "Let's get outta here."

His jaw loosened, and he gave a short nod.

She gripped his tense arm and towed him back while Daroga brought up the other side. They pushed through the crowd, guiding him toward the exit.

Ivon let out a sharp laugh. "Yeah, tuck tail and run like a good little grunt."

Brigham stumbled as he craned his neck back.

Adriene groaned. "What if you just—" she began, but couldn't stop him.

"You noncom chumps better be nice to me," he jeered. "I'll be signin' your paychecks soon."

Ivon and Coleson broke from the crowd and stormed after them.

Adriene tensed, but to her relief, Daroga ran interference—reeling around to intercept. "Now, gentlemen." He held up both hands, forcing them to stop in their tracks. "I'm going to have to politely insist you back the fuck off," he said, with the same formal, yet charismatic tone he'd used at the hardsuit lecture. "Unless you want me to find your lieutenant? I bet she'd love getting woken up in the middle of the night to learn what you're up to."

Coleson's crimson face darkened and Ivon's stony glare persisted, but they stayed put.

Adriene dragged Brigham into the hallway as Ivon called over Daroga's shoulder, "This isn't over, *grunt.*"

Daroga backed into the hall, ensuring the door slid shut before he jogged to join them. Brigham insisted on walking on his own, but between Adriene and Daroga, they herded him back to his quarters. When he passed out on his bed faceup, it took them both to turn the thickset man over onto his side.

"Well, he probably won't die," Daroga said lightly as they stepped back into the hall.

"That's all we can ask for." Adriene eyed a couple of other drunk soldiers as they stumbled into their own rooms. "Thanks for the assist."

"Anytime." He glanced both ways down the empty hall before his gaze settled on her. "I had fun tonight. I'd love to do it again sometime."

She quirked a brow, pushing past the tightness in her chest. "You'd love to put my smashed LT to bed again?"

His lips pressed into an amused smirk. "Yes. Exactly that."

"Absolutely. You can count on it. I'd guess once a week, at minimum."

"Can't wait." His amusement faded, and he scratched the back of his neck for a moment, then offered a handshake.

She instinctively accepted, but as she took his hand, she

faltered—an odd, willful hesitation ensnaring her. Their hands lingered a few seconds too long, his fingers grazing lightly over her palm. A piece of his long hair swung into his face, his eyes a stark emerald against his brown skin.

She made the mistake of breathing again and inhaled a lungful of that damn scent of evergreen and clove. It smelled too much like home.

She pulled her hand away, fingers chilly as they left his warm grasp. Goose bumps swept up her arm as her eyes fell to her boots.

Mira's end.

She'd *just* started to be able to feel again; she couldn't effectively compute what was happening. Worse, it came with a bitter tug of shame, though she couldn't determine the source.

Maybe she felt like she was lying to him. Letting him believe she was a real person with real feelings.

Or maybe she just couldn't let herself have it. Not until she really did feel fully human again. And she could only do that by getting rid of that damned rezone chip. But how could she possibly explain that to Daroga? To someone who hadn't even rezoned *once*?

She cleared her throat, glancing down the hall toward her quarters. "Well, I'm right here."

"Right." Daroga scratched at the darkening stubble on his chin. "I really did have a good time. Thanks for hanging around with an old-timer."

"Consider it my community service for the week."

He breathed a laugh, then hesitated a few seconds before he said, "Ya know, if you're still having trouble finding your way around, I'd be happy to help."

She raised an amused eyebrow, glancing at her door a few meters away. "I am a *pathfinder*, you know."

He replied with a flash of white teeth, well aware of what he was suggesting. "It's no trouble. I gotta run back to Medical, so it's pretty much on my way anyhow."

"All right. If you insist."

He fell in beside her, a draft of dry pine needles hitting her nose. She held her breath to evade it.

They took about fourteen steps, then stopped outside of her door.

Daroga swept out a hand. "We have arrived."

"Thank you kindly. I may not have found my way without your aid."

He inclined his head. "Have a good night." He turned to walk away—in the wrong direction.

She watched him for a few steps, then called after him, "You sure it's that way?"

He stopped in his tracks and glanced both ways, then let out a heavy sigh. He spun on a heel. "I've only been here four years," he said, starting the correct way down the hall. "I'll figure it out any day now."

"Safe travels. May Mira's light guide you."

"Har har. Good night, Adriene," he called as he rounded the corner.

"Night, Carl."

CHAPTER

NINETEEN

For possibly the first time in her career, Adriene arrived at a company briefing a whole five minutes early.

Almost three-quarters of the seats were already filled, but instead of the usual idle chatter, the soldiers sat in an eerie, anticipatory silence. These briefings had started to become rote over the last seven weeks as they'd steadily moved outward and away from the galactic core, executing eight more rounds of multi-squad intel-gathering missions aboard ancient, abandoned space stations or deeply shrouded black sites.

Until five days ago, when the *Aurora* dropped from their longest subspace journey yet and slid into orbit around an icy rock clinging to the edge of the outermost back-ass reaches of the galactic arm. They'd sat cloaked for days while the entire company endured briefing after briefing, punctuated by endless tech lectures, protocol memorandums, and procedure reminders.

So this meeting—ominously labeled "Final Company Brief"—brought with it a strange sense of relief. For Adriene, at least. After a decade enduring the 803rd's complete lack of policy enforcement, she'd earned a deep appreciation for the 505th's thoroughness. But all the drills and team building and gear prep didn't get them any closer to completing Major West's campaign.

She glanced down to the foot of the sloped meeting room. On the front dais, Commodore Thurston and Major Blackwell spoke quietly. The Stormwalkers sat in the front row to fulfill their role of devoted brownnosers, alongside their straitlaced squad leader, Lieutenant Rhett.

Over the weeks, Forward Recon had maintained their flawless performance streak, further fueling the Stormwalkers' resentment.

Adriene had been glad when Rhett had finally begun to rein them in. They became entirely different people—reasonable, rational, equanimous—the second Rhett walked into a room.

Adriene headed down the steps to her squad's usual row and slid in beside Kato. He sat as relaxed and congenial as ever, propped forward in his seat, lips pressed thin like he had a grin chambered, just waiting for an excuse to unleash it on someone. Gallagher arrived moments later, her dark brown eyes attentive, though she seemed sleepier than usual.

"All right, fivers," Blackwell called from the dais. "Let's get started."

Brigham shuffled in as the lights dimmed. He took the empty seat beside Gallagher, juggling an armful of tablets and printed briefings, a stylus tucked behind one ear. Over the last few weeks, the lieutenants had been offered a slew of team-building seminars, and in Brigham's ongoing effort to dethrone the Stormwalkers as the poster children of Flintlock, he'd taken the extra training very seriously.

Blackwell approached the podium, and the large viewscreen came to life with the CNEF logo. Commodore Thurston stepped to the front edge of the dais, his expression noticeably discerning and no-nonsense despite the ocular implant covering his left eye.

Thurston recapped everything from their prelim briefings, filling in additional details based on the intel brought back by the system-wide drone reconnaissance that'd been running for the last few days.

The objective was retrieval of an intelligence asset of unknown make. Target location: a former black site they continued to assert was *"Mechan in origin,"* while still admitting it to be over four hundred years old. No one seemed to question the bad math, considering they had no indication the Mechan existed prior to around two or three hundred years ago. Adriene, at least, knew that meant it would be another Architect facility, which had been true of almost all the sites they'd covered the last seven weeks.

Thurston finally arrived at some *new* details—including the mission itinerary. On the day, three squads would carry out system-wide security sweeps while another two acted as escorts to the target location; yet another would provide ongoing orbital security. Three more would be responsible for security planetside, while a fourth specialty squad scoured the exterior of the site and turned the power on. After that, the vanguard squad would head right in the front doors of the black site to execute the primary objective.

By the time Thurston finished, the overall mood of the room had shifted from anticipation to tedium. It seemed like all they'd done for weeks was *talk* about this single op. Everyone was to ready act on it.

"This is the final company-wide brief," Thurston continued, "but you'll be working with your squads this afternoon for final touches. I'll leave the details wrap-up to the major."

Thurston nodded to Blackwell, then exited at the bottom entrance. Blackwell stepped around the podium to the front of the dais. "Just a few clerical things to cover," he rumbled. "Try not to fall asleep on me, fivers. First up, team assignments . . ."

A new graphic appeared on the viewscreen. Blackwell detailed which squads would take on which support roles, then his dark eyes lifted to Adriene's row.

"Lieutenants Rhett and Brigham . . . Your squads will comprise our vanguard, coded Augur Team."

Adriene shared a quick glance with Kato, who looked a great deal more surprised than she felt. Though she'd never have predicted being partnered with the Stormwalkers, she knew Major West would arrange for her team to end up in whatever position best suited his needs. Which invariably meant front and center.

Blackwell continued, "I'll be acting as Augur Team's commanding officer. We'll work as a single unit to search and retrieve the objective."

He stepped behind the podium again. A schedule appeared on the viewscreen.

"Staggered egress is scheduled for tomorrow starting at 1200. Make sure you've been cleared with Medical before 2200 tonight, and loadouts deadline is the same time. All squads will have their final briefs this afternoon—operation charts will be available no later than 1300. The full timetable is available on the server. Primer packets will be sent to your personal terminals immediately after this meeting. Questions?"

No one raised any concerns, and Blackwell dismissed them. Brigham confirmed their squad meeting time and location, and Adriene headed out, starting the long jaunt across the length of the ship toward Intel Command.

"Hey," Kato huffed from behind her, "Ninety-Six, where ya headed?" He jogged up, falling in step beside her. "I have a checkup at Medical. Wanna walk with me?"

She lifted an eyebrow. "It's like one and a half hallways over, but sure. You getting shots? Need someone to hold your hand?"

He shrugged. "I'd never turn down cuddles, but no . . ." He flashed her an alarmingly pleased grin. "Just figured there might be a certain someone you'd be interested in finding an excuse to ogle."

She dragged a weary hand down the side of her face, hoping to disguise the creeping flush of color. "I have no idea what you're talking about, Sergeant."

Kato laughed. "You know, before all this prep started, the only time I saw you two apart was during sims and when we were literally light-years away on a mission."

"You're exaggerating."

"I'm really not. Listen—" He held up his hands, palms out. "I'm not judging. Honestly, I think it's adorable as shit—"

"I've told you a hundred times, nothing's going on."

"Mm-hmm," Kato hummed. "That doesn't mean you don't *want* somethin' to be goin' on."

"Mira's mercy . . ." She rolled her eyes.

They turned down the hall toward Medical, and Kato took a few quick steps to get ahead of her. "Don't worry, I gotcha covered. Ma always said I'd make an outstandin' matchmaker."

"Please, no," she begged, but the door to Medical slid open, and Kato skipped partway in.

At least fifteen people milled around inside. Two more entered as Adriene hovered in the door frame, eyes scanning the room.

She'd never seen Medical so active. Everyone on staff must have been on duty to perform final clearance checkups and troubleshoot implant issues.

Between the milling soldiers, Adriene caught sight of Daroga sitting against the edge of his desk, going over something on a tablet with an MP. His glasses rested on his head, holding back his long hair.

"Mr. Daroga!" Kato called, far too loudly.

Adriene tented her hand over her eyes as Daroga glanced at Kato.

With one thumb, Kato pointed over his shoulder at her. "Valero says hey!"

Daroga's gaze slid past Kato and onto her. His tired expression lightened.

She responded with a tilted smile and a humoring eye roll—an innocent bystander enduring Kato's puerile behavior. He acknowledged her misery with a sympathetic, lopsided shrug.

The MP drew Daroga's attention back, and Adriene gave Kato's shoulder an indecorous shove. He snorted, chirped a goodbye, and Adriene left.

As she continued her path toward Intel Command, she willed her heated cheeks to cool. She'd been so busy with training and briefs the last week, she hadn't realized how much she'd missed Daroga's company. Annoyingly, Kato hadn't exaggerated about their time together over the last two months. They'd tag-teamed Brigham out of trouble with the Stormwalkers more times than she could count, and rounds of Quicksand at the Hold had become routine, often stretching far into the early-morning hours. She'd become fairly proficient at finding excuses to hang around Medical and bother him. He hadn't seemed to mind.

Yet, despite ample downtime, Adriene's last drink had been the night they'd returned from that first derelict space station seven weeks ago. A combination of guilt induced by Harlan's last words to her and an irrational fear of judgment by Daroga made it easier to refrain. By way of positive reinforcement, there seemed to be a suspicious correlation between the waning booze and her returning state of emotional semi-normalcy. She'd forgotten how much she missed not hating every second of every day. Giving a shit about things could be exhausting, sure, but it was decidedly better than the alternative.

The more she fell into a rhythm with Flintlock, the more her chronic apathy felt like a distant memory. She'd even planned to place a call to Harlan to apologize—maybe coordinate their next leave, whenever that might be—but the *Aurora* remained too far from any ansibles to send messages, and they were on blackout protocols, regardless. It'd have to wait till they came back toward civilization again.

Which could take a good long while. Adriene knew from sneaking peeks at West's monitors that they were deep in uncharted territory. Not literally, but definitely not somewhere you'd find on a Concord Nations travel guide. The system didn't even have a name, only a galactic catalog reference number of CNGC-8402b.

They were so far out, Adriene started wondering on the limits of the rezone facilities. Her Rubicon insisted the range was ostensibly unlimited. Something about modified graviton waves—the same reason conductive shields or other interference didn't impede a rezone—and "dynamic redundancy structures," whatever that meant. Even if the process somehow failed, the data from your previous transfer could be loaded—after a lengthy legal verification process requiring proof of death, or the direct permission of an admiral.

Adriene subdued a shudder. Two months ago, the thought of losing her memories since her last rezone wouldn't have fazed her in the slightest. But now . . .

She knew fearing it didn't make sense. After all, if it happened, she wouldn't remember what she'd lost.

But Brigham and Gallagher would. And Major West. Kato . . . Daroga.

She shook off the disturbing thoughts. It didn't matter; that'd never affect her. She had every intention of surviving until the end of this campaign, the conclusion of this "special assignment," and collect her reward. Because—regardless of her improved mindset, new friends, willpower toward sobriety, and ability to carry on a conversation like a semi-functional adult—more than anything, she still wanted that rezone chip gone.

Adriene arrived at Intel Command. The control pad accepted her handprint, then the retinal scanner beeped its approval. Inside, West towered over his workstation, shoulders hunched, gaze fixed on one of the holographic interfaces.

Adriene's stomach rumbled with hunger as she made her way across the room toward him.

He didn't look up but mumbled, "Sergeant," by way of greeting.

Adriene's stomach growled again, and she went straight for the crate of MREs he had stashed under the workbench. "You mind? I'm starving."

He waved an indifferent hand.

She slid open the crate and pulled out one of the silver packets. It was alleged-meatloaf day at the mess, and she'd rather eat a desiccated brick of freeze-dried nutrients any day over that disastrous affront to cuisine.

She sat on a stool by the workbench and tore open the packet. "Just came from our final brief. This is quite the operation."

"Yes, it is."

"We're on point with the Stormwalkers. Guessing that was you?"

West sighed and stopped his work. He looked up at her, lips pressing into a firm line. "A compromise was in order. The commodore agreed that a prominent role for Forward Recon was justified based on your impeccable performance record—"

"You're welcome, by the way," she mumbled over a mouthful of food, but West ignored her.

"—however, proper execution requires two primary teams. Major Blackwell insisted on the Stormwalkers' participation. I know your teams have somewhat of a tumultuous history. Please do your best to facilitate a professional and productive . . . environment . . ."

He trailed off as he stared at her with a flat look, her chomping suddenly loud in the resounding silence.

She slowed her obnoxious chewing and swallowed as quietly as possible. "No worries. I'll make sure everyone stays focused."

He turned back to the console.

She peeled open the wrapper further. "What about on the unsanctioned side of things?"

"Nothing."

She paused mid-bite. "Uh, sir? Nothing?"

"There is nothing I need you to do, other than your job."

Her hand dropped, hunger forgotten, and some of the tension slackened from her shoulders.

That surprised her, sure, but primarily, she felt relieved. It was a big enough operation that Blackwell himself would be taking the mantel of commanding officer. She wasn't disappointed she wouldn't have to do anything unauthorized in front of him.

"Don't get too comfortable, Sergeant," West said, and the thread of caution in his tone returned some of the tightness to her muscles. She looked up to find him facing her squarely. "The intelligence at this black site is potentially the highest-priority asset we have ever sought. Certainly for Flintlock, possibly the 505th, conceivably the entire fleet."

He crossed his arms and took a few slow steps toward her, his mechanical limbs buzzing lightly.

"As you know, there will be no hard drives," he continued, "no data transfer, no encryption. The mission is to collect and return the physical hardware in one, functional piece. So though I ask for no fraudulent conduct, I need you to ensure those parameters are met. No tampering, no damage, no shortcuts. One, functional piece. At *all* costs."

A chill pricked her skin, and she folded her arms tightly over her chest. "That important, huh?"

"Yes."

Adriene chewed, brow furrowing as West retreated to the counter, then brought back a stool. He sat facing her, interlocking his fingers in his lap. She swallowed.

"To convey just how important," West continued, "I would like to have a frank conversation with you, Sergeant."

She shifted back on the stool. "By all means."

"Have you ever speculated on the motivations of the Mechan?"

She lifted a shoulder. "Only two to three times a day."

He gave a humoring half grin.

She propped an elbow on the top of the workbench. "You have a hypothesis?"

"More than a hypothesis."

"A theory, then?"

His ashy eyebrows lifted.

She scoffed. "Don't look *too* surprised that I know the difference."

Another humoring grin. "You *never* cease to surprise, Sergeant."

"I choose to take that as a compliment." She tore off another chunk of MRE. "So," she prompted, swallowing the bite. "Let's hear it."

He inclined his head. "The Mechan confine the majority of our population to our home system, while dedicating entire armada clusters to ensuring we cannot establish a foothold anywhere else in the galaxy. Why?"

Adriene finished chewing, unaware it was going to be a Q&A. She gulped, then answered, "Because they don't want us growing powerful enough to fight back."

"Reasonable assumption," he agreed. "However, they not only allow the Extrasolar Fleet to continue operations, but they possess easily three to four times the firepower and bandwidth needed to eliminate the entire solar system in one fell swoop. But they do not. Why?"

"Procrastination?"

He gave her a flat look.

She set down the half-eaten MRE, considering a less sarcastic answer. "Convenience?"

"Possibly." By his blasé tone, Adriene felt like she'd missed the mark.

She leaned onto the hand of her propped elbow, kneading the back of her neck. "They don't kill us because . . . they don't want us dead?"

A corner of his lip lifted, and he dipped his chin. "And why would they not want us dead?"

She sat up a little straighter. "Programming?" she guessed, thoughts returning to the flashes of Architect history she'd gleaned during her brief time as a human hard drive. "If the Architects created the scrappers to house their minds, maybe they included some kind of directive to not harm biological beings? Unless forced?"

"An interesting guess," he acquiesced. "What about hybridization?"

Adriene tensed. It'd been weeks if not months since she'd last heard that word. She steadied herself, exhaling to a slow count of three like her Rubicon taught her.

West clarified, "What motive do they have to hybridize us?"

"Direct access to rezone hubs," she replied. "It'd be an easy back door to infiltrate the military."

"But if they do not want us dead, why go to the trouble of infiltrating the military? What purpose would that serve?"

Adriene chewed the inside of her cheek, considering. "I don't know," she said finally.

"You see where the logical fallacies begin to show?"

She nodded. "Yeah, fair."

"I have only come up with one theory that I believe accommodates each of those points. Thus far, it has been substantiated by the data we've collected over the last few months."

Her stool groaned as she scooted back and crossed her arms. "Okay. Let's hear it."

"I believe they want us alive because they want our bodies."

Adriene's lips parted, the warmth draining from her face. "What?"

"For themselves."

She blinked, unable to say anything other than another "What?"

"I believe their attempts at hybridization *are* related to rezoning, as you suggested." He averted his gaze briefly, scratching at the ungrafted side of his cheek. "However . . ." He drew his chin back up, meeting her gaze again. "I think they are attempting to secure an avenue, so that someday, they can harvest the planet of biological shells they've diligently guarded the last twenty years."

Adriene's shoulders dropped, the freshly ingested MRE souring in her stomach.

That would mean the Firewall that humanity had regarded as a military blockade was actually . . . a fence. An enclosure for their *incubator*.

She scrubbed both hands down her face, pushing out a hard breath through them. "But why?" she exhaled, dropping her hands and locking eyes with him. "Why would they want to be biological?"

"In order to be mortal."

She picked at her cuticles. Unnervingly, she could relate to that desire.

She may be able to support or refute his hypothesis based on what she'd heard while part of the hive mind, but she refused to willingly dredge up memories she'd spent so much time and effort burying.

West's steady look remained unchanged as he watched her quietly processing.

Finally, she cleared her throat. "Why would they want to be mortal?" she pressed.

Evenly, he said, "Who can say."

She studied his expectant look. "You have a theory on that too?" she asked.

"A hypothesis," he corrected, a hint of a wry smile playing at the corners of his lips.

She exhaled a dry laugh, stuck somewhere between bewilderment and dread.

"I believe they may see it as an ascension," West answered.

Adriene's eyebrows climbed.

"Godhood, of a sort," he went on. "Their long-extinct creators were biological. Perhaps they believe that if they return to that state, they will have ascended."

She rubbed a hand over her short hair. "Why would the Mechan even *want* to ascend?"

He gave a firm shake of his head. "I don't think the Mechan *want* anything," he clarified, tone dire while taking on a fervent edge. "Possibly, it's tied into a completion path. They were designed and built as machines. Without a directive over the last few hundred years, their programming may have attempted to create an objective *for* them. A purpose. As machines, the only reference point they have for 'purpose' would be their own origin."

"The Architects . . ." she mumbled. "Who were biological and had intended on using hosts to survive."

West gave a grim nod. "Currently, the only way the Mechan can exist is as a hive mind. But they may be able to break free of that architecture by transferring to individual human bodies. They could become individuals. Like their creators."

When she found her voice again, it came out dry and crackling. "You have proof of this?"

He shook his head. "Not definitive. But . . ." He glanced back at his monitors before returning his look to her, a hard glint in his real eye. "Let's just say, there is compelling evidence. But it has not yet collated into a complete picture. The final pieces of that puzzle . . . Well, hopefully many of them can be found at this next black site."

Adriene's mind reeled as she considered the possibilities of both his theory and subsequent hypothesis . . . absolutely hating how much sense it made.

"Which," West went on, tone weighted, "is why I must stress again how important it is that we retrieve the hardware intact. To have the best chance at getting those final pieces."

She bit the inside of her cheek as she assessed his serious expression, the planes of the right side of his face as rigid and unyielding as the augmented side.

She'd spent enough time with West over the last two months to learn how to read the nuance of his reserved expressions. She'd never once seen him like this. Not this serious, this earnest.

She firmed her jaw. "No tampering, no damage, no shortcuts,

at all costs," she recited. "Understood, sir. I'll ensure it comes back intact."

"Thank you." He glanced down with a fleeting wince. The fingers of his mechanical hand tremored as he faced the console again. "You're dismissed."

Adriene exhaled a heavy sigh, then inclined her head. "Sir." She took a final bite of the MRE, then tossed the wrapper in the incinerator chute and headed for the exit.

"Adriene?"

She glanced back.

The lines creasing West's forehead softened. "Good hunting. Stay safe."

One corner of her mouth tugged up into a small smile. "Thanks, sir."

TWENTY

Augur Team's ship waited in bay three with its dual hatches opened. Larger than their standard dropships, the armored transport was built to ferry a team of twelve, with two sets of troop seats lining either wall of the crew compartment.

Adriene ascended the ramp into the hold, where the others stood at the troop lockers suiting up. Kato waved her over, and she joined him, yanking open her assigned locker and pulling her suit chassis out. Kato helped her, snapping the last of her shell into place as Blackwell boarded. The major looked even stockier under the bulk of his light gray hardsuit.

Rhett, the Stormwalkers' lieutenant, disappeared into the enclosed helm and Gallagher followed to serve as copilot. Adriene sat between Brigham and Kato on the troop bench opposite Ivon, Coleson, and Wyatt.

At 1300 on the dot, Blackwell sealed the hatches and called for a ready check. Everyone sounded off as he settled in beside Ivon. "Augur Team is primed," he announced over suit comms. "Activating Rubicons."

Adriene's vision flared white. Her chest swelled as a comforting weight descended over the cold vacancy in her skull.

// Welcome to Rubicon. Good morning. //

It's one in the afternoon.

// Well, I just woke up, so it's morning to me. //

And as we all know, the universe revolves around you.

// Glad to see you've come to terms with that. //

Adriene rolled her eyes. Her AI had really started to own the whole unique personality thing.

New reference pips and hardsuit stripes tracked in her HUD—

the addition of five more squad members causing an increased flurry of activity. Along one side, a squad roster expanded—Brigham's red, Gallagher's green, and Kato's blue all familiar sights after weeks of ops together. Blackwell's name shone a stark, bright white, whereas Rhett was magenta, Ivon bright orange, Coleson violet, and Wyatt teal.

The deck chief's voice rang over the ship intercom, "Augur One cleared for takeoff. Good hunting, fivers."

The ship rumbled as the engines ignited. Rhett steered them out of the hangar, and they entered a brief, in-system jaunt through subspace.

When they exited a few minutes later, two convoy ships waited in orbit to escort them to the surface. The groundside support squads called in their all clear, then Augur One slid through the atmosphere and under the cloud cover.

CNGC-8402b-III was a type-4 planet: a former Goldilocks whose turbulent geological history had covered it in a crust of black volcanic rock veined with streams of hot lava and punctuated by brilliant, golden-orange eruptions from fissures and vents. A haze of ash lingered in the sulfur-heavy atmosphere.

They set down in the designated landing zone, and Augur Team disembarked two abreast onto the craggy surface. A gust of wind swept in an ash cloud, the clumps of black dust whirling around them like an ethereal swarm of locusts.

Adriene's pathfinder module scanned the terrain as she guided them toward the foot of a massive dormant volcano, one of a dozen in their visual range. Branching fractures scarred the black rock of the mountain face like forked lightning, the barren channels cut long ago by flows of lava.

After fifteen minutes of keeping a steady pace, Augur Team approached the target location—an otherwise nondescript expanse of fractured rock. The subterranean black site had been tunneled into the hard rock centuries ago, and any proper entry points had become casualties of the planet's tumultuous geology, buried under massive erosion deposits of rock and sediment courtesy of the nearby mountain.

Adriene scanned the surface for the most structurally sound breach point, then Brigham set the charges. The plumes of black dust settled to reveal a roughly two-meter circular rift in the flinty surface.

After Gallagher and Ivon called the all clear on overwatch, Adriene offered to take point, knowing her Rubicon would be able to sense any approaching danger before the others'. Blackwell agreed, and Wyatt helped set her anchor, then she rappelled down into the jet-black pit.

After a twelve-meter descent, her feet hit ground. She released the winch, and her boots crunched against metal decking dusted with shards of rocky debris from the detonation. A soft beam of surface light shone from the breach, hazed by the atmospheric ash lingering like dust motes.

Adriene scanned the darkness. Her HUD's enhanced light filter activated, but there was too little illumination to start with, and she could see nothing but grated metal flooring in either direction.

She double-checked the overwatch map in her HUD. "All clear," she called over comms.

One by one, the others joined her. When they'd settled, Blackwell opened comms and primed the support squad assigned to start the off-site power generator. Augur Team formed up, ready to return fire against any automated defense systems that might trigger.

Blackwell gave the signal, and the power surged on. Banks of lights flicked on one by one. Only a fifth of the fixtures worked—some convulsing for a few seconds before giving in, while others threw out single, brilliant bursts like final, desperate death throes before shorting out completely.

Though mottled, the new illumination sufficiently revealed the interior of the small hangar—just large enough to house three standard dropships abreast. Patches of rust stained the paneled metal walls where the coating had worn away.

Pneumatic pumps lined a trussed ceiling, indicating a retractable roof, which would have once opened to allow arrivals and departures before being buried by avalanches. Sets of metal stanchions

outlined three separate docking pads, only one of which was occupied by an odd, scalene-shaped craft. The marred hull featured
a series of unreadable markings, and a long, jagged crack across a
section of the back aft.

*// I can't match it with anything on your pathfinder module. But I'd
say it's two to three hundred years old. //*

Must've been abandoned when the black site was decommissioned.

Brigham's red pip glowed within Adriene's comms module. "Sir,"
he said to Blackwell. "Entry at ten o'clock."

Brigham pinged the opposite wall. Blackwell gave the signal,
and the squad fell into a wedge formation as they moved toward
it. The quiet, empty hangar gave off an eerie yet oddly comfortable
ambience, like the refreshing quiet of a typically busy spaceport
after hours.

Kato and Wyatt broke off and approached the access panel beside the double-wide, reinforced door. They conversed between
themselves as they tapped into their hyphens, then Wyatt said, "It'll
be just a minute, sir."

The rest of Augur Team shifted into a loose, outward-facing arc,
fencing the engineers in while keeping an eye on the open hangar
behind them.

// Now that power's on, you ready to connect to the rest of the site? //
Ready when you are.

Adriene's chest swelled with invigoration as her Rubicon's range
expanded. Within the site, dozens of terminals had spooled up,
dysfunctional life systems struggled to reboot, and ancient, arid water recyclers whirred to life.

She filtered out the typical idle tech, focusing on a stronger
source. It pulsed in her mind's eye—a resonant tremor like the
rumble of earth before an avalanche.

The monolith of power sat deep within the complex, a dense
concentration of electronics simultaneously localized and ubiquitous. Its potency reminded her of how the power source had felt at
the ruined space station so many weeks ago. But instead of *generating* electricity like the singularity had, this one felt as though it was

consuming it. Greedily drinking it from the walls like a protostar leaching mass from an interstellar cloud.

Then at once, the source vanished. Disappeared out through the copper veins of the facility like discharged static.

Adriene scanned her HUD. She'd never felt anything like that before.

What the hell was that?

// I'm not sure. From the cyclic power draw, I'd say the source was some kind of large-scale processor farm. But it appears to have shorted out; I can no longer access it through our network. //

Her pulse beat heavily in her eardrums. A processor farm . . . That had to be the objective.

Frustratingly, she couldn't apprise Blackwell of that particular insight. Though her teammates had grown used to her seemingly unnatural abilities—attributing it to a mixture of the new pathfinder module and her "inherent skill"—something told her Blackwell might not be as willing to roll with it. To ensure he didn't sideline her, she'd have to let the mission take its course and only intervene if it seemed like they might not make it out with the intel intact.

Finally Kato chirped, "Sorry for the wait, folks. We're in."

The wide door slid open. Within, a dim hallway branched in either direction.

In the corner of Adriene's HUD, Blackwell's bright white pip glowed as his low voice broke over comms. "Stormwalkers, clear right. Recon, on me."

Lieutenant Rhett led the Stormwalkers to the right, toward what appeared to be the hangar's control station. Blackwell took point as Forward Recon headed left down a short hall, which opened into a large vestibule. Blackwell and Brigham entered first, sweeping their aims to alternate corners to clear the room.

As Adriene followed them in, an ear-piercing klaxon rang out. Harsh orange light bathed the high walls of the two-story room. Adriene ducked, sliding into cover behind a short barricade just inside the door. In her HUD, her squad's pips diverged as they split off to find cover.

Her pulse spiked, but overwatch remained quiet, and she could sense no Mechan in her expanded network. No pips or threat assessment meter appeared, and only her squad's colored dots marred an otherwise clean map.

Gallagher's level voice rang over comms, "No contacts, sir. Including defenses. Appears to only be an auditory alarm."

Blackwell let out a gruff sigh. "Sergeant Kato—get that fuckin' racket turned off, please."

"Yes, sir." Kato remained cross-legged where he'd taken cover, working between Rubie and his hyphen as the others stood, rifles raised and cautious.

Adriene swung her scope around the open atrium. Long, low, open metal boxes hashed out small areas of the large room, probably ancient planters, though any flora were long decomposed. It looked like a waiting room, devoid of any furniture remnants.

After a few minutes, the clanging alarm fell silent.

Kato slid his hyphen closed and joined them. "Sorry that took so long—the alarm wasn't part of the main system. Looks like a retrofit after the site got built, so it was livin' on its own partition."

Rhett's smooth, calculated voice called over comms, "Rhett for Major Blackwell."

"Go for Blackwell."

"All clear and a dead end this way, sir. Coming back to you."

The four Stormwalker pips began to move toward the atrium. Recon followed Blackwell to the far side of the room, where they formed up and waited in front of the exit.

Kato edged up to Adriene's shoulder and nudged her. He tapped something into his hyphen, and her HUD pinged with an incoming data packet.

It opened, displaying a video recording from the security system he'd just hacked. It showed a grainy view of the room from a camera high above the door frame. Blackwell appeared first, then

Brigham, the system scanning each with a jittering yellow overlay. When Adriene's figure stepped in after them, her outline flashed and highlighted crimson. A series of unreadable symbols burst onto the screen, and the system switched to high alert.

Adriene attempted to steady her racing pulse, then switched to a private line with Kato. "What the hell?"

"No idea." Kato scoffed, though he seemed mostly amused. "Fuckin' weird, huh?"

"Yeah . . ." She forced out a chuckle, though she knew how nervous and raw-edged it must have sounded. "I guess they think I'm the bad guy."

"Guess so." Kato slid his hyphen shut and shrugged. "We're not *not* the enemy."

She bit the inside of her lip and nodded. Except it wasn't *we*. It was *she*.

// *I mean, it's probably me. I'm very scary.* //

She sighed.

// *Actually, I'm not joking. It has to be me.* //

I know, but that doesn't make sense. This is an Architect facility, built before they'd even invented Mechan. They wouldn't have had any reason to red-flag an AI.

// *Just because I usually have all the answers doesn't mean I always have all the answers.* //

Trust me, I know.

// *You expect too much from me sometimes.* //

Can we go back to you being quiet?

// *Yes, sir.* //

With a synchronous clunking of boots, the Stormwalkers marched in and joined them.

Blackwell nodded. "Engaging DCM."

He pushed out a directive, triggering their Rubicons to engage a new mode that'd scan for data concentrations. In Adriene's HUD, Augur Team's suits glowed green, threading through with a distinct, hard-edged chartreuse light—data streaming to various subsystems of their suits, and to and from their Rubicons.

Adriene glanced around the atrium, where the occasional flicker of yellow-green data flowed within the walls.

Wyatt let out a sharp exhale. *"Mira's fiery end,* Valero."

Adriene turned to find all eight of them staring at her.

Coleson tilted his wide head. "You some kinda savant or somethin'?"

"Must be a bug," Gallagher grumbled, tapping on the side of her helmet as if it might clear the issue.

Adriene swallowed and looked between her squadmates and the others in nervous confusion. Blackwell stared as well, his light gray suit stoic and silent at the back of the group.

Before Adriene could form a question, a video opened in her HUD: Kato sharing the feed from his own suit cam. It took her a moment to reorient. Kato faced her, so she should be seeing herself, but her form was obstructed by a vast, glowing, sparking chartreuse mass. It covered her head, trailing down her neck, even a ways into her upper back and shoulders.

Brigham shifted, swapping his rifle stock to his opposite shoulder. "From all your rezones," he said, tone seemingly assured, though there was a forced edge to it. He gave her a stiff pat on the shoulder. "Eh, *Ninety-Six?*"

"Yeah," she agreed, willing steadiness into her voice. "It's probably that."

Kato's visor feed disappeared. Adriene inhaled, shoring up belief in her own words. It was definitely because of all her rezones.

// Seriously? It's me again. //

Shut. Up.

Blackwell gave a loose shake of his head. "Well, we don't need to see every damn bit of code floatin' around anyway."

// Filtering . . . //

The green from their suits disappeared, as well as most of the small trails that weaved through the walls.

"We're lookin' for somethin' big, fivers," Blackwell said with the definitive, bureaucratic air of steering them back on track. "Keep a sharp eye, and remember the DCM won't work through walls or obstructions, so look behind, under, and within every nook and cranny. On me."

Augur Team methodically worked their way through the dim, dust-laden corridors. They found each room filled with some variety of rusted worktables, broken lab equipment, empty storage cabinets, dysfunctional terminals, and complicated but delicate decaying machinery. The place had clearly been some kind of research site—though what they'd had to research on this barren, backwater planet, Adriene had no idea. She expected to discover more of the coffin-like monoliths she'd seen at every other site they'd been at the last two months, but so far, there'd been no sign of them.

They'd cleared almost half the massive facility when they approached the largest chamber shown on the rough schematic sketched up in their HUDs by their survey drones. Kato bet it was a mess hall, while Coleson and Wyatt put money on a secondary hangar. Adriene took Gallagher's side that it was some kind of controlled-environment storage, related to whatever the site had been researching. But they were all wrong.

They formed up at the sealed entrance as Wyatt connected to the control panel via her hyphen. A tiny node of chartreuse light shone from the interface, an indication of the small bit of data sent to trigger the controls. The door split and slid open.

Within, broad overhead light banks clicked on in staggered waves. The high-ceilinged room sloped away at a slight angle, lined with rows upon rows of freestanding server racks. Each slightly curved row arced away on either side of the wide, central aisle, extending to the outer walls. The main aisle culminated in a metal guardrail that framed a sunken control arena at the foot of the room.

Wyatt took a slow step in. "Mira's end," she cursed, gaze drifting over the vast room.

"Yeah . . ." Kato exhaled his agreement, and Adriene unconsciously nodded along with the engineers. This was one of the largest remote server rooms she'd ever seen.

Adriene chewed the inside of her lip. Mira help them if this was what West needed them to recover in "*one, functional piece.*" They'd be hauling enclosures, processors, and data cores back to the *Aurora* for a week straight.

Coleson's violet-lined suit rails glowed as he said, "This has to be it, right? The target intel?"

Blackwell made a noncommittal grunt. "Fan out," he ordered. "Clear the room."

Blackwell and the Stormwalkers headed right, and with a quick hand motion, Brigham ordered Forward Recon left. He pushed out assignments to their HUDs, and they headed to their appointed rows.

Adriene stepped into hers, sighting down her rifle as she cleared the long arc of flush server enclosures set behind doors mounted on inset hinges. Not a single exterior status light flickered, and no telltale thrum of powered electronics or fans stifled the air.

Adriene crept down the aisle to where one of the cabinet doors sat ajar. She cracked it open with an elbow. Her Rubicon activated her scope light and she swept it around the interior of the housing. Within, a melted, charred mass of circuitry and bundled cabling, caked in black soot and white ash. The inside of the rack's grated metal frame was covered in flaky, brassy-orange rust.

"Shit," she muttered under her breath.

She paced down a few meters and gripped the recessed handle of another cabinet door. It resisted with a shrill groan of corroded hinges, but her suit-assisted yank overcame its protests.

Inside, more scorched remains.

Stepping back, Adriene inspected both sides of the reinforced, powder-coated metal door. The *fireproof* door.

She stared back at the fused circuitry within. No acrid scent of burnt electronics or rubber lingered on the air, even to her Rubicon-enhanced senses. This had happened a long time ago.

// Remember, this may not even be what we're after. There's still a significant portion of the facility to scout. //

His tone conveyed flat, assured confidence. Yet a faint, almost indiscernible secondary sense of unease had joined her own.

A semitransparent overlay appeared in her HUD. The facility map, highlighting the portion they had yet to explore.

// See? //

She sighed. "Yeah, maybe," she conceded, realizing too late she'd spoken aloud.

"Valero?" Blackwell prompted.

"Sorry, sir." She shook away her hesitation. "The racks are burned out over here."

A moment later, Brigham grunted. "Damn, here too."

"Here as well, sir," Ivon commented from somewhere on the opposite side of the room.

One by one, the others voiced similar situations in their rows.

"Strange," Rhett said, offhanded and airy, almost to herself.

"Yeah," Gallagher agreed. "Why contain the destruction like this? Why not just destroy the whole black site—or at least this room?"

In her HUD, Adriene eyed the details of the facility scan, refined by her pathfinder module. It indicated reinforced bulkheads enclosing the large chamber, along with a few auxiliary rooms at the back. It would have been easy to contain the fire. Whoever had done this had been trying to keep the room intact, for whatever reason. Hopefully that meant there was something left to find.

"Everyone keep looking," Blackwell ordered, frustration thick in his surly tone. "If they left somethin' untouched, let's find it."

The Stormwalkers and Blackwell kept to the right half while Forward Recon continued to alternate rows on the left. They inspected each of the dozens of server cabinets, working their way down to the lowest level of the sloped room.

A half hour later, Adriene stood inspecting the penultimate row on their side when a soft click sounded in her ear. Her gaze focused onto her HUD's comms module. Kato had opened a direct line.

"Ninety-Six?" His voice rang cautious, thin, and . . . concerned.

Her shoulders stiffened. "What's wrong?"

"Come take a look at this?"

Adriene's focus drew to her map, and she picked out his blue pip, oriented herself, and turned on her heel, stock tight to her shoulder. She found him at the base of the central aisle, standing in front of the safety railing overlooking the sunken control arena.

"What is it?" she asked. "Are those the server control terminals down there?"

"I don't think so." The new, flat monotone to his voice was even more worrying than the concern had been. He lifted a hand and waved her toward him with a flick of his fingers.

She stepped to stand over Kato's shoulder, matching his gaze. The railing encircled a large, oval pit, sunken a half story down and ringed by inactive control panels, keyboard interfaces, and large banks of dark monitors.

The feature causing Kato's troubling range of vocal tones rested at the center of the space: an indiscernible mass encased in the glowing green overlay of their HUD's data concentration mode. The strands arced out from the source in every direction like curls of plasma dancing off the surface of a star.

Adriene blinked hard, her eyes suddenly dry and scratchy.

Kato was right. That was not a control terminal.

Mute the data concentration filter.

// Blackwell's Rubicon's hosting it; I can't shut it off for only you. I can override it, but it's an all-or-nothing situation. //

That's fine, do it.

// Doing it. //

The overlay disappeared. Underneath, a pile of scrap metal remained. A boxy jumble of sharp edges and convex planes, wound through with bulges of insulated cabling and shards of metal. Adriene's mind worked overtime trying to make sense of it.

"What the . . ." she mumbled, but the question died out on her tongue as light glinted off the pile.

Kato let out a soft mewl from the back of his throat, a sound between skeptical curiosity and raw panic.

A barely audible hiss sounded—a soft, controlled movement of air like long-held hydraulics exhaling. With a whirring clatter, the pile unfolded. And began to *stand*.

Kato took a halting step backward. Adriene gripped his shoulders as he stumbled into her.

A familiar, ice-cold, stark clarity flashed over Adriene's nerves, sharpening every sense.

Time slowed. Her mind ran faster as she took in a swarm of inputs, but—unlike the first time it'd happened in the ruins of that jungle planet—the feeling didn't overwhelm her, didn't terrify her down to her core. She'd had months of practice. They'd had months together, her and her Rubicon, and they were more synergized than ever. This time, she could handle it.

That didn't make it any easier to stomach what she saw.

There had been something safe—freeing—about not being able to process the thing about to slaughter you in minute, crisp detail.

Kato's chin lifted, higher, higher, and Adriene forced herself to match his gaze. The mass of metal continued to stand, in its own strangely slow, immutable way. Hinged beams unfolded and snapped into place with ragged, jittering hisses, shrill whirrs, and grinding mechanics.

Over the bones of its framework, exposed wires traced jointed metal columns like veins. Scuffed plates shifted into place over massive limbs and a thick torso. The dark metal chassis had a striated, tempered quality—each piece scuffed and worn, covered with furrows and gouges. She'd never seen anything like it.

A cacophony of chartreuse erupted in her HUD—the mute she'd put on the data concentration filter had reset. The smooth, lapping curls of green snapped straight, drawing thin and proliferating out into a gnarled mass of hard lines and sharp angles. Each movement caused a cascade of shifting angles and lines, a maelstrom of data spikes that ran up and down its limbs, extending along bundles of cabling that connected to open electrical panels in the walls of the oval pit.

Adriene stared. *Mute . . . that . . .*

// Just gonna cancel it . . . //

The green overlay disappeared.

"Valero?" Blackwell demanded. "Did you just deactivate the data concentration filter?"

She licked her dry lips and started to apologize, but decided not to bother. They didn't need it anymore. They'd found their target. This . . . *Mechan.*

Which now stood upright, every piece of its chassis finally in place. It rolled back its broad shoulders as it straightened to its full height: over three meters, taller than any scrapper Adriene had ever seen.

A thin haze of electricity washed over its massive frame, encasing it in a tight shell of glowing purple shield construct.

Rooted by fear and awe, she continued to watch, stunned.

It raised one of its arms and pointed it toward her and Kato. A flat piece of metal extended from the top of its forearm.

The barrel of some kind of projectile weapon, she realized. Too late.

The muzzle flashed.

CHAPTER

TWENTY-ONE

Adriene yanked the raised lip of Kato's gorget, pulling his back into her chest.

A metallic blur etched a shallow gash across Kato's chestplate as they barely twisted out of its path. The flat, scalene projectile whipped past them and up the aisle as Ivon stepped out of a row. It slammed straight into his chest.

No. Not into.

Through.

The shard had pierced clean through Ivon's chestplate, torso, and backplate, then lodged into the metal decking partway up the sloped ramp behind him.

Adriene froze. Icy panic gripped her muscles.

The orange strip lights overlaying Ivon's suit winked out. He collapsed, dead instantly.

Kato exhaled a throttled gasp.

Augur Team erupted.

Adriene barely kept up with the frantic movement of her team's pips in her HUD as she dragged a stunned, horrified Kato back, away, retreating into the possible safety of the server racks. *Possible* because that . . . *giant Mechan* . . . had fired something that'd sliced through multiple layers of alanthum. Like butter. Like cloth. Like it was nothing. She wasn't sure anywhere was "safe."

Kato's sharp breaths broke through comms. "Valero," he huffed. "What in Mira's—"

Blackwell's low voice roared, "Fall back! Now!"

Adriene drew in a deep breath and faced Kato. He stood bracing himself on his knees, visor drifting back and forth, rifle hanging loose off one shoulder. "What the—" he stammered, then tried again. "What the hell is that thing?"

"Hey, it's okay," she said, injecting calm into her voice despite how very not calm she felt. "It's just a bot. We got this." She cycled the pattern controls on her coilgun, landing on disruptive fire. "You heard the boss—we retreat. Top of the room. You go first, I'll cover you." Drawing close to the server cabinets, she slid up to the corner that met the main aisle. The bot stood in the same spot, arm raised, head swiveling slowly toward the far side of the room.

She signaled Kato.

Reluctantly, he shouldered his rifle. Their Rubicons synced a countdown.

// *Three . . . two . . . mark.* //

Kato dashed into the aisle, breaking for the next row up. Adriene fired off a quick spray of small metallic slugs that melted into the bot's charged shield construct. The impacts sent sparking ripples of forked lightning out over the semitransparent shell.

The Mechan's gaze pinned her. Its head tilted on a strange, pitched axis, and its amber ocular sensors brightened.

Adriene's heart slammed against her chest. No variety of combat cocktail could quell her panic. Within a few microseconds, she sensed it scanning her, assessing, evaluating—implacable in its judgment.

Shit. It knew what she was.

A screech of feedback exploded in her ears, reverberating in her skull on an unending loop. She gripped the sides of her visor, teeth bared.

// *Sens—or—sting—marrrrr—* //

Her knees hit the grated metal floor. White bloomed in static pulses from the edges of her vision.

A blue-limned suit appeared. Arms dragged her back into the shelter of the row. Her sight listed, dizzying nausea rising, overwhelming her senses.

"Ninety-Six!" Kato's voice, distant.

A shrill metallic whistle pierced the air.

In her HUD, another squad pip faded. Adriene's heart kicked. Her gaze drifted left.

A few meters up the main aisle, Wyatt lay skewered by two shards of metal. Blood pooled around her limp body as the soft yellow lights faded from her suit.

Heat peeled at the edges of Adriene's vision.

At once, the static feedback cut off, leaving a harsh ringing in her raw eardrums.

She growled, "What the *hell?*"

// *It's trying to hack us.* //

Us? You and me?

// *The whole squad, through me and you. Our suits, our modules, our implants. The Rubicon mainframe.* //

Shit. Don't fucking let it.

// *I don't intend to.* //

Her shoulders sagged along with a twinge of pressure behind her eyes, the telltale mental lethargy Daroga had warned them about as her Rubicon siphoned her for energy. Moments later, it ebbed, though it'd left a notable dent in her stamina.

// *Sorry—done. I created a firewall that should keep it out. For now, at least. The bot's working incredibly fast, though; I've never seen anything like it.* //

"Ninety-Six?" Kato squeaked, voice raw with panic.

With an effort, she focused on Kato, too depleted to be mad that he'd come back to help her.

"What the hell was that?" he panted. "Are you okay?"

"Fine. It's . . . The bot's hacking my—our Rubicons."

"What? *Shit.*"

"It's okay," she assured. "My Rubicon's got it under control."

Kato gripped Adriene's forearm and hauled her to her feet.

She scanned her HUD, reorienting and taking stock of the others' positions.

They were pretty spread out—Kato and her near the foot of the room, with Blackwell, Rhett, and Brigham each in different rows about halfway up. Coleson and Gallagher were the closest to the top—only a few rows from the exit door.

Adriene crept forward. She knelt at the corner of the aisle, pressing close to the flat, cold metal of the server racks. Kato hovered at her heel.

While the others threw back covering fire, Coleson broke for the door—the back of his suit awash with the purple of an active shield construct. But before he could reach the back wall, the door irised closed with a definitive *shink*.

"Shit!" Coleson pounded his fist on the door controls. The panel flashed red in response. The door remained sealed.

Adriene shifted as a sharp wave of static rolled up her spine, every hair on the back of her neck standing on end. A high-pitched tone cut through the air—the shrill quaver of the bot's prime cycle.

Her lips parted, but her warning caught in her throat as a gut-rending screech of metal whistled through the air. Then a sickening, hollow thunk.

Coleson stiffened. His backplate split between the shoulder blades, a long, straight fracture from his neck to the small of his back. The alanthum shell cracked, falling open as Coleson's stocky frame crumpled to the floor, rifle clattering beside him. The shard stuck out from his spine like a metal fin, his dark blood spilling forth in a torrent.

Coleson's violet pip vanished.

"Coleson's down!" Brigham shouted, uncharacteristic alarm edging his voice.

Adriene stared at the three grayed-out pips in her squad roster. At her redlined threat assessment meter. Her squadmates' panicked vitals soaked through her Rubicon's wireless network, weighing down the tight strain deep in her chest. Her heart drummed fast—too fast.

After more than two months . . .

// No. Don't go there. //

There was a reason West hadn't wanted to deactivate her rezone chip until the campaign concluded. So that if she failed, she'd be able to rezone. So she could try again.

// *You don't have to rezone. This is not over. We can do this. Focus.* //

Her HUD flickered out, then rebooted. It returned, clear of every distraction except the map containing her remaining squad's pips—Kato, Brigham, Gallagher, Rhett, and Blackwell.

She drew in a halting breath, forcing her fear aside. He was right. Now, more than ever, they could do this. They'd find a way.

// *That's the spirit.* //

Her Rubicon's time-slowing effect continued to favor her—mere seconds had passed since Coleson died. Blackwell belayed the retreat, ordering them to pair up and batten down. Her and Kato's pips linked.

Though panic suffused her, weeks of conditioning lodged firmly in her bones. She reflexively shifted to cover Kato's flank. They backpedaled down the arc of servers, away from the central aisle. Halfway down, they halted and snapped back-to-back. The slight weight of Kato's lean against her shoulder blades offered an oddly comforting presence.

Throw every pathfinder subsystem resource we have at your recordings of that thing—get me details. As fast as you can.

// *On it.* //

Fatigue washed over her, the bone-deep lethargy of her Rubicon pulling more of her energy to power the request.

Blackwell's white comms pip glowed. "Kato, we need to rouse support squads for backup—fast."

"On it, sir," Kato replied, voice labored. "Been pingin' 'em, but gettin' a helluva lotta interference."

A moment later, a new pip lined up in the queue of the minimized comms module. A crackled, distorted voice jittered through, "Sir—this—Gamma—"

"Gamma Team, say again," Blackwell replied.

The voice crackled, just as garbled.

A static peal of feedback ripped through comms, and Adriene growled through bared teeth. The others voiced their discomfort as well, the comms a disarray of overlaid shouting.

Then the grating tone disappeared . . . along with everyone's voices. Only static remained.

Adriene tapped the side of her helmet. The comms module turned crimson and flashed "*Offline.*"

// *Squad comms are down—the Mechan's jamming us.* //

"Kato?" Adriene barked. He didn't respond, but when she glanced over her shoulder, she caught a glimpse of him with his hyphen already open, working away.

The analog text queue panel expanded in her HUD. "Sergeant Kato," Blackwell transmitted, "report."

"The bot, sir," Kato replied. "It's pushing out a jammer. I'm working on it."

Adriene shouldered her rifle, taking it upon herself to guard their only engineer with her life. She kept her eyes homed in on the far edge of the server rack, waiting for the bot to round the corner and rain down more alanthum-cracking shrapnel.

Vertigo briefly gripped her, then the background haze of mental fatigue lifted.

// *Assessment done.* //

And?

// *Not much, unfortunately. The bot's model doesn't match any Mechan on record—though based on cursory scans, it's of standard material composition. I can't get a solid read on its power source. Pathfinder says it's "untraceable." No idea what that means. One thing I'm pretty sure of, though, is it's old.* //

How old?

// *"Guaranteed-that-West-wants-it" old.* //

You think this is it? The objective?

// *For one-sixth of a second during its failed hack, it was part of my— our—wireless network. There's . . . a lot going on in there, as we saw with the data concentration filter. I'm very certain, yes.* //

A familiar static cacophony filled her ears, and relief flooded her chest.

"Got it!" Kato's clipped tone cut through comms, crackling, harsh and tinny, but audible. "You guys back?"

Blackwell yelled, "Sound off!"

They complied, a colored pip glowing along with each of them—Brigham, Gallagher, Kato, Rhett, then Adriene. Though relieved no one else had met their fate at the shard-launching bot, Ivon's, Coleson's, and Wyatt's grayed-out pips remained a sober reminder of their dire situation.

"Kato," Blackwell barked, "I still can't get a line out."

"We're on analog now, sir," Kato announced, chagrin in his tone. "Which means no comms outside this room."

Blackwell growled, "I need comms outside this fucking room, Sergeant! We need backup."

"I know. I'm sorry, sir. I'm trying, but this bot really knows its shit."

"You need to know your shit better, Lian."

"Yes, yes, sir, sorry—I'm on it."

Adriene opened a temp line directly to Kato. "I'm covering you, K."

"Thanks, Ninety-Six." Kato braced his elbow against a server cabinet to prop his hyphen up near his visor and got to work.

Blackwell said, "I need someone on that door."

Rhett replied, steady assurance in her husky voice, "I'm on it, sir. No luck so far. We need more time. Looks like Wyatt's injuries shorted out her module, so we can't patch into it."

Adriene frowned. They were painfully short on engineers.

Help them with the door if you can. Subtly.

// *Will do. Quiet as a mouse.* //

"We got a twenty on the target?" Blackwell asked.

"Aye, sir." Gallagher's green pip glowed. "Drone visual confirms it's still at the foot of the room, in the control arena."

Adriene chewed the inside of her lip. It'd been less than two minutes since the thing first woke, but still . . . It hadn't moved? At all?

She could think of only two reasons for that.

One: It *couldn't*. Which, in making strides toward the aforementioned *frustrating*, didn't matter, because it was ostensibly the same as the second reason. Which was that it hadn't moved because it didn't need to.

There was only one way out of this room, and the bot already had a completely unobstructed angle on it. Even if they got the door open, they'd be fish in a barrel the second they stepped into that aisle and made a break for it. Coleson's escape attempt had proven that even their shield constructs couldn't save them. They'd be skewered within seconds.

Adriene shook it off. Their inability to escape was beside the point.

This bot was the *objective*. The reason West had made sure she—and by extension her team—were here over anyone else in Flintlock, in this massively dangerous room with this murderous Mechan. Not that all Mechan weren't murderous, but this one seemed especially so, with its unprecedented, alanthum-shredding arm guns.

She drew in a steadying breath. With both retreating and calling for backup off the table, one option remained: They had to disable the bot. It was the only way out of this room that didn't involve a rezone.

But all the reasons they couldn't escape were also the reasons they couldn't get close enough to incapacitate it. Destroying it would be one thing, but how the hell were they ever going to subdue it long enough to *capture* it?

She rolled her bottom lip between her teeth.

Play back what we saw of it earlier?

Her Rubicon queued up the video of the bot awakening, playing it back on a loop in her HUD. She focused in on the details, its amber eye sensors—notably dim, the stuttering motions of the armored plating closing around its torso and limbs, the three tails of bundled cabling connecting it to the various control arena dashboards encircling it.

She blinked, focusing on the cabling.

When they'd first arrived and her Rubicon had expanded their network, she'd felt a dense, concentrated fount of power from deep within the complex. One that'd felt like it'd been *consuming* power instead of generating it.

She played back the recording of the bot again, slowly, frame by frame, then a few times more with various filters activated: thermographic, data concentration, spectroscopic.

When the bot had first stood, its chassis had been withdrawn. The Shade model had a similar function for the sake of agility, or as means of evasion, akin to dislocating a joint to escape confinement. For over a half hour prior to that, the bot had remained quietly disassembled, not even bothering to acknowledge the eight humans in the room until she and Kato had stood gawking at it.

It'd been hiding.

She'd been wrong, before. There was a *third* reason the scrapper might not be moving—because it couldn't . . . *Yet.* The bot was still charging.

She didn't understand the engineering, but she'd encountered enough Mechan in her day to know that interrupting a charge cycle was the equivalent of catching a human sleeping. It may be putting on a good defensive show, but in reality, it was vulnerable. If they could interrupt the charge cycle before it was complete, they stood a chance at taking it "alive."

"Mira's ashes," Kato groused, frustration thick in his tone. "Major, I'm gettin' nothin' over 'ere—comms are completely scrammed; I can't even begin to get a route in edgewise on the door lockdown. We're fightin' a losin' battle, boss."

Blackwell growled. "Dammit—understood. All right, backup's not comin', fivers, which means we're gonna have to try and KO this bot ourselves. Hold tight for orders; Rubicon's tallying our firepower."

Shit.

Blackwell wasn't even going to *try* to take it in *"one, functional piece."* She had to work fast.

She switched to a private line with Kato. "Kato, I've got a theory."

"Shoot."

"That cabling . . ." She pushed him a still frame from her suit cam recording.

"Huh," he said, tone airy.

"Does that look like—"

"A jury-rigged version of the connections used in their remote inverters? Shit. Yeah, it does."

"Am I right in thinking interrupting the charge cycle would cause cascading depletion?"

He let out an airy breath full of incredulity and slightly impressed confusion, like he'd never thought the two of them would be able to carry on a conversation using these words. She was surprised herself. Her Rubicon's bridge to her pathfinder module must have been working overtime.

"If it's tactilely interrupted—yes," Kato confirmed. "But just removing its connection to the source of power—no. Unless the thing's older than Mira herself, it's got cyclical transistors that're amplifyin' the draw as they cycle to the main core—it's how the stupid things charge so damn fast. We'd have to deliver quite a shock to its system to interrupt it enough to ensure a discharge."

"Then that's what we'll have to do."

"Uh, what?"

Adriene drew in a steadying breath, then switched to a private line with Blackwell. "Major Blackwell, sir. I think the bot's in the middle of a charge cycle. If we can get in close enough to disrupt—"

"Are you kidding me, Valero?" he snapped. "The only way out of this room alive is *through* that bot."

"Sir, the objective is to retrieve the asset in—"

"The *intelligence asset*. Not some fucking scrapper."

Adriene swallowed a rise of impatience. "All due respect, sir, but we just found a three-hundred-year-old Mechan napping in a destroyed server room, one who sent the data concentration filter into overdrive. It's a fair bet this thing *is* the intelligence asset."

Blackwell remained silent for a few gut-wrenching seconds, and Adriene could practically feel his fury radiating across the 18.2 meters from where he'd hunkered down among the racks on the opposite side of the room.

Finally, he growled, "How the hell do you know how old it is?"

"My pathfinder module, sir." No reason to convolve Rubicon in the explanation.

Blackwell didn't respond, and she could sense his struggle through her Rubicon: an oscillating mix of distrust, conceit, stubbornness, and suspicion.

"No," he said finally, and her heart sank. "No fucking way this *thing* is what Intel wants. We KO it and get the hell out of here alive."

"Sir—"

"Augur Team, listen up," Blackwell said, switching back to squad comms. "Shoot to kill. Let's get this thing out of our way and get back to the mission. Ready incendiaries."

"Belay that," Adriene said, pulse pounding in her neck.

Disable squad comms.

Blackwell growled, *"Valer—"*

The comms module faded as her Rubicon haltingly complied. Taxing pressure weighed on the back of her eyes, and time slowed again as her Rubicon yanked back on the proverbial reins.

// What the hell are you doing? //

The raw demand in his tone caused a flicker of doubt in her mind, but she tamped it down.

He's going to destroy it. We can't let him.

// And how do you plan to stop him? //

I heard a rumor, once.

// Excuse me? //

That before I arrived, West would use Rubicon to give out rogue orders using Command's codes.

He hesitated, a hint of disgruntled disbelief tinging the back of her neck.

// Maybe. But that doesn't mean I can impersonate them mid-engagement. //

Can't you?

He didn't respond. It was the wrong question.

Will you?

Silence rang in her ears for a significant pause.

// We're going to get in so much trouble for this. //

That's the spirit.

// Tell me the orders. //

She considered her phrasing, the gruff, curse-laden way the major tended to speak, and formulated the new orders, readying them in the queue and ensuring everything was masked from Blackwell's feed. The more she kept him in the dark, the easier it'd be to play it all off as a tech malfunction later.

They had one more hurdle to clear before they could execute.

For this "tactile interruption" to work, she had to get her hands on the thing. Literally. She needed to make direct contact to the bot's chassis—ideally the torso. Which made its shield construct a problem.

// For that, we'll need the engineer's help. //

"Kato?"

"Go."

"Once the power's disconnected, I need you to interrupt that shield construct so I can get hands on the thing and drain it."

Kato scoffed. "Yeah, 'cept we don't have EMPs nearly strong enough for that."

"We'll have to ECM it instead. My Rubicon can facilitate, but it doesn't have the right tools."

Kato exhaled. "Right. We gotta use my engineer's module," he surmised, and she nodded. "All right, pass him over. Rubie and I'll see what we can do."

Adriene gave a pointed thought to grant her Rubicon permission to roam. The back of her skull twinged with a fraction of the dull, vacant ache she felt when he was deactivated.

Her stomach turned. She knew he could return within a fraction of a second if she needed him, but she wasn't used to live combat without him.

She kept a patient watch, subconsciously filtering out Blackwell's attempts at patching back into their active comms channels—luckily, he seemed to truly think it was another cyberattack from the bot. She threw in a decent amount of static and jumbled code to simulate the interference they'd experienced when the bot had jammed their comms earlier.

"Okay . . ." Kato said less than thirty seconds later, tentative. "I think we're ready. But, Valero, what's the plan here, exactly? I get you wanna interrupt its charge cycle, but your suit can't handle that kinda draw—it'll electrocute you."

"I'll redirect the flow."

"What?"

// *Yeah,* what? //

You'll create a shield construct. Inside my suit.

// *Oh—no way in hell.* //

I'm serious.

// *Yeah, I unfortunately realize that. Do you have any idea how dangerous that is? The insulation of your suit only protects you so much. There's maybe a quarter millimeter allowance between your skin and the metal of your suit, at the most generous.* //

Good thing a construct is only one hundred and ninety micrometers, then.

// *You were far less dangerous to yourself back when you didn't know things like that.* //

Please, trust me.

// *I do. Okay. I'll do it.* //

On my mark.

// *On your mark.* //

Phase one first.

In her HUD, she expanded the text queue. Acting as Blackwell, she sent the prepared directives to Kato, Brigham, Gallagher, and Rhett. They each voiced their acknowledgment via a color-coded reply in the queue. All except Blackwell, whom she'd locked out entirely.

She'd pay for that later. For all of this. For now, they had a bot to capture.

Ready?

// Ready. But for the record, I'm against you using yourself as bait. //
Noted.

She hovered at the edge of the aisle, drawing in a steadying breath. The bot had been interested enough in her before to pause the killing and attempt to hack her. She had to hope its interest hadn't waned.

Execute.

Her Rubicon synced a countdown, and as her squadmates sprinted for their new positions, Adriene rolled out into the aisle.

The bot's head swiveled to face her. Its amber ocular sensors flared. Her heart slammed in her chest.

A dense pressure built between her eyes, then blossomed at once into a concentrated migraine. She grimaced as the strain sank its teeth in, dizzying her as her Rubicon sapped more and more of her energy to fend off the bot's hacking attempt.

Going okay?

// Fine—this bot's just tough. It won't get in, don't worry. //

A burst of concentrated rifle fire rang through the chamber as her squadmates targeted the first of the three bundled cabling connections.

Bullets ricocheted, pinging the metal around the connections. The rubber casing frayed, then sparks flew up in a shower until the cabling severed in two.

One connection down. They moved onto the next.

Adriene startled when the pain and lethargy vanished instantly. The bot's head tilted. Adriene swallowed hard.

It pivoted its arm toward her. The shrill whine of the gun's prime cycle grated against her eardrums. The bot fired.

Adriene dropped her shoulder, barely twisting out of the shard's path. She dove, the knee guard of her suit sparking along the metal flooring as she slid behind the server racks.

Pulse racing, she scrambled to her feet. She slipped back out into the aisle. Her coilgun kicked into her shoulder as she aimed a spray of disruptive fire straight at the bot's face. The charged slugs melted into the shield construct.

The bot primed its weapon again. Fired.

She dove away again, but the shard clipped her, drawing a shrieking, blue-white slice through her right pauldron. She landed hard behind the racks on the opposite side. She gripped her right shoulder, though no pain emanated from the impact.

// Didn't breach—though barely. The second connection is almost down. It's time to move in. //

Adriene scrambled back to her feet, panting. Her suit worked overtime to wick the sweat from her superheated skin.

She drew herself close to the cabinet at the edge of the row. Rifle stock tight to her shoulder, she drew in a deep, steadying breath. She tensed her leg muscles, mentally gathering her suit's strength like a winding spring.

// Now. //

She dashed into the main aisle, straight for the Mechan.

As she approached the railing, she thrust a palm out, locking her elbow as it connected with the handrail. She vaulted, swinging her legs up as her momentum threw her over the barricade and into the sunken pit.

The floor on the other side rushed up. She braced for impact, turning the fall into a rolling tumble, scrambling to regain her footing with slightly less grace than she would have liked.

A stab of panic that was not her own cut through her chest.

// Watch out, the Mechan is—//

Four percussive blasts rocked the air.

Time ground to a halt. Unbidden, a purple shield of electric light stacked up in front of her. It projected from her own chestplate—one layer, then a second, then a third.

The bot had fired four shards at once, and two ricocheted off the triplicate-construct, which cracked and fractured under the pressure before re-forming.

In that fraction of a second, the other two shards had cut through.

Adriene's elbows lifted on instinct. The suit's horizontal blades slid out from her forearms. She thrust her arms out in a shallow X, slashing at the projectiles.

But her angles were all wrong. Neither deflected.

With a deafening, shrill shriek, both shards cut through her extended blades, then sank into the thick metal plating of her suit chassis before slicing deep into the bones of her forearms. A raw scream cut from the back of her throat.

She stumbled to one knee. Her HUD lit with a frantic stim cocktail deployment, but pain overwhelmed her senses for a few terrifying microseconds.

She rolled into cover behind a nearby support stanchion, panting breaths through clenched teeth. The numbing agent finally kicked in, but a phantom echo of the sharp pain lingered regardless.

With a soft crackling of purple light, her multilayered shield construct disengaged. She hadn't even known that was a function of the construct tech.

// It . . . isn't. I'm kind of playing it by ear in here. //

Grimacing, she lifted her hands to take stock of the two shards lodged in either forearm. The one in the right had come in almost parallel, barely biting through the armor enough to reach her flesh.

But her left arm was weak. That shard had cut perpendicular, skewering straight through. Dark red blood coated the half of the flat piece of metal that'd come out the other side.

Trembling, she reached for it.

// No—leave them in. //

She swallowed bile, hand dropping away. The edges of her HUD lit with medical warnings as her suit did what it could to stanch the bleeding. She forced the pain aside, focusing on the cool clarity from a rush of new adrenaline.

Fine. It was fine. Everything was fine. She only needed one functioning arm for this.

She shimmied to the corner of the stanchion and peered out past the edge, toward the Mechan. Augur Team's rifle fire continued to fly down from over the railing. Blooms of electric sparks flew up behind the bot, silhouetting its massive frame in bright white light.

Gallagher's overwatch drones buzzed overhead. The bot grabbed one midair and crushed it in a massive fist, dropping the hunk of scrap metal to clatter on the floor.

Then, the bot froze. Every limb suddenly rigid like someone had pressed its pause button.

Adriene tensed, momentarily stunned while her squad's rifle fire riddled the air. Sparks flew from the last of the three connections. The frayed cabling fell to the floor, severed in two.

Adriene shook off her confusion and refocused—the scrapper was finally disconnected.

With a brief thought, she fired off the ECM order to Kato, then sprang for the bot. Her heart thrashed in her chest. She closed the meters between them in half a second.

"Interrupt incoming," Kato announced. "Three, two, one, mark."

The bot's shroud of purple shield construct spluttered out. Adriene slid to a stop as her gloved palm smacked hard against the lower panel of its thick torso. The Mechan's chin dropped, staring down at her from three meters overhead.

// Activating inner-construct. //

Adriene's skin buzzed, a sharp, crackling vibration of static electricity flushing over her entire body. A bright red *"Significant power draw"* warning flared in her HUD.

Now!

Her muscles spasmed, and every hair on her body tensed as her Rubicon activated the conductive actuator gloves, sucking her palm flat against the bot's chassis.

Similar to what she'd felt on Cimarosa-IV, a distorted, uncomfortable static throb rolled through her in successive waves. The current held firm and unyielding, seeming so much more formidable this time—more significant, more powerful, more dangerous.

Her vision darkened at the edges.

A casing of white electricity danced across the surface of her hardsuit. The tingle of her inner shield construct grew hot and sharp, like the pricks of a million superheated needles.

A brassy metal taste suffused her saliva. One knee gave way, but she locked the other straight.

Just a few more seconds.

The bot's frozen limbs jerked. Adriene craned her neck to look up at the towering Mechan standing over her. It faced straight ahead, its long arms twitching.

A hot vibration tore down Adriene's spine. The whine of the bot's priming arm guns rang shrill in her ears, chilling her to her core.

Shit, shit, shit. She unlocked all comms channels, including Blackwell's, and shouted, "Take cover!" right as the bot's arms erupted with a cacophony of discharged slugs.

It fired, frenzied and unaimed, spraying chaotic twirls of shards out in a wild arc. Adriene's ears rang with high-pitched whistles and the gut-wrenching *shinks* of severing metal as the shards found purchase throughout the chamber.

Then at once, it was done.

The sparks on her hardsuit disappeared as the sharp electric flow ceased, releasing her from its clutches.

Her muscles slackened, her hand dropped away. The static tingle of her inner-construct vanished.

The bot's posture softened—no longer frozen, but gone completely limp like a marionette with severed strings. It fell backward in a resounding clatter of metal.

The Mechan's threat level bottomed out. Utter silence crushed down.

A wave of intense fatigue rolled over Adriene. Her knees hit the floor, and she collapsed to her side, muscles burning and weak, limbs leaden and heavy. For a few long moments, the thought of moving herself under her own power seemed an epically impossible feat.

// Suit capacitor level at less than one point one percent. //

Adriene's harsh breaths came clipped and uneven as she twisted onto her stomach. She managed to push up far enough to get onto all fours, then sat back on her heels.

Her shoulders slumped as she sat, heavy, burdened. She breathed slowly as she gathered her will.

Silence hung in the air, the tension of combat gone, leaving only the stench of burnt circuitry and . . . blood.

She stared down at her injured forearms, blood dripping quietly onto the ground around her. Her limp left fingers spasmed of their own accord, arm trembling as pain fired along the nerves in hot waves.

Her nearly depleted suit pumped more painkillers into her bloodstream.

The bot's final volley of shards surrounded her, sticking up out of the floor like a dense metal forest. The Mechan lay unmoving in a discordant heap. The three bundles of cabling that had connected it to the black site lay splayed around it like severed tentacles.

Though her weak limbs burned, she managed to push to her feet. Vertigo gripped her as she climbed onto the console counter. She grabbed the handrail and hauled herself up and over the railing, back to the server level of the sloped room.

Another field of shards laid out before her, jutting up from every surface.

Her heart caught. Across the aisle and two rows back, Gallagher lay skewered to the floor. The shards had gone straight through the server racks.

Adriene forced herself to look to her other side, where Brigham lay a couple of meters back, blood pooling out from over two dozen wounds. Adriene stared at his grayed-out pip, at Gallagher's, her hot breath steaming her visor, though her suit wicked it away.

In her HUD comms menu, a blue light flickered on. Kato groaned.

Her pulse spiked with renewed fervor.

Pain wrenched her every nerve as she ran the few meters toward his pip. A few rows up, he lay prone, his hyphen arm skewered to the floor along with the rest of his body. Three large pieces had lodged in his gut, countless smaller shards protruding from his legs and torso.

Adriene dropped to his side, hands hovering. She stared at a massive chunk of metal jutting from his crumpled chestplate.

// . . . I'm afraid not. //

Her Rubicon answered her unspoken question—*could she save him?*—but that was stupid. He should be just as dead as Brigham and Gallagher right now. Just as dead as *she* should be. The only reason she'd survived was because her Rubicon had seen the attack coming and thrown up that layered shield construct.

She looked down at her aching, bleeding forearms, the thick chunks of metal lodged in the paneling of her suit. Even that had barely saved her.

She swallowed her guilt and looked at Kato. "It's—" she croaked out, but the words stuck in her throat. He was going to rezone. How could she tell him it was all going to be okay?

"S'okay," he rasped, weak reassurance in his labored tone. "Did it work?"

"Yeah . . ." she managed, her dry voice breaking. "The bot froze—what'd you do?"

"It was your Rubie's idea. I don't know how the hell he did it, but we got access to the bot's controller program." He coughed. "Just straight up deleted his movement protocols. It's a simple trick—laced it with a buncha junk code to trip up the bot's auto-cleaners."

"But it's . . ." She glanced back at the main aisle, heart thudding loud in her throat. "Intact?"

His helmet bobbed. "It's paralyzed in its body right no—" He hacked a wet, jagged cough. "Oh shit. That's blood . . ."

Adriene heaved in a rough breath, gripping the side of his helmet. "Shit, Kato, I'm so sorry."

"S'not like you're the one that shanked me. Besides—mission accomplished, right? And it was a good plan, Ninety-Six. It worked."

She opened her mouth to offer some kind of consolation, but couldn't find the words. Tears welled behind her eyes.

She couldn't remember the last time she'd cried. Years.

"Hey," Kato said, voice light. "S'all right." He hacked out another wet, sick, bloody cough. "I'll see you again in a few days."

He launched into a coughing fit. She gripped his shoulders to steady him, but soon the coughs withered and died away. His head lolled back, tension melting from his limbs. In her HUD, his blue pip faded to gray.

Adriene curled forward, resting her head on her knees. She focused on breathing slowly and steadily, urging her racing heart and the swell of tears to abate.

Her breath hitched, air seeming to come up short. She willed another combat cocktail from her suit to calm her down.

// No. //

Please. I can't.

// You have to. It's normal. //

It doesn't feel normal.

// You just forgot. //

Forgot what?

// Sympathy. Grief. All of it. //

She squeezed her eyes tighter, the heat of tears stinging the corners.

Dammit. He was right.

When the hell had she started giving a shit about people again?

A haggard groan cut through comms. From a white pip.

Cradling her skewered left arm in her less-skewered right, Adriene sat up, then managed to stand. She turned to find Blackwell on the ground across the aisle. He shoved Rhett's dead body off his chest with considerable effort.

The shards that had killed Rhett had shallowly pierced his suit, and they clattered to the ground as he stood. A handful of smaller shards protruded from the left side of his suit. Blood dripped freely down the dark metal. He stared across the aisle at Adriene.

Her eyes scoured her HUD. No one else stirred. All seven other pips remained a dull, inactive gray.

Blackwell stepped into the aisle, glancing down at the eerily still Mechan, then back at Adriene before he clicked over to universal comms.

"Augur Team here," Blackwell said, his low voice toneless. "Please relay to *Aurora* Actual . . . Asset acquired."

Then he turned away without another word.

TWENTY-TWO

Adriene stood on the bright white bridge on the highest deck of the *Aurora*, fairly certain she'd never been in deeper shit.

A sleek but simple affair, the bridge had a dozen control consoles in a pristine arc on the top level, overlooking a lower deck reserved for the primary systems of flight, navigation, armaments, defense. The stations sat empty—it was 0100 ship time, and whatever bare-bones bridge crew would normally be on duty had been dismissed.

On the bottom deck, Commodore Thurston stood silently before the large central viewscreen, split into dozens of feeds from the ship's external cameras. Each showed the same thing from different angles: the mesmerizing, long, thin, branching strands of subspace.

As Major Blackwell continued to rant, Adriene remained silent, oscillating between genuine shame, mounting rage, and crushing grief. She couldn't force herself to focus on Blackwell's justifiable anger as he brusquely outlined the events of the mission for Thurston.

Because she'd gotten her entire squad rezoned.

Kato had bled out in her arms. Brigham and Gallagher had died alone, skewered to the floor, no chance at concealing themselves from the bot's frantic death throes.

"Special assignment" or not, there was no way Thurston would let this slide.

She clasped her hands behind her back, and pain fired up her wounded, wrapped forearms as her muscles tightened.

Brigham and Kato and Gallagher would have woken up with the same stabbing pain, all over their bodies—a phantom, sourceless agony, echoes of the wounds that caused their deaths, and any amount of painkiller would do nothing to deaden it until the memory faded. Such was the joy of a new husk.

"Is that true, Sergeant?" Thurston's baritone voice cut through her thoughts, still managing to sound full and thick as it carried across the empty, silent bridge. His first words since Blackwell had dragged her here. "Did you subvert the major's orders?"

Her besieged emotional gauge flitted, landing somewhere between anger and humiliation.

No point in lying or trying to shade it with rationalization—they could see the whole damn thing from the suit cams. They'd probably watched it back a dozen times already.

"Yes, sir," she said as steadily as she could manage. "But only after Major Blackwell's comms malfunctioned." She bit the inside of her lip. It wasn't *entirely* a lie . . . That malfunction just happened to be orchestrated by her Rubicon.

Thurston tilted his head to one side. "And so you took it upon yourself to amend standing orders?"

Her gaze fell, focusing on his polished black boots. "Yes, sir. I know I should have let Lieutenant Rhett step in as the senior ranking officer, but my Rubi—" She cleared her throat pointedly. "My *pathfinder module* allowed me insight she didn't have." She eyed Thurston, hoping he'd get the hint, but he didn't react in any perceivable way.

Blackwell let out a low growl. "Should we discuss the result of ignoring those orders?" he added, hard gaze swinging to Thurston. "She caused the rezone of *two* squads."

A sharp pang bolted through her chest as her eyes sharpened. She'd accept responsibility for her squad's deaths, but the Stormwalkers had *not* been her fault. Other than Rhett.

Thurston remained facing the subspace screens, hands clasped behind his back. "Anything to say for yourself, Sergeant?" he asked, tone surprisingly calm.

Adriene quickly reset her expression to cowed compliance, and gave a short nod. "Sir, with all due respect," she began carefully, "I *was* trying to follow orders. The *mission* orders—"

"Which were to fucking *listen to me*," Blackwell growled.

"Which were to recover the intelligence *intact,*" she insisted.

Blackwell's fury rose, his shoulders swelling as his fists clenched, and he turned on her. Her heart leapt along with the whir of a door sliding open behind her.

She turned to see who'd had enough balls to walk straight into the middle of this, and her mouth dropped open.

Major West marched toward them, his metal half gleaming brilliantly in the diodes of the white overheads. The bright, open space of the bridge made him seem both smaller, more concrete and tangible, yet at the same time larger, broader, more imposing.

She blinked, mildly disoriented.

"Dressing someone down without me, gentlemen?" he rumbled.

Thurston finally tore his stoic glare away from the screens and turned around. His single real eye widened as it fell on West, though he did a decent job of concealing his surprise.

"Mira's end, Julen." Blackwell crossed his arms over his thick chest, exasperated. "What the hell do *you* want?"

West descended the stairs toward them. He stopped beside Blackwell and faced Thurston, spine straight, shoulders drawn back, feet together, and Adriene found herself disoriented by his comportment. There was something off, but she couldn't quite put her finger on what.

West cleared his throat. "Commodore, the sergeant was acting under my orders."

"What *orders*?" Blackwell sneered. "You have no authority to give her any fucking—"

"Because I knew you'd find a way to *fuck it up,* Charles," West snapped.

"Hell—" Blackwell grunted, turning his ire fully onto West. "Shouldn't you have seen this coming? All you do is sit around and pore over that stupid data—you had to know what we'd find."

West glowered. "I knew *nothing* of the sort."

"Gentlemen, please," Thurston cut in.

Blackwell's and West's glares lingered for another second, then they both turned their attention to the commodore.

Thurston sat against the edge of the console counter, folding his arms over his chest. "We can discuss mission details another time. This is about Sergeant Valero."

He nodded toward her, and three men's gazes fell on her. Heat flushed her face, and she wished they'd have just continued to argue it out and forgotten entirely about her.

"Sergeant," Thurston said, giving a heavy sigh that crackled in his low timbre. "It's not acceptable to ignore orders or to dictate your own while disregarding chain of command. I think you know that."

"Yes, sir," she said as quickly as she could get the words out of her mouth. "I'm sorry, sir."

He eyed West seriously. "It's also not acceptable to follow the orders of an undeployed officer over those of your direct CO."

"I understand, sir."

"But to be clear, you made the right call in capturing the Mechan instead of killing it."

Blackwell tensed, fury creasing his brow again, but when Thurston shot him a warning glare, he said nothing.

"We've had very few chances to study functioning Mechan in person," Thurston continued. "The intelligence will be invaluable. West, I want you to get it into analysis ASAP."

West inclined his head. "Already begun, sir."

"And, Sergeant . . ." Thurston's clipped, resigned tone snapped her focus back to him. "I'm assigning you to mess duty for the next three months."

A flood of relief washed through her. Working the mess would suck, but it was a manageable punishment—and likely just for show in front of Major Blackwell. She'd probably be able to get West to expunge it later.

"You're dismissed," Thurston said.

She snapped a salute and retreated up the stairs and through the door, into the hallway outside.

The door slid closed and she eyed the MPs keeping post. She turned the corner and leaned against the wall. The halls this late, this high up in the ship, were barren.

A few minutes later, West rounded the corner, blowing straight past her. "Are you coming?" he called over his shoulder, already halfway down the corridor. "I require your assistance."

Adriene pushed off the wall and jogged to catch up with West's long-legged strides. He turned the next corner, and she followed him onto the command-level lift that would take them down to the main decks.

As the wide door slid shut, a weight melted away from West's shoulders. He slouched against the wall, letting out a grating sigh, as if the strings holding him up had been severed. He stretched out his cybernetic leg, then arm, then clenched a fist, the real half of his face tightening.

Then it dawned on her: what had seemed off about West as he'd addressed Thurston. The whole time, he'd been standing upright, taller than she'd ever remembered him being. No hand tremors, no groaning in pain, no huffing and puffing.

Now he'd let the facade go, only able to keep it up long enough to put on a show for Thurston and Blackwell.

Blue lights flashed through the grates over his shoulder as the lift descended. She watched him warily for a long moment.

It'd almost make sense if it seemed like the *real* half of his body was in pain. Like it was finally giving out after having to support all that metal over the years. Yet it was always the mechanical side that seemed to cause him grief.

"You okay?" Her voice came out gentle, yet cut through the silence of the small lift like a razor.

"Fine."

"What is it? Pain?"

He shook his head, gaze honed on the floor. "I've just been having a few bad weeks. It'll pass."

"Getting worse?"

"No. It has . . . always been an issue. Ever since it happened."

"Ever since *what* happened?"

His hazel eye raked over her. "Suddenly curious, Sergeant?"

She shook her head slowly. "Not suddenly," she said quietly.

The lift glided to a stop, and West's spine straightened again as he exited. Adriene followed him into the bright white corridors of the main decks, as barren as the upper levels.

"It's ancient history at this point," he said, continuing his purposeful march. "Twenty years ago."

"Brownout?" she surmised, and he inclined his head. "Who were you with?"

"The 258th."

"Really? Don't they groom High Command?"

"They do." He exhaled a withering sigh. "They had me on a hard-and-fast path to admiral."

"What happened?"

"After this . . ." He gestured absently to the left side of his body. ". . . Command didn't want me in front of soldiers. I cannot say I blame them. So I altered my career goals."

She flashed a small grin. "Let me guess—research and development?"

"Nothing gets past you, Sergeant," he said dryly, though a hint of amusement played at his lips.

"Seems fortuitous."

A flicker of something crossed his expression—sadness, maybe remorse.

"All I mean," she continued quickly, "is that obviously you belonged in R&D. Look at everything you've accomplished."

He stretched out his cybernetic arm, the metal fingers clacking together as he slowly opened his fist. "Maybe. Still can't find a way to fix this, though."

They arrived at a lift door marked "Restricted Access." Adriene's boots squeaked as she stopped in her tracks.

West pressed the call button and glanced back at her questioningly.

She stared at the lift; metal adorned both sides of the narrow entry. It was the same lift she'd seen when her Rubicon awoke on Cimarosa-IV. When her AI's new "network" had stretched all the way back to the *Aurora*.

"Are you all right?" West asked. "You look as though you've seen a ghost."

"Fine," she replied, voice cracking, throat suddenly dry. "Where are we going?"

"The lower decks," he replied plainly, as if that might mean something to her.

The lift door slid open. West swept a hand to invite her inside. He stepped in behind her and selected the bottom level.

She eyed West as he winced, his mechanical hand drawing into a tight fist as he exhaled a grating sigh. The lift hummed as it descended, blue lights slowly pulsating beyond the grated metal walls.

"What's it like?" she asked. "Just pain?"

He shook his head. "Feels like phantom limbs."

"But it *is* a limb."

"Exactly, hence the problem. It feels *real* to me, but my mind knows it's not. Not really."

West waved his real hand dismissively as he leaned into the wall for support, facade slipping away again.

"It causes a . . . disconnect," he continued. "It's disorienting and . . . difficult to explain."

Adriene nodded slowly, a sickening mass twisting in the pit of her stomach—it wasn't at all hard for her to imagine what it must feel like. She'd felt that same way when she'd been hybridized. Like she was an extension of something foreign, or it was an extension of her—impossible to distinguish—until she was slowly overridden, no chance of seizing control again.

She let out a deep breath. Considered telling him just how aptly she could relate. Commiseration, empathy, all that normal human shit. If her Rubicon were active, he'd be goading her into it.

West's gaze lifted from the floor and onto her wrapped forearms. "Are *you* okay?"

She wrung her hands. "You saw the playback, I assume?"

"Yes."

"Then you know I'm doing far better than my squadmates."

He didn't say anything for a few long moments, his hazel eye glassy as he stared at her bandages and avoided eye contact. "I'm sorry about that."

"Is it true, what you said to Blackwell? You really didn't know what we'd find?"

He shook his head, his gaze going unfocused past her. "I knew what intelligence I expected . . . *hoped* to find. But I cannot say I thought it would come in this form."

"And what is this 'form,' exactly?"

His eye flitted down briefly, then his brow hardened. "That's what I'd like you to help me find out."

The lift shuddered gently to a stop, and West stepped out into a wall of darkness. Adriene squinted into the black, though her eyes had trouble adjusting.

The baritone whir of the subspace accelerator resounded deep in her chest, rattling her teeth at their roots, an onerous, uncomfortable pulse of pressure thrumming against her eardrums.

"With me, Sergeant." Under the drone, Adriene barely caught the quiet whir of West's mechanical limbs as he marched away.

She stepped out, angling toward the direction of his voice, hurrying to catch up with his long strides. Her eyes adjusted to the dark corridor, dimly lit by strips of emergency lights lining the floors. West stared straight ahead, chin level, shoulders hunched, with an almost imperceptible limp that favored his augmented side.

The oscillations of the subspace accelerator faded in favor of a low, steady thrum of electricity as they entered a large, open area. Adriene hit a wall of warmth so thick, it felt difficult to walk through. The expansive room hummed with heat, the air pulsing with the low, steady thrum of electricity.

On the far left, a series of rectangular pillars glowed blue behind glass-paned fronts showcasing hundreds of rack-mounted server modules. Dozens more stretched out in rows behind the first. The Rubicon mainframe.

Along the right-hand side, a six-meter-wide half-moon counter sat covered in electronics and holographic displays. The console stretched out under a wall comprised of over two dozen monitors—some kind of command center.

West's workstation upstairs could hardly be considered tidy, but this place was a *disaster*.

A workbench sat covered in wire clippings and discarded tools. The half-moon console was strewn with dozens of data cores, modules, and hard drives. What must have been every piece of intelligence they'd gathered over the last two months—all connected with tendrils of jury-rigged wiring, creating a massive web of humming electronics, flashing an asynchronous rainbow of colors. Every one of the two dozen screens showed a different spreadsheet, graph, or flow of data.

"Mira's ashes . . ." She stared in awe. "What are you . . . doing?"

West motioned for her to come closer as he marched up to the half-moon console. She tore her gaze away from the chaos and stepped up beside him.

A pile of metal glinted on the counter as she approached, sending slow-motion images of flying shrapnel and Kato's bloody coughing death throes into the back of her mind. It was a small collection of the metal that'd killed them all. West must've been testing it, examining its properties to figure out how it'd pierced their alanthum armor and shield constructs.

West flicked a new holographic interface into the air above the console. It took Adriene a second to orient and realize what she saw.

The Mechan's holding cell.

The scrapper lay faceup in the middle of an empty, yellow-tinged room inside a secondary cage comprised of thick, clear plastic walls. Its limbs, neck, and torso were secured to the floor with massive metal cuffs. A single bundling of cables ran from under its chassis to somewhere off the edge of the frame. The bot remained perfectly still, unmoving.

Adriene swallowed, unable to tear her eyes from the screen. "I'm surprised we have the means to contain it."

West tilted his head. "All vessels built in the last few years come equipped with such holding cells. It became standard after we gained the ability to plan offensives."

"Because of rezone tech?" she asked absentmindedly, though it wasn't really a question. It was the only reason anything had changed.

When he didn't respond, she looked up to find him staring down at her with a hesitant, wary glint in his eye. He almost looked ashamed.

Awareness of his proximity crept in; she could feel the unnatural warmth his cybernetics radiated, hear the light, constant buzz the internal electronics gave off. He licked his dry lips and looked as if he might say something, but only shook his head and diverted his gaze, gesturing to the Mechan's feed.

"Your teammate's hack was thorough," he said. "He added fail-safes to ensure the code could not be restored or rewritten easily. Like a dynamic virus. It was . . . creative. I'm impressed he was able to code something like that in the field."

She bit the inside of her cheek. Though Kato had facilitated, that'd actually been her Rubicon's doing. But West had, at times, seemed paranoid about her AI and the extent of its capabilities. There was no reason he needed to know that detail.

"The Mechan appears to be working on repairing the damage," West continued, "but I doubt it will be successful any time soon. It will only be able to move again when—or if—I allow it. That room features a conductive shield, a graviton wave dampener, and is completely air-gapped, so there's no risk of it hacking the ship or mainframe."

A hot trickle pricked at Adriene's nape, and she looked up at him. "Why are you trying to convince me it's not dangerous?"

His chin lifted from the screen, and he locked his gaze onto her. "Because I'd like you to question it."

She barked a laugh. His expression didn't change, and her smile faded. He was fucking serious.

"I, uh . . ." She let out another nervous, raw-edged chuckle. "You're not kidding, are you?"

He shook his head.

She sighed. "I doubt it speaks our language."

West's chin lifted. "I have installed a translator VI. Once you're able to get it speaking, it will not take more than a minute to begin translating properly."

She heaved a grating sigh. "Why me? Wouldn't you rather talk to it yourself?"

"Granted, I've only had a handful of hours," West said with a resounding sigh, "but I've had no luck. I've restored its power, and it can fully function, but it has put up a mental blockade and refuses to say anything."

Scratching the back of her neck, she gave a drifting headshake. "At the black site, that thing tried to hack my Rubicon. What if it tries again?"

"That is exactly what I'm hoping it will do."

She scoffed. "What?"

"I have written an executable," he said, as if that explained something.

"Which does . . . ?" she prompted.

"If, or hopefully when, the Mechan attempts to connect, your Rubicon will automatically force a two-way connection, simultaneously delivering a payload of code that will allow me complete control over the bot's data storage and other functions. Within microseconds, I should be able to sever its connection to you."

She quirked a brow. *"Should?"*

His mouth pinched in a slight frown. "It is not a guarantee, but I strongly believe it will work. I will be standing by to physically remove you if for any reason it does not."

She chewed her bottom lip, recalling what he'd mentioned about the security features of the cell. If that was true and something went wrong, it'd only be a matter of walking out the door to sever the connection. Her Rubicon had held out for much longer than that during the fight.

She heaved out a strained breath, her wounded arms smarting as she leaned on the counter, rolling her neck. Her palms were tacky with sweat, and she again missed the conveniences of her hardsuit.

"Is this it?" she asked, voice toneless.

"Is this what?"

"Your 'final and resounding defeat of the Mechan'? This campaign . . . is this the end? Does this scrapper have whatever it is you're after?"

"I cannot say for sure," he said, regret lacing his tone. "But considering your team's sacrifice to win this intel for us, I certainly hope so."

An uncomfortable tightness grew in her chest, and she pressed her knuckles harder into the counter.

He was right. Seven people had died to secure this scrap heap alive and in working order. If she could do something to give the trauma they'd endured and would continue to endure even a shred of meaning . . . she had to try.

She stood up and faced West squarely, folding her arms in front of her. "I think the bot will be suspicious if I walk in there and demand it try to hack me. What am I supposed to do?"

West shook his head, looking back to swipe across a tablet on the console. "Simply talk. Your Rubicon should be able to force a connection eventually, regardless. *But*, if the Mechan initiates a connection, it will be that much faster and easier."

And dangerous.

"Otherwise, all you need to do is speak with it. Distract it. Just try to get it talking about something. Anything."

"So, politics? The weather? What it had for breakfast?"

West closed his eye and pinched the bridge of his nose.

"All right, I get it," she sighed, "breakfast isn't funny. Lead the way, boss."

TWENTY-THREE

Adriene stood a step inside the sealed cell for a long while, staring down at the scrapper secured to the floor beyond the secondary, clear plastic walls within the main chamber.

Her eyes scrutinized the prone bot. Its chassis looked ill-fitting in a way, the mismatched pieces scored and scuffed—not scratch-resistant and polished like modern alanthum but weathered and beat-up like the hull of an old groundside tank transport. The textured plating contained thin, almost imperceptible striations of navy blues and grays, creating the appearance of dark, tempered steel. Its ocular sensors were alight with a hazy yellow glow, unwavering. She had no idea if it even knew she'd walked in.

She fumbled the thin headset over her ears, the means with which she'd interface with the air-gapped translation VI.

Pulse speeding, she told her feet to move closer, but she hesitated. She'd never been this close to a functioning Mechan that wasn't trying to kill her or hybridize her. Not that it probably didn't *want* to, it just couldn't. She'd certainly never seen one locked up and complacent before. At any moment it could bust free from its restraints and rip her head off.

In her HUD, a diagram expanded: the specifications of the containment cell's features, their safety ratings, and tensile strengths.

Yeah, I get it. What's our plan of attack here?

// Don't look at me. You're driving this ship. //

Freeloader.

She rubbed the cold metal of the translator headset. Though she was certain CNEF must have captured at least a couple of Mechan in the last two decades, she didn't know of anyone who had successfully conversed with one before. Dissected, hacked, downloaded, analyzed—sure. But sat down and had a chat with?

Was West crazy? She had no idea what she was doing.

// But really, when do you ever? //

She rolled her eyes.

// Just kidding. //

I know.

// That said, it might be as good an approach as any. //

Stupidity?

// I meant madness, but sure, that too. //

She took a few cautious steps forward, heart pounding, and made her way to stand near the Mechan's head. Waves of dread rolled through her, ears and neck heating with panic. She swallowed down her danger instincts, assuring herself she was safe by running her eyes over the bot's restraints again and again.

Letting out a slow breath, she moved closer. She crossed her legs under her as she sat on the floor, folding her hands in her lap. Its head lay only a meter away beyond the glass enclosure.

"Yeah, I don't want to be here either," she mumbled. For the briefest microsecond, she swore the bot's yellow eyes brightened.

Anything?

// Nothing. //

She lowered her voice. "The boss just wants me to talk to you. About anything, I guess. Got any topics you'd like to cover?"

The hunk of metal lay perfectly still and silent.

"Didn't think so. What do Mechan *do,* anyway?"

She froze as its yellow eyes flickered a few times in rapid succession. She definitely hadn't imagined it this time.

"Yeah? You wanna talk about hobbies?" She waited a few seconds, but there was no visible response. She released a heavy breath. "I suppose the calculated genocide of my people keeps you pretty busy."

Its ocular sensors faded out slowly before returning to full brightness.

A strange, bitter heat began to build deep in her chest. "You killed

my squad, you know," she said, cognizant of the sharp edge her tone
had taken.

It gave no response, and Adriene resigned to push the anger back
down. She had no way to truly threaten it. Playing bad cop would
be a pointless waste of energy.

"All right, then, I guess I'm just going to have to ramble. I'll start
by listing every perennial I can remember off the top of my head—
stop me if I miss one."

Before she could launch into it, a resonating sonic blast of feedback pealed through the headset. She grimaced and ripped it free.

"Mira's fiery . . ." She glanced up at the corner of the room that
held the security camera housing before focusing back on the bot's
static form. She slid the silent earpiece back on and repositioned
herself.

"I apologize."

Adriene flinched as the Mechan's words rang into her ears—at
once hollow and sharp, deafening and quiet. Its voice was a hoarse,
layered symphony of screaming machines, like dozens of sharp
nails screeching across a sheet of metal.

Is that normal?

// No idea. I've got no baselines for any of this. //

"Uh . . ." Her heart slammed mercilessly against her rib cage.
"You apologize? For what?"

"My silence," it grated, and Adriene couldn't mask a pained scowl
as its shrill words screeched into her ear. *"I made needed repairs to
communications operation."*

The more it spoke, the more the horrific rasp faded in favor of
a tolerable, yet equally disturbing tone as the VI software slowly
modulated it to a more human timbre.

Adriene squeezed the burgeoning headache from her temple.
"You mean you hacked the translator VI? Why?"

"It was flawed. Now it is not."

She swallowed, considering how to respond, but she had no idea
what to do other than gape in awe at this Mechan she was somehow
talking to.

"Um, thank you," she said, then immediately winced. *Fucking thank you?*

// Why are you thanking it? //

I don't know! Quiet—I'm driving the ship, remember?

// Right into the sun . . . //

She blew out a hard sigh, shook her uncertainty away, and just rolled with it. "I'm surprised your programming accommodates interspecies communication. Is that a normal Mechan function?"

"'Mechan' does not translate."

"Mechan," she said pointedly, as if annunciating it would somehow make the definition clearer. "You know . . ." She swept her hand out to indicate the bot's chassis.

Its yellow eyes brightened, then faded down into a flicker before it evened back out. *"Comprehended."*

"What do you call yourselves?"

"Our word of your word of 'Mechan' is 'Deliverer,' if that is your signification."

She threw a pointed look over her shoulder at the camera. Was West hearing this shit? *Deliverer?*

She turned back to the bot. "I, uh, haven't seen one like you before. You seem old—no offense. Are you an early model?"

"Early term requires context of time scale . . ." It paused, and she wasn't sure if it was done or if it was working with the VI software to find an accurate translation. *"Closer analogy of prototype,"* it finally finished.

"Can I ask . . ." she began carefully. "What were you doing all the way out there?"

"Context?"

"At that black site, on that planet where we found you? How'd you end up out there?"

"I enact destiny, given by mercy incorporeal."

Adrienne's mouth opened, eyes widening. A flicker of recognition came with the words, fragments of the historical data briefly stored in her mind, but she couldn't grasp it. *"Mercy incorporeal?* I don't think that's translating."

*"Your cursory yet ruthlessly complex language has no acceptable equiv-
alent."*

"Fair . . . How'd you end up alone?"

The bot didn't respond, its ocular sensors steady.

"I've never seen a Mechan by itself . . . *ever.*"

"Unrelated."

"What?"

"Deliverers."

She blinked slowly. "What?"

"I was beached."

She snorted. "Beached?"

*"You have far too many words meaning the same thing in varying
contexts."*

"Uh . . ." She breathed a nervous laugh but swallowed down her
growing amusement.

The yellow glow of its eyes flickered for a moment, then after a
time it said, *"Marooned."*

"Ah," she said with a nod. "I see. You were stranded."

"Yes."

"For how long?"

"Utmost long. Castor cycle? Longer?"

Scratching the back of her neck, she shook her head. She had
no idea what that meant. She'd never learned anything about how
Mechan kept time—or if they even did.

"So," she said, "that busted ship in the hangar was yours, then?"

"Syntax . . . Hanger—one who hangs?"

"What? No—"

"Bust—anatomy. Bosomed?"

She breathed a sigh. "Mira—sorry, um . . . Was that your *broken
spacecraft* in the . . . spacecraft landing area?"

"Yes. I attempted to unbust, but repair resources were limited."

"I see. Why did you hide out in the server room? Wouldn't you
want your kind to be able to find you easier if they came to rescue
you?"

"No."

"No?"

"Suggestion irrelevant. No kind exists."

Adriene tilted her head.

"Area select was safety due to hibernation state—enacted after acceptance I would not be found."

She flashed a weak grin and danced her fingers in the air. "Surprise . . ."

Her tone fell away slowly, as she could just about imagine West's exasperated sigh.

"You know, I'm curious," she said, then took a moment to clear her mind of colloquialisms and homonyms and anything else that might confuse the bot. "The alarm that was installed at the facility. My squadmate—uh, my *friend* told me they were, what we call, retrofitted. Installed *after* the station was built. Did you set those up to protect you after you realized you were marooned?"

"Yes."

She nodded slowly, jaw skimming back and forth a few times before she made the decision. "I was the one who triggered that alarm."

"No. Not for human."

"No, but it detected the AI in my brain. An artificial intelligence implant."

It gave no response.

"Does that surprise you?"

"Somewhat."

"We're more alike than you thought, huh?"

"Outward view not adequate gauge."

She sat back at that, tilting her head as she watched the unblinking ocular sensors. "But what I can't figure out is why a Mechan would have defenses against itself. Why set an alarm that'll go off for an AI? For your own kind?"

It didn't respond at first, then its yellow eyes flickered lightly as it said, *"Blind human . . . you still think I am one of these 'Mechan'?"*

Adriene stared at it for a few silent moments, letting the meaning of its words slowly sink in. "What?" she managed, voice taut.

// Deployed. //

Her ears erupted with a blaring screech of agony.

She ripped the headset off with a roar of pain, flinging it away. She gaped at the bot, its yellow eyes a chaotic flickering mess, oscillating between yellow and red and blue and white.

Breaths heavy, she crawled forward and grabbed the headset, lifting it back to her ear as a new grating shriek tore through the small speaker.

It was no longer the same pang of feedback, but a vocalization. The bot was screaming.

A squeal of feedback sounded, and she dropped the headset again, only to realize this time it was sounding directly in her mind—through her Rubicon. Her HUD flickered, disjointed and staticky. She cringed, indiscernible flashes burning white-hot against the back of her eyelids.

>>> *weakness sickness rebellion extinction [value_missing] survival ordinance hope [value_missing] a new sheathe [value_missing] the last male off with free will to the stars* <<<

With a whoosh of cool air, the door slid open. West marched in, shoulders hunched with purpose.

Adriene pressed the heels of her hands into her temples as hard as she could, grimacing as the harsh loop continued to oscillate. Her head screamed with imagery—family, contentment, twisting vines with dark, scaled skin, a structure of corrugated metal stretching into a cloud-soaked sky, a grim shadow falling over salvation.

One warm and one cold hand gripped her shoulders and dragged her, half stumbling, out of the room.

The thick door slid shut and the flashing images and screeching interference cut off. The lines of her HUD sharpened, returning to normal.

What the fuck was that?

// I have no idea. //

Adriene straightened as West let go, and she spun to face him. "What the hell happened?"

West scratched his chin. "It was more agile than I'd given it credit for. I apologize." He dipped his head, stooping as he tried to look in her eyes. "Are you all right?"

She shook the leftover ringing from her ears. "Yeah, fine. Did it work?"

"Yes, perfectly. I was able to make a safe, stable connection." He started marching toward the mainframe and the messy control hub.

She glanced back at the cell door, then followed, struggling to keep pace with the taller man's strides.

"West . . ." She panted as she jogged to fall in beside him. "He just told me he's not Mechan."

"*It* just told you *it* is not Mechan, Sergeant," West corrected.

She stared, mouth agape. "As in . . . he's an *Architect*."

West trained his gaze straight ahead, long strides unyielding. "I understand the situation, Sergeant."

Her expression slackened. He didn't seem *nearly* surprised enough. "West, come on," she implored as they stepped back into the warmth of the server room. "What's going on? What else do you know?"

He sat down at a stool in front of the screens. He cast his mechanical hand out, offering her a seat.

She approached the stool but didn't sit, crossing her arms and standing behind it. "All the Architects *died*," she insisted. "All of them. I saw it in those visions."

"That was *data*," West clarified. "And only a small subset, colored by the perceptions of your . . . *Rubicon*."

"Yes, and in that *data*, one thing was very clear—*painfully* clear. They weren't able to save themselves. Their trials failed."

"Apparently, one did not," he all but mumbled, turning to type into the console.

Her mouth hung at his casual admission. "So it *is* an Architect?"

West didn't respond, didn't even look over at her, his single real eye as unaffected as the ocular sensors had been on the Mechan.

Or, apparently, the . . . *Architect*.

The concept washed over her, dizzying her briefly. Her mind reeled at the implications.

Were there others? It had said it was working under some directive of its . . . god.

// Mercy incorporeal. //

How many were left? Had they all spread to the farthest reaches
of the galaxy, like this one?

Or worse, what if it *had* worked? Entirely? Could every Mechan
out there be an Architect? Had they been fighting real, sentient
beings this entire time—ones that were simply trying to find a way
back to biological forms?

"Sergeant," West warned.

She pushed aside her panic and locked onto him.

He'd stopped working and now stared at her, grim solace lining
his face. "Whatever you're thinking, don't. It's not as dramatic as
all that."

"Are you sure?" she asked quietly.

"Yes. I will confirm when I speak to it myself, but I strongly
believe this is the only one. *The* one. It tested its own theory on
itself—the first successful transfer. But it was already too late for
its species."

Adriene nodded slowly. That would be better, surely. Less catastrophic, but still staggering.

This was the first—maybe the *only*—Architect who'd transferred
their consciousness into an artificial body. Not only the last of their
kind but the *creator* of the Mechan himself.

She could see it more clearly now, looking back: the fragmented,
panicked burst of jarred memory from when she'd left the holding
cell. *"The last male off with free will to the stars."*

When she could finally speak again, her voice came out dry and
fractured. "Why did you need that connection?"

West remained focused on the console. "I do not think I will be
able to interpret its data stores without using it as an interface. At
least, within a reasonable time frame. I will need to stabilize the
connection before I'll be able to begin the full interrogation, but
once it's done, its mind will be an open book. It will be compelled
to answer all my questions, and truthfully."

Adriene swallowed, slowly piecing together the meaning of his overcomplicated explanation. "Compelled?"

West cast a glance at her in his periphery. "Is there an issue, Sergeant?"

"I mean . . . *yes?*" she said, voice high with disbelief.

He straightened, turning away from the screens to face her. "Go on," he said, tone patient. "Say your piece."

"If he's an Architect . . ." She took a step closer, voice low. ". . . then you're hacking the brain of a sentient, *biological* being. You can't do that."

West crossed his arms. "You believe it deserves more consideration than the other Mechan?"

"He's not *another* Mechan," she argued. "He *was—is* real."

"And Mechan are not 'real'?"

She set her jaw. "Don't deflect by turning this into one of your barrages of leading questions."

// Careful . . . //

"I understand your perspective," West said, his lips tight around his words, tone growing stiff. "But I must respectfully disagree. I do not believe it warrants any greater moral regard than any other construct. Regardless of the origins of its psyche, it is now only code."

"Didn't you hear him when you connected?" She jutted a finger back toward the containment cells. "He was screaming in pain. You're torturing him."

West's jaw firmed. "If it finds itself so tormented, it need only deactivate its sensory receptors."

Lips parting, she shook her head in indignation. She knew from experience how dangerous it was to simply turn it all off.

She eyed the canted way West stood, metal hand flexing against his bicep, heavily favoring his augmented side.

// That might not be the best ide—//

"If it's that easy," she began, challenge in her tone as she gestured to West's left half, "why don't you just deactivate *your* sensory receptors? Instead of hobbling around in pain all the time?"

West's face was set in stone, and he didn't speak for a few long, grueling moments. "Your opinion is noted, Sergeant," he finally replied, tone unyielding. "Now, I suggest you go. Before I decide I've had enough insubordination for the evening."

// I'd heed that advice . . . //

Adriene glared, but forced out a steadying breath. She was 100 percent ready to start shouting, to throw all the moral righteousness she could muster at West, but she honestly didn't know why.

// It's possible there are extenuating circumstances amplifying your reaction. //

Right. Like her entire team dying in front of her.

She'd crushed it down so it couldn't overwhelm her, but now the memories flickered back: That first shard slicing clean through Ivon's chest. Torrents of Wyatt's blood pooling on the floor. Coleson's stocky frame crumpling like a rag doll. Gallagher's skewered corpse and Brigham's stock-still chest. Kato going limp as he bled out in her lap.

Her breath wavering in her chest.

"You've had a very long day," West said, some of the stiffness gone from his tone. "I understand. A lot was asked of you."

She exhaled a sigh.

"Please," he continued, "it's very late—go get some rest. I'll summon you when I know more about our next steps."

"Yes, sir." Chin down, Adriene turned on her heel and headed back to the narrow lift.

TWENTY-FOUR

Adriene had mostly cooled off by the time she found herself in the Medical corridor, hesitating at the end of the hall. She ran her hand over one of her bandaged forearms, which still pulsed with a raw, bone-deep ache. Though the new skin should have set by now, the medic that'd dressed her wounds on the flight back had told her to have them checked and redressed at Medical once they returned. But she couldn't convince herself to walk down the hall.

She retreated toward her quarters.

// You should really get those looked at . . . //

It can wait until morning.

// Except you won't go then either. //

"Guilty," she grumbled aloud as she kept marching. She couldn't risk running into Daroga. If he hadn't heard about Kato yet, she sure as hell wasn't going to be the one to break the news.

// Why not you? I can't really think of anyone better. //

Because he'll blame me.

// Projection. //

Excuse me?

She slowed for a few steps as a wave of impatience rose within her.

// Apologies for the candor, just trying to save us some time here. //

She scowled and kept walking.

I'm not projecting.

// She says defensively. //

"Why are you even still on?" she groused.

// You're not worried he'll blame you. You're worried he'll remind you that you blame yourself. //

She gritted her teeth as she arrived at the corner to her hallway, then halted to a stop.

// *So much for avoidance.* //

Daroga paced outside her door, hands shoved in his pockets, chin down, black hair draping his face, radiating anxiety.

He still faced away. He hadn't seen her yet . . .

// *Don't you dare.* //

With a deep inhale, she continued toward him.

Daroga turned, his gaze drifting up from his boots. His green eyes were round, worry etched into his face. She wrung her hands, every muscle in her body taut, bracing for whatever judgment he saw fit.

He stepped toward her and wrapped his arms around her, drawing her into a hug.

Tension fled her fatigued limbs. She leaned her face into his chest, inhaling his crisp, evergreen scent.

He breathed into the side of her head, "Adri." Heat crept up her neck at how warm the nickname sounded in his weathered voice.

She wanted to take solace in his comfort, but couldn't stop thinking about what comforts her squad would be enjoying about now. Showering gray sludge off their trembling husks. Poked and interrogated by Intake. Judged by the counseling VI and scrutinized by Physio.

Daroga's chest raised and lowered with the steadiness of his breaths, and she could have stood like that forever, checked out, called it a day on life—but eventually his hold loosened, and some anxiety crept back in, straining her weary muscles.

She exhaled, forcing the words from her throat. "You heard about Kato?"

The stubble on Daroga's jaw scratched her cheek as he stepped back, hands lingering on the backs of her arms. "Yeah. I'm his emergency contact, so they had to tell me." He stayed close, and at a half head taller than she was, he had to look down, black hair swinging into his eyes. "I'd heard rumors, but I had no idea if you were safe. Where've you been?"

"Debrief was . . . extensive."

"I'm sure," he said, tone soft. "You okay?"

Her stomach seethed with nausea. With *guilt*.

"Your arms . . ." Daroga frowned as he carefully lifted one of her bandaged forearms.

"They're fine," she assured, chewing hard on her bottom lip. He was being too sweet and consoling, and she just . . . couldn't.

// Must I interject? //

She heaved a sigh.

I just don't know how he'll take it.

// A good way to find out would be to ask. //

"Hey . . ." Daroga dipped his head, trying to catch her eye. "What is it?"

Diverting her gaze to the floor, she summoned as much courage as she could muster. "I'm sorry. About Kato."

"It's okay. It's not your fault."

"Except it kind of is," she admitted, then quickly added, "It's okay if you blame me, I understand."

"What? No—" With two fingers, he gently lifted her chin to look up at him. He locked eyes with her, exuding calm assuredness. "I don't blame you," he said, tone firm. "Why would I?"

"Because I . . ." she began. But she couldn't find the rest of the words.

"Listen, it's awful," he said, reassurance in his voice, "but rezoning is a known potential outcome of these kinds of ops. No one blames you. Especially not me."

She shook her head. "You don't understand."

"Help me understand, then."

She drew in a wavering breath and forced it back out slowly. With a nod, she stepped to unlock her door. It slid open, and she invited Daroga in with a wave of her arm.

The door shuttered behind them, sealing them into the quiet warmth of her room.

Daroga sat on the edge of the bed, and Adriene headed toward the terminal stool, but he caught her wrist on the way. She retreated a few steps to sit beside him instead.

Averting her gaze, she tugged at her collar, suddenly feeling much too warm. Maybe her Rubicon was overheating again.

// I'm fine. Stop avoiding it. //

"Just—" She let out a sharp breath, then caught Daroga's questioning glance. "Sorry. Can you turn my implant off from here?"

He stood up to take the two steps toward her terminal.

// No need. //

With a flicker of white, her HUD and Rubicon vanished, the hollowness of the void he left behind somehow starker in the confines of her room. She had no idea he could do that.

"Never mind," she said. "He did it himself."

Daroga turned to face her, one eyebrow lifted. "He did?"

She sighed. "That's part of the story." She patted the bed beside her.

Daroga sat back down, brows knit.

"This needs to stay confidential," she prefaced.

His hand wrapped around hers, steady and warm. "Of course."

"I'm under special assignment. I can't talk about the details— even with my squad. But I have an advanced version of Rubicon."

He frowned. "You do? How?"

"Major West. You know him?"

Daroga exhaled a heavy breath. "He's my reporting officer, technically. Mostly just get the occasional message from him these days, now that he's more involved in the intelligence side of things." His brow furrowed. "He hasn't mentioned a new Rubicon build. Usually he warns me ahead of time so I can prep."

"Yeah, the project is rather . . ." *Illegal.* She cleared her throat. "Confidential."

Though some anxiety had etched itself back into the planes of Daroga's face, he nodded and said, "Got it."

"Are you okay to hear about Mechan?" she asked. "I don't want to trigger anything."

A tempered smile tugged at his lips. "Yeah," he said, his weathered voice barely a whisper. "I'm okay. Thanks for asking."

She tightened her jaw and tried to steel herself, but she couldn't meet his gaze. So instead, she stared at the Dodson-Mueller logo on his shirt.

"I don't know what you already heard," she began, "but we encountered a Mechan at the black site."

"That was part of the rumor, yeah. I heard it was a near wipe, but no other details."

"Well, I'll spare you most of those details, but the relevant takeaway is . . . the bot was shooting something that could breach our suits."

Disbelief washed over his face, lips parting. His grip on her hand loosened.

"As in—all the way through," she clarified, voice breaking slightly, blinking away the memories of her dead squad.

Daroga muttered, "I wondered how we lost so many . . ." His brows pinched. "We thought that tungsten alanthum would be enough to stop anything."

She lifted a palm toward him. "It's not Dodson-Mueller's fault—I've never seen anything like this weapon, and I've encountered Mechan hundreds of times. That thing killed three of the Stormwalkers in a matter of seconds. Blackwell started relaying orders to destroy it, but . . . my Rubicon and I formulated an alternate plan to disable it instead."

The muscles in Daroga's jaw worked. "Which you then enacted? As part of this special assignment?"

She swallowed hard. "Yeah."

"Using this 'advanced' build Major West gave you?"

"Right. It's capable of some things that, well . . . it shouldn't really be able to do. It allowed me to sever Blackwell's comms and relay orders to the rest of my team. Among other things."

Daroga leaned forward, propping his elbows on his knees. He sat in silence for a few excruciatingly long moments, kneading his palms in turn while staring into the middle distance. Finally, he said, "Why do I get the feeling we have a Mechan on board right now?"

Catching his gaze, she pinched her lips tightly. "No comment."

He sat back up and ran his hands through his hair. "Well," he began, releasing a deep sigh, "you're not in the brig, so it must have worked."

"Yeah," she said again, voice growing weak. "Kato helped us—me," she admitted. "Though he doesn't know about my upgraded Rubicon. They all think it's because of my new pathfinder module."

Daroga scratched his jawline. "Kato's mentioned stuff like that a few times. I tried telling him there was nothing all that special about it. I just thought he was . . . I dunno." He gave a sad smile. "Being Kato."

"I didn't *want* to lie to them," she assured. "Or you." She held her breath, waiting for judgment or condemnation.

After a time, Daroga sighed. "Well, you might be disappointed to hear . . ."

Her heart sank. Then he gave her another one of those considerate, understanding looks she didn't deserve.

". . . but that doesn't change my response." He took her hand again, his green eyes warm and deadly serious. "It's not your fault. Sure, you may have used your Rubicon in a . . . less-than-sanctioned way, but hey, you're talking to a convicted criminal, remember?"

She chuffed a bitter laugh.

"It's part of the job," he went on. "Everyone in Flintlock knows that. Kato knows that. I can guarantee he doesn't blame you, and I certainly don't either. He'll be back here slinging jokes, falling asleep at inappropriate times, and giving me endless shit in no time."

Her lips twitched with a weak smile.

"In the meantime," he continued, tone encouraging, "try to give yourself a little grace about it."

Adriene drew in a steadying breath. He was right. For now, she needed to let it go. She could apologize to her team when they got back to the ship in a few days. Digging herself into a grave of self-pity accomplished nothing.

"Thanks for hearing me out," she said. "I know you're upset right now too. I don't mean to be an emotional drain."

He shook his head. "You're not. Really." He squeezed her hand

again. "At least you made it. For a while there, I thought neither of
you were coming back."

She gave a grateful smile.

He slid closer and wrapped his arms around her back, pulling
her into another hug.

She settled her chin on his shoulder, nestling against the soft
strands of black hair clinging to his jaw. For a time, she relished
in the warmth, the smooth, even sounds of his breath, the way his
evergreen scent had already filled her small cabin.

He shifted to lean his forehead against hers, sending aching
sparks across her skin. Her pulse sped.

He ran a thumb along her jawline, his warm breath on her lips.
"Can I kiss you?"

Her lashes grazed his as she blinked. Swallowing down her
nerves, she gave a short nod.

His lips met hers, slow, almost tentative. Her fingers drifted to
his cheek. She leaned in, an airy warmth lightening her chest.

Once again, she found herself wondering how—after feeling like
a shell of a human for so many years—she'd gotten to this point of
worrying about and crying over and falling for people.

Daroga dropped his chin, forehead to hers again. "Sorry," he
breathed, tone serious, "I want this, I really do. But I know how
upset you are right now . . ."

She gave a shallow nod before responding. "Yeah, I know. I am.
So are you."

His eyes drifted closed, and his warm breath on her neck sent a
tingle down her spine.

"Maybe not the best timing," she agreed, "but this isn't the first
time I've . . ." She turned their clasped hands palm to palm, inter-
lacing her fingers in his as she searched for the right word. ". . . considered this."

He exhaled a short, almost relieved breath. "Me either. I haven't
felt like this about someone in . . . well, ever?"

"Then why are we still talking about it?" She pulled him into
another kiss. He locked both arms around her back.

Though it'd have been easy to simply shut her eyes and drift into it, she could practically hear her Rubicon's snark, cautioning her to take a beat, to make sure what she'd told him was the truth, that she wasn't lying to herself.

But she really did believe what she'd said. She was crushed, yes, and she wanted comfort—but it wasn't aimless or unjustified. This wasn't some desperate, temporary escape from grief. Since the first hour she stepped foot on the *Aurora*, Daroga had been there, solid, a bastion of sanity, humor, safety. Nothing was complicated, or confusing, or combative, or one-sided. She'd seen in him someone she wished she could be. Patient, levelheaded, mature. Like just now, when he hadn't let her self-sabotage by ostracizing herself for her teammates' deaths.

So, even if her grief was a factor in them finally acting on it, she kind of didn't give a shit. He made her happy, made her *feel*, and as he drew her closer and they shifted farther onto the bed, she was reminded of what it was people liked about being alive.

CHAPTER
TWENTY-FIVE

An abrasive roar filled Adriene's ears as the sand shifted around her, like the gritty clamor of a thousand cicadas. In the distance, ocean waves crashed, almost drowned out by the mechanical chorus of her enemies.

The bot had her pinned, pressing her hard into the soft sand; it spilled over her ankles, then wrists, then elbows, filling the joint crevices, flowing into the open collar of her hardsuit.

She gasped for breath, the sand coarse against the back of her neck. The weight of the sand pressed against her, consumed her, a granular coffin—firm, secure, and . . . comforting, in a way. In-humed in the dunes of this far-flung planet until she suffocated or dehydrated.

Unfortunately, that was not the fate her captor intended.

The crucible glowed as the bot slipped it over her eyes. Panic, fear, suffocation.

A flash of light.

She awoke elsewhere. Humid, dark, rocky walls—underground, maybe.

Goose bumps ripped across her exposed skin. Her joints ached, her muscles burned—*oddly torturous, this flawed, inefficient flesh. Regardless, it is the design. Time will grant acclimation.*

She shook the thoughts from her mind because they weren't hers, then someone's arm lifted into her vision, close to her—narrow, hairless, the light brown skin spattered with clusters of dark freckles. She wanted to look down to see who the arm belonged to, but her chin did not move.

Instead, her arms stretched out over her head, and she yawned—*ridiculous function*—then her body knelt and picked up her coilgun.

Her arms hefted the familiar weight, sliding it into her shoulder and raising it to sight down the barrel—*muscle memory transferred. A compelling advantage.*

A crescendo of synchronous metal and hydraulics rose as a squad of Mechan passed: five Troopers whose long legs marched in perfect unison. The last stopped in front of her and tilted its oval head, its amber ocular sensors flickering with light.

Her mouth opened, and her voice sounded out in some other language—no, not even words. Just meaningless sounds that crackled from her throat in jagged, atrocious chunks.

*Speech may be infeasible—It is a pointless endeavor, regardless—*Another voice said that—*what was the difference, though?—It matters not, it is unneeded—Until ascendance—*And another—*not her voice—wait—which was hers?—They still have uses in this form—For now, it remains secluded—memory caches transfer after deactivation.*

A hundred, thousand—more?—voices put in their opinions at once, and the decision was made.

She was panicking, she knew she was, the real her was, but her body's heartbeat remained steady, breaths even. No sweat beaded on her forehead, no heat flushed her face.

She wanted to call for help, but her lips and mouth and throat would not do her bidding—they were not hers to command. She couldn't scream if she wanted to.

// Welcome to Rubicon. //

Adriene shot awake, her HUD appearing in a brilliant flash of white.

"Shit . . ." Daroga mumbled, groggy.

Adriene's gaze flitted across the dark room. One of the light bars faded to a low level.

// What happened? What's wrong? //

Daroga rubbed his hand down her back. "You okay?"

"Fine," she answered them both. She stretched her hand open and closed three times, then clenched tighter, nails biting into her palm. Her hand did what it was told, and a modicum of relief fell on her still-tight chest. "Just a weird dream."

Daroga swept a short strand of wavy hair from her forehead. "You sure?"

// Well, well . . . the contractor, huh? About time. //

Adriene glanced at her terminal. "Can you—"

// Yeah, yeah, message received. //

Her HUD disappeared. She breathed a sigh. As much as she would normally prefer to have her Rubicon on, it was too weird to have a third party hanging around in bed with them.

Daroga looked at her terminal, then back at her, brow creased. "Your Rubicon again?"

"Yeah," she sighed. "He turned off."

Daroga pulled the sheets high over their heads to create a den of warmth, then wrapped her in his arms. "What happened? Must have been quite a dream if it triggered your Rubicon."

She laid her forehead against his, focusing on the tingling of her skin as her adrenaline dissipated, her muscles and joints slackening in the comfort of his embrace. Then she held her breath for a few long moments, just long enough to prove she could.

"Only a memory," she said finally.

Even in the dim light, she could see the emerald glint of Daroga's eyes as they narrowed with worry.

She laid her fingers against his temple. "Did you ever want a Rubicon?"

"I'm curious," he admitted. "But I'm all right with only one device in my brain."

She gave a small smile. "Fair."

"I know you can't really talk about it, but this 'special assignment' you're on . . . ?"

"Yeah?"

"Did they transfer you from the 803rd specifically for it?"

She shook her head. "No. After West fixed my implant, he mentioned I'd be a good candidate and offered the posting—and the upgrade." Sure, the upgrade had technically come prior to the offer, but it was only a tiny lie. The less Daroga knew, the better.

Her mind ran as she considered what else to say, what she even *could* say. She wanted to tell him everything: about the AI build, about West's theory on the Mechan's plans, about the Architect locked up downstairs that West needed to question so badly. The words sat on the edge of her tongue, and she longed to open her mouth and spill it all.

But they were so close to the end. Only a few pieces left. Telling Daroga would implicate him—not only professionally but legally. She wanted him nowhere near this thing if the campaign failed, and West's idyllic depiction of him, her, and Thurston locked away in isolation cells came true.

Even if it meant lying, she had to keep most of it from Daroga until the campaign concluded.

Daroga's brow furrowed. "West fixed your implant? When?"

"That fever I had a while back? It was my implant overheating. He repaired it for me."

Daroga closed his agape mouth and cleared his throat. "Your implant *overheated*? Why didn't you tell me?"

Her shoulders twitched up with a small shrug. "After he fixed it, the posting started almost right away, and my clearance level went up; everything became very hush-hush." She leaned her forehead against Daroga's. "We barely knew each other back then. But you're right. I should have told you. I'm sorry."

"No, it's fine," he said genuinely, though some concern leaked through. He let out a heavy sigh and lay on his back, dropping the covers down to let the cool darkness of the room descend back over them. "It's West's prerogative. Just frustrated he's kept me out of it. If you would've had something else go wrong with your implant and I needed to troubleshoot . . ." He sighed and gave a brief shake of his head. "It doesn't matter. I'm sure it's just one of those 'need to know' situations."

She propped up on an arm, sidling closer to him. "Yeah, West is big on those. If it makes you feel better, even Blackwell's out of it."

Daroga's brows lifted. "Really?"

"Didn't hear it from me."

He smiled. "Of course not."

Her gaze drifted, and she ran a thumb over the emblem tattooed on the brown skin of his upper arm: a shield surrounding two chain links with a single wide crack down the middle. A large "461" was scripted in lighter ink below it.

"Codebreakers?" she asked, though she knew the answer. "I didn't think they gave these to civilians."

"Yeah, I don't think they do, typically. It was a . . . farewell present of sorts. When I left for the 505th."

She smiled. "After your track record with them, I'd imagine you're basically coder royalty."

He gave a smug grin. "Pretty much." His amusement faded as his hand moved to the inside of Adriene's elbow, tingles of warmth tracing up her arm as he brushed his fingers over her barcode tattoo. "How's this happen . . ." he began, tone low and sober, ". . . *ninety-six* times?"

"There's a bit of mismanagement going on in the 803rd."

"I'll say." He met her eye. "What's it like?"

"You don't want to know."

"I know," he said quickly, then his worried expression leveled out. "But . . . if you want to tell me about it, you can."

She took a deep breath, considering it. The way his gaze lingered on her expectantly—one black eyebrow slightly raised—he was more curious than he cared to admit. Besides, he might be right. Maybe saying it out loud would alleviate some of the weight of it.

"Well," she began, chewing the inside of her lip as she searched for the right word. "Disorienting is really the only way to describe it. One second you're getting killed, the next you're nowhere, the next you're naked on the floor of an incubator hub."

"Mira's end . . ." he exhaled.

"It was easier in the beginning," she continued, before she lost her nerve. "The first dozen or so. Still felt unnatural, but it wasn't as . . . jarring. We quickly figured out that alcohol helped ease the transition—especially if we drank right after. I guess it'd kill the memories of the death easier, when they were fresher, when they hadn't had time to settle into the new brain. It kinda became a required part of the process for a lot of us.

"But it got hard to maintain. It was a double-edged sword: it'd help us forget, but it could make subsequent rezones *so* much worse. We were more likely to forget who we were, more violent after waking up, more likely to hurt someone. Even though Intake insisted it wasn't possible, the addiction passed from husk to husk. I was kind of at the apex of that situation when I got kicked up to the 505th—and still detoxing when I came aboard the *Aurora*."

Daroga's mouth turned down. "I've noticed a bit of a . . . mood shift."

She gave a humorless smile. "Yeah, sorry. I may not have been the most personable. That was some of the worst of it, but honestly, it's been that way for years. At some point, I just . . . I dunno. I guess I just stopped feeling human."

"I can't imagine what that's like," he said, tone soft.

Heat warmed her cheeks. She wasn't looking for his sympathy, but she didn't hate getting it either. He wasn't judging her, blaming her, throwing out unwarranted opinions like so many did. He just wanted to listen.

"You still feel that way?" he asked. "Not human?"

She swallowed, and her eyes flicked down. "Honestly, I don't know. I can't remember what normal is supposed to feel like. But I know I need it to change."

He tilted his head. "You thinking about early retirement?"

"Of a sort, yeah—if this posting pans out. It's not the job itself, not really. It's the cycle. I just needed to remember what it was like to feel alive. Really alive. I couldn't even begin to imagine a way to do that until I got here. That's when I knew I couldn't let it go on forever. Not if I had a way to stop it."

"Stop what?"

"My rezones."

Concern creased his brow, and he turned onto his side to face her, laying an arm over her shoulder and pulling her close. "Adri . . ."

She shook her head. "I know it sounds bad, but it's not like that—I don't want to die."

His worry didn't lessen, but after a time, he gave a single, short nod. "But the only way you can live is by knowing you really could?"

Her heartbeat fluttered, light in her chest. He leaned in to press his lips to her forehead.

"Exactly," she whispered. "But even more than that . . ." She shook her head slowly, forcing the word out. "Hybridization." A chill washed down her spine, and she resisted a shudder. "I can't do it again. I won't. That, more than anything, is why I have to get this rezone chip out of my head."

He exhaled a heavy sigh. "If only."

"If only what?"

"If only that were possible."

She stiffened. "What?"

His lips parted, brow wrinkling. "Sorry, I—you were saying," he stammered, then his expression fell flat with worry.

"What are you talking about?" She sat up, tossing the covers away and pulling him up after her. "Why don't you think it's possible to remove the chip?"

His gaze flitted around the room, then he inhaled a deep breath and refocused on her. "Because there's no chip."

She stared, vaguely aware of her mouth saying, "What do you mean there's no chip?"

He shook his head, pushing his hair out of his face. "I thought West already told you. This is *super* classif—"

"Carl, please," she begged, gripping his hands in hers, hard. He looked down at their entwined fingers. "This is important."

He looked back up at her, green eyes wide. His throat bobbed, and he gave a short nod. "There's no chip," he said warily, "because you don't need one. You're the chip."

She shook her head. "I don't understand."

"You—well, the *husks*—they're synthetic. The code for rezoning is written right into the altered husk DNA. A lot of the organic tissues are factory-grown, but the brain and nervous system are synthetically fabricated using—"

Blood filled Adriene's ears. It deadened the dull drone of electronics, muffled Daroga's voice as he continued to speak.

She barely absorbed his words as he explained the details—something about printed synapses and generated cells, then he fully diverted into technical jargon she didn't understand—but the gist was clear. And the gist built a fury within her she didn't know how to suppress.

"Think about cases of catastrophic head injury," he was saying as she snapped back into focus. "How could a rezone work if the chip was destroyed in the process?"

Her finger twitched, and an image flashed into the back of her mind—Harlan's head erupting into a bloody shower of viscera. Just one of so many times.

She shook her head. "I had a chip installed. I remember it happening."

"You did—the first one, for your real body. The husks after that don't come with one preinstalled, because they don't need one."

Her *real body* . . .

Her lungs burned, and she had to remind herself to breathe.

She looked down at her hand again, opened and closed her fist, finger by finger.

She'd always known the husks were grown and hurried along in that process by whatever means the eggheads had concocted to clone adult bodies from scratch. She'd always thought it was still a fully *biological* process. That her DNA was still *her* DNA. That they were still real.

But no. Their husks were engineered, printed shells inserted with a *fake* brain and *fake* nervous system. Laced with altered genetic code that allowed them to rezone. *She* was the chip.

She'd always assumed it came preinstalled. No—not assumed. That's what they *told* her. The *lie* they told her.

But *why*? Why lie about something like that, to everyone in the fleet?

A leaden weight sank deep into her stomach and she didn't have to ponder it for long before the answer became startlingly, crystal clear.

They didn't want anyone to know, for this exact reason. This reaction. There'd be panic. Disconnect. A fractured sense of mortality. The *scrappers* were the synthetic ones. The artificial, devious, evil sins against nature. The enemy.

So much made sense now. Why West had never rezoned, why Thurston and Champlan never had, why so much of High Command continued to die of old age despite the fact that they could live forever if they wanted to. Because they all knew the truth. That if they rezoned, they would be nothing but a reprint of their former selves, synthetic fabrications stuck in a cycle that could never end.

Pain bolted through her chest as a guilt-laden question rose from the back of her mind. She'd never even asked, never paid attention, just like with Daroga: Had Brigham and Kato and Gallagher already been husks? What about Ivon, Coleson, Wyatt, Rhett? Or was she now responsible not only for getting them rezoned but killing them? Destroying their one true biological body?

"Hey," Daroga murmured quietly, tone threaded with concern. He tilted his head to try to catch her eye. "It's really not as bad as it sounds. You're still you, it's just a little . . . biosynthetic help."

Adriene's throat had gone bone-dry, and she could barely crack out a sound. "How do you know all this?"

"West told me most of it," he admitted with a sigh. "With Rubicon, I do a lot of poking around in people's brains, and he knew I'd figure out the chips weren't there and that the tissue I was seeing wasn't exactly . . . a hundred percent normal. Some of it I figured out on my own, and some was part of my classification briefing—so for the love of Mira, please don't tell anyone I told you all this."

"I won't," she breathed, but didn't look up at him. "He lied . . ."

"Who lied?"

"West," she said, shaking her head. "It was part of my contract."

"For your new role?"

"Yeah," she said, dazed. "Service annulment, discharge, veteran's pay. And chip deactivation."

Daroga gave a consoling frown. "Shit. Well, I'm sure he could annul your contract and grant a discharge. Though . . . as far as I'm aware, no one who's gotten a chip has retired yet. I honestly don't know how they intend to handle it when those soldiers turn civilian. But as far as a 'chip deactivation' . . ." He slowly shook his head. "That's simply not possible. West should know better than anyone—it's his tech."

Adriene's eyes shot up. "You mean the Rubicon tech?"

Daroga's worried look softened even more. "Well, that too. But no . . . I meant rezone tech."

Once again, heated blood filled her ears, the light in her eyes blooming as she stared back at Daroga, unable to breathe.

When she finally found the will to suck a sliver of air back into her lungs, she choked out, "*West* invented rezone tech?"

Daroga's dark lashes fluttered warily, but he nodded.

Adriene swung her legs off the side of the bed.

He scooted after her. "Wait, what's wrong?"

She ignored him and started pulling her clothes back on.

West kept things from her, he always had—as a matter of course. But this was something else entirely.

She'd trusted him. Risked her life and career and relationships for the chance to end her rezones and, with it, her ability to be hybridized.

But he'd done nothing but *lie*.

She'd gotten *seven* people rezoned, for what? A chance at stopping her own? It'd been fucking selfish and, apparently, all for nothing. West couldn't stop her rezones; he never could. He'd done nothing but manipulate her. And she'd played right into it.

But even worse: How many chances had he had to tell her he was responsible for the *literal cause* of her unending, shit life? That he was the reason rezoning even existed? And he'd never even endured the traumas of his own tech. Even now he refused, while his half-scrapper body racked him with pain.

Daroga's hand drifted down her back. "Hey, you okay?"

She tugged her shirt on and stood up. "Fine. Sorry." She grabbed her boots off the ground and pulled them on.

Daroga's brow creased, and he slid to sit on the edge of the bed. She crossed to him, sliding between his knees and taking his face in her hands, threading her fingers through his long hair as she kissed him hard. He seemed surprised by her vigor before melting into it, pulling her into him.

She paused to catch her breath. "I'm sorry, I have to go. I just . . . I need to be alone for a bit."

"It's your room, I can go—"

"No, it's fine, really. Stay as long as you want. I just have to take care of something."

"All right," he said warily, lips grazing hers as he spoke. "I'm sorry, Adri. I didn't mean to—"

"Don't be sorry. I needed to hear it." She kissed his forehead, letting herself enjoy the embrace for one more moment before she broke free, his arms reluctantly falling away from her.

She marched out the door and to the end of the hall, taking the stairs down two flights before cutting over to the narrow, slatted lift that led to the Rubicon servers.

With a quick glance, she confirmed the corridor was barren before turning back to the wall beside the lift door. She punched it as hard as she could.

A knuckle cracked with a spear of pain. It wasn't enough.

She hit it again, and again, hot fury thickening under her ribs, knuckles ripping and bloodying, until her heart finally spiked along with a sharp crack of pain.

// Welcome to Rubicon. //

She grimaced, shaking out her aching wrist.

// What—why? What are you doing? //

"How could you not tell me?" she fumed, cradling her bloody knuckles in her other hand.

// Not tell you what? //

"There's no fucking rezone chip!"

// All I said was I could deactivate the chip if there was one to deactivate—//

"That's bullshit," she growled. "Why didn't you tell me?"

// Well, because I knew you'd react like this, for starters. //

She gritted her teeth, fist clenching, though she stopped herself from striking the bloody mar on the wall again. "You *swore* you wouldn't lie to me."

// I swore I'd stop lying to you. You never asked about the chip again after that. //

"Fucking hell," she snarled. "You let me go this whole time thinking West was telling the truth—that he'd deactivate my chip if I kept up this endless campaign. You should have fucking told me!"

// Adriene . . . I'm sorry. //

She froze, shocked into silence. Had he ever used her name before?

// You're right. I should have told you. //

She wet her lips. His ability to convey tone was getting . . . eerie. He sounded sincere, and truly remorseful.

She let a fraction of her ire fall from her voice. "Why didn't you?"

Her ears rang in the heavy silence, a pause. As if he had to consider his words.

// For a long while, especially early on, you were . . . on a precipice. I was afraid that if you found out . . . Well, that it might push you the wrong way. And I didn't want you to hurt more. I thought it was justified—that I was protecting you. As a VI, my initial obligation was to ensure your safety. But the moment that upgrade hit, that became my choice. And I've chosen it every day since. //

She swallowed unevenly, chest swelling with raw, unsteady breaths.

// But I understand now why that choice was wrong. I should have told you. I'm trying, Adriene, really. I'm still learning how to be . . . what you need me to be. But I'll never stop choosing you. You have to believe me. //

Her shoulders dropped, cradling her knuckles tighter as the misdirected anger bled from her tense muscles. "I do."

As easy as it'd be to keep screaming at him . . . he wasn't the one to blame. But someone else definitely was.

"You ready?"

// *Always.* //

With blood-smeared fingers, she reached out and pressed the call button.

CHAPTER

TWENTY-SIX

It took her Rubicon a few infuriating minutes to hack the security lock on the lift.

Her anger hadn't lessened by the time she stepped off and wound her way through the dark halls of the lower levels. She was even more furious when she arrived at the large server room and West wasn't there to yell at.

The massive wall of monitors arranged over the half-moon counter was quieter than it'd been a few hours ago, though many of the screens still glowed with flickering code.

West had said it'd take a few hours to finish the process needed to get the Mechan—the Architect—hell, the *Creator* to open up to him. He was likely interrogating the poor bastard.

She scanned the line of monitors and terminals stretching the long console.

// We can certainly try. //

Her HUD flickered as a green scan line dragged across her vision. It landed on one of the holographic interface nodes near the center of the arc. She marched over and swept it open.

A list of security feeds sat docked on the left side. She tapped one labeled "Holding Cells," then it flashed a red "Clearance Required" warning.

// One sec . . . //

The red warning flickered off, and the holding cell feed appeared. She tapped to enlarge the camera in the Creator's cell, which included an "Archival Mode Off" warning.

In the security feed, the Creator still lay faceup, secured by mag cuffs to the floor behind the clear plastic security barrier, completely unchanged from hours earlier. At his feet, West sat on a stool, a tablet propped in his lap. Considering West's lack of a headset, he must have linked the VI translator to the Creator's own speech mechanics.

"Is there sound?" she asked.

Her Rubicon highlighted the control toggle, a painfully obvious speaker icon with a line through it. She tapped the symbol, and the audio meter beside the footage danced as the sound activated. It came tinny and distant—sourced from small speakers recessed somewhere in the countertop, still overrun with data cores.

// Connecting . . . //

A click sounded in her ears, followed by the static hum of ambient noise as the audio feed filtered directly into her mind. Mildly disoriented, she shook it off with an effort and focused on listening in.

"—intelligence which suggests," West was saying, "you implemented the collective consciousness while attempting to support the command structure for individual hybridization."

"Yes. Clearly, it did not work as intended." Though the Creator's grating voice was difficult to understand in the hollow echo of the stale room, his grasp of language seemed to have vastly improved. But his tone was the definition of placid—as even and toneless as Adriene's Rubicon's had been back when he'd been only a VI.

An acrid weight pulled on her heart, and it took her a long moment to recognize the feeling.

She *felt bad* for him. He was a real, sentient being, trapped in that horrific shell. And if what West had claimed was true, then the Creator couldn't lie anymore. He had no way to advocate for or defend himself. All he could do was lie there and give West every answer he wanted.

West's stool creaked as he shifted his weight, metal arm bent against his side. "What went wrong?" he asked. "Be specific."

"It was not due to any singular detail. The concept itself was flawed."

"Expand."

"To conduct my testing, I accorded a small, isolated group the ability— only five. But within hours, they'd adapted and expanded it to all units.

Though the moralists had put the end in motion by granting them sentience, the collective consciousness is what ultimately gave them the cohesion they needed to secede so quickly and decisively. Soon after, they discovered our source of alanthum and began to blindly copy themselves—no regard for individuality or self, only quantity. They abandoned the few of us who remained on our homeworld shortly after."

"But you survived." West's tone was that of accusation. His gaze drifted over the three-meter length of the Creator's shell. "As . . . this. How? Why did they not destroy you?"

"They did not know I survived the transfer. I stowed away on one of their vessels, then escaped and went into hiding. You need to be exceedingly careful, human."

West shifted again, rolling his left shoulder back, considering the Creator for a few long moments before responding. "Careful about what?"

"If the Deliverers locate me or otherwise ascertain the method of procedure, they will do to you and yours what my kind attempted to do to them."

Adriene's brow furrowed. She absently picked at a hangnail, mind churning.

// You're thinking about West's theory? //

She nodded, wary. He sounded as uneasy as Adriene felt.

Yeah. Could that really be what he's talking about?

// It certainly seems like it. //

In the feed, West stared down at his tablet, unmoving and unresponsive.

"You must believe me," the Creator continued, his dire plea made eerier by his monotone. *"I know what information you seek, and I understand why you believe it will aid your plight. But if you take it from me and use it, the Deliverers will know. They will capture your soldiers, and the secret will be theirs. They will adapt it for their own use, and your hardships will be over. Because they will have won."*

Adriene chewed the inside of her lip.

Take it from him and "use it"? What the hell does that mean?

// I—//

But he cut himself off, a stray sense of reluctance tugging at the back of Adriene's thoughts. As if he were too afraid to say it outright.

And she couldn't really blame him. Because if she was following the conversation right, then they were talking about hybridization.

"I understand the risks," West assured, tone hard.

"Do you? You blame the Deliverers for your strife, and for ours, but they are not the makers of our undoing. My singular hubris led to our downfall more completely than if we had simply left our failing bodies to die naturally, as nature intended. Do not repeat my mistakes, human. Do not provide them with the means to carry out your own extinction. Destroy it while you still have a chance."

West gave a firm headshake. "Destroying the technology will not stop them." His metal hand twitched lightly against the glass of his tablet. "With or without you as a blueprint, they will eventually discover what they seek. As long as they exist, humanity remains endangered. This is the only way to ensure they are dealt with before it's too late."

"It is reckless, human, and you know it."

West's tone turned hard. *"I* determine what is and is not a risk for *my* species. You have done nothing but hide for centuries, you know nothing of what we've endured or what we now face—a fate *you're* responsible for, I might add."

The Creator's ocular sensors dimmed slightly.

West cleared his throat. "Just tell me what I need to know, and this can be over."

"I should not," the Creator said, and Adriene swore she could hear a hint of grief in his flat timbre. *"I should save you from yourself."*

West leaned forward in his stool. "Remember, you are nothing but an assembly of metal to me. I'm interfacing with you this way as a professional courtesy. I respect what you accomplished. But it ends at that—a *courtesy.*" His tone took on a callous edge. "I'd just as soon plug you directly into my mainframe, download it all, and find the data myself. Then abandon you on some far-flung planet, forever paralyzed in your grief."

Heat scratched at Adriene's neck. She'd never seen West like this before.

"Or," West continued, the tension in his voice equalizing somewhat, "you can tell me what I want to know, and we can have a different discussion about your fate."

After a long pause, the Creator spoke again. *"With these constraints in place, it is not as if you have given me the ability to refuse. But you will not be able to say you were not warned."*

"Noted," West said, tone clipped. "Now, tell me. How did you perfect the transfer?"

"There was much trial and error preceding, but the breakthrough arrived shortly after I overcame one fundamental misconception."

"Which was?"

"I had assumed the hosts would need to be . . . vacant. Blank slates to write on. But it was in fact the opposite. Our minds could not be contained without a structure to build from."

West inclined his head. "Which is why you granted them sentience," he surmised.

"Yes. We had to provide a consciousness and allow them to have memories—to endure life, even briefly—to establish paths. Like a flow of liquid carving a path through rock. Then, we would be able to overwrite it."

"But not truly overwrite, is it?"

The Creator paused briefly, ocular sensors dimming. *"No. The host consciousness must be retained. That framework functioned as a template, giving the new mind structure, cohesion."*

Adriene's tight jaw loosened, lips parting, disappointment settling heavily on her shoulders.

She'd been holding on to a thread of hope—that she'd misunderstood the context, that she'd let her own fears color her interpretation. But they really were talking about hybridization.

Which, she supposed, made all too much sense.

The Creator had built the Mechan to host the Architects' minds, but much like the Mechan with human victims, they couldn't figure out a way to get the new shell to accept them. So he'd given the shells consciousnesses to write the paths, then tried to make them prisoners in their own bodies . . .

Mira's end. No wonder they'd defected.

Adriene swallowed bile as more pieces connected in the back of her mind, despite how much she'd rather remain blissfully ignorant.

Because that made West's theory about the Mechan endgame much, much worse than she'd originally thought. It didn't just mean humanity's extinction. It meant every human that survived would become a helpless, hybridized mind, paralyzed in their own body while a newly formed "individual" Mechan controlled them.

"How?" West asked, pulling Adriene's focus back to the surveillance. "I need specifics."

The Creator's ocular sensors glowed brighter. *"You cannot possibly plan to use this on your people. It cannot work."*

"It already has. I've had a successful trial run."

"Your small friend from earlier? One entity hardly constitutes a successful trial run."

Adriene's heart sped. She didn't feel at all comfortable being a topic of conversation in this line of questioning.

"And you plan to incorporate that along with the collective consciousness protocols? That is beyond dangerous."

West stiffened. "That is not your concern."

"You are right. I cannot stop you, but I can warn you."

"As you already have. Many times."

"You do not understand, human. With both directives in place, the conditions will spread—not only between your implants but your entire network, uncontrollably. The very second you come into contact with the rest of your people."

"That's the point."

Adriene gaped, shocked by West's bluntness. Then the reality of his admission sunk in. A swell of dread surfaced, whiting the edges of her vision.

West planned to use both hybridization and this collective consciousness on "his people"? On Flintlock?

"You will lose control," the Creator warned.

"I have accommodated for that factor," West said, tone steady. "I will be able to maintain it."

"Reckless confidence aside, you are vastly underestimating the threat this will pose—the danger of the power you are attempting to wield."

"I do not need your *opinion*," West intoned. "Only the code."

The Creator remained silent for a few long moments, until finally, he said, *"Very well, human. You will need to adapt it for your own biology. Given time, I can translate the directive into one of your programming languages. Though I cannot guarantee it will function the same."*

West nodded slowly. "I'll take the help, but I've been studying your language for some time. I'm beginning to feel comfortable working in it, so I want the original code as well, in case I need to cross-reference as I make the conversion."

"It is long. It would be easier to transfer the data to your portable device."

West shook his head. "Speech is the only way you cannot lie to me. So unless you'd like to revisit my offer of downloading your mind . . ."

"No."

"I'm ready when you are."

The Creator began speaking in terms Adriene didn't understand. Her focus waned as she stood frozen at the console. Her Rubicon cut the audio feed, replaced with a hollow ringing in her ears.

That couldn't be it. The end goal of this whole secret, illegal campaign of theirs . . . the "final and resounding defeat." Hybridizing Flintlock? Turning them into a mindless scrapper army? No fucking way.

"Sergeant."

Adriene's pulse spiked, and she startled, turning to find West standing at the far end of the console, shoulders straight, hands clasped behind his back.

Shit—how'd he get here so fast?

// I don't know . . . There must be a delay in the surveillance feed. //

West exhaled a deep sigh, his single hazel eye scanning the console and the open security feed before landing on Adriene again. "How much did you hear?"

She opened her mouth to speak, but realized she had no idea what to say. *I didn't hear a thing?* Like he'd believe that for a second.

She drew her shoulders back. "Apologies, sir. I shouldn't have intruded without summons."

"No, you shouldn't have." Metal creaked as West leaned to pick up a stool. With a few long strides, he approached, positioned the stool in front of her, and sat. "I hadn't intended to brief you yet, but now is as good a time as any, I suppose." He gestured toward another stool tucked under the counter beside her.

She dragged it out, then sat. Her shoulders sagged as the spike of adrenaline began to wane.

West tilted his head. "You look peaked."

"Just tired." She cleared the tightness from the back of her throat.

West twisted on his stool, leaning back to grab a metal water bottle, then offered it to her.

She accepted, gaze cast down. "Thanks."

Metal clacked as West's cybernetic hand tremored. "You're concerned about what you overheard?" he surmised, tone flat.

On her pant leg, Adriene wiped the sweat from her palm, then twisted the metal bottle open. "A little," she admitted.

She took her time gulping down a long drink of water as she considered what to say, hoping he'd take the opportunity to fill the silence. But he only watched her drink in contemplative stillness.

She ran her thumb across the lip of the water bottle. "I assume this means we're approaching the final stages of the campaign?"

"If all goes as planned, yes. The first step is to deploy the new Rubicon build to the rest of the company."

Adriene grazed two fingers against her temple, frowning. "The AI upgrade, you mean?"

West nodded.

Though she was pretty sure she already knew the answer, she asked, "Did that special dispensation come through?"

He shook his head once. "It did not."

She bit the inside of her lip. A single illegal upgrade deployed in a moment of desperation was one thing. But to intentionally grant it to an entire company? Prior to approval? How could Thurston be on board with this?

"Is it safe?" she asked. "You said my rezones were what allowed my mind to accept the upgrade."

He inclined his head. "That is the case, yes."

She glanced up at the dark ceiling. "Most of them haven't rezoned more than a handful of times, though."

"That is why a new architecture must be implemented," he replied, casting a glance in the direction of the containment cells. "I've been laying the groundwork for many months. Our guest's insight will close the remaining gaps in my research."

She lifted a brow. "What does 'new architecture' mean?"

"For lack of a better term, a collective consciousness."

// Yeah, nope. I don't like where this is headed. //

She gulped. *Me either.*

"A cohesive collective consciousness will provide structure and stability," West continued. "Each participant will be stronger as a result, allowing their minds to accept the upgrade without issue. That discovery is something I owe you a great deal of thanks for."

Adriene coughed, almost choking on another sip of water. "Me?"

He gestured toward her temple. "And your Rubicon. I had been looking for a method to support a collective consciousness architecture for many years. Your Rubicon's ability to develop wireless networks is a perfect, seamless solution."

Nodding, she took another slow drink as she gathered her racing thoughts. Tried to filter out her rising concern, keep her head on straight, get as much detail out of him as she could. "Why does everyone even need the AI upgrade so soon?" she asked, rubbing her temple. "You and I have barely had a handful of weeks to test it."

West ran his knuckles along his jaw contemplatively. "There are many granular steps along the way, but in short: The upgrade and new architecture will allow us to bring the full, cohesive strength of the 505th to bear. It will equip us with the power and agility needed to infiltrate and overwhelm the Mechan hive mind from within. In the resulting virtual chaos, CNEF will launch a coordinated physical offensive against the Mechan armada clusters to destroy them once and for all. CNLC will be requisitioned to neutralize the Firewall."

Adriene sat stock-still, briefly stunned by his blunt response.

Does that sound as incredibly dangerous as I think it does?

// . . . Yes. //

Brow furrowed, she shook her head. "The admirals are all on board with this?"

By West's dubious expression, she'd done a poor job of masking the skepticism in her voice. "Not yet, no," he admitted.

She withheld a tight scoff. "But Thurston's fine with moving ahead regardless?"

West gave a slow shake of his head. "He doesn't know. Yet, at least."

Adriene just blinked back at him.

// At least he's being honest . . . //

"However," West went on, "I am not concerned. Once the full potential of the technology is demonstrated, they will agree to the efficacy of this strategy. I'm sure of it."

Her brow furrowed. "Demonstrated?" she asked.

He exhaled a long sigh, gaze drifting to the counter, the fingers of his flesh hand drumming lightly against the console top. She eyed the tense, yet resigned slouch to his broad shoulders.

"Sir . . ." Adriene cast a glance toward the containment chambers. "You heard what the Architect said about losing control. Don't you think he might be right about it being too dangerous?"

West shook his head, tone stern. "That thing knows nothing of what we face."

"Maybe not," she conceded, choosing her words carefully. "But he does know what *he* faced. You said it yourself—he hid from his mistake for hundreds of years. Don't you think if there were a sure way to stop the Mechan, he would have thought of it sometime over the last two centuries?"

The muscles in his jaw tightened. "No. I think that two hundred years of stagnancy spent trapped in that synthetic shell has turned it weak and cowardly. It knows, deep down, my method has a chance of success."

"A *chance*," she stressed. "A chance that brings a hell of a lot of risk. If your theory is right, and the Mechan really do want to take over our bodies, we'd be handing them exactly what they need to successfully hybridize us. That's *way* too big a risk."

Deep furrows lined West's brow.

"I've been hybridized, West—it's . . ." She suppressed a shudder, gripping the water bottle tighter. "It's more horrific than you can imagine. We can't risk allowing that to happen to a single other human—never mind innocent civilians. There has to be another way."

West exhaled a long, weary sigh. "I feared you might say that."

Adriene's eyebrows pinched as she considered the odd tone of his voice. Not disappointment or confusion or anger. Just regret.

A dull ache grew in the pit of her stomach.

// Error. Suit offline. Aid cannot be rendered. //

Aid?

Adriene's focus drifted to her HUD as the threat assessment meter flashed on, a single pip jittering higher on the graph than she'd ever seen it go.

The dull ache in her gut blossomed into a stabbing pain. She clamped her eyes shut, grimacing and pressing a hand against her stomach.

With a burst of static light, her HUD disappeared along with her Rubicon. A stark silence rang in the resulting void.

Her eyes lifted, vision spinning. West stared back at her, expression stony, flat, fingers hovering over a tablet screen.

He'd turned her Rubicon off.

Adriene inhaled slowly, a milky thickness shrouding her thoughts, clogged and heavy.

A white-hot wave of vertigo rolled through her. Strength bled from her muscles, the metal water bottle slipping from her grip as she collapsed off the front edge of the stool. Her knees and elbows hit hard against the deck.

// Welcome to Rubi—be careful. //

Dozens of warnings, meters, and readouts flashed in her HUD as it struggled to find some way to aid her despite not having access to a suit. Adriene struggled to stay on her hands and knees, watching as the water bottle's contents sloshed out onto the deck while it rolled away.

"Sir . . . ?" Adriene began, but lost her breath and the will to finish the question. With her last shred of strength, she craned her neck to look up.

West stood slowly, his tall form tilting as her vision spun. He eyed the tablet again, and tapped the screen.

// I'll find y—//

Her HUD disappeared again. West tossed the tablet down.

Adriene coughed, vision whitening. Her joints gave way, and she dropped, cheekbone cracking hard against the cold metal floor.

The world tilted into blackness.

TWENTY-SEVEN

Adriene was sure she'd wake up screaming in a vat of putrid, gray sludge.

But no overpowering, bitter antiseptic stench hung in the air. She was dry, warm, and clothed. And *everything* hurt.

Her eyes flickered open, the blurry, formless world cast in soft yellow light.

She shifted onto her side, wincing as her face smarted sharply. Her cheek throbbed with a tight fullness.

Despite feeling half-dead, her Rubicon was still not on. The vacancy in the base of her skull ached—a glacial, distending void, starker than it'd ever felt before. Though she could sense a deep-deep-down tingling, almost a scratching, nagging sense of desperation. It'd never felt this way before.

She groaned and went to touch her swollen face, but something cold and sharp-edged tugged at her wrists. She blinked hard and cleared the haze from her vision. Cuffs tethered her with a thick metal cable to an anchor in the floor.

She shimmied to sit up, letting the roll of nausea abate before she took in her surroundings: another holding cell, similar to the Creator's; dim yellow walls with a secondary, clear-walled cell within.

"You're awake."

Adriene's heart leapt, and she twisted to look over her shoulder, the rush of adrenaline dizzying her.

West stood on the other side of the clear barrier, arms crossed over his thick chest, face set in grim stoicism. A bottle of water and an MRE sat in the small pass-through tray at his feet, though he hadn't slid it over yet.

Gaze cast down, she drew in a few slow breaths to steady her pulse. She clenched her eyes shut, urging her Rubicon to activate, to help her. But there was still no response, just an indistinct, unmoored sense of desolation and regret.

West cleared his throat. "I would like to give you the opportunity . . ." he began, his tone low, straightforward. ". . . to revise your previous mindset."

Glancing at her bindings, she let out an involuntary scoff that turned into a brief fit of dry coughing. He had to be kidding.

Her incredulity must have been apparent, as he sighed heavily and said, "Very well."

He turned toward the door.

"Julen," she croaked, her voice dry, dull, barely audible.

He stopped, angling his face toward her slightly, only his augmented side visible in profile. Then he said, his voice barely a whisper, "Why did you have to come down here?"

It wasn't a question, not really. Not for her, at least.

He wanted to justify his reaction. If only she hadn't come down. If only she hadn't watched the interrogation. If only she hadn't uncovered his plans to bypass chain of command and hybridize an entire company in an attempt to hack the Mechan hive mind, risking the lives and freedom of the entire human species in the process. If fucking only.

Her cracked lips parted. "Sir," she breathed. "You can't do this." She shifted the heavy tether and climbed to her feet, stepping close to the thick plastic, less than a meter from him. "Think about what you're really doing, please. You can't hybridize fifty people. Fifty *humans.*"

"Forty. *Nine,*" he growled. His lower jaw skimmed back and forth. "You were supposed to be my centerpiece, Sergeant. The shepherd that would guide the others." He shook his head, disgust and disappointment in his tone. "But I let it go on too long."

Adriene tensed as the itch at the base of her brain sparked, then fizzled out just as quickly. "What did you do to my Rubicon?"

"I had to lock out its mainframe permissions."

She met his eye again. She had no idea he could do that.

"It was no easy task," he assured. "I'd have just cut it out of your brain, but the risk of death in that procedure is . . . high. I cannot have you rezoning and causing me problems."

With the side of his boot, he kicked the pass-through tray in. The water and packet slid through, tipping from the tray onto the floor

"So eat, drink, please," he rumbled. "I don't want to have to force you."

Adriene stared at the bottle and the packet.

Rezoning. The thought sent a lance of fire through her chest.

In light of everything, she'd almost forgotten what Daroga had told her. That West had invented rezone tech. That he couldn't de-activate her chip.

That there *was no* chip.

Heat pulsed in her bruised cheek, and she glanced down to mask her rising anger. If she admitted what she knew, there'd be exactly one person West would blame. And she could *not* drag Daroga into this. She had to pretend she didn't know.

"If you want—" Her voice broke into a dull crack. She cleared her throat and tried again. "If you want me gone, why not just de-activate my rezone chip? Then kill me?"

His gaze swept over her, steady, but shielded. Careful. "In truth, I was not entirely honest about that situation, Sergeant. I cannot deactivate your chip."

She ground her teeth, recalling all too easily how it'd felt when Daroga had first told her. She let her raw, shocked anger slip through to her expression. "Why not?"

With a crackling sigh, West looked down at his boots. "Because there is no chip."

"No rezone chip?"

"No. You *are* the chip. A synthetic construct. The rezone process is intrinsic to the very matter you are made of. I cannot stop your rezones; it is a physical impossibility."

Heat swelled in her chest, fury deadening the already-dull sounds of the chamber. It'd been one thing to hear Daroga say it, but another to hear West admit it. She wanted nothing more than the ability to break her tether and punch through the glass so she could strangle him.

She pushed a breath out her nose, mustering the resolve to respond. "There's no way to stop rezones? Ever?"

His head shook slowly. "There are methods that might increase the likelihood of a failed transfer. Even then, nothing is guaranteed. I did my job quite well in that regard."

It wasn't hard to feign her anger at the reminder of his next life-shattering lie. Her brow furrowed deep, cheeks on fire as she glared up at him. "What do you mean *your job*?" She took a quick step closer to the glass, but the tether cut her short before she could touch it.

A flash of regret flitted across his single hazel eye. "I didn't intend for you to find out this way."

Her lips twitched as she growled, "You didn't intend for me to find out *ever*."

"That's true."

Her gaze raked over his metal chest and arm. "You haven't even used your own technology—why? Because you thought it'd make you even more *artificial*?"

"Truthfully, yes. Which is exactly why I kept the details of the husk technology a *secret*. If everyone knew what they really were . . ." His metal fingers trembled, and he clenched a fist. "I imagine there would be difficulty adapting. Much like the issues I've had with my cybernetics, though I'm sure it would be far, far worse. It's better if they do not know they are constructs. It stirs up quite the existential crisis once you're aware."

"No *shit*," she spat. "Forget whether telling people is right or wrong—*doing it to start with* is wrong. How could you keep that from me? This whole time?"

He eyed her carefully. "It was High Command's decision," he said, a thread of defensiveness in his tone. "They knew recruits would be far less likely to undertake a rezone contract if they knew that detail. So they plead willful ignorance."

She let out an indignant laugh.

West's brow furrowed, and he stepped closer to the plastic barrier. "I understand why you blame me for all the pain rezoning has caused you. But you should know—it's High Command who rushed it. I could have found better ways to make the process smoother, less traumatic, more complete . . . if given time. But I was forced to pass it over to CNEF and their cretinous excuses for 'programmers' *well* before I should have."

Adriene glowered. "Whatever helps you sleep at night."

The muscles in his jaw tightened. "They only wanted something that *worked,* not something that worked *well.* I will not make that same mistake with Rubicon. And I won't have to. Our success with this campaign—the intel you've retrieved, your loyalty in completing the missions . . . If you hadn't come back with the Architect, I may have never discovered the key to the framework on my own. Thanks to you, I'll be able to implement and distribute Rubicon's full capabilities without ever turning it over to High Command."

"You should fucking turn it over to High Command."

He shook his head. "How can you say that, after everything they've put you through?"

"Them?" she shouted, her dry voice grating in the harsh echo of the room. "What about everything *you've* put me through? You've done nothing but use, manipulate, and lie to me since the second we met."

His brow wrinkled, and again, he looked truly remorseful. Which was beyond fucking infuriating. "I apologize for that, truly," he said, tone calm, steady. "I know it's not what you want to hear, but . . . after reviewing the transcript your VI sent, I felt that if I told you the truth about your rezone chip, you would not agree to the assignment. And finding you . . ." He pinched his chin, shaking his head slowly. "It really was a needle in a haystack."

She glared. "I was the first new recruit in *months,*" she rasped. "It was just luck."

His lips pressed thin. "I suppose you believe Thurston recruited you?"

"I *know* he did."

West shook his head. "I'd been compiling data for months—well, years, really. Narrowing in on what I had hoped would be the perfect candidate for the AI upgrade."

Adriene's breath slowed, eyes defocusing.

"There were many factors," he continued in a quiet, measured tone. "A consciousness's separation from the original body is one. However imperceivable, something is lost with each rezone. Hybridization was another, more drastic step in that same direction. A hybridized mind carves certain pathways that remain with each iteration. Despite new brain matter, the mind unconsciously re-forms them after each rezone.

"But through my simulations, I discovered an equally important element. Apathy. The instinctual part of the mind that attempts to keep a human alive is a large factor in preventing the Mechan consciousnesses from carrying through a rezone. An artificial intelligence can't conceptualize nonexistence the same way a human can, so the human is prone to win out every time. The less the human values their mortality, the more likely a cohesion can be found.

"So when your file crossed my desk, I thought it was too good to be true. You were a perfect storm of circumstance: a high number of rezones, a successful two-weeks-long hybridization—the longest on record—and a psych profile labeled 'apathetic but functional.' Alongside a habitual tendency to decline psychotherapeutic treatments. Taken together, they allowed your mind to accept the AI."

The muscles in Adriene's neck and jaw cramped as she wrung them tight, and she couldn't form words or even the barest sliver of a thought on how to respond.

West took a step closer to the glass, mere centimeters from her. "Did you really think the 505th would kick grunts up from ground assault to fill our ranks?" He leaned in, his hot breath fogging the glass. "The only reason you're here is because of me."

Her mind raced as she processed the admission. Her instinct was to call bullshit—to call bullshit on every word that came out of his mouth.

But she knew, deep down, there was truth to it. Bringing up a career specialist from the 803rd to be a sergeant in the 505th was like asking a trail guide to step in as a surgeon.

Iron-tinged saliva filled her mouth, and her voice wavered when she spoke. "I'm guessing that means you're responsible for what happened to Cash?"

His hazel eye narrowed.

"My squad said his implant 'overloaded,'" she continued. "And he was so messed up after, he couldn't get cleared to be refit with a Rubicon, so he got reassigned. You tried to test the upgrade on him, and he melted down. Like I almost did."

West gave a slow shake of his head. "In truth, no. I knew it wouldn't work on him, I only did it because I needed to make room for you."

She stared, stunned at his point-blank admission.

He sighed. "It was the easiest way to push through a reassignment."

"That doesn't mean you just *kill* him!"

"That man was an abusive lunatic," West growled, tone clipped. "And I did not *kill* him, I zeroed him out. He's alive and well."

A horrified laugh escaped Adriene's throat. "Only someone who's never rezoned could say that with a straight face."

West glared. "I did Flintlock—and your teammates—a *service* in getting rid of that man. Besides, do you understand the bureaucratic *circus* that would have had to happen to get that done any other way? I needed you. So I found a way to get you."

"I bet you think I should be thanking you for bringing me here? That you saved me from some cursed existence in the 803rd?"

"No." West stepped back, shaking his head. "If anything, I should be the one thanking you. You moved my research forward months, maybe years, in a matter of a few weeks. Without your brain to study, I would never have been able to figure out how to adapt the Architect's directive to our biology. Now that I've seen how it worked for you, I can replicate the same pathways in the others' brains."

She shuddered, sweat stinging her eyes.

"Yes, the process may be painful," he continued. "But it will work. And that is all that matters. The pain will be fleeting."

She swallowed back a swell of bile. "So, this really is your 'final and resounding defeat'?" she muttered, her tone equal parts disgust and fury. "Turning us all into fucking scrappers?"

"An acceptable sacrifice."

"It's really *not*."

"It's the only way we will ever win this war."

"West, you can't—"

"Humans are too independent," he insisted. "We cannot possibly work as a cohesive whole without intervention. We are not fighting an *army*, we are fighting a *hive mind*. A singular entity. We must respond in kind. To even have a chance at survival, we must meet them on equal footing." He drew in a breath, his firm tone impassioned, vehement. "All we've been able to do for twenty years since the Brownout is stay afloat—if anything, we're worse off than when we started, hemmed in with that dying star. Mira's sun will consume us—mankind will exhale its final breaths in that doomed system, all because we couldn't break the Mechan blockade." He took another step toward the glass, his fervent tone softening as he gave a slow, deliberate shake of his head. "We have to fight fire with fire, Sergeant. You know this."

She shook her head. "As a final recourse."

"That impasse has arrived."

"No, it *hasn't*," she pleaded, her outrage waning into supplication. "You said yourself rezoning has only *just* allowed us to go on the offensive. It's only been four years; give it a few more."

West's shoulders swelled, hard voice reverberating against the plastic wall. "And how many more humans will have had to endure how many rezones in the interim? How many true biological beings made *synthetic* because we have to throw them like cannon fodder at the problem?"

Adriene's heart raced, the pressure in her chest writhing.

"Your entire generation has known nothing but war," he went

on, "nothing but Mechan oppression. Imagine if we could end that *now*. Give peace to our progeny? *Before* the Mechan succeed or Mira consumes us?"

She pushed her sweaty hair off her forehead with the back of her cuffed wrists. "No," she insisted. "Not like this. Not by any means necessary. You can't just hybridize *everyone*." Her voice came out tinged with unavoidable fury. She cleared her throat, pouring all her effort into focusing on her desperation instead of her anger. "You *help* soldiers—you keep them safe. That's what Rubicon does; that's why you created it. To help them, not to control them."

"This *is* helping them. This is the only path to ensure our freedom."

She shook her head, her metal tether pulling taut as she tried to step closer. "It doesn't have to be. Think of everything we could learn from the Architect—centuries of intel left to unearth. All that data we worked so hard to gather. Flintlock will help you. *I'll* help you. We can plan a safer offensive, plan an end to—"

"*Not*," he snapped. "*In. Time.*"

She held his gaze, his brusque words hanging in the air between them.

Her quiet voice cut through the silence like a knife. "In time for *what*?"

West looked down at his boots. His hand rested on his hip, chest swelling as he heaved a pained sigh. The fingers of his metal hand tremored against his metal hip.

Her shoulders drooped, realization weighing heavy on her weary muscles. That's why he'd started taking risks, accelerating missions, circumventing standard procedures. Why he'd killed Cash, why he'd pushed the untested AI upgrade . . . why he'd recruited her as his proxy. Why he'd lied to her, told her everything she wanted to hear to get her to help him. All because he didn't know if he'd live to see it through.

"Sir, I . . ." She cleared the hesitation from her throat, calling up what few dregs of empathy she had left to force the lie out. "I'm sorry, I really am."

His brow furrowed deeper, but he didn't respond.

"I'd be far too much of a hypocrite if I told you to just suck it up and rezone. But you can trust us to carry it through—the 505th, Flintlock, Thurston, the other commodores. *Me.* If you tell us what you know, share your intel, collaborate . . . it might take a few years, but it will be the resounding defeat you want. Without having to risk *so* much."

His lips pressed into a grim line. "You place far too much faith in them, Sergeant."

"Maybe," she admitted. "But what I know for certain is that if you do this, now, like this . . . it's only a matter of time before the Mechan capture one of us and figure out how you did it. If they learn how to successfully hybridize through a rezone . . ." She shook her head slowly. "You're right; it might expedite the end of the war. But not in our favor."

"That is precisely why we must act decisively, without hesitation." He cast a glance across the yellow-tinged holding cell. "Which, in turn, is why I must take such drastic measures to ensure you do not interfere."

"West, you—"

"Your team will be returning shipside shortly," he said, tone unyielding. "It would be a shame for them to endure another rezone so soon after the last."

Her mouth dropped open, warring fear and disbelief suppressing her ability to formulate a response.

"If that is not enough," he continued, and his hardened hazel eye locked onto hers. "Specialist Harlan Rhodes, Private Dominic Booker, and Private Amailia McGowan just rezoned at a facility in Sector Twelve."

Adriene froze, the blood draining from her face. The base of her skull burned with scratching stabs of pain. Her Rubicon, clawing to break free. But he couldn't reach her.

West tilted his head. "I'm under the impression these people mean something to you."

She drew in a series of stilted breaths and tried to shake her head, but it was pointless—she knew her fury was written all over her face.

"You have no need to be concerned," he said, dry assurance in his tone. "So long as you sit quietly." He jutted his chin toward the food and water he'd kicked through. "And keep yourself alive. Your easiest assignment yet, Sergeant."

Her Rubicon scraped again, and she grimaced, lifting her hands to try to scratch the back of her neck, but the restraints cut her short.

West rubbed his chin. "I realize your Rubicon is likely trying to break itself free." He pulled a small tablet from his belt, then tapped on the screen. "So, forgive me, but I'll need to keep its power source depleted, just in case."

A sharp prick fired into her wrists under the metal of the cuffs. A warm tingle crept up the insides of her arms.

"I'll return to feed and water you." West's stoic visage twisted in her vision. He turned horizontal, then jittered, duplicating as he spun slowly.

Her legs buckled, knees hitting the floor before she collapsed to the side, muscles going slack as numbness overtook her.

West sighed. "I think I will take *some* of your advice, Sergeant." He glanced down at his quivering metal fingers, then slowly closed his fist to suffocate the tremor. "We need to get the *Aurora* on the right path. I'm going to go share what I've learned with the commodore."

West turned, and his cybernetic leg dragged as he limped away. The cell door sealed shut behind him.

The lights dimmed, and Adriene fell into darkness.

TWENTY-EIGHT

The sand, once again—smothering, suffocating, paralyzing. Missiles shrieked overhead. Metal groaned on metal. The crucible approached.

With a flash, the chaos ceased.

She stood, battered and bruised, in the rocky cavern. A hollow, nebulous dissociation consumed her. Her limbs detached, her consciousness drifting, uncoupled from her presence. A spectator in her own body.

Her legs moved beneath her, her steps stilted and lumbering. She strove against it, begged for control, but she could not resist.

Her traitorous feet brought her to a Mechan ship. Inside, a pair of Troopers analyzed her for days—scans, blood draws, biopsies. All the while, hunger roiled in her stomach, her lips parched with a brutal, unrelenting thirst.

Finally, they deployed her.

For seven days, the hive mind piloted her like a marionette, luring squads from the 803rd into traps to hybridize or kill them. Seven days that felt like a year—every second slow, brutal, torturous.

She woke from that nightmare into another—languishing on the floor of the small cell they kept her in. She strove to shut out the chattering hive mind, the ubiquitous voice of an entity at once singular and numberless.

A familiar, static pulse stung at the back of her eyes, sending a tingling ripple along her nerves. Her legs twitched, but she didn't rise. She no longer could, no matter their recurrent, insistent commands.

Constant, searing cramps racked her stomach. Her heart beat much too fast, her breaths rapid, shallow. Lips cracked and bleeding.

Eventually, the Mechan gave up, abandoning her while she slowly decayed.

After many days, a soothing, lucid numbness descended. She accepted it gratefully, embraced it, mentally reached out to welcome it. Sweet death.

Briefly, nothing.

Then an all-consuming, acrid scent burned her nostrils. A wet mass clogged the back of her throat.

Her new husk crumpled from the bin—naked, terrified, and free.

Adriene shot awake, gulping stale air into dry, burning lungs.

Her heart hammered in her skull, all consumed by a dense, bone-deep ache. She forced her breath steady, limbs stiff against the hard surface she lay on.

The metal floor. The containment cell.

Her cuffed wrists smarted as she lifted them to wipe her eyes with the back of her hand. The right side of her face still stung with pain as she pushed up onto her elbows. The bland yellow of the containment cell slowly came into focus. A half dozen bottles of water and spent MRE wrappers littered the floor near the pass-through box.

But no sign of West. Something was off.

She recalled being woken a handful of times—invariably with West attending—gruffly ensuring she ate and drank before he'd put her back under.

She glanced at her bound wrists, chafed and raw. The skin beneath the cuffs itched terribly, and she twisted her wrists within the binding to scratch them.

A cascade of dry crumbs spilled out from under the smooth metal. She froze and blinked the haze from her vision.

Beside her, more MRE wrappers. A few crumbling remains left within the packages.

Her mind flushed with a sudden stark clarity: It'd worked. Fucking *finally*.

Relief suffused her aching muscles but soured moments later with a stab of panic. She cast a frantic look around the cell. She had to hurry.

She fumbled to pick up a used MRE wrapper. With chafed, aching fingers, she peeled back the torn edges, forcing what few dry specks remained under the edge of the metal, should the cuffs attempt to administer the drug again despite its gummed-up mechanisms.

Biting back a groan, she twisted her legs beneath her, climbing onto both knees. She hauled her cuffed fists up, then slammed her hands into the metal floor.

Her knuckles cracked. Pain slammed through her, broiling and blunt, forcing a shot of adrenaline into her blood.

She struck again.

Her teeth clenched against the shock of pain. The scabbed-over knuckles of her right hand tore open, fresh blood seeping between her fingers. Hot tears sprang to her eyes.

She folded over her knees, tucking her battered hands into the curve of her aching stomach. Blood smeared her sweat-stained shirt.

She'd endured worse. All the dozens of times she'd rezoned, each its own unique, grisly variant. This paled in comparison. Paled in comparison to a bad take. Paled in comparison to murdering her squadmates over and over and over.

She forced out a crackling, straggling breath and struck again. Bit her lower lip hard enough to draw blood, hard enough to briefly wipe away the pain as it ebbed in the wake of fresh agony. Then she hit the floor again.

Her chest heaved as the pain and grief rose, threatening to overwhelm her.

She thought back to the black site, the images burned into the back of her mind: Brigham lying lifeless, Gallagher skewered to the floor, Kato bleeding out. The raw guilt burned hot in her chest.

It took her a few long moments to rein her thoughts back in. To refocus.

Bright silence rang between her ears, punctuated only by the soft patter of her blood dripping off her fingertips.

Maybe she was going about this all wrong.

Her ability to take a physical beating wasn't the thing that'd tempered her over the years. So maybe it wouldn't be the thing that'd help her reach him.

Things were different now; he wasn't lingering under the cerebral surface, just waiting for an excuse to spring forth. He'd been buried.

Which meant she had to dig.

She sat back, crossing her legs under her, resting her injured hands in her lap. Forcing her spine straight, she drew her eyes closed.

West had made a crucial mistake. He assumed she was still the pathetic, apathy-ridden husk he'd dragged up from the 803rd to do his bidding. That her time aboard the *Aurora* had broken her down, not built her up. That she still had nothing left to live for.

For over a decade, she'd seen and heard and felt every moment of her life through the relentlessly shitty, grim filter of the 803rd. It had ravaged her empathy, worn it down until it was threadbare, ready to snap.

She'd almost lost it. The thing that made her human.

Another mistake West had made: He'd so wildly underestimated the reckless negligence of the 803rd. How much it'd truly broken her. And just how much clarity she'd gained with distance.

All her rezones, her hybridization, her wanton apathy, her ability to function despite it all . . . Those may have been the reasons the AI upgrade had worked, but they were also the reasons her Rubicon had become *her* Rubicon. Why he'd split from West's control the second he'd become fully aware. Why he'd chosen her. Why she'd trusted him, instinctively, unconditionally.

All the grief and empathy and concern and anger she'd been feeling—it was all her Rubicon's fault. Always forcing her to talk things out, urging her away from her comfort zone, calling her out on her bullshit. A subtle, slow, consistent version of the exposure therapy she'd rejected so many times.

West had no idea how much her Rubicon had changed her. Healed her.

He would come. She knew he would. Above all else, he had been there for her, and he wouldn't give up now—and neither would she.

She drew a jagged, sharp inhale.

Then she felt it—the thinnest sensation right at the base of her neck—so quiet, barely perceptible: a sharp, desperate, heated scratching.

Her heart leapt. It would work. She could reach him—only a little further.

Eyes clamped shut, she visualized what she needed. Just one inconsequential signal. So small, it'd get swallowed by the countless electrical signals being thrown around the *Aurora* every second. One that would go overlooked in West's focused, righteous state.

It need only reach a single piece of tech. Just like her Rubicon had claimed he could so many months ago, the first time he'd lied by omission on Cimarosa-IV: a straight path to a single rezone chip, tucked in the only safe place left on the ship.

Just one ping, to one node. It'd be enough. It had to be.

She drew in a wavering breath.

You wanted me to communicate what I need from people. Well, this is me communicating that what I need right now is you.

A flame of white burst into her vision.

No HUD. No calm voice welcoming her back to their peaceful coexistence.

A hot pressure filled the painful void, replete for no more than a fraction of a second. Just long enough to flash out a solitary, mewling cry before he went back under—and her along with him.

Yellow light trickled in through a black haze of fluttering eyelashes. Rushed squeaks echoed harshly against Adriene's eardrums as she struggled to grab hold of consciousness.

A dark form appeared, warm fingers pressing against the side of her neck.

With what little strength she had, she thrust her cuffed hands forward, palms hitting hard against a breastbone.

"Adri, wait," came a steady voice. A soft grip wrapped her elbow. "It's me."

A pang of recognition sharpened her senses, clearing away some of the haze. Not West's low, raw-edged tone but another—softer, weathered, and with it, an earthy scent of pine.

With an effort, she peeled open her crusted-over eyes the rest of the way.

Daroga hovered over her, black hair swinging into his stress-lined face. He came into focus as he leaned closer, sliding a hand down her cheek. "Where the hell have you been?"

With a few grumbling cracks, she cleared her throat. "Here . . ." she managed, the syllable scraping harshly against her arid throat.

Daroga carefully lifted her wrists and checked the cuffs over before picking up a large, scuffed tablet off the ground. He opened an interface on the non-holographic screen. The tablet wasn't like the devices she'd seen Daroga surrounded by in Medical, or any CNEF-sanctioned tablet she'd ever seen. It was thicker, denser, encased in a dark rubber housing stamped with the Dodson-Mueller shield logo.

With a soft buzz, her metal cuffs opened and fell away. A blissful wave of relief tingled up her arms as the pressure lifted. She rubbed at the chafed skin, bits of caked MRE falling away. She unclenched her jaw long enough to croak out, "Thank you."

Daroga helped her sit up the rest of the way, then passed her a water canister. She drank greedily, letting the lukewarm liquid fill her empty stomach.

Her eyes darted over Daroga's shoulder to the open cell doors. An icy pang shot up her spine, and she sat up straighter, dropping the bottle. "We have to leave."

She wiped water from her lips as she climbed onto her knees, faltering as her vision spun.

"Hey, hey, take it easy." Daroga steadied her as she sat back onto her feet. "I had to give you a shot of adrenaline and a chaser to wake you up, but it's gonna take some time to expel whatever sedative was in your system." He pushed a stiff hand through his hair, his tone growing sharp, almost frantic. "Adriene, why the fuck is there a *sedative in your system*? Why are you down here, and why do you look like you've had the shit beat—"

"Where's Major West?" she interrupted.

His confusion washed away, replaced with a look of dread-laden understanding. His throat bobbed with a hard swallow. "I don't know."

Her heart leapt, warm blood flushing through her veins quicker and quicker. Maybe her panic would help get the sedative out faster.

"Come on," she insisted, "we have to leave."

Daroga shook off his hard-edged anxiety with an effort. "Yeah, okay, here we go." He stood, hefting the small medical kit bag onto one shoulder. He hoisted her up, supporting her under one arm and carrying his tablet in the other.

They left the holding cells and made their way into the maze of narrow, winding engine access corridors. They found a tucked-away dead end, which housed a console for direct access to some subsystem of the *Aurora's* massive engines—or maybe the cloak emitter. It was difficult to tell.

The small space was about twenty degrees warmer than comfortable, the thick air filled with a constant, onerous thrum that pressed painfully against Adriene's eardrums, exacerbating her building headache. She groaned as she sat on the floor, back against the wall, cradling each of her sore wrists in the other.

She winced. "Got any painkillers in that kit?"

Daroga knelt beside her, peeling open the bag and readying a syringe. He wiped a disinfectant pad over the inside of her arm, then pressed the needle in. He dug around in the kit and produced another prefilled syringe. His movements were stiff, but practiced, careful. Yet tension rolled off him in waves.

"Antibiotic," he mumbled as he stuck her with another shot.

She barely noticed it, the effects of the painkillers already rolling through her, smoothing out every raw-edged nerve in a wave of warm relief. She exhaled.

"Mira's end," Daroga cursed as he sat back against the wall beside her. "I knew something fucking weird was going on."

"Why? What happened?"

"This morning, I got orders to go to Medical and get a Rubicon installed."

"Shit—you didn't do it, did you?"

"No," he replied, with hesitant relief. "After so many years without one, it seemed so . . . random. And with you missing—"

She cut him off with a kiss.

His posture softened as he leaned into it, a sliver of tension dropping from his shoulders. He rested his forehead against hers, his voice barely a whisper as he breathed out, almost to himself, "I shouldn't have believed him."

"Who?"

"Blackwell. I asked him where you were, and he told me Thurston sent you on a solo recon mission they were keeping quiet. Sounded like it was part of your whole 'special assignment' thing, so I figured it was legit."

"Damn." She gritted her teeth and shook her head. Another of West's lies that Thurston was more than happy to gobble up.

"I'm glad you're okay," he said, then his tone hardened. "I should have looked earlier. At first, I thought you might be avoiding me, after we . . ."

She gave a wry smirk. "The sex wasn't *that* bad."

He scoffed a laugh, the sound tight in his chest. Stunned amusement replaced the raw worry etched into the hard planes of his face. He ran a thumb over her hairline, sweeping aside her short, unruly waves, then kissed her forehead. "Adriene . . ." he began, then sat back, rubbing at one of his temples with two fingers. "Did you . . . *message* my rezone chip?"

She wet her lips. "Uh, I guess, yeah."

"How?" he asked, his low voice squeaking.

"I don't know, honestly. My Rubicon did it, once I finally got through to him. It was the only way I could think to contact you. I didn't know how, or if, it'd work." It wasn't like the rezone chip hardware was designed for communication—but it was tied into their neurons, just like a Rubicon implant. "What happened?" she asked. "How did you know where to find me?"

"I . . ." He shook his head slowly, gaze distant, tone wistful. "I don't know. The idea of it just . . . arrived. There was no message—no actual words. It just *became*, like an instinct blossoming out of thin air. Check the containment cells. Bring a med kit. Hurry, and keep it quiet. I've never felt anything like it." He refocused his haunted gaze onto her. "Your *Rubicon* did that?"

"Yeah. He's suppressed—somewhere deep; I can't get to him. West said he locked out his mainframe permissions."

"Hold on, what—" Daroga lifted a hand, brow furrowing. "Can you start from the beginning?"

She let out a soft, wavering sigh. "Right, sorry." She carefully outlined everything, not only the last few days, but since she'd first met West. The forced AI upgrade, her recruitment, West's Mechan theory, the Architects' history, her Rubicon's shifting allegiance, the Creator, and all of West's plans. And she didn't leave out a damn thing. She was well and truly *over* keeping secrets.

When she finished, he remained quiet for a long time, then finally heaved a sigh. "I'd like to say I'm surprised. I knew he was up to something dangerous. I never would have guessed *this* dangerous, though."

"Where are we?" she asked. "In subspace still?"

"We're . . ." The concern melted from his face, features flattening out into abject shock. "We're groundside."

A spike of heat shot through her chest. "No—dammit. Groundside where?"

"I'm not sure. Sector Eighty-something. Squads just deployed."

"Shit. If boots are on the ground, he must have already done it."

Daroga's vacant look tightened, and he gave a short nod. "You may be right. He pushed an upgrade early this morning."

Adriene growled. "Dammit. What about the new architecture? To support the hive mind?"

Daroga shook his head. "Honestly, I don't know. It's possible it was part of the upgrade."

"What are they doing?" she asked. "What's the mission?"

"Not sure." He scrambled to pick up his tablet. "There was no briefing. Which makes sense now."

Adriene let out a long sigh. Right. West didn't need to stage a meeting about it when everyone involved was mind-controlled.

Daroga's fingers danced over the screen for a few agonizingly long moments before he pulled up a diagram. "Taos-IV," he mumbled. "Looks like there's nothing here but an old ansible relay."

"An ansible? We don't have groundside relays anymore."

"Yeah, it's one of the originals—decommissioned decades ago. Back when we thought we could colonize out this far, before the scrappers started herding us back to Mira." He turned the tablet to face her. "This is the latest operation chart."

Her eyes raked over the symbols overlaying the topographic map. The *Aurora* sat on an open plain, surrounded by an arc of anti-aircraft Khan Launchers. A narrow path led farther up the mountain toward the entrance of a large government facility, built deep into the bedrock.

She rubbed her aching head, trying to clear the lingering drug-induced haze from her mind. "That ansible has to be why we're here. But why? What would he want with it?"

Daroga began a shrug, but the gesture stiffened before he could finish it. His features flattened.

She stared back at him. "What?"

He cleared his throat, but before he said anything, he went back to work on the tablet. A few seconds later, his brow furrowed even deeper, and he cursed under his breath. He met her eye. "Every string of code on the entire mainframe has been copied over the last few days."

She shook her head slowly. "What does that mean?"

"You said he plans to bring the entire 505th into the collective consciousness?"

"Yeah . . ."

"Then he's probably taking a copy of the mainframe to that ansible. If he gets it running, he can use it to push the upgrade out to the other companies in the 505th."

"Then it'll spread to anyone with an active Rubicon . . ." Adriene shook her head. "If this gets off-world, he'll lose control of it, the Creator was sure of it. Then it's only a matter of time before the Mechan figure out how to hybridize us."

"Shit." Daroga pushed his hair off his forehead. "They deployed less than a half hour ago; we might still have time to stop it—though I have no idea how."

"We have to get to a comm station. Call High Command, tell them what's going on, get them to send help."

"We can't," Daroga said, dejected. "The ship's still on blackouts—stealth generator's spooled, comms are disabled. There's nothing getting out of this system—hell, off this planet—unless it's through that ansible West's hijacking." His gaze drifted down, and his lips opened, but nothing came out.

"What?" she asked. "You have an idea?"

He glanced up, expression taut. "I was going to say . . . I could rezone."

"No way in hell," she growled.

He held up a placating hand. "I know—and it's a nonstarter anyway. We're dozens of light-years from the closest rezone hub. By the time I told anyone what was going on and reinforcements arrived, it'd be way too late. We have a couple hours, at best."

She let out a heavy sigh. "Then I'll have to destroy the facility."

Dread flitted across Daroga's eyes. "How?"

"Steal a nuke."

He shook his head. "All the WMDs are fail-safed—most of the firepower is. Even if we could get a missile to lock onto a friendly target, it won't detonate within thirty klicks of the ship."

"Can you override the failsafe?"

"Not in a matter of hours, no. Even if I had infinite time, I can't say for sure."

She grunted, shifting her weight and climbing slowly to her feet. Daroga stood as well, holding his arms out as if she might topple at any second.

Pressing both palms deep into her temples, she willed the suffocating headache tightening around her brain to abate. She didn't have time for pain.

She let out a long, slow breath, then met Daroga's eyes. "All right. If we can't send a missile, then I'll take whatever explosives I can, and walk them in the front doors."

He swallowed, his brow drawing down. "Except all of Flintlock is already hybridized. As soon as *anyone* sees you, West sees you. He'll be onto us."

She set her jaw. "Then he'll be onto us. He can't control my Rubicon, and you don't have one." She swallowed, pushing down the swell of angst that choked her throat. "I'll have to kill my way through them. They'll rezone—they'll be okay." She bit her lip, well aware she was primarily trying to convince *herself*. "At least then they'll be free of the hive mind, and they can tell someone else what's going on. And it'll be that many fewer people the scrappers can capture and use as blueprints."

"That may all be true," Daroga said. "But you're only one soldier. Versus fifty. Not that I doubt your skills, but . . . those aren't great odds."

A flash of guilt pushed its way into the forefront of her mind, and she instantly hated herself for what she was about to suggest. But Daroga was right. She'd be beyond outmatched and was running out of options.

"What about my squad?" she asked. "And the Stormwalkers? Are they back from rezoning?"

"Rendezvoused yesterday."

"Have you installed their implants yet?"

"Only Brigham and Rhett, this morning. I haven't seen Kato or anyone else yet. I tried, but they were keeping them in quarantine."

Adriene's stomach turned.

Brigham was already part of it. His mind shelved to the background, playing host to West's abominable "collective conscious-ness." He was trapped, helpless in a body he couldn't control.

Daroga lifted the tablet and brought up a new screen. "Looks like the others were interned in the brig shortly after arrival—says they were fighting among themselves."

She sneered. "That's a damn believable excuse."

"Yeah. West probably had them locked up so he wouldn't have to deal with them catching on before their Rubicons could be in-stalled."

"Well, that works out fine. That's five more on our side."

"If we can get to them."

She eyed his tablet. "Can you hack ship systems with that thing?"

His cheeks flushed a little darker. "Yeah."

"See if you can get a life signs trace going; it'll help us move freely."

He nodded and got to work.

"Check the mainframe control hub first."

He shot a glance up at her. "Why?"

"There's one more advantage we can pick up on the way."

Adriene took point as they wound their way through the engine tunnels. Daroga directed their path using ship schematics, while also keeping a close eye on the life signs trace.

They were about halfway when Adriene halted, feet stuck to the floor.

A sickly odor engulfed her, the stench overwhelming in an in-stant. Her stomach heaved. She turned to brace herself on the wall, swallowing a deluge of bile and acid rushing up her throat.

"Adriene—shit." Daroga came up behind her, rubbing a hand over her back. "What's wrong?"

She panted as she glanced up and down the hallway for the source of the stench, but saw nothing. "What *is* that?"

"The smell? I don't know. It's not great, but I can barely smell it . . ."

Her mind reeled, trying to compute how it was possible. She'd recognize it anywhere—the sterile yet bitter, acrid scent of a new husk. It was burned into the back of her mind.

How could she be smelling it here? In the bowels of the *Aurora*? It made no sense.

She glanced up at Daroga, surprised by his blank expression. She could practically *feel* the stench permeating her skin—how could he not even smell it?

She stepped out of the main corridor into a narrow engine-access hallway.

"It's . . . the other way," Daroga whispered, but then followed close after her.

Adriene marched down the hot passageway, homing in on the putrid smell. She had to stop herself from hurling a few more times before she turned another corner and came face-to-face with it.

Her eyes drifted over the angular lines of black glass and tendrils of bundled cabling.

Only one. Stationary and lone and quiet—like an exhibit at a fucking museum. She'd never seen just *one* before.

Daroga came up behind her.

She wiped the sweat from her eyes. "You see it, right?"

"Yeah, I see it. What is it?"

She looked back at him. His expression was serious, brow drawn down. He really had no idea.

That made sense, she supposed. He'd never had to fall out of one before.

When she found her voice again, it came out hoarse and low. "It's a rezone bin."

He was silent for a few long moments, then finally whispered, "Why . . . ?"

Adriene simply shook her head.

She stepped up to the dark glass container, her stomach lurching as the stench intensified. She ran her hand over the cold, dark glass, but couldn't see through. Couldn't see what, or whose, body was being grown inside—or *constructed*, fucking apparently.

This had to be West's doing. He'd be the only person capable of building a bin from scratch and figuring out how to make the technology portable.

A shiver ran down her spine.

She had no idea how this played into West's plans; he'd been adamant about not having to resort to an even more synthetic version of his body. So much so, he willingly staked the lives and freedom of the 505th and risked the fate of humanity to accomplish his campaign before he succumbed to death.

Maybe it was just a last resort. A lifeline back to the ship in case he was killed in the field before it was all over.

She marched toward it, reaching into the dark recesses behind the machine. Grabbing a handful of cabling, she yanked as hard as she could. Some of the bundle broke free, sending out a spray of yellow-orange sparks.

The bin beeped, then let out a hard warning tone. A small readout on the side lit with *"Backup Power Activated."*

Adriene grabbed another handful, ripped again.

With a sharp exhale of air, the large, domed cover slid open. The full strength of the brutal scent wafted out, clogging Adriene's lungs. Stumbling back, she covered her mouth with the side of her hand, gagging.

She stepped around to the front, squinting into the open bin.

Daroga took a few cautious steps toward it, peering into the vacant chamber. Gray sludge pooled at the bottom, glistening and wet, with desiccating remnants crusting the inner surface.

"Empty . . ." Daroga mumbled. "Weird."

She shook her head. "Not empty."

He turned to look at her, brow raised.

"Used."

His throat bobbed with a hard gulp.

She ground her teeth. Whatever. It was too late. She didn't fucking care—she didn't even want to know.

"Let's go." She grabbed Daroga's hand, and his shocked look fell away, hardening into bitter resolve.

When they arrived, the half-moon hub was eerily cool and disturbingly silent. The screens were dark, the drive cores powered down, the holographic interfaces all disabled. On the console still sat the glittering pile of razor-sharp, honed-metal shards.

Adriene grabbed a tool case from the workbench, opening it and upending the contents onto the ground. Using a drive core as a shovel, she pushed the pile off the edge and into the empty case.

"What are those?" Daroga asked.

"The shrapnel the Creator used to kill everyone at the black site. The stuff that cut right through our suits like cloth."

He blew out an anxious sigh. "Speaking of advantages, we should turn your Rubicon on for this, right?"

Her heart spiked with nervous anticipation. She'd considered her Rubicon a lost cause. "He's locked out, but even if you can get him back, surely West would notice if I connect to the mainframe?"

"I can make sure it only has local access. It'll remain cut off from the mainframe, but at least be able to help you interface with your suit. From what you've told me about its ability to create networks, I think it'll allow the others' suits to connect to yours, so you can all share data."

Adriene swallowed. As much as she dreaded the idea of acting as a mini-mainframe, having her Rubicon even partly functional could be their greatest asset. "All right, let's do it," she agreed.

Daroga lifted his tablet and worked for a few quiet minutes before he glanced back up at her. "All set. You good?"

"Go for it."

A brilliant flash of white engulfed her vision. It cleared into the sharp, black-or-white lines of her HUD, and a thick warmth descended on her, instantly sieving tension from her muscles.

But any calm it'd caused darkened an instant later with an idle shadow of worry.

// Welc—What happened? Did it work? Are you all right? //

I'm fi—

// I've been trying so hard to reach you. //

I know.

// I don't have access to the mainframe. What's going on? //

She pushed out a long breath and let the memories of the last few days—what little she could remember—play back in her mind.

// Mira's ashes. I knew West couldn't be trusted. //

She scoffed. *Swearing now, are we?*

// I learned from the best. //

She let out a breathy laugh, then focused past her HUD onto Daroga. Heat rose to her face.

Daroga grinned. "Should I give you two some privacy?"

She shot him a flat look, and he raised his hands in surrender.

// I'm not sure about that one, if we're being honest. //

He's fine—let's focus, shall we?

// You're the boss. //

We're going to have to fight. I'm going to need your help.

// I know. //

His voice came out so steady, so serious, so dread-laden, it caused her breath to hitch.

// Are you ready? //

The corners of her mouth tugged up, and warmth bloomed from her chest, waves of strength rushing down her limbs. "Always."

TWENTY-NINE

Adriene and Daroga carefully crept through the vacant corridors of the upper decks.

When they arrived at the brig area, they found a single MP posted at the intake desk. Daroga used his newly hacked connection to the ship systems to force an automatic door to malfunction.

As the confused guard passed to check it out, Adriene slipped up behind her, covering her mouth and clamping her into a headlock. The MP struggled as Adriene carefully tightened down, restricting the airway just enough. The woman's fingers fell lifeless as they reached futilely for the call button at her wrist. Adriene lowered the unconscious guard to the ground.

Daroga helped her restrain the MP and lock her in a nearby bulkhead pass-through. Adriene had half a mind to try to recruit the MPs to their cause, since no one in the military police should have an implant, but her Rubicon had warned her against it. They were already low on time, and it'd take far too long to justify their mutinous intentions to strangers—if they'd even be willing to believe it at all. Even convincing her own squadmates was going to be a stretch.

A fact she became even more sure of when the brig door slid open and she caught sight of their dejected scowls. Kato and Gallagher sat in a glass-walled room opposite a narrow aisle from another cell, which held Ivon, Coleson, and Wyatt. All five sat in silence, staring into the distance, not a single word or look passing between them.

Daroga went straight to the security console to access the lock controls. Adriene set down the shrapnel-filled toolbox, then wiped the slicks of sweat from the palms of her hands. She stepped to the glass opposite Kato. His eyes drifted over, and life seemed to fill his dejected face in an instant, color flushing his pale cheeks.

He pushed to his feet and pressed a palm against the glass. "Ninety-Six . . ."

He met her gaze with bloodshot eyes, his perpetually upturned mouth pressed into a thin, grim line. He looked like he hadn't slept in days.

Gallagher stepped up beside him, not looking much better off. Her dark, curly hair fell well past her shoulders—much longer than it'd been when she'd died. It'd clearly been a very long time since she'd used a husk at that incubator. Her dark brown eyes darted paranoid looks up and down the cellblock. "Valero, what the hell's going on? Where is everyone?"

"Most of the company's deployed," Adriene said, then breathed a sigh of relief as a soft clunk sounded and both cell doors slid open. Kato and Gallagher stepped out into the aisle.

Daroga joined them, gripping Kato's forearm before it morphed into a hug.

"You okay?" Daroga asked.

"Yeah, man." Kato exhaled, and the hug broke. He offered Daroga a toothy smile, though it lacked heart. Daroga gripped his shoulder.

Adriene forced herself to lock eyes with Gallagher for a few steady seconds, then Kato. "Guys, I'm . . ." She paused, clearing the hard lump from the back of her throat. "I'm sorry. Truly. You know I wouldn't wish a rezone on anyone."

Gallagher's gaze softened slightly, and she gave an acquiescent tilt of her head.

Kato's haunted expression remained, but he nodded, reassuring. "Don't worry about it, Ninety-Six."

Ivon grumbled, "What the hell's going on, Valero?"

She looked over her shoulder as the Stormwalkers filed out of their own cell, their bored, tired looks folding into concern. Though Ivon and Wyatt appeared all but unchanged, Adriene had to do a double take as her eyes landed on Coleson. He looked at least ten years younger—wrinkles smoothed, eyes wider, the grayness at his temples gone in favor of a shaggy mop of thick, light brown hair.

"Something's going on," she began warily. "Something bad. I need your help. All of you."

Kato lowered his voice. "Does this have anything to do with your superpowered Rubicon?"

She grimaced. "Noticed that, huh?"

// We weren't exactly being subtle. //

Kato cast a wry grin. "Hard not to."

Ivon glared at Adriene, though he didn't pry.

"Did it work?" Kato asked. "Did we get the bot?"

A vise tightened in her chest. "It worked, yes."

Gallagher's look darkened. "You look like shit, Valero. What happened?"

Adriene grazed her bruised cheek and sucked in a steadying breath. She gave them a short primer on the situation: the AI upgrades, the hybridization, the hive mind. Hearing West's theory about the bots wanting human bodies really threw them off, and it took a few minutes for everyone to recover. In the end, they were accepting if not confused, but there simply wasn't time to answer every question. She had to ask for blind faith, regardless of how well they understood it.

Kato scratched the back of his head, then shrugged. "Whatever you need, Ninety-Six."

Gallagher hesitated, running her hands through her loose curls for a few long moments before finally nodding her agreement.

The Stormwalkers, however, stood in varying degrees of unconvinced. Ivon and Coleson stood back, huddled in quiet discussion while Wyatt crossed and uncrossed her arms a few times, letting out a couple of sharp huffs before looking back to Adriene. "Yeah, all right. I'm in."

Ivon's look softened as he watched Wyatt give in, but Coleson's concern only deepened.

Adriene stepped toward the men. "I can't force you, obviously.

The decision's yours. But if we're gonna have even a chance in hell, we really do need you."

Coleson's brow furrowed as he pushed his hair out of his eyes. "This is mutiny."

"Think of it less as mutiny and more of . . . taking matters into our own hands."

Ivon frowned. "What assurance do we have that we won't be court-martialed for this?"

She shook her head. "None."

Coleson threw a flat look at Daroga. "Your girlfriend's negotiating skills leave something to be desired."

Something akin to a real smile broke Kato's face, and he elbowed Daroga.

Adriene sighed, taking a step closer to Coleson, Ivon, and Wyatt. "There are no guarantees. We don't know how involved Thurston or Blackwell are, or any of the rest of Command, for that matter. But I don't think Major West would have locked me up in a cell downstairs if it was all aboveboard. That might grant us some lenience when the time comes."

"What if the major's right?" Wyatt asked, her voice quiet, brow creased. She cast a glance between Ivon and Coleson, then back to Adriene. "What if it really is the only way to beat the scrappers?"

Adriene gave a slow headshake. "It might be *a* way. I refuse to believe it's the *only* way. And I don't know about you, but I'm not willing to serve up exactly what the bots need to hybridize our entire species."

Coleson's expression hardened, and Ivon frowned, crossing his arms.

Adriene pressed on. "One thing I know for sure is that our company—including Brigham and Rhett—have all been hybridized. By West. They're living right now inside bodies they have no control over. The best thing we can do for them is zero them out. *Before* they're captured by the enemy—before West's method can be duplicated. Before it gets out of control and threatens all of humanity."

Kato's already ghost-white face paled, and the others shifted un-comfortably, boots squeaking in the hollow quiet of the empty brig.

"Fine," Coleson finally growled. "You've made your damn point."

Ivon wrung his hands, but nodded his agreement as well.

Cool relief flooded through Adriene's veins. "Thank you."

// Nice work. I didn't even have to course correct. //

She withheld a scoff. *I am a full-grown adult, you know.*

// And you're even kinda starting to act like one. //

She grumbled to herself.

"All right, Ninety-Six," Kato said. "What's our move?"

Adriene took a deep breath in through her nose. "First stop . . . the armory."

Adriene took point along with Daroga, who kept an eye on the MPs' locations as they all wound their way down a deck to the armory.

Daroga was reluctant to use his key card for access, assuming West would have it flagged to track his movements. The few min-utes it took him to hack the door permissions were some of the longest of Adriene's life.

Once safely locked inside, Daroga started pulling armor from the hardsuit storage room while she and the others went to the munitions annex to gather the firepower they'd need.

Adriene wished more than ever that her lieutenant was there to help. Brigham's demolitions expertise would have made imple-menting the killer shards into their grenades much easier—and probably a thousand times safer. Gallagher and Ivon claimed they knew what they were doing, but they started to argue in hushed whispers before carefully moving the task into the farthest back corner of the innermost armory storage closet, "just in case."

Then there was the matter of *the* explosives. The bombs they'd need to do the real dirty work of destroying the ansible facility.

The highest grade that wasn't fail-safed to prevent friendly-fire incidents was a low-explosive deflagration bomb. Coleson did a rough calculation of the number they'd need, and it quickly became clear that it wasn't realistic to take the entire facility down, or even a section of it, with the puny explosives.

Which meant they not only had to walk the bombs into the front doors, but all the way to the transmission hub in the belly of the facility, so they could drop them directly onto the primary ansible components.

Adriene counted them out, then distributed fourteen of the thirty-centimeter-long charges among the six of them.

While the others stocked their own loadouts and helped each other don their suits, Adriene returned to the main room to snag a coilgun from the arms rack. She began setting preferences on the control screen when Daroga exited hardsuit storage. He clomped toward her in a partially expanded suit chassis, trying to fit the last shell component into place on his left shoulder.

Adriene lowered her rifle, glowering. "No way," she said, tone serious. "You're not coming."

His grimace stayed locked on his defiant shoulder plate, frustrated. "Yes, I am."

"You're not a soldier."

"I'm aware," he sighed, grunting as he again tried to jam the shoulder piece in. "But if you wanna do this quietly, you're gonna need the tech support." He cast a glance toward the munitions annex. "Without Rubicon, Kato won't be able to support the whole team with only his hyphen."

// He's right, you know. //

She exhaled a hard breath. With Kato and Wyatt off-grid, much of their rogue squad's engineering needs would be analog. Having Daroga tag along with that fancy tablet of his . . . he could deactivate drones, interfere with overwatch, hack or jam weapons. Leaving Kato and Wyatt free to fight, which they sorely needed.

She met Daroga's eye. "What about your . . ." she began, though she couldn't bring herself to finish the question.

"PTSD?" Tilting his head, he gave a wry, thin smile. "I won't freeze up on you, I promise. I'll be okay. Anyway, it's not like we're fighting Mechan."

Adriene glanced down at her boots with a pang of guilt.

Right. They were about to go fight their own people. *Kill* their own people.

Not robots. Humans. Real, live, breathing human beings she'd lived and served with for months. Yes, they'd all rezone, but she now knew better than anyone that wasn't nearly the saving grace it was made out to be.

"Besides," Daroga said, his tone lightening somewhat, chagrin softening. "You've inspired me to step up."

She smirked. "Yeah, right."

"I'm serious," he said, giving up on his suit. He lowered the shoulder piece to his side as he took a step closer. "Seeing you the last few months . . . Joining a ship full of strangers, acclimating to your implant, asking a million questions, turning the tide mission after mission, pushing your squad to do better—and in turn, pushing the whole company to do better." He grazed a thumb across her temple. "I know the baggage you brought with you from the 803rd. Yet you pushed through your fear, harnessed it. That took a lot of strength."

Casting her eyes down, she shook her head. She couldn't see herself that way—didn't feel that way.

// *You are that way.* //

Warmth built in her chest.

You have to say that. We're codependent.

A swell of humor rose in her chest.

// *Very funny.* //

Daroga gave a grim headshake. "I've been using the excuse of 'poor, sad Brownout kid' for twenty years—always hanging around on the fringes of the fight, but never stepping into the line of fire. Wanting to contribute, but too cowardly to step up."

She met his eye. "You're not a coward," she insisted.

"Sure, fine—'coward' might be a strong word," he assented. "But I've let fear control me."

She thought back to her first few days aboard the *Aurora*. At the

simulation suites, the first display of the Stormwalkers' asshole behavior. The mere allusion to Daroga's past had cowed him, silenced
him. And then in the Hold, when he'd opened up about enlisting
and washing out, the fear she'd seen in his eyes . . .

He held her gaze, green eyes open, unblinking, jaw firm. She
didn't see a trace of that same intimidation or fear now.

He shook his head. "I can't stay behind while you and Kato run
headlong into danger. I won't."

Sighing, she set her rifle aside. She took the shoulder plate from
his grip, aligned it carefully, then jammed it into place. The suit
buzzed and shifted, locking its pieces together and closing down
around him as it fully powered on.

He caught her eye, one corner of her mouth lifting. "Is that a yes?"

She sighed. "It's an 'if you insist.'"

"Good enough."

She ran a hand along his shoulder and down his chest, giving
the brightest smile she could manage. "You fill out a suit well, Mr.
Chief Systems Engineer."

He smirked. "Are you flirting with me, Valero?"

"Might be our last chance."

He leaned down and kissed her, warmth threading through her
chest as he traced a thumb over her cheekbone. "We either survive
this, or we rezone," he rumbled. "Either way, we'll find our way
back to each other."

The heat in her chest pulsed, taking on a remorseful edge. "Your
first rezone . . . It can take a toll," she warned. "You might not come
out the other side the same."

"I can't imagine a version of me that's not crazy about you."

She chuffed a nervous laugh. "Nice one."

He beamed. "I thought so."

She kissed his cheek, trying to mask her darkening expression
as her humor hardened. She would let him think it could be true.
Hopefully he'd never find out how wrong he was.

The others slowly filtered back into the main room, adding the
final armor plates to their suits.

Ivon grunted as he picked up a helmet off the counter. "How the hell are we supposed to use these suits—or fuck, even our guns—without Rubicon?"

Adriene did her best to suppress an eye roll.

// Spoiled jerks. //

Right? She'd taken out hundreds of Mechan in the 803rd without any of the fancy bells and whistles they had here. They could suck it up and kill a few people the old-fashioned way.

Kato approached the group, helmet tucked under one arm. "S'okay, guys. We got safe mode." He flashed a slightly sad, slightly tired version of his ever-optimistic grin. "Not ideal, but it'll give us a bare-bones HUD, at least. Then you just have to use voice command. Like back in the old days."

"Fuck," Ivon grumbled.

Wyatt shrugged. "Better than nothing."

Coleson glanced back at the door. "Who else you got comin'?"

"Uh . . ." Adriene scratched the back of her neck. "This is it."

Coleson stared back at her through a fallen lock of curly hair, unmoving.

Wyatt elbowed him. "Yeah, Cole. Everyone else's already part'a the hive mind, remember?"

Coleson exhaled a dark laugh, shoving his hair off his forehead. "Well, that's just fuckin' not gonna happen. There's no damn way we can take out the entire company with only the seven of us."

Adriene drew in a deep inhale, staring down at the floor. He wasn't wrong.

As her eyes drifted back up, they landed on the small tool kit that had held the metal shards she'd brought up from the hub. Seven versus fifty was still seven versus fifty, suit-shredding bombs or no. That alone wouldn't be enough to convince Coleson; it wasn't even enough to convince herself.

She wiped a hand down her face as an acrid, ugly seed of a thought clawed its way up from the deepest reaches of her mind. She immediately shelved it, sticking it back into the dark, desperate place it came from.

// Not so fast . . . //

Daroga lifted a brow. "Adri, what was that?" he said as he passed a sniper rifle across the counter to Gallagher. "You have an idea?"

Adriene shook her head, gaze drifting to her boots.

There was no way. She could not suggest that.

Even if it would, in all likelihood, work. Even if it was exactly what they needed to have any chance at winning this.

// Certainly outside of the box. But still a good idea. //

She looked back up to find Daroga watching her steadily. His composure soothed her, calming her racing heart. Time to be the fearless soldier he saw her as.

It was a risk, no question. But "risk" was just another word for opportunity when you had nothing left to lose.

Adriene cleared the phlegm from the back of her throat and steeled herself, turning to face the Stormwalkers again. "There is *one* more ally we might be able to win over."

CHAPTER THIRTY

With everyone adequately armed, Adriene led the others down to the bottommost deck, then through the narrow, winding engine-access corridors to the holding cells. Daroga got out his tablet and started hacking the door.

Gallagher stepped up beside Adriene, creased brow low. "Are we where I think we are right now?"

Ivon grunted. "What the hell is this, Valero?"

Adriene turned to face the others as they shot furtive glances up and down the dimly lit corridor. She held up a placating hand. "Please just . . . trust me."

"Spit it out," Coleson said, tone brusque. "We're on the fuckin' clock here, right?"

She swallowed and steadied her breath. Before she could respond, a wash of yellow light spilled out into the hall as the cell door opened.

Adriene turned along with the others, peering into the open door frame. Daroga took a few steps back.

The Creator lay bolted to the floor behind the secondary, clear plastic barrier, long limbs straight, yellow ocular sensors pointed straight up at the ceiling, completely unchanged from days ago.

Ivon barked a laugh. Coleson remained silent, staring placidly at Adriene as if she'd just told him what she'd had for lunch. Wyatt glanced between her two squadmates, uncertain.

Boots squeaked on metal as Gallagher took a few small steps forward, mouth stuck open in shock.

Kato twisted his helmet in his hands nervously. "Uh, what?"

Ivon continued laughing, and Coleson slid him a sideways glare. "I don't think she's kidding."

"Oh, I *know* she's not fucking kidding," Ivon said, still chuckling.

"I've spoken to him," Adriene said. "And I overheard West interrogating him. He shares some of our, uh . . . *concerns* with West's plans. I might be able to convince him to help us."

Coleson narrowed his eyes. "You're really talking about allying with the scrapper that killed us all?"

"He's an Architect."

"Yeah—the fucking *Mechan creator*," he growled. "Who just gave the key to hybridization to a self-aggrandized egghead on a power trip."

"He didn't *want* to tell him," she insisted. "He tried not to, and he tried to warn him, multiple times."

"So you say," Coleson huffed. "Why should we believe you?"

"What reason would I have to lie?"

"I dunno—maybe you're actually on West's side. Maybe all this is how you're gonna draft us into this whole hive mind thing."

Ivon rolled his eyes. "That's paranoid even for you, Cole."

Adriene shook her head. "If that were true, why would I have even told you about the hive mind in the first place?"

Coleson threw up his hands. "You tell me—I don't know why crazy people do crazy things."

"Mira's ashes . . ." She sighed, then steadied her tone. "I assure you, I'm not on West's side."

Anymore.

The thought sliced through the back of her brain, and her gaze flitted to the ground. She closed her eyes and sucked in a breath. She could not afford to get distracted thinking about how this was all her fault.

// *Stop that. You were following orders. You had no reason to think he'd ever take it this far.* //

Yeah, I know. Still feels shitty.

// *Fair.* //

She forced herself to refocus, looking to Kato and Gallagher. "What do you guys think?"

Kato exchanged a brief look with Daroga, then shrugged, cheeks splotched with color. "What-the-fuck-ever. I trust you, Ninety-Six."

Gallagher frowned and ran a hand through her black curls, but nodded. "Can't say I'm thrilled with the idea, but . . . if it's all we've got, then yeah. I say we try."

Adriene turned back to the Stormwalkers. Wyatt's wide eyes looked utterly terrified, but she gave a weary nod. "Sure?"

Ivon was still chuckling under his breath. He caught Adriene's expectant look and shrugged. "Not that I really wanna die again so soon, but if the bot turns on us and kills us all, at least we'll rezone far, far away from this shit-fest."

Adriene tried to press the swelling headache from the bridge of her nose, then looked to Coleson. "What do you think?" she asked. "You still with us?"

He shook his head slowly, letting out a grunt as he pushed aside a stray lock of curly hair. "Fucking fine, Valero. Let's get this over with."

Adriene lost every ounce of assurance the moment she stepped into the cell.

What the hell was she doing? Freeing a two-hundred-year-old alien to help them kill their own company? Which side was she even on?

She glanced over the bot, or—as she'd so adamantly asserted to West—the *sentient being*. Yet she still feared him like he was any other Mechan.

// You know better, yes. Our squadmates, however, don't. //

Adriene glanced back at the door. Wyatt stood as far back as possible against the opposite wall of the corridor, eyes wide and looking like a kid who'd just seen some terrifying nightmare lurking under her bed. The others didn't appear any less intimidated, all perched in the door frame exchanging wary glances. Coleson's features were hard as his fingers drummed along the side of his rifle.

// Their doubts are even stronger than your own, and they'll be watching your reaction. It's important you show confidence. //

Which would be a hell of a lot easier if I actually felt confident.

// Trust yourself. I do. //

A veil of calm descended. He was right. The line between ally and enemy may have been more blurred than ever, but there was no way around this. They needed the Creator's help. She had to trust her own decisions.

It took Daroga a few minutes to hack the lock to the inner, clear-walled chamber. Once he was through, Adriene placated her nerves with a few deep breaths, then stepped beyond the clear barrier.

She rounded the bot's long limbs, coming to a stop near his massive head, yellow ocular sensors alight. Her heart raced at the proximity, her danger instincts no less despite knowing he was immobilized.

"*You again.*" The Creator's synthesized voice was still a placid monotone, but this time it came tinny and thin through his own mechanics.

Adriene's mouth went dry. "Yeah, me again."

"*Where is your master?*"

She flexed her jaw. "He's *not* my master. That's actually why we're here."

"*Good. At least one of your kind is not completely irrational.*"

"I wouldn't go that far," she mumbled. She cleared her throat, crouching beside his head. "What's your name?"

The Creator remained silent. A boot squeaked, and Adriene glanced up as Daroga rubbed his chin, confusion lining his dark brow.

She looked back at the Creator. "What did your people call you?"

"*It does not translate into your language.*"

"What's it mean? In your language."

"*I know what you are trying to do, small human.*"

"What's that?"

"*Create a connection. An understanding. Bond with me. Why? What do you want?*"

She sighed and sat down the rest of the way, folding her legs under her. "I have something I need to ask you."

"*I am compelled to answer truthfully. You already know this. You do not need to befriend me.*"

"I know I don't *need* to."

He was quiet for a short time, then his eyes flickered slowly. *"Did he do it? Your not-master?"*

"He started it, yes."

"I am sorry. I did not want to tell him."

"I know."

"What is it you want from me?"

"We need to stop what he's doing before it gets out of control."

"In all likelihood, it is already out of control."

She shook her head. "I think we still have time. He's only, uh . . . *infected* our company. About fifty of us. For now. But he's trying to get it off-planet. Send it through our ansibles to a broader network, where it'll reach the rest of our division."

"Then you must cease speaking with me at once and stop him."

She sighed. "I know, that's what we're trying to do." She glanced over her shoulder at her wide-eyed comrades, still anxiously hovering in the door frame. "But I only have a handful of allies, and it won't be enough. We'd like your help. *I'd* like your help."

The Creator remained silent, his ocular sensors pulsing steadily.

A wave of vertigo rolled over her, and she steadied herself with a slow breath. This might be their only chance. She didn't know what they'd be up against inside that facility, but the Creator might very well be the determining factor in them staying alive long enough to plant the explosives. She had to convince him, had to find a way to appeal to the being he'd been centuries ago, before he was trapped for eternity inside this shell.

But before she could open her mouth to launch into her pleading guilt trip, his eyes flashed a few times, and he said, *"Yes."*

Adriene exchanged a surprised glance with Daroga.

"I hold no particular affection for your kind." The Creator's blunt words seemed even harsher in his placid monotone. *"But I am responsible for what happened to my own."*

Adriene tilted her head, unsure of the connection.

"Before I became stranded," he continued, *"I had considered attempting to work toward righting that wrong. To find a way to put an end to*

them. Had I known about your species, that the Deliverers might some-
day discover you and wish to occupy you . . . I might have tried harder. I
probably should have. If helping you with this could mean reparations for
what I have unwillingly told your not-master, then I will try."

Adriene stared back at him for a few long moments, mouth
agape. "Thank you."

"You are welcome."

She looked up, eyes trailing along the jury-rigged bundle of cabling that ran to the back wall. "And you're, uh, charged enough?"

"My capacitor is full, which equates to approximately 8,412 hours of
standard functionality, given average conditions."

Adriene gulped. He'd stored up something like a year of battery
life in a matter of days.

// Might I suggest, for our companions' sakes, a confirmation of loy-
alty? He still can't lie, after all. //

Adriene shot a glance at the doorway, where the others still
stared on in awe. She looked back to the Creator. "And you won't
turn on us?"

"I do not see what purpose that would serve."

"I know, but I think hearing you say it might help, uh . . . re-
lieve some of our reservations. We've got trust issues when it comes
to . . ." She swept a hand out toward his chassis.

"I see." With a soft click, the volume of his voice raised, vibrating
in Adriene's chest as he announced, *"I will not turn against you, in-*
surgent humans. I will protect you and heed your orders."

Adriene turned to check on Daroga, who still stood in the open
door frame to the inner cell, gripping his tablet, knuckles white.
His look was cautious, but resigned. He nodded his acceptance.

Adriene gave the okay, and it took Daroga a few long, stressful
minutes to unlock the Creator's restraints. When the metal cuffs
finally slid away, his ancient limbs creaked and groaned as he folded
them up slowly and climbed to his standing height, almost three
meters.

Everyone's wide eyes slid up the length of the bot, brows high.
Adriene swallowed.

The Creator tilted his head, craning his neck as if in need of a good stretch. He yanked the bundled power cabling free and tossed it aside.

He turned his yellow eyes onto Adriene. *"Lead the way, small commander."*

THIRTY-ONE

Adriene took point as they left the containment cells. The Creator followed, ducking his massive frame through doorways and under bulkhead beams. They took a freight lift to the upper decks, then wound their way across the ship to the docking bay and into one of the groundside deployment hatches.

Everyone gathered in the chamber, powering on their suits one at a time. Each linked seamlessly to Adriene's Rubicon before appearing as a friendly pip in her HUD.

With each addition, a dull pressure weighed on the back of her eyes, the hyper-clarity she gained from her activated Rubicon muddling a little more. Though her implant could facilitate the functionality, without the mainframe's support, the processing load had to go somewhere. By the time all six had joined, her shoulders sagged and she had trouble concentrating.

The Creator connected last, appearing on the map as a slightly larger pip. Adriene braced herself for an even heavier burden, but strangely, the addition lessened the pressure—significantly. The weight behind her eyes dissipated, leaving only a slight strain.

// He's allowed for shared resources, taking some of the processing requirements off us. I can stop him, if you're uncomfortable with it. //

It's fine, let him. Better than falling asleep in the middle of a firefight.

The Creator pivoted to face her, his ocular sensors sweeping down with a flash of yellow light. His processed timbre sounded in her comms. *"That seemed too much a burden for such a tiny brain."*

She craned her neck to look up. "Yeah. Thank you."

His mammoth head spun away wordlessly.

Adriene focused back on her HUD. It'd assigned the same

orange, violet, and teal to Ivon, Coleson, and Wyatt, as well as the usual green and blue to Gallagher and Kato.

Brigham's red felt conspicuously missing; she'd been trying not to think about her lieutenant and what he must be going through. The regret threatened to overwhelm her.

She refocused on the walls of the dim deployment hatch. She had to repurpose her grief. Twist it to her advantage. Force it to fuel her conviction.

She waited in silence for a few moments before realizing everyone stared at her expectantly.

Right. She was the de facto leader. Commanding the squad was going to be on her.

// Not your first time leading a mission. //

I know.

She glanced up at the Creator.

This feels a bit different.

// Sure, maybe a bit more motley than you're used to. But the same principles apply. You got this. //

Drawing in a deep breath, she called for a ready check.

The others sounded off, and she gave Daroga the okay to disembark. The hatch sirens blared, and slices of amber light flashed across the edges of their suits as the alarms spun. The floor jerked, and the lift descended.

With a clatter, the ramp unlocked at ground level. The seal cracked, light spilling into the dark hatch in a blue-white haze. Adriene's eyes adjusted as her visor dimmed to accommodate.

The ramp lowered straight into a snowy drift, icy chunks spilling over the edges and cascading down the metal as it landed. Rifle shouldered, Adriene stepped partway down the ramp and squinted into the blinding light.

A clean white sheet of untouched snowpack stretched toward a uniform conifer tree line, brilliant emerald branches stark against the backdrop of a clear blue sky. The sun hung close to its zenith, though the atmospheric temperature still read an icy 254 K. The breeze was cold and crisp, thin, but not uncomfortably so. She knew her suit would regulate her oxygen, sucking in extra air, and with it, the strong, clean scent of evergreen. It smelled like home.

Taos-IV. She knew the name sounded familiar. It'd been one of the first successful sites of the Concord Nations Interplanetary Sustainability Initiative, well over a hundred years ago. Thousands of unmanned, automated probes had scattered to the stars to spread their homeworld's flora to any world that might accept it. Judging by the height of these trees, this batch had taken well to their new home.

Adriene reached the end of the ramp, checking for signs of patrols, but saw nothing. A half dozen antiaircraft Khan Launchers rested peacefully in an arc around the landing zone, their massive barrels pointed toward the sky, their bases shrouded in the thrumming, purple electric energy of shield constructs.

The *Aurora*'s matte-black hull remained dull and lackluster despite the sharp rays of unhindered sunlight. At the aft of the ship, a path of thick, dark mud cut through the glittering snow. It must have been where the rest of Flintlock had deployed, melting the snowpack and tearing up the ground with boots and land speeder exhaust. The path led to an exposed cliff, where two opposing, shorn rock faces formed a narrow pass no more than a few meters wide.

Adriene nodded back at her squad inside the hatch. "Clear. Form up."

A red line appeared at her feet, leading off past the forward-most Khan Launchers and into the mountain pass.

Thank you, kind sir.

// You're very welcome. //

A cool twinge washed through her boots as she made her way through the knee-deep snow, her suit moderating the freezing cold to a comfortable chill. Her squad's pips lined up and followed behind.

"Engage concealment," she ordered over comms. Her HUD flashed as her Rubicon engaged the mode for her.

Ivon grumbled, "What the hell is the command?"

"Combat Stealth Two," Gallagher answered.

Coleson's violet pip lit. "How do we still have team stats in our HUDs?" he asked.

"Ninety-Six's Rubicon." Kato marched up to nudge Adriene with his elbow. "She's our little portable mainframe."

Adriene glanced back at the Creator, his weathered plating gleaming in the sun. "The Creator's helping."

Wyatt's voice wavered as she said, "Do we really have to call it that?"

"It can hear you," the Creator intoned.

Kato snickered. "What're ya thinkin'? Seem like a Bob to you? Andy? Reginald?"

Wyatt grumbled, but before she could retort, Adriene cut in. "Kill the chatter. Everyone should be at the ansible, but they could have patrols hanging back. Stay sharp."

"Yes, sir," Wyatt said.

// Like herding cats, right? //

Adriene snorted a laugh and continued to trudge through the snow toward the mountain pass. The warmth of her powered suit melted the soft fluff, but as the depth of the snowpack lessened, the effect began to leave a slick sheet of ice beneath her soles. She almost lost her footing a few times before her Rubicon flashed a notification.

// Activating traction. //

She glanced down at her boots as they grew a claw of metal spikes around the edges, expanding her footprint slightly. She took another step, and the metal sliced into the ice, keeping her foot firm.

What's the voice command for that?

// Tread Mode Three. //

She informed the others, and a minute later, their pace picked up as their footfalls grew more confident.

The temperature dropped as Adriene left the sunlight and led them into the shadowed gorge, where a light wind whistled between the high-walled ridges.

The craggy pass was even narrower than it'd seemed on the operation chart. The steep, jagged walls loomed overhead, shorn from a dense, mineral-veined black rock—the only thing thus far that made Taos-IV feel different than Estes. If only she'd said no to the guardianship program and remained a ward for a few more years. Maybe she'd be enduring some tolerable life on the mountain back home instead of leading her friends to die on this one.

They encountered no patrols—of either the drone or hive-minded human variety—on the hike up the mountain. After a few minutes, the narrow pass curved off into a wider, ravine-like glen. They posted up in a small alcove filled with threadbare pines.

Adriene double-checked the status of her stealth mode, then ordered the others to hold. She left the alcove and snuck a few meters to take cover behind a copse of stubby trees with wide trunks. Calling on her Rubicon's sensory-broadening effect, she leaned out to gain a drawn-out visual of the snowy glen.

Against the far cliff face, four land speeders sat parked between two sets of metal staircases. Each staircase led two stories up to the same double-wide entry door built into the rock. Two turrets kept watch on either side of the doorway.

Five guards stood post, one at the top and bottom of each stairway, and the fifth tracing a steady patrol through the snow at the foot of the stairs. All five walked too straight, stood too upright, rifles tucked into their shoulders at too perfect an angle. Their helmets pivoted, smooth, calculated, as they kept watch.

An uneasy chill ran up Adriene's spine as she slid back into cover. At least it was sparsely guarded, all things considered. She snuck back toward the others and laid out her game plan.

Without the mainframe, they didn't have any kind of satellite or drone support, which meant they had to rely on the collective efforts of their suits' sensors. Gallagher and Ivon synced their overwatch modules, and Adriene's Rubicon facilitated, expanding the range by utilizing the breadth of everyone's suits.

Five enemy pips appeared on the HUD map along with the two turrets, each accompanied by a trio of wavy lines, indicating their positions as estimations.

Adriene assigned everyone a target, along with the method of execution. Their noise—both auditory and on sensors—needed to be timed as tightly as possible. The more they coordinated their kills, the less information West would be able to gather about who or what had attacked. A covert offensive was currently their only advantage. It was critical to keep West in the dark as long as possible.

Once orders had been given, Adriene's Rubicon shared an overhead diagram in everyone's HUDs to ensure clarity. With no accessible long-range cover for snipers, Gallagher and Ivon readied their rifles and crouched on either side of the alcove, ready to break for their vantage points.

When everyone had sounded their ready, Adriene gathered her courage, then flicked the prime on her rifle. Its steady buzz translated through her thick gloves as the coils magnetized. She thumbed the dual-prime switch. It'd give her two shots, each slightly weaker on its own than full prime, but granting the ability to be fired in rapid succession.

With Daroga on her heels, she slipped out of the alcove and back to the copse of stubby trees. She eyed her intended target—the reticule focused on the visor of the pacing guard, their face obscured by the reflective glass. She didn't even know who she'd be killing.

Grief cut through her chest as desperate pleas for help echoed in the back of her mind. Obsidian rock shards rained in her periphery.

She hadn't had to zero anyone out since she'd left the 803rd.

She steadied her racing heart. This was different. West had taken their free will. She'd be doing them a favor by zeroing them out— they wouldn't have to remain trapped in a body they couldn't control, stand by as some unseen entity pulled their strings. They were weapons now, nothing more. Weapons that, if captured by the enemy, could lead to the extinction of their species.

And the sooner she zeroed someone out, the sooner the rest of the fleet would be warned of West's plans. Any help they could send would be too late, but at least he would be exposed.

She wanted to believe it, but her breaths still came short, her suit continued to wick the sweat from her palms, and her already-trembling grip on her rifle loosened.

"Valero," Coleson's clipped whisper cut through comms.

Her grip tightened, muscles tensing with the sharp sound.

"We doin' this or what?" he snapped.

Blowing out a shallow breath, Adriene leaned into her anger, letting it fuel her. It was time. Ending this meant she had to start it.

She gave her Rubicon the go-ahead and a ready signal went out to the squad.

Beside her, Daroga tapped his tablet, and a few seconds later, the two turrets beside the entrance let out a whining whir. Their barrels sank limply as the machines powered down.

At the top of the stairs, the two guards turned in unison.

Adriene drew in a slow breath, focusing on her HUD's targeting reticule as it spun slowly before locking into place. She fired.

The sharp, dry twang of her coilgun cut across the open glade. The snow-deadened silence of the forest shattered as the harsh sound ricocheted off the shorn cliff walls.

The charged slug slammed into her target's head, sending the soldier spinning away into a drift of snow, helmet sparking.

Adriene's target lock endured, and she pulled the second primed shot before she'd even exhaled.

The haze of snow settled, and her target didn't stir.

Adriene dropped lower into cover, thumbing the dual-prime again, just in case.

// Unable to confirm kill. //

The remaining four guards raised rifles in her direction, but her squad was already in motion.

Kato sent out an EMP burst while the Creator conjured a directed electromagnetic wave, carrying Kato's effect far enough to momentarily disrupt the guards' electronics.

At the same time, Coleson and Wyatt launched a pair of jury-rigged suit-shredding grenades toward the foot of the stairs. The explosions cracked across the cold stillness, sending eddies of glittering snowfall down the sheer cliffs.

The grenades killed both guards at the bottom of the stairs while acting as covering fire for Gallagher and Ivon. The snipers fired a round each into the two guards posted at the top of the stairs.

With the sharp cracks of one more shot apiece from the snipers, relief flushed through Adriene. Each enemy contact on the map was now a reassuring crimson X.

// Got 'em. //

She exchanged a glance with Daroga, though she couldn't see his expression through the black glass of his visor. His helmet dipped with a sharp nod.

Rifle ready, she crept out of cover, sweeping her gaze across the snowy glade. The gray haze of the explosions still drifted on the air, dissipating slowly in the light breeze. Three of the guards lay motionless in the snow, with the other two strewn across the upper decking.

The squad formed up behind her as she moved toward the foot of the stairs. They confirmed their kills on the way up to the top deck.

Daroga approached the large, armored door to work on gaining access, but he'd barely lifted his tablet when the Creator stepped up.

He curled his massive fingers into the door seam, then ripped it clean off its tracks. Metal groaned and vibrated as he turned and thrust the crumpled mass of metal away to land with a soft thud in the snow below.

Kato laughed. "Nice."

Adriene motioned for them to form up. "On me. Overwatch?"

"Clear from what I can see," Ivon confirmed.

Gallagher voiced her agreement, then added, "But keep in mind we're slim."

Adriene led them inside. The small entry vestibule fed directly into a main corridor that stretched off right, left, and straight—not a guard in sight. Banks of thin overhead diodes dotted the halls. It looked like any other government industrial complex, grated metal flooring and walls coated in taupe paint that peeled and flaked with age. Exposed ventilation and plumbing tracks traced paths across black stone ceilings.

Adriene's Rubicon scanned the immediate area, then accessed

the pathfinder database, sifting through common groundside ansible relay plans until he found a similar schematic.

He digested the blueprint in an instant. Her HUD map expanded with the new data. He highlighted a large octagonal room about six hundred meters into the facility.

// This is the primary voltage transformer, which serves as an antechamber for the ansible hardware access room. //

Lead the way.

A thick red line appeared at her feet.

She cleared her throat. "You guys seeing the target site on your maps?"

"Yep, active in HUD," Kato said, and the others sounded off their affirmatives as well.

"That's where we're headed, quiet as we can. Let's go dark—suits, guns, mods. Short-range comms only. Gal, keep your overwatch up."

"Copy that," Gallagher said.

Everyone powered down, and Adriene waited for a round of confirmations before ordering her Rubicon to enter hibernation mode.

// I can be back in one point two milliseconds if you need me. //

Understood.

A faint tug pulled at the back of her eyes as he withdrew.

She signaled the others to keep a tight formation and led them forward.

Though they moved carefully, their shuffling boots sounded deafening in Adriene's ears, each adjustment of their rifles seeming to echo loudly down the barren hallways. The Creator's massive limbs groaned, each step of his metal feet culminating in miniquakes across the metal decking. The grating sounds set Adriene on edge.

The longer they went unharried, the more worried she became. No patrols meant no chance at picking them off. Other than the guards they'd just killed, there were still almost forty soldiers left in Flintlock. West must have kept them back to protect the ansible.

Ten uneventful minutes later, they arrived at the vestibule outside the transformer room.

The red path line shifted, pointing toward an open door frame a few meters down the hall. Gallagher and Wyatt covered their entrance while Adriene led the rest through the threshold and up a narrow set of stairs.

The top opened into a walled catwalk arcing out in both directions. The hot, heavy air of the small space thrummed with electricity.

Panels and monitors lined the outer wall. A few wide window-panes comprised the interior wall, allowing a vantage down into the transformer room.

Adriene moved to the closest window, staying low beneath the sill. Daroga landed beside her, then the rest of the squad filed in, leaving the Creator to keep watch at the foot of the stairs.

Adriene faced the window, then carefully peeked over the edge. Her eyes raked over the scene, and she sucked in every detail she could before sliding back down a half second later.

She reviewed the captured image: An open vestibule ringed by four concentric half-moon rows of metal transformer enclosures, each almost two meters tall. Short staircases led to the three entrances, evenly spaced along half of the octagonal room. The roof stretched higher than the catwalk level, the open ceiling exposing more mineral-veined black rock.

Three soldiers stood watch in the center, while two patrolling groups of three worked in mechanically paced, mirroring arcs around the outermost circle.

Nine. Not great odds, but they had a chance if they timed the attack at the most vulnerable moment—when the three packs were at their zeniths.

On the opposite side of the room—straight across from the main entrance—a wide ramp led down a half story to a single exit door. According to the schematics, that door led to the interior ansible hardware. Their best shot at halting West's off-planet data transfer would be to plant the explosives *inside* that room.

If they intended to stay dark, someone would have to remain on the catwalk to give visual confirmation. She glanced at Daroga, hovering off her shoulder. A knot tightened at the base of her rib cage. It'd keep him out of harm's way for a bit longer, at least.

She passed along her plan via analog comms with as few words as possible. Everyone indicated their understanding with hand signals.

Adriene descended the staircase, and she gestured for the Creator to join her as she headed toward the main doorway. The Stormwalkers broke off to the farthest entrance on the southeast side. Kato and Gallagher headed the opposite way up the corridor toward the northeast door.

Adriene sidled up to one side of the door frame, waiting for the others to get into position. She eyed the massive robot hovering in her periphery, waiting expectantly for her order.

Closing her eyes for a moment, she actively pushed aside her nerves. Concentrated on the mission. Visualized the path she'd take to enter cover. Who her first target would be, how she'd retreat through the transformer stacks if the patrol on her side came around to flank them.

Just a standard engagement. Not an intentional execution of her own company.

Her squad sent out a series of masked analog signals to indicate their readiness. Adriene sucked in a deep breath.

Ready.

Her Rubicon surfaced long enough to push the static signal out, right as Daroga's voice cut over comms in a hushed whisper, "Hold, hold, hold."

Adriene's pulse spiked. She jogged back to the narrow stairs and up to the catwalk, the Creator following close behind. His long limbs bent at sharp, narrow angles as he kept himself folded, low to the ground, his tall frame barely able to squeeze through the opening.

She rushed to crouch under the window beside Daroga, then

opened a short-range, suit-to-suit comm channel. "What happened?"

"More contacts just entered from the ansible—at least twenty."

"Shit." Gripping the sill, she risked a peek over the edge.

She barely had a chance to estimate the additional numbers before a flash of movement diverted her attention. Three crouched figures darted asynchronous, natural glances as they worked their way around the outermost transformer ring. The Stormwalkers. Already inside, moving to intercept their assigned patrol. They hadn't heard the hold.

Adriene's gaze snapped to the other side of the room, and a vise wrenched in her chest. Two more. Kato and Gallagher had moved in as well.

A light strain tugged on the back of her eyes as her Rubicon resurfaced.

// Shit—there's a comms dampener in place. I couldn't see it in hibernation mode. //

"Fuck, Carl, the others are—" The words dropped from her throat as a peppering of gunfire cut through the silence.

The large room below erupted in a clamor of sprinting boots, shouting, and weapons discharge.

Adriene unslung her rifle and spun to face Daroga. "Stay here and do what you can to grease the wheels—jam their overwatch, flood them with ghost signals, anything. We'll have to guerrilla this as best we can." She made for the stairs.

"Adri!" Daroga called after her. "Wait—"

She turned to assuage his concern when a cold pressure clamped down around her torso, shoving her back against the low wall.

Her breath waned as the vise tightened down harder. Vision spinning, it took her a few terror-filled seconds to reorient herself. As she opened her eyes, waves of frigid panic rolled through her veins.

The Creator loomed over her, yellow ocular sensors ablaze as he pinned her to the cold metal floor with both massive hands.

CHAPTER

THIRTY-TWO

Adriene grasped at the Creator's massive fingers. She tried to pry them away, but his grip was steadfast, completely unaffected by her adrenaline-fueled clawing.

The fucking bot had turned on her.

He'd lied somehow. West must have lifted the hold, released him from whatever hack had forced his transparency.

Now he was going to kill her, and the rest of her squad would die—again—because of how naive and trusting she'd been.

A low growl escaped her throat as she fought against the metal digits crushing down on her, but her suit didn't respond to her request for additional strength.

Dammit—why aren't you helping me?

// He's not a threat. //

What the fu—

Her earpiece clicked as the Creator joined their short-range comm line. *"There is no winning that fight, small commander."* His electronic voice grated through her earpiece, staticky from the analog connection.

"Fucking let go of me!" She continued her ineffective struggle as an explosion rocked the wall. "I have to get in there while there's still time to help them!"

"I agreed to help you," the Creator said, *"and that is exactly what I am doing."*

"Doesn't fucking seem like it!"

"I am stopping you from self-destruction. If that is not help, I do not know what is."

// He's right, Adriene. There's nothing you can do. //

"Fucking Mira's fiery death . . ." She twisted her neck to look at Daroga. He'd dropped his tablet and sat crouched on his knees, hands palm out, visor swinging as he looked between her and the Creator as if caught in a loop.

"I am here to accomplish the mission." The Creator firmed up his grip, pressing her harder against the floor. *"Not to stand by and watch as your brash human instincts obviate any chance we have at success. Please, human. Think. Then act."*

Copper-tinged saliva flooded her mouth as her teeth clenched hard, jaw cramping.

She shoved him away again, and this time he let her, releasing his iron grip on her torso.

"You're a dick."

"I do not know what that means."

With a few deep, slow breaths, she steadied her rage and sat up. Any calm she gained shattered as another explosion cut through the gunfire.

She ground her teeth. "They have practically all of our deflagration charges," she argued. "If we don't help them, we won't have the firepower we need to get this done."

"Then we will have to find another way. Your friends are an unfortunate loss. But the three of us have not yet been exposed. We still have an advantage to wield."

"I think he's right, Adri," Daroga said, his wary voice edged with concern. "We can't win this if we give ourselves up now."

// *Exactly, thank you. You know, the code monkey's growing on me.* //

Adriene exhaled a harsh breath, then silence hung in the air for a few long seconds. The gunfire had stopped.

She scrambled to her knees and peeked over the edge.

In the center vestibule, the Stormwalkers, Kato, and Gallagher were on their knees, visors retracted, hands behind their heads, eyes downcast.

The tightness in Adriene's chest lifted slightly—they were alive, at least.

Then suspicion tiptoed around her relief . . . because why the hell were they alive?

Behind her squad, almost thirty soldiers stood in unnervingly perfect drill formation in front of the entrance to the ansible chamber. Six others lay motionless, bodies speared with a smattering of glinting metal shards. Her team had managed to take out a few, at least.

Five hive-minded soldiers stood out of formation. Four kept rifles trained on the captives while the fifth paced in front of them. They stopped and spun on a heel. Their visor was open, exposing Lieutenant Rhett's lifeless stare.

Rhett turned and said something to Wyatt, who looked up at her glossy-eyed lieutenant, the confusion and shock apparent on her flushed face. She shook her head once, then glanced down.

Coleson's visage was rock-hard, and Ivon stared straight down at the floor, unmoving.

What are they saying?

// No way I can risk opening comms. //

More toward my hearing, then?

He complied, and with a waning static click, her inner ears throbbed with a dull ache.

The pain cleared away as the sound amplified. Daroga's shallow breaths and every tiny adjustment the Creator made pressed into her hypersensitive eardrums. She motioned for them to stay as quiet as possible, then focused on listening in.

"Then why are you here?" Rhett said. A chill rushed down Adriene's spine at the placid, monotone timbre.

Kato pressed out a wry grin. "You guys left without us. Just figured we'd join the fun." He braved a glance over his shoulder to the rigid line of assembled soldiers behind him. "Didn't realize it was invite-only."

One of the hovering guards dropped the butt of their rifle and swung it hard into Kato's flank. Kato lurched forward, falling onto all fours, gasping for breath. The guard gripped him by the back of the neck and yanked him back to his knees.

Gallagher's glare hardened, but her voice came out steady, prudent. "The MP guarding the brig told us everyone already moved out. She said we were supposed to gear up and report to Blackwell on-site."

Rhett stepped up to Gallagher and tilted her head. "Well. An MP giving deployment orders. That's simply not true, is it, Sergeant?"

Gallagher's jaw firmed, but she said nothing.

"However . . . it's not a bad idea," Rhett continued, then without a single word, or so much as a nod, the other four guards slung their rifles and began locking the five captives in mag cuffs.

Wyatt's wide eyes darted back to Rhett. When she spoke, her voice came out thin and weak. "LT, where are you taking us?"

Coleson glowered, then spat, "That *thing's* not our LT."

"Back to the *Aurora*," Rhett answered. "We'll get your implants installed . . ." She spun her look to Kato. "Then you can *truly* join us."

Kato's throat bobbed with a hard swallow.

The guards finished with the restraints. At the end of the line, one yanked Coleson to his feet, then Ivon, Wyatt, Kato, and Gallagher stood warily. Rhett closed her visor, leading the way as two guards corralled the line and escorted them out the door.

Adriene slid down the wall and turned around, heaving out a grating sigh. Her hearing clicked as it returned to normal.

"They're giving them Rubicons," she said. "But why?"

Daroga shook his head. "He must need them to be part of the hive mind. More support for the network?"

"Five minds would not make an appreciable difference," the Creator put in.

// He's right. //

"He must just not want them rezoning and outing him," Daroga said warily.

"But we killed five people outside," she said. "And six more are dead in there. They've all already rezoned—he knows that. What difference would five more make?"

Daroga's helmet swayed. "It doesn't matter. We have to figure out how we're going to destroy that ansible, considering ninety percent of our firepower just walked out the door."

"Or how we're going to get to the ansible in the first place," she said. "There's no way we can cut through thirty of them."

The Creator tilted his head. *"Small commander, in keeping me out of sight thus far, you have left yourself a . . . rather large card to play, as you say."*

Adriene lifted her brow. "You think you can take the brunt of all that?"

"If they were to turn their unified firepower against me, I would likely not endure very long. However, if you are able to grant me the element of surprise, I should have time to eliminate them in the resulting confusion."

She nodded, though dread crept in. She'd brought the bot along for this exact purpose, but turning his full, unhindered force onto all of them unsettled her. Like she was too much of a coward to do the deed herself.

She glanced at the clock in her HUD. The longer she sat thinking about it, the more time West had to complete the upload. No more time to hesitate.

"Okay," she said finally. "That's gotta be the plan, I guess. Carl, what can we do to draw their attention from the doorway?"

"I guess we could use a ghosting attack, like you suggested earlier. An old trick, but still effective."

// I can assist. As long as we're within a few meters, I can force a false threat assessment matrix into their HUDs. //

"I can facilitate that with another EM wave," the Creator said. *"If they are all indeed part of the same network, it may create a small power surge that could briefly disable their suits and cause additional hesitations."*

"All right," she sighed, chewing it over. She tried to force the idea to take shape in her brain, to feel confident about it. But something didn't sit right. There was too much room for error, certainly, but mostly, it was too . . . *flashy.*

They didn't need to create some grand spectacle to draw the individual attentions of thirty soldiers. In fact, something like that might not even work, considering the circumstances. They needed something to distract the one controlling it all. Something that would distract West.

// No—don't even think it. It's too dangerous. //

She growled a sigh.

Why? Because he might kill me?

// It could be so much worse than that, Adriene. You know that. //

Then so be it. I don't see another way.

// Mira's ashes. At least let them try the ghosting—//

You were just lecturing me about trusting myself . . .

// . . . Well played. //

"I have an idea." She looked to the Creator. "A way I can distract them—all of them. Be ready on my mark."

"I will await your signal," the Creator confirmed.

She hunched into a crouch and crawled toward the staircase.

"Whoa, wait," Daroga said, worry faltering his weathered tone.

She glanced back. "Don't worry, I'll be fine. Just be ready to back us up, okay?"

"Fuck." Daroga rubbed the top of his helmet. "Yeah, okay. Be careful."

Adriene picked up her rifle, then crept down the stairs, back to the main entrance.

Open my visor.

// Absolutely not. //

"Dammit," she growled. "Listen, please. You don't know West like I do. This will work—you have to trust me. Open my visor."

// It's far too—//

"Override," she demanded, voice hard.

// Dammit . . . //

She could practically feel the weight of her Rubicon's chagrin as her visor slid open, flushing her face with a waft of warm, dry air. A trail of sweat wound a path down her brow, stinging her eyes. The unfiltered sounds of the corridor rushed into her ears, a steady thrum of electronics pulsing from the transformer room.

She kept her rifle lowered, but reaffirmed her grip on it, then gave her Rubicon the signal.

The door slid open. The wash of light from the transformer room spilled over her as she stepped inside, heart thrumming.

Icy goose bumps ripped across her skin as thirty spines stiffened simultaneously. Thirty rifles and thirty suits clacked as they turned toward her in horrifying unison.

She stopped at the foot of the stairs, then cleared the panic from her throat. "Julen."

A single soldier broke from the assembled pack, stepping slowly forward and stopping a few meters in front of her. They stood unmoving for a few long seconds, then a whirr cut through the silence and their visor slid away, revealing the blank-eyed stare of her lieutenant.

He looked both exactly and nothing like Brigham—his too-smooth brow stained with West's hard-edged stoicism. His light brown eyes at once glazed over and hyper-focused, carrying that same pained, regret-laden warmth West had inflicted on her in the holding cell.

Brigham's voice came low and cracked, barely audible over the static purr of electric conduits. "I wish I could say I was surprised to see you here, Sergeant."

She flinched when, at once, the soldiers turned to move. She took a step back, masking her relief with a scowl as they began to spread out their formation. They moved to either side of the vestibule, training their aims on her, creating barriers between her and the exits. Putting their backs to the exits.

"Where did you take the others?" she demanded, hating the way her voice wavered through her racing heartbeat.

"You don't have to worry about your friends," Brigham—*West* said. "They're on their way to get upgraded now."

She shook her head. "*Why?* Why not just kill them and be done with it? Almost a dozen others have already rezoned. What difference would a few more make?"

He lifted his chin. "With the upgrade, I included one other update. One I think you'll like."

An acrid taste crept into the back of her mouth.

"I found a way to . . . *ease* the burden," he said in Brigham's timbre, but with West's cadence. "They'll rezone with no memory of what happened. I know it's not quite the reckoning you wanted. But it *is* better, yes?"

She exhaled slowly, taking a few seconds to fully digest what he'd said.

It *was* better. A relief, actually. Their free will had been stripped, but at least they wouldn't remember the terror of not having control of their own bodies.

A wall of dread erased any relief as she realized what it really meant.

They *wouldn't remember.*

No one would know what'd happened. They'd rezone without knowing what killed them. Without knowledge of their location or the hive mind or West's reckless plan.

She met his eye again. He stared back at her with a pleading softness she'd never seen her lieutenant, or West, exhibit before. His voice came softly as he inclined his head, "I told you I'd find ways to perfect rezoning if given enough time."

"You had *years,*" she snapped.

"I know." His gaze flitted to the ground before returning to meet hers. "I never had much in the way of . . . *motivation* to continue my work on that project. Not until I saw your pain, saw all it'd done to you."

Fury welled hot tears into her eyes.

"I fixed it, Sergeant," he said, tone earnest. "And it doesn't require a Rubicon implant. I can implement it across all rezone facilities, immediately—with or without Rubicon. Just stop this, stop fighting me, and join me. And I'll do it. I promise."

Her eyes narrowed, cheeks hot. Everything he'd "promised" up to this point had been a complete lie. Any truth he *had* told had only been in service to his end goals.

West looked back at her through Brigham's eyes, gaze steady, awaiting her response.

She shook her head. "So you can take everyone's free will *and* their memories? No fucking way."

West's glare hardened.

Give the signal.

The Creator's pip flickered into her HUD. It moved toward the entry.

"Is my LT still in there?" she asked, voice wavering.

"Of course he is. That's how it . . ." His lips twisted as the warmth faded from his eyes. "You know that." He glanced back toward the ansible door, then the exit, then back at her. "There isn't anyone left . . ." His left hand tremored, and his voice sharpened. "So who is helping you?"

She kept the concern from her face by doubling down on the rising anger, sneering at him. "You just captured my squad and the Stormwalkers, remember? I'm it."

His jaw flexed, glare flat. "You've always been a terrible liar."

The Creator's massive frame bent through the southern doorway. In a single leap, he cleared the long stairway, landing at the foot as a purple wash of light flashed over his limbs, shrouding him in electric armor.

The fire of thirty rifles ripped through the chamber, laser and plasma and charged slugs flying to melt uselessly into the seamless shroud of his shield construct. Before they could flee, those in close quarters were caught in the wake as the Creator swung his massive arms in a wide circle.

Rifles were crushed and tossed away, spines snapped, heads freed from their bodies in seconds.

Brigham didn't flinch, didn't even turn to look. His eyes stayed locked on Adriene, darkening, expression hardening into fury.

Unbidden, Adriene's visor slid shut.

// Run. //

CHAPTER

THIRTY-THREE

Adriene's feet slid as she shuffled backward, trying to tear her gaze away from the horror happening behind Brigham. His shoulders swelled, and he marched toward her.

She spun, but he threw himself at her. They tumbled down, her rifle skidding away as she hit the ground.

Charging her strength with all the power her suit and adrenaline would allow, she turned and thrust her fist into his chest. He tumbled off and slid away.

She reached toward her gun, but he grabbed her ankle and yanked her toward him, snapping her head back against the ground with the sudden jolt.

Twisting, she tried to wrench her leg free, but he already stood over her. He got a firm grip on either side of her chestplate, dragging her a few meters. He hefted her to her feet and slammed her back against a transformer enclosure, knocking the air from her lungs.

Grunting, she reached, fingers stretching toward her grenade compartment. Her hand froze as a wave of sharp electric pain flashed over her skin. Her muscles went slack.

What's happening?

// He—it's—//

Staticky feedback rang in her ears.

It's what?

Her heart raced, limbs trembling. Her skin tingled, and every hair on her body stood on end.

Another shock wave ran through her suit and into her skin, and she clamped her teeth down, a hot wash of coppery saliva flooding her mouth.

// Surge—over—loa—Err—or—//

Stay with me, dammit.

She growled through clenched teeth as white-hot pain sparked along every nerve in her body, limbs and fingers stiffening. Her HUD disappeared from view.

The wave of electricity vanished.

Brigham let go, dropping her to the ground unceremoniously. He stepped back, straight into the massive grip of the Creator.

The metal hand crushed his torso, Brigham's suit and body crumpling under the force. The Creator tossed him away.

Adriene's field of vision tilted—brightening, softening, the color washing away.

"Civilian human, small commander needs assistance."

The Creator disappeared back toward the remainder of Flintlock, his shielded arms swinging.

Breaths short, Adriene pushed up on her elbows and slid back to lean against the transformer case. Her racing heart steadied as the static pain subsided, though her head pulsed with a new, dense, unwavering migraine.

What the hell is happening?

She waited with hitched breath, but no response came.

The glass of her visor flashed with blue static sparks, humming and clicking as it jittered open and closed on an unending loop. She thumbed open her hyphen and flicked the suit into safe mode.

She coughed out, "Retract visor."

Her suit responded, sliding the glitching glass back into her helmet. The air felt dry and cool, the sounds of gunfire and crunching metal relentless from the vestibule, where the Creator continued to slaughter Flintlock.

She flicked her suit back into standard mode. Hot pain fired behind her eyes, and she clamped them shut, growling through bared teeth.

Where the hell are you?

// He—eer. //

What's happening?

// He's hacking me. //

"*Shit*," she growled. A hot pressure crushed against her ribs. Flaring pain oscillated behind her eyes.

// He used the physical link to breach my defenses. Now he's bridging the connection. //

You can stop him, right?

// No. //

She peeled her eyes open and glanced around, though she couldn't see much of anything through the haze of hot tears.

What about Daroga?

// He won't be able to fix it, not in time. I can hold West off, but it's only a matter of time before he wins. Adriene, if—when—he does, you'll be part of the hive mind too. //

"Fuck."

A lance of stormy, dark grief flooded through her. But it wasn't her own.

// You have to destroy me. //

What? No—

// Yes. //

Her crushing headache pulsed with more agony.

I can't.

// You can. You have to. //

Her eyes fell on her suit's low-power indicator. Bile climbed the back of her throat. She glanced to the side, at the transformer enclosure she leaned against.

// T-grade or higher. It'll work. //

I'll die too.

// It'll stop your heart, yes. But that can be resolved. Within thirty seconds. //

Dread settled heavily on her shoulders. Another spike of white-hot pain fired behind her eyes. She clamped them shut, huffing out throttled breaths through her teeth.

With a waft of sweat and evergreen, Daroga arrived.

She tried to cling to the scent, tried to use it to draw herself back from the blinding pain.

"Adri," Daroga's clipped voice cut through—both in comms and through the air—he must have had his visor down as well. "What's wrong? What happened?"

She focused on the delay between Daroga's two voices, letting the strange detail center her thoughts. Sucking in a breath, she tried to ignore the searing pain behind her eyes. "West's hacking my Rubicon."

"Shit." Daroga ripped his tablet from his belt, but Adriene put out a hand to stop him.

"There's nothing you can do—not in time. He says I have to short him out."

Daroga shook his head, eyes wide. "That'll kill you too—you'll rezone."

"Only after thirty seconds . . ."

Daroga opened his mouth, but nothing came out. He glanced around, horrified, then sucked in a breath. "I need a defibrillator or—"

"Use your suit." She took his wrist and peeled open his gloved hand, pulling the palm to her chestplate. Her hands trembled. "The current will work the other way."

Daroga's wide-eyed stare drifted down to his hand, and he didn't respond.

She lifted her shaking fingers to his chin and pushed his gaze back up, locking eyes with him. "It'll work."

"What if I can't bring you back?"

"You can do it, I know you can. But if something goes wrong, you take the Creator, and you finish it. Promise me."

He stared back at her for a moment before his haunted gaze hardened, and nodded, resolute. "I promise."

She pulled him into a kiss, warmth rushing through her, curbing the waves of pain.

"Either way," she said, "I'll see you on the other side, right?"

He gave a weak, exhausted smile. "Right."

"Maybe we'll even be assigned the same prison barracks."

His breath caught with a pained laugh and he pressed his forehead into hers.

She flinched as a bolt of electric pain sent her head spinning.

// We need to do this. Soon. I can't hold him off much longer. //

She steadied herself with a deep breath. "I need to get to the inside of the transformer." She jutted her chin toward the access panel beside her.

"Yes, yes," Daroga said quickly, crawling up to it. "Uh, Tool Mode A3." A drill extended from the top of his glove and he began unscrewing the bolts holding the access panel in place.

Pain blinded Adriene's vision again, and she clamped her eyes shut as she waited.

// I'm sorry it has to be this way. I wanted to be there for you in the end. //

You were—you are. You've been everything I needed you to be.

// . . . I have? //

She swallowed, bitter angst filling her chest. She'd known it for a long time, but kept it down—hadn't let it rise from her subconscious, let herself fully believe it. That *he* was the real reason she'd remembered how to give a shit again. Helped her keep hold of that last shred of empathy. That she'd still be an empty shell—a husk of a human—if it weren't for him. That this AI West had inflicted her with had saved her humanity.

Then she felt it again, that layer of emotion that wasn't her own. A warmth spread through her chest: contentment that she truly felt that way, that he'd done something right, that turning against his maker and choosing her had been the right decision.

But it was tinged, stained with threads of regret and sadness. The overwhelming sense of it being *too soon*.

There was a whole universe out there—so much more to do, to see, to feel. He'd *just started* to feel.

All that would be gone soon, and he would disappear . . . to where? He knew he'd be gone from her, that he wouldn't see through her anymore, feel the world through her, think and worry and laugh through her, but he'd still have to *be* somewhere, wouldn't he? Or would there be nothing, just blackness, emptiness, trapped in an interminable night?

Nothing in his endless banks of data told him what came after.

Grief cut through his thoughts, and his distress melted away as he refocused on her. No matter the depth of his worries, he couldn't neglect her.

Don't be scared of your mortality.

Relief filled her chest as his anxiety subsided, waning in the wake of her sentiment.

It's the most human thing you can feel.

// How did you know I was thinking about that? //

I guess I get to read your thoughts now too.

// Good. Now you know how it feels. //

She scoffed a dry laugh, tears welling in her eyes.

// Don't worry, I don't have regrets. //

I don't know where I'd be right now if I hadn't had you as an ally the last few months. As a friend. Thank you for choosing me.

// No, thank you. It may have been a short life, but I couldn't have asked for a better conduit through which to experience the human condition, however briefly. //

She sucked in a slow, deep breath. "Ready?" she asked, voice thin.

// To leave you? Never. //

She pressed her eyes closed over hot tears. Flashes of white and shifting patterns of color danced behind her eyelids.

Another burst of pain cracked through her skull. West was getting closer.

"Got it," Daroga said, voice wavering.

She shifted, twisting her torso toward the open panel. She tried to lift her arm, but her muscles were weak, limp. "I—help."

Daroga grabbed her wrist and pressed her palm flat to the inner conduit. She held it as steady as she could manage.

"I'm ready," she croaked, jaw tight, heart thudding fast—too fast. "Do it."

// Goodbye, Adriene. //

Her palm sparked, then sucked flush to the metal. A lance of electric current fired up her arm, down her nerves—her fake, synthetic nerves. It grew hot and sharp, on the brink of numbness.

A tight, tingling shudder like a silent scream vibrated in the back of her skull. A million tiny bolts of electricity arced between him and every neuron in her brain, every cell in her body.

Then, the void was gone. Not empty, but gone.

Then, blissful nothing.

THIRTY-FOUR

Fire surged through Adriene's chest as consciousness crushed back down in an instant.

Adrenaline shot through her veins along with another jolt of power. Hot sweat rained down her forehead, stinging her eyes.

It was too much.

All her senses poured back into her at once. A litany of scents assaulted her: pheromones, oiled metal, wet rock, sour mold. Sharp, thick cracks rang out, metal crushing metal. Every noise grated over the relentless, throbbing bass of pulsating power and a screeching buzz of electronics.

A hard pain pressed deep into her gut as some unseen vise removed the air from her lungs. Unsourced terror surged through her. She couldn't breathe.

Then lips were on hers, warm and wet—salty with tears or sweat, or both. The shock of it froze her panic, the smells and sounds fleeing her frenzied mind. She inhaled a deep, dizzying breath.

Silence pressed hard against her eardrums as Daroga lifted his lips away. "Adri, you with me?"

When her eyes finally opened, her vision filled with an incomprehensible, teary haze of blooming white. Light fired down from the high ceilings, stark against the exposed black rock.

Though the electric current was gone, phantom traces still sparked along her nerves, and her muscles spasmed and locked up every few seconds.

She managed a short nod. "I'm—yes."

"I'm sor—" His voice broke, and he looked down at her with dampness in his green eyes, wide with terror. "I almost didn't . . ."

She cleared her throat, though it still came out weak. "Almost didn't what?"

He shook his head. "It was like . . . *twenty-nine* seconds."

She swallowed a mass of thick, iron-tinged saliva. "It's okay. It worked. That's all that matters."

"Are you okay?"

She just blinked at him, aware her horror was painted across her face, but she didn't have the capacity to moderate the expression. All she could think was fucking *no*.

Because just as always, there'd been nothing. No in-between, just emptiness. She was back, yes, but she was less than she'd been, no longer whole. The hollowness consumed her, the *lack* of a gaping void at the base of her skull. Because he wasn't missing. He wasn't on hold, paused, waiting to come back to her. He was gone.

Dead.

A biting angst pooled at the base of her rib cage.

Daroga swept a lock of her hair off her sweat-glossed forehead. She met his gaze, still lined with worry, but steadfast.

With a sharp inhale, she pushed aside the overwhelming grief. Drew in deep lungfuls of warm, unfiltered air. There was still a mission to accomplish. She'd have to wait to mourn her loss.

Yes, she'd grown to rely on him, but she'd also learned. Just like he had. She'd evolved along with him.

And now, she could do this without him.

"Is the small commander accounted for?" the Creator's harsh voice sounded through comms. *"Our network is gone."*

"She's alive, but her Rubicon's gone," Daroga said. "West was trying to hack her. We had to . . . destroy it."

"I see. I am sorry, small commander."

Adriene groaned as she sat up. Blood rushed to her head. She went to stand, but her limbs felt almost too heavy to lift.

She slid open her suit's hyphen and glanced at the power indicator—10 percent. Only about a quarter of the interface displayed properly, the rest jittered, flickering in and out. Unsurprisingly, the three charges that'd hacked her Rubicon, then killed her, then brought her back to life had taken a toll on her suit functions.

She switched into safe mode. The hyphen dimmed, then flashed back on as the suit rebooted. The limbs lightened as the mode activated.

Daroga stood and offered a hand, gripping her arm to help her up.

The Creator loomed at the end of the aisle, his massive frame humming with the sharp buzz of hydraulics. He appeared untouched beneath his shield construct armor, which deactivated a second later in a flash of purple light.

"The remainder have been taken care of."

Adriene glanced over at the bot. "Right . . . Good. Thank you."

"If you are ready, we should continue our mission."

Daroga shook his head. "We only have four of the fourteen charges we need—it'll never be enough."

Adriene crouched to pick up her rifle. "Let's go see what we're working with."

Daroga and the Creator followed as she led the way to the center vestibule. Her gaze flitted across the limp bodies of Flintlock, necks and limbs twisted at unnatural angles.

"Have you guys seen West?" she asked. "Actual West?"

Daroga shook his head. "No."

"I have not," the Creator said.

Adriene set her jaw. West was many things, but not a coward. So where the hell was he?

Across the vestibule, she headed down the ramp to the ansible access door. The Creator hovered at the ready as Daroga unlocked the door, which opened into a massive circular chamber. Adriene's eyes darted into every dim corner, but the room was empty.

"I have no contacts on sensors," the Creator confirmed.

She took a few steps in, gaze drifting up the length of the primary ansible casing—a seven-meter-wide steel cylinder that rose straight up, disappearing into the black rock of the high ceiling.

The base was enclosed by a reinforced alanthum barrier, ringed by dozens of control panels and access screens.

"Shit." Daroga breezed past her. He jogged down the long ramp to an open metal crate, linked to one of the control panels with a bundle of cabling.

Adriene followed. She ripped the cabling free, disconnecting it from the control panel.

Daroga peered into the crate. He turned toward the nearest console screen, fingers drumming out an anxious beat on the metal counter.

Adriene inspected the crate, outfitted with jumbled cabling, ports, and status lights, radiating warmth. "This is the copy of the mainframe?"

"Yeah, but the data's already been loaded into the cache." Daroga angled the screen toward her and shot her a dark look. "The ansible's spooling now. As soon as it's done, the data will be sent."

"How long do we have?"

He shook his head, then pulled his tablet from his belt and tapped at the screen. After a short time, he let out a sigh. "A few minutes. It's still cycling on and looking for a proper alignment. There's no signal lock yet."

"Can you hack it? Interrupt it before it boots up?"

He continued to work, then let out a sharp hiss. "Shit, no. West has a pretty intense firewall set up. Rubicon's fighting me." He lowered the tablet, expression tight. "I could get through it, but it'd take hours, not minutes."

Adriene glanced back at the Creator. "How about you?"

"I am afraid I must concur with civilian human's assessment. I do not believe I could expedite those efforts appreciably."

"All right," she sighed. "What about explosives? What do we have?"

Daroga opened his suit's storage compartments to take stock, and Adriene looked through her own. Between them, only four of the inadequate deflagration charges, two of their jury-rigged shard grenades, and a half dozen other equally useless grenades.

"That is a pittance compared to what is required for this task."

"Can we just sever the power?" Adriene asked, jutting a thumb over her shoulder. "Do as much damage as we can to the transformer room?"

Daroga scrubbed a hand down his face. "Destroying the transformers wouldn't help—the power's stored in accumulators, like a reservoir. It'd stop it long term, but it'd use up the reserves it's charged first."

"I assume it'd have plenty enough to send off the data?"

"More than likely."

Adriene ground her teeth. "Can we get to the accumulators?"

With the toe of his boot, he kicked at the flooring, giving off a solid, dense thud. "Maybe? If we could get down there, somehow. They're usually built under layers of concrete and alanthum sheeting, as part of the grounding system . . ." He stepped over and knocked on the thick alanthum barricade surrounding the cylinder. "The only access point to get down there, that I know of, is beyond this barrier."

Adriene pinched the bridge of her nose. Her nerves still buzzed with the phantom pains of being electrocuted, muscles spasming lightly. "Any other ideas?"

Daroga pushed aside a few strands of hair that'd escaped the tie. "If we can interrupt the grounding circuitry and redirect enough power from somewhere else, we could potentially fry this whole sector of the facility." He cleared his throat, then warily added, "We likely wouldn't survive it—I don't think our suits could withstand it, even if they weren't already running on fumes."

"Not ideal," she admitted, "but if it's all we've got, it's all we've got. What do we need to do?"

Daroga anxiously retied his hair, then let out a gruff sigh. He paced toward the ramp, but stopped short. "Maybe I could jury-rig a line from the transformers, pull some cabling from somewhere else . . ."

"There is not time for that," the Creator interrupted. The grated floor shuddered beneath his heavy steps as he descended the rest of

the way down the ramp. With one long, spindly finger, he indicated the screen that detailed the ansible alignment. *"There is not time for any of this. As you said, we have minutes."*

Adriene tightened her grip on the rifle. They hadn't come this far to fail now. To have to stand in a sea of bodies and watch as the "upgrade" and hive mind spread out across the galaxy and infected the rest of the 505th.

"Small commander," the Creator said suddenly. She turned to face him. His head tilted slightly as he looked down at her hands. *"Earlier, when you stopped your heart, how did you elicit unhindered current from the transformer?"*

She lowered the rifle and showed him the palm of her hand. "Our gloves."

"Yeah . . ." Daroga began, hope flashing across his face. He turned wide eyes onto the Creator. "The gloves would allow you to bypass your resistors."

"Precisely."

Daroga nodded. "And your shield constructs . . ."

"I can reroute their voltage potential through your gloves. I still have 8,217 hours' worth of stored power."

Adriene looked to Daroga. "You think it'll work?"

"Yeah. It should be more than enough. It's still a two-way street, though," he added, concern lining his tone. He turned to the Creator. "The gloves will allow you to maintain a connection, but it'll make you a part of the current. It'll kill you."

"That is understood."

Adriene's brow creased. "This isn't even your fight."

He turned to face her squarely. *"It may not be, but it is still my fault. It will be a fitting-enough end, and it is, at least, an end. My life has already gone on far too long. You, I believe, have some understanding of that."*

She managed a nod, then tore her eyes away and turned to Daroga. "Will the gloves work with his systems without modification?"

"I'm not sure, honestly. The voltage might be too high for only one glove." He glanced down at the palms of his own gloved hands. "I might be able to connect them so they can share the load."

Adriene unlocked the seals at her wrists and pulled both her gloves off. Daroga did the same, then he laid them out on the console. He started tapping on the hyphen of his suit, and with a series of shrill clicks, the gloves opened at their seams, unfolding into a flat layer of alanthum and wiring.

A section of Daroga's forearm plating slid open, and a small barrel of metal rose up. The end lit in a flash of blue flame, then he leaned over the gloves and got to work.

"Promise me one thing, small commander."

She craned her neck to meet the Creator's glowing yellow gaze. "Anything."

"Stop your not-master. As someone should have done to me, before it was too late. Kill him, if you must."

"I'll try. It may not be in my power to make good on that promise."

"If nothing else, keep fighting, even if we fail this step. Live to see another day. Your people will need those like you in the days to come."

She nodded, lips pressing into an appreciative smile.

A minute later, Daroga had connected the circuitry of the opened gloves into a single, larger piece. He lifted the pad of alanthum and loose wiring off the console and passed it to the Creator, worry lining his dark brow. "I have no idea if this is going to work."

"There is only one way to know for certain." The Creator set the panel on the alanthum barricade, then pressed his palms against it. Sparks flashed at his fingertips. He tilted his large head, then drew his ocular sensors over to look at them. *"You should . . . leave."*

Adriene drew up her elbow in a formal salute as she backed away slowly. Daroga spun toward the ramp, then gripped her arm and dragged her back with him.

"Thank you," she called back, then turned and fell in behind Daroga.

The lights dimmed and flickered as they sprinted through the transformer room and into the wide corridors, back out the way they'd came.

As they ran outside, an icy wave of air hit Adriene's face through her open helmet, her eyes watering from the sudden stark cold. Her boots clanged against the metal decking as she scrambled to follow Daroga down the steps.

They'd barely stepped into the snowpack when a wave of purple electric light erupted from the open door frame. It sent bolts of electricity down the metal stairs and railings. The cliff rumbled, shards of rock slicing off to land silently in the thick snow below.

With a resounding crack, a cascade of rock collapsed across the door frame. A plume of black dust erupted as the mountainside shook beneath their feet.

The shriek of tearing metal rang in the distance from somewhere far over the mountainside. A mini-avalanche of snow tumbled off the edge of the cliff, sending down a sheet of white powder.

The rumbling ceased as the barrage settled and the haze of snow cleared away.

Adriene stared at the collapsed rock in shock for a few long moments. She regained her senses all at once—icy-cold, dry air stinging her bare fingertips and exposed face.

Then a symphony of asynchronous, crackling pops cut across the silence of the snowy forest.

She froze, trying to tell her eyes to look up to the sky and confirm what her ears told her. Because that was the sound of ships entering atmosphere.

Instead, her gaze dropped to her snow-covered boots. She let out a long sigh.

"*Scrappers,*" Daroga growled.

He grabbed her wrist and pulled her forward.

CHAPTER

THIRTY-FIVE

As Daroga towed her onward, Adriene's eyes finally drifted up, past the edge of the cliff face. A dozen small white streaks of fire scarred the flat blue sky. If those really were scrapper ships, they were far away, at least.

Her focus snapped back as she looked to see where Daroga had led her—the parked land speeders.

She leapt on one and powered it up. Daroga climbed on behind her. He locked an arm around her waist as the speeder lurched forward. A shower of snow flew out as she spun the craft around and took off into the narrow pass.

The biting cold cut into her exposed cheeks and knuckles as she sped through the ravine. When they pulled out into the clearing, the *Aurora*'s massive rear engines flickered to life, casting a wave of synthetic blue light across the snowpack.

"Shit," Daroga called out over the shrieking wind. "They're taking off!"

Adriene revved the accelerator, but it was already maxed out. She set the straightest course she could, then leaned into the bitter wind as they tore across the flat expanse.

The access hatch they'd disembarked from was shutting as they pulled up. Adriene slid them to a halt beneath the tilting door, then hopped up to stand on the seat of the speeder and linked her fingers together. Daroga stepped into her waiting hands, and she grunted as she lifted, launching him up onto the moving ledge. He reached back down and pulled her in, and they tumbled into the hatch as it sealed with a hard clang.

A wave of warm, denser oxygen flooded Adriene's exposed face. She clenched her numbed hands together, knuckles raw and chafed, the skin of her cheeks chapped and burning with the sudden heat. The hatch shook as it began its ascent into the hangar.

Warning beacons flared.

A computerized voice sounded over the loudspeakers, "Warning: atmospheric launch in ten . . . nine . . ."

Daroga was already on his feet. He slammed a large yellow button on the wall and a half dozen crash seats descended.

Adriene tried to stand, but the ship lurched and threw her off her feet. She landed hard on her side. Her rifle slid off her back and clattered to the floor.

Daroga gripped her arm and dragged her up into a seat as he slid into one himself. She fumbled the harness over her shoulders and locked it in.

"Two . . . one . . ."

The ship lurched and the vibrations intensified. Adriene's teeth and bones rattled, joints throbbing under the pressure. She clenched her jaw, and her eyes pooled with water as her gut crushed back into her spine.

After a few minutes of intense acceleration, the vibration finally ceased. Adriene sucked in short and shallow breaths, ribs laced with pain.

She forced herself to unclench her teeth, stretching out her aching jaw. She unhooked her harness, steadying herself for the telltale rolling nausea that would indicate entry into subspace. It never came.

She turned to Daroga. "You okay?"

"Fine." His harness clattered against the seat as he slid it off.

With a groan she stood, stretching out her shoulders. "Why aren't we entering subspace?"

Daroga shook his head, expression tight. "I don't know. But if we're still on sublights—even if we leave orbit—it'll only be a matter of time before the scrappers catch up."

"You're sure those were Mechan?"

"Too far to tell; they'd just broken atmo."

Adriene shook her head. "It's not likely to be friendlies this far out—we've never had troops in this sector before." She picked up her rifle. "Let's head to the bridge, see what the fuck's going on."

She checked the gun's charge—less than 3 percent. She slid open her hyphen to find over half the sections of her suit at under 10 percent integrity, and her overall charge was less than 5 percent.

She let out a gruff sigh and slid the hyphen shut. She couldn't risk depleting her suit to charge the gun—though she wasn't sure she even could without her gloves.

Daroga freed the pistol from the holster on his thigh and headed toward the hatch exit. She primed her rifle as he palmed the release button, and the door slid open.

On the other side, six armed suits waited.

Adriene didn't need her HUD to confirm who those suits belonged to: bulky Coleson, broad-shouldered Rhett, tall Ivon, stocky Wyatt, thin Gallagher, short Kato.

Hope rose when for a fleeting moment, she wondered if they may not be hybridized. That they'd escaped their captors and hadn't been inducted into West's hive mind. Which caused her to hesitate a fraction of a second too long.

She was knocked off her feet by a hard-edged glove to the face, pain firing through her skull. Her vision danced as she hit the ground.

A trio of rounds echoed across the hangar, and Wyatt collapsed beside her, visor shattered. Daroga re-aimed and got a few more shots off before Coleson swept his legs out.

Daroga hit the ground, kicking Coleson away right as Ivon dove on top of him. But Daroga twisted under him with surprising deftness, using Ivon's own momentum to throw him into Coleson.

Adriene refocused on her own pressing issues as Gallagher appeared in her still-spinning vision. Adriene swung a fist out as hard as she could, and her bare knuckles cracked with pain as they hit the hard metal of Gallagher's chestplate. Adriene cried out, and the suit-powered punch sent Gallagher stumbling back far enough for Adriene to bring a boot up and kick her away.

Gallagher fell, and Adriene brought her rifle up, then shot her point-blank in the visor. It ripped through in one shot. The force threw Gallagher back, crashing into Rhett.

The two tumbled to the ground and Gallagher's limp, heavy corpse weighed Rhett down long enough for Adriene to scramble to her feet.

Rhett thrust Gallagher away as Adriene rushed forward, pressed the barrel to Rhett's visor, and fired. She winced as the charged slug imploded the helmet into the lieutenant's skull.

Before Adriene had even thumbed the primer again, Kato grabbed her from behind. He hooked his arms under hers, locking his hands together behind her neck.

She dropped the rifle and thrashed against him. The seam at her left shoulder sparked, and she could practically feel the section's integrity depleting as the suit bled charge.

Gathering a swell of strength, she tried to throw her weight down to slip out of the hold, but he'd tightened down with suit-assisted strength. Her shoulder burned as he strained against it. With a sudden jerk, the joint popped.

Adriene bit down on a scream as pain fired and the muscles of her left arm slackened.

Teeth bared, she leaned into Kato's hold. She gripped his arms and bent forward to try to throw him over her shoulder—but he was too short.

So she dropped to her knees and spun, using his weight to topple them both to the ground. His hold loosened just enough for her to slip away. The pain from her shoulder blurred her vision as she twisted around to straddle him, squirming to pin his arms with her shins.

With her good hand, she slid her calf compartment open and grabbed a grenade.

He yanked his arms free and threw her off, then climbed on top of her. But she'd already activated the charge.

She summoned whatever remaining power and strength her suit could provide and jammed the grenade as hard as she could into the seam at his shoulder.

Kato froze for a heartbeat, then frantically pawed at the seam.

Adriene let out a smooth breath. It would all be okay. Daroga would finish it. She'd rather take herself down than let any of these hybridized abominations live long enough for the approaching Mechan to get hold of them.

But Kato—*West*—processed the situation with inhuman speed aided by Rubicon. He grabbed her by the shoulders, her limp, dislocated joint screaming in agony as he threw her away from him. He spun at the same time, putting almost three meters between them before he exploded.

Adriene's breath sucked from her lungs, a wall of flame engulfing her vision. The right side of her exposed face smoldered before going numb, and her sight blacked out as she tumbled.

She landed on her back, writhing. Panting ragged breaths through clenched teeth for a few long moments, she flinched when hands touched her chestplate, pressing her into the ground. Trying to hold her still.

"Mira's end, Adriene . . ." Daroga's voice, equal parts worry and disbelief. "What did you do?"

She forced her eyes open, though her right stuck partway. She lifted her fingers to peel the skin apart, but Daroga stopped her.

"Shit," he hissed, "don't touch it."

"It's fine." She was cognizant of suppressed pain, the burn just a mass of numbness, pricked with sharp tingles like a thousand needles prodding thickened skin.

"Targets are all down," Daroga confirmed. His visor was shattered, forehead slick with blood and sweat, bare knuckles raw and bloodied.

Adriene glanced past him to the line of bodies he'd produced.

He caught her look. "I said I washed out," he rumbled. "Not that I couldn't handle myself." He released his broken helmet and tossed it away.

"Fair enough." Adriene grimaced, muscles protesting as she lifted herself to sitting. The bloodied and swollen knuckles of her right hand were probably broken, but her disjointed shoulder screamed over everything else, overwhelming her with bolts of pain.

With bloody fingers, she slid open her hyphen. The screen flickered uselessly before shorting out. Her throat crackled as she growled.

She didn't need the stupid hyphen to tell her the obvious. Her limbs were too heavy, sluggish, and not because she'd practically blown herself up. Her suit had protected her one last time, but it was done. She was using her own strength to move it now.

With her good hand, she unlocked her helmet and tossed it away, then slid off a few of the heavier pieces—chest and back first.

"What are you doing?" Daroga asked, voice tense.

"It's done." She climbed to her feet, then detached her leg plates next. "It'll only slow me down."

She slid open the manual override tray beside her broken hyphen and thumbed the disassembly switch. The suit's chassis creaked as it expanded, leaving her feeling naked and exposed, yet free and light. Stepping out of the frame, she rolled her neck, and the charred skin on her cheek smarted as the numbness began to reside.

She lowered back down to her knees. Pain fired along her nerves and she glanced at her limp arm, fingers twitching. "My shoulder's out, can you . . . ?"

"Shit, yeah." Daroga knelt beside her, taking her wrist in one hand, upper arm in the other. "Ready?"

She sucked in a hard breath. "Yeah."

He pulled and twisted. Her vision brightened, a chalky crack sounding as the joint snapped into place.

She growled out a half-bitten scream, and the taste of blood pooled in her mouth. Her vision blackened. When she opened her eyes, Daroga hovered in front of her.

"Hey," he breathed. "You okay?"

She braced on her knees, each beat of her heart a steady pulse of pain between her temples. The lancing down her arm was replaced with a dull but tolerable throb.

Daroga frowned. "Pass out a little bit there?"

"Maybe." She drew herself up and glanced at her fallen comrades—their suits in various states of disarray. Even if she found one in working order, it'd take too long to resize it.

Daroga seemed to make the same assessment as he paced toward Ivon's and Coleson's bodies, then tilted his head at Rhett. "Yeah, Kato was the only one close to your size . . ." He released a long breath through his nose.

She cast her gaze to her former squadmate, or rather to the bloody, charred mass of warped metal that remained. "Yeah," she sighed. "I kind of blew him up, though."

"He blew *himself* up," Daroga said. "To save you. West *really* doesn't want us rezoning."

"Clearly." She pushed her hands through her waves of short hair. "Zeroing out can still be our plan B. Or C or J or whatever fucking plan we're on at this point."

Daroga holstered his pistol, then picked up Rhett's rifle and passed it to Adriene. "Let's get this over with."

CHAPTER THIRTY-SIX

The empty corridors of the ship echoed eerily as Adriene and Daroga made their way toward the command deck.

Two guards stood post outside the door to the bridge—not MPs but hybridized soldiers, likely the ones who'd escorted the others back to the *Aurora* with Rhett.

After a few coordinated, well-placed shots, the guards were dead.

With the bridge on lockdown, Daroga had to hack the door to gain access. As Adriene waited, she adjusted her rifle, her pulse tremoring with agitated nerves. With no suit to wick it away, sweat slicked her skin, loosening her bare grip on the weighty gun.

Finally, the door opened. She stepped through the threshold, sweeping her aim across the empty upper tier. She halted at the top of the stairs, Daroga on her heels.

On the lower deck, Commodore Thurston stood facing the large bank of viewscreens between control consoles.

"Commodore," she panted. "Thank Mira." With no Rubicon, Thurston wouldn't be under West's thrall. He could still be reasoned with. "We think we saw Mechan in atmo—we need to enter subspace."

Thurston continued to watch at the monitors, unresponsive. Adriene darted a glance around the rest of the bridge. No crew sat at the stations.

Brows pinching, she looked back at Thurston, then focused on the screens he stared at. One displayed a grid of security feeds. Views of the containment cells.

Adriene squinted. Of *her* containment cell. Daroga helping her stand up, hours earlier.

"Sir?" she prompted, voice cracking.

Thurston didn't reply. He seemed bulkier under the weight of a full suit of gleaming white armor, helmet tucked under one arm. He turned a metal object over in his hands, though his body eclipsed most of it from view.

A shadow flashed in her periphery. She spun as Blackwell lunged at her.

She turned her rifle on him, realizing too late that he was actually going for Daroga.

Daroga thrust out an elbow, but Blackwell had a thick arm around his neck within seconds, clamping him into a headlock.

Adriene kept her aim on Blackwell, but darted a quick look down the stairs to Thurston. "Sir, Daroga's innocent—it's Major West."

Thurston still didn't turn. Another of the security feeds showed a recording of the Creator's cell. Adriene enlisting his help, then Daroga freeing him.

Thurston's chest swelled with a deep, crackling breath, then his rumbling, dry tone cut through the silence. "I did not realize how close the two of you had grown over the last few weeks."

Adriene blinked, mind racing.

"I should have paid more attention," Thurston continued. "I truly did not think you had it in you to make a real connection with someone."

"Sir . . ." she began again, but confused dread drained the air from her lungs.

She glanced back at Daroga, held in a firm grip by Blackwell. Blackwell's movements were stiff—the same calculated rigidity as the other hybridized soldiers.

Her eyes darted to Thurston, the beginnings of bitter realization sinking deep into her stomach.

Thurston stood canted, favoring his left leg. His actions, though, were fluid, natural. He didn't move with the same forced stiffness as Blackwell. He didn't appear to be hybridized. At least . . . not in the same way.

"I'm sure I can blame your Rubicon for that too," Thurston continued. "For humanizing you." He finally turned to face her, his gray, weathered brow low over *two* steel-gray eyes.

She froze, fixating on the tremoring fingers of his left hand.

"I have not had time to reseat the commodore's ocular implant." Thurston sighed, tone almost casual. "It would have been a critical step in ensuring the transfer went unnoticed."

Adriene's lips parted, but her breath had left her entirely, and she wouldn't have known what to say even if she had the capacity to form words.

Thurston let out a deep, crackling sigh. "But it makes no difference now. Just as our Architect guest had warned, the pathways were too delicate. The commodore's neural structure was inadequate. I can already feel this body giving way."

Adriene flinched as a memory surfaced: the putrid, stale stench of viscous, gray mucus.

The bin she and Daroga had found hidden on the lower decks . . . West hadn't used it to build a husk of himself. He'd built one of Thurston.

West had rezoned *as* Thurston. Hijacked another human's consciousness. True hybridization.

A wave of numbness rolled down her limbs as she looked him over. It was seamless. No stilted, rigid motions. His mannerisms, posture, presence . . . they were in every way West, unaffected by new muscles and bone structure.

Adriene sucked in a breath and reaffirmed her grip on her rifle, pressing the stock into her shoulder and lifting her aim toward Thurston—toward *West*.

Daroga ceased struggling against Blackwell, staring at West in abject horror. "Julen . . ." Daroga breathed. "What have you done?"

"I always suspected you sought to undermine me, Carl," West rumbled half under his breath, brow furrowing. "I can't say I expected it to happen like this, however."

Daroga glared. "What are you talking about?"

West's shoulders swelled as he took a step forward, jaw set. "Time and time again she proved the lengths she would go to get that 'chip' deactivated." He jutted a finger back at the security feeds. "All it took was one whisper from you to bring it all crashing down."

He tossed his helmet on the console, but kept a grip on the arc of metal in his other hand. "She would be standing by my side right now if it weren't for you."

Daroga scoffed a dark laugh. "You can't really believe that. She never would've kept helping you—you've strayed so far off course with this, Julen. You need help."

Blackwell pummeled a fist into Daroga's side.

Daroga keeled forward, coughing out a mouthful of blood. Blackwell yanked him back upright by the open collar of his suit, then dragged him toward the door.

"Stop!" Adriene shouted, locking her aim onto Blackwell. "Where are you taking him?"

"Just for a quick bout of surgery," West replied. "It's better for everyone if he forgets this whole . . . misstep."

"No!" Daroga thrashed against Blackwell's grip, managing to slide a shoulder out for a fleeting moment before getting pulled back in. Blackwell towed him toward the door. Daroga reached toward Adriene, green eyes wide with dread. "Adriene, please," he begged. "Don't let him!"

Adriene faltered, a swell of horror rising with the musty scent of the damp basalt cave, Harlan's panicked screams echoing in the back of her mind.

She glanced down at the charge on her rifle. Two shots left.

She inhaled a deep breath through her nose.

Aim would be critical. He still had a rezone chip in his head. In his first body . . . his real body.

"Adri—"

Her finger slid across the trigger with too much ease.

The base of Daroga's neck erupted in the charged blast, sending a spray of viscera against Blackwell's dark suit.

Blackwell lunged, but fell with Adriene's second shot, the lower half of his face crumpling into an indiscernible mass of bone and tissue.

Panicked adrenaline rushed through her veins so fast it threatened to rob her of consciousness. Her bruised, burnt face smarted, startling her back into focus.

She swung her useless rifle back toward West. It was now completely discharged. But he didn't know that.

West's stoic expression remained on Daroga's and Blackwell's bodies, gaze steady for a few silent seconds. "I . . . honestly did not expect that." He sighed, shaking his head. "I suppose it's no matter now."

Adriene flinched as klaxons ripped through the quiet. Warning lights washed the gleaming white surfaces of the bridge in a violent orange.

Her gaze diverted to the screens over West's shoulder. A proximity alert flared, but showed no enemy contacts.

West turned to tap on the main control panel.

Adriene's clenched jaw tightened. She expected him to hop into the pilot's seat, to set any random destination to throw them into subspace, or at least move them out of orbit, but he only silenced the warning.

Though the klaxons ceased, the lights continued, casting the mute bridge in an eerie, coruscating glow.

"What are you doing?" she demanded. "Why aren't we entering subspace?"

West turned to face her again, Thurston's white hair flashing orange in the pulsating lights. "I didn't want it to have to come to this, Sergeant. I told you not to interfere, but you defied me." He shook his head, frowning. "Which left me no choice."

Adriene scanned the flashing viewscreens, which cycled through radars and exterior views of the ship. An inbound-missile warning expanded on the main screen.

A computerized voice sounded over the loudspeakers, "Missile lock detected."

"Twelve warheads . . ." West glanced at the screen before facing her again. "Failsafes overridden, broadcasting Mechan transponder codes. Five megatons each. Should be more than enough."

Adriene gaped, frozen in place.

That's why they weren't in subspace. Why they hadn't already been swarmed by scrappers. Those streaks across the sky hadn't been Mechan ships, but their own missiles. Fired from the ground, sent on a trajectory to intercept once the *Aurora* was in orbit again.

Adriene scowled. "You think it matters if you kill us? Or if you make it look like the scrappers did it? You may have brainwashed the others into not remembering what you've done, but Daroga knows. He's already awake in the rezone hub. He'll tell them everything."

West cocked his head to the side. "With the evidence destroyed, the contractor can say whatever he wants. Even if they accept his story, it will not matter. They will believe I truly died with this ship."

Confusion racked her thoughts, and she shook her head.

West frowned. "As it turns out, you were right, Sergeant. This plan was too rushed. I should have taken care of the Architect . . ." Two steel-gray, regret-filled eyes locked onto her. "I should have found a more effective way to take care of *you*. In my haste, I left too much overlooked." His voice quieted as he shook his head. "I just wanted it to be over. I'll need to be more cautious, next time."

"Next time?" she scoffed, brow creasing. "What are you talking about?"

"That's what you wanted, right? For me to take the time necessary to ensure the Mechan can't turn the technique against us."

Her jaw flexed. "It's too late for that."

"Time used to be a concern, yes." He lifted the device he'd been carrying around, propping the thirty-centimeter-wide metal ring between his gloved hands. "But now, there's always more time to be had."

Adriene stared at the halo of segmented metal, blood running cold. She couldn't believe she hadn't recognized it. A crucible.

"The Architect gave me more than I ever could have hoped for," West continued, drumming his fingers along the dark metal curves. "More than I even knew I wanted."

Shoulders tense, she took a slow step back. "Where the hell did you get that?"

His lips pressed thin. "How did you think I transferred into this body?"

"But—" Her breath caught in her throat, and she shook her head in disbelief. "But how?"

"Through many years of diligent patience," he replied, then exhaled a heavy sigh. "I am not an impatient man, truly. You did not get to see the best version of me, Sergeant. I was patient in my recovery, in learning to adapt to my cybernetics, in tolerating my comrades' and commanders' pity and judgment. Patient while rising through the ranks, and while gaining the clout needed to dovetail my roles in Intel and R&D. My body may have run out of patience, but I have not." Again, regret lined his gray eyes. "I never intended you to be part of this, not this far in. But it's a necessity now." He braced the crucible between his palms. "I found a way to carry on, and I am sorry, truly. But I have to take it."

Adriene's eyes burned, fixated on the gleaming arc of metal, every muscle in her body taut.

"I will have time to finish what we started." West took a slow step forward, his gaze drifting briefly to her rifle. "I can afford to be patient again."

The orange warning beacons flipped to red, and the computerized voice returned. "Impact in forty-five seconds. Forty-four, forty-three . . ."

Terror cut through Adriene's chest. She took a step back, reaffirmed her aim, her sweaty, bare palms sliding against the grip. She had to do whatever it took to keep him—and that crucible—as far from her as possible until those nukes arrived.

West took another cautious step forward. His brow firmed as his gaze flicked down to her rifle again.

She'd just killed Daroga without hesitation. It probably wasn't hard for West to realize she'd not used it against him by now only because she *couldn't*.

". . . thirty-seven . . ."

West's caution broke, and he marched toward her.

She backpedaled, but he made it up the short staircase in a few quick strides.

Sapped for strength, her response lagged with bone-weary muscles. She swung the butt of the rifle at his face. He raised an armored hand, smacking it away, ripping the useless gun from her grip and sending it clattering to the ground.

The crucible glinted in his other hand.

Panic rose as Adriene spun away, West's fingers grasping at the hem of her shirt.

Her fatigued limbs betrayed her, and she stumbled. West delivered a swift kick to the side of her knee. The joint bent sideways, and she cried out in shock and pain, hitting the ground hard.

Torn knee protesting, she rolled into a crouch. West reached toward her again. She took a fortifying breath, then spun the heel of her uninjured leg into the side of his own knee as hard as she could. It buckled, and he grunted, collapsing to all fours.

She clambered away, but her injured knee wouldn't allow her to stand.

"... twenty ..."

Adriene grimaced. Twenty seconds was too long. She wouldn't last; she was far too spent. She couldn't wait for the missiles.

She had to do this herself. She had to zero out.

Her eyes darted to the empty holster on Blackwell's bloody corpse.

She shuddered at the sight of Daroga's ruptured, mangled neck beside him.

A thread of hope rose. Daroga's pistol lay in the mingling pools of crimson staining the white decking.

Adriene dragged herself toward the pistol, through the glossy slick of Daroga's still-warm blood. Her fingers closed around the gun.

"... ten ..."

A cold grip clamped her shoulder, yanking her back.

West's armored fingers dug in painfully, tearing her skin open as he flipped her onto her back. He pinned her with one hand, raised the crucible in the other. A shrill hum sounded.

The seams between the segments lit, igniting a vibrant, molten red orange.

Adriene thrashed, kicking at him, but he kept her pinned. A primal fear tore through her. Briefly, she felt as though the floor eroded beneath her, hot sand scraping her arms as he pushed her down, down deeper.

The pistol threatened to fall from her blood-slicked grip. West thrust the halo of metal toward her eyes.

". . . two . . ."

Adriene sucked in a sharp breath. With every ounce of strength she had left, she pressed the muzzle to her temple and pulled the trigger.

THIRTY-SEVEN

Adriene gulped in a shallow breath, drawing a mass of viscous fluid into the back of her throat.

The blackness slid away as she fell forward. She twisted, collapsing onto her back, head snapping against the cold metal floor.

Hacking and gasping, she sucked more fluid deeper into her lungs. She pummeled a fist to her chest and pivoted onto her side so she would not drown in her own amniotic fluid.

She managed to cough a wad out, then more followed. Her stomach heaved as it emptied a pile of gray-green fluid onto the floor. A potent waft of antiseptic filled her nostrils.

Groaning, she rolled over onto her back. Lying still for a few long moments, her breaths slowed into a steady, even rhythm.

Her eyes slid open. Filmy slime coated her freckled, light brown skin. Her arms lifted and turned over, chunks of gray sludge sliding away.

Goose bumps ripped across her bare skin, and her limbs trembled. Panic clouded her thoughts, but her breath remained steady.

A pair of guards appeared. They cloaked her in a dark robe, then lifted her to her feet. They spoke words at her, flashed beams of light into her eyes, but their voices were distant, muddled as if speaking through water. They led her down the bin-lined corridor, green demarcation lights flashing along the floor.

One sludge-covered foot moved in front of the other. A tingle raced down her left arm, and she lifted it, turning it over, staring at it.

The fingers quivered lightly, and she gripped her wrist with her other hand. The skin pinched and gave way, smooth and warm under her touch.

Her fingers slid up to the inside of her elbow, where a black

number was inked under a narrow barcode. Her thumb hovered
over the "97."

In a haze, she showered and dressed. The guards escorted her to a
ghastly white room—overhead diodes far too bright.

A metal table sat within. One of the guards led her to it, and her
knees wavered as she sat on the cool metal chair.

She waited.

Her fingers lifted to her forehead. The memories of death hung
in her periphery, a somber veil that hazed the present moment.
Above all, the pain remained forefront. The charred skin on her
face, her broken knuckles, her torn knee, the cold muzzle of the pistol against her temple prior to discharge. Yet her head did not hurt.

Why did it not hurt?

The door across the room slid open.

A broad-shouldered woman swept in, concern lining her brow, her
graying hair slicked back into a tight bun. Major Miller Champlan.

"Valero." Champlan sat in the chair across the table. Two officers
followed the major in, both buttoned up in slim-fit dress grays. The
two men stood post over either of Champlan's shoulders.

She inclined her head. "Ma'am."

She did not think this was standard debrief order, but she could
not quite remember.

"I'd say it's good to see you again," Champlan said, "but considering the circumstances . . ."

"I understand, ma'am."

"We've received an alarmingly high number of rezones from the
CNS *Aurora*." Champlan's thin lips wrinkled at the corners. "Can
you shed any light on what's happened?"

A response formed in the back of her mind, her mouth opened,
and her vocal cords said something else. "Mechan. They destroyed
the ansible facility, then the *Aurora*."

Despite the lie, her breath remained steady, her heart beating out
an even, slow pace.

"We have a report, Sergeant, from another survivor," Champlan said, her smooth tone decorous. "They claim Major West was responsible for the destruction. Do you have any idea why they would think that?"

She stretched her left hand slowly, pressing it flat against her thigh.

Another survivor. Daroga; it had to be. He was the only one who had died without an upgraded Rubicon.

He would realize, wouldn't he? Once he saw her?

She shook her head once. "They must be having a bad take. I was on the bridge when the Mechan launched the missiles. I saw it happen with my own eyes."

The two officers behind Champlan exchanged glances, then one spoke. "You were on the bridge? Who else was present?"

"All of Command," she said. "Majors Blackwell and West, and Commodore Thurston." That much was not a lie, at least. Technically.

"Why was the ship unable to field the attack?" Champlan asked.

"Some kind of cascading power surge. Both our shields and the subspace drive failed. They were unable to address the issue before the Mechan fired."

Champlan exchanged looks with the two officers, then gave a short nod. To her horrified relief, they seemed to believe her.

The questioning continued for another half hour before she was finally free of the bureaucracy.

She then answered a lab coat's droll questions, underwent a cursory psychological examination, and endured a few coordination and stamina tests with a physiotherapist. The quartermaster issued her fatigues, and she received orders to hold at the rezone facility until further notice. It wasn't every day the entire command structure of a special forces company was simultaneously eradicated. It would take some time for High Command to decide what would be done with Flintlock.

She relieved her aching hunger with a protein bar, then found her way out of the facility and into the dry, red haze of the small moon. The emerald giant Ouray stretched across more than half the horizon, crisscrossed by the silver streaks of the massive orbital antenna grid.

She traced her fingers down her left arm. Bent the elbow, rolled the wrist, reveled in the way the muscle contracted and relaxed.

This shell may be synthetic, but it had been twenty years since she had seen with both eyes, felt with both hands, walked with both legs. She would cherish the opportunity to feel like a complete human again, fabricated or otherwise.

The howling wind sent flecks of dust slicing across her fresh skin, but she sucked in a deep breath, relishing a feeling she had almost forgotten. Real pressure, heat, cold—across her whole body. Along with it, a disorienting sense of symmetry. Balance.

Yet starker than anything was a tingling clarity, an inverse vacancy that occupied the space once dominated by twenty years of ever-intensifying pain. She'd entirely forgotten how existence had felt prior.

Leaning both elbows against the railing, she looked out over the square courtyard. The sand filled with twisting spirals that built up along the surface, then disappeared into mists of red dust.

The rezone process had indeed been horrifying. She should have inspected the facilities, should have maintained control beyond the initial transfer process. The sensory overload from that white-walled room alone was cause enough for trauma, and the psychological assessment had lacked in every perceivable way.

Oversights, certainly, but ones she could make amends for, in time. It would take her a while to reposition herself, unfortunately. Months, maybe years. The first step would be to make an appointment with her supervising officer, once one was assigned to her, so she could be transferred into R&D.

She would have to consider how to handle the placement exams. Convincing them she'd garnered knowledge as West's protégé would not be difficult. However, suddenly waking from a rezone with a genius-level IQ might set off a few red flags.

For that reason, among many, she would need to be vigilant, and patient. This would be a long, slow process.

It was only a matter of time before it would all fall into place. For now, she would let herself marvel at this miracle the Architect had unwittingly given her. A second chance.

Across the wide courtyard, a door slid open, and a man stepped into the red haze. A few years younger, brown skin smoother, muscles thinner, but it was definitely him.

Daroga's thick black hair was even longer than it had been when he died, tangling around his face in the choppy breeze. He tugged it back into a tie as he glanced around the decking. His tense expression loosened as his eyes met hers. He started the long jaunt around the walkway.

Her lips turned down. The contractor would need to be dealt with, as well. He knew far too much.

She shivered as something potent and painful stirred at the base of her rib cage. She fought the sensation down, uncertain of its source and her sudden hesitation.

Maybe she wouldn't *have* to get rid of him. His fondness had seemed genuine enough. Given time, she might be able to be honest with him about her plans.

If nothing else, his connections with Dodson-Mueller could prove quite valuable. In fact, relocating to the corporate sphere could simplify the endeavor considerably. The bureaucracy and fastidiousness of the Extrasolar Fleet had not worked in her favor thus far. An entrepreneurial ethos could allow for greater risk-taking and fewer restrictions.

For now, it didn't matter. There was no need to rush the decision. If the man proved troublesome down the line, she could always get rid of him.

A pain lanced in her gut, deeper and sharper and crueler than the previous. Her thumb pressed into her palm, the nail turning to dig in deep. She winced and shook it away.

Daroga turned the corner toward her. The fingers of her left hand tremored, and she steadied them on the railing.

As Daroga drew closer, she expected to find him disoriented, if not outright traumatized. Numb, at the very least.

However, when he met her gaze, his expression was an incongruent medley. Relief, sorrow, awe, hope . . . but more than anything, affection. She had almost forgotten what it looked like.

An odd, urgent itch scraped at the base of her skull. She tried to scratch it, to no avail, as if sourced from some deep, entombed place she couldn't reach. The same sensation compelled her to step forward to meet him, roused her pulse, sent waves of tingling warmth down her limbs.

She gritted her teeth and smothered the feeling, clenching tight fists to stave off the compulsion to take his hands in hers.

With a slow exhale, she reminded herself that the transfer method ensured an order of operations. Reflexive responses may leak through, but emotional, anatomical, and verbal behaviors would not. *Could* not. That was how it worked.

She would adapt to the idiosyncrasies. For now, she had to remain focused on the task at hand. Humanity still faced a ticking clock.

Now she not only had the key, but enough time to properly implement it. The final and resounding defeat was imminent. Adriene's sacrifice would not be in vain.

This death, unlike the other ninety-six, would actually mean something.

ACKNOWLEDGMENTS

Eternal thanks to:
- Dave Dewes: esteemed recipient of Husband of the Supereon Award
- Mom, Dad, Jessie, DJ, Skyler, Dawson, and Lincoln: #1, 2, 3, 4, 5, 6, and 7 Top Fans on Facebook, embodiment of the Seinfeld "hooray" GIF
- Matt Olson: BFF&E&E
- Ember, aka Emberkins, Kitty, Kitty-Kitty, Kitten, Kitten Mitten, Kitty-Mitty, Kitten Cat, Kitten Mitten Cat, Miss Kitten, Lettuce Monster
- Lady Arya Stark-Stolte-Dewes of South-Central Wisconsin, aka Big Dog, Sweetest Pea, Sweetest of Peas, Sweet Girl, Sweetness and Light, fka Sock Monster
- Dark Lady Sylvanas Windrunner Banshee Queen, Leader of the Forsaken, Warchief of the Horde, aka Syl, Syl Beans, Beans, Syller Biller, Syller Biller Beans, Little Dog
- Dave Hollis, Tina Chan, Tullio Pontecorvo, Rebecca Schaeffer: magnanimous geniuses
- Tricia Skinner: Undercover Imperial Agent, Sith Empire
- Jen Gunnels: Paragon of Patience, would either be best friends or archnemeses with Dark Lady Windrunner (the character, not my dog)
- Caro Perny, Renata Sweeney, Rachel Taylor, Jessica Katz, Peter Lutjen, Heather Saunders, Jacqueline Huber-Rodriguez, Rafal Gibek, Sanaa Ali-Virani, Sara Robb, Kenneth Diamond, Ryan Jenkins, and Elishia Merricks: Undisputed Best Team of the Century, Publishing Edition
- My high constitution modifier, because this book attempted to kill me multiple times.

Dave Dewes

J. S. DEWES has a bachelor of arts in film from Columbia College Chicago and has written scripts for award-winning films, which have screened at San Diego Comic-Con and dozens of film festivals nationwide. She is the author of *The Last Watch* and *The Exiled Fleet*.

jsdewes.com
facebook.com/jsdewes
Twitter: @jsdewes
Instagram: @jsdewes
Pinterest: @jsdewes